P

THE L

"Yarros's novel is a deeply felt and emotionally nuanced
contemporary romance..."
—*Kirkus Reviews*, **starred review**

"Thanks to Yarros's beautiful, immersive writing, readers will
feel every deep heartbreak and each moment of uplifting love in
this tearjerker romance."
—*Publishers Weekly*, **starred review**

"*The Last Letter* is a haunting, heartbreaking and ultimately
inspirational love story."
—**InTouch Weekly**

"I cannot imagine a world without this story."
—**Hypable**

"A stunning, emotional romance. Put *The Last Letter* at
the top of your to-read list!"
—**Jill Shalvis,** *NYT* **bestselling author**

"This story gripped me from start to finish. *The Last Letter* is
poignant, heartfelt and utterly consuming. I loved it!"
—**Mia Sheridan,** *NYT* **bestselling author**

"*The Last Letter* is so much more than a romance. It's a testament
to the strength of bonds forged from trauma and loyalty. It's an
exploration of motherhood and the importance of family. But
above all, it's a story of survival, forgiveness, and the healing
power of unconditional love."
—**Helena Hunting,** *NYT* **bestselling author**

Praise for
GREAT AND PRECIOUS THINGS

"A moving story that is sure to please."
—*Publishers Weekly*

"A poignant and skillfully crafted second-chance romance."
—*Kirkus Reviews*

"Without a doubt, *Great and Precious Things* is Yarros's best
work to date."
—*USA Today* **bestselling author Adriana Locke**

"A heart-wrenching, sincere, and beautifully emotional story....
Our hearts broke and soared in equal measure."
—**Totally Booked blog**

"As perfectly, devastatingly beautiful and haunting as all her
other stories. Bring tissues."
—**Readers Retreat blog**

the things we leave unfinished

the things we leave unfinished

#1 *NEW YORK TIMES* BESTSELLING AUTHOR
REBECCA YARROS

Entangled Publishing, LLC
644 Shrewsbury Commons Ave., STE 181
Shrewsbury, PA 17361
rights@entangledpublishing.com

Amara is an imprint of Entangled Publishing, LLC.

Visit our website at www.entangledpublishing.com.

Edited by Stacy Abrams
Cover design by Bree Archer
Cover images by CatLane/GettyImages,
cappels/GettyImages,
pkanchana/GettyImage
Interior design by Toni Kerr

ISBN 978-1-68281-566-3
Ebook ISBN 978-1-68281-588-5

Manufactured in the United States of America

First Edition February 2021

11

ALSO BY REBECCA YARROS

The Last Letter
Great and Precious Things
The Things We Leave Unfinished

THE EMPYREAN SERIES

Fourth Wing
Iron Flame

THE FLIGHT AND GLORY SERIES

Full Measures
Eyes Turned Skyward
Beyond What Is Given
Hallowed Ground
The Reality of Everything

THE RENEGADES

Wilder
Nova
Rebel

To Jason—

For the days the shrapnel works
its way to the surface and reminds us
that after five deployments
and twenty-two years in uniform,
we're the lucky ones, my love.

We are the lightning strike.

CHAPTER ONE

Georgia

My dearest Jameson,

This is not our end. My heart will always remain with you no matter where we are. Time and distance are only inconveniences to a love like ours. Whether it's days, months, or even years, I will be waiting. We will be waiting. You'll find me where the creek bends around the swaying aspen trees, just as we both dreamed, waiting with the one we love. It's killing me to leave you, but I'll do it for you. I'll keep us safe. I will wait for you every second, every hour, every day for the rest of my life, and if that's not enough, then eternity, which is exactly how long I'll love you, Jameson.

Come back to me, my love.

Scarlett

Georgia Ellsworth. I brushed my thumb over my credit card, wishing I could wipe hard enough to erase the letters. Six years of marriage, and the only thing I'd walked away with was a name that wasn't even mine.

In a few minutes, I wouldn't have that, either.

"Number ninety-eight?" Juliet Sinclair called out from behind the plexiglass window of her booth, like I wasn't the only person at the Poplar Grove DMV and hadn't been for the last hour. I'd flown into Denver this morning, driven into the afternoon, and hadn't even been to my home yet—that's how desperate I was to rid myself of the last pieces of Damian in my life.

Hopefully, losing his name would make losing him and six years of my life hurt just a little less.

"Right here." I put my credit card away and walked up to her window.

"Where's your number?" she asked, holding out her hand and wearing a satisfied smirk that hadn't changed much since high school.

"I'm the only one here, Juliet." Exhaustion beat at every nerve in my body. If I could just get through this, I could curl up in that big armchair in Gran's office and ignore the world for the rest of my life.

"Policy says—"

"Oh, stop it, Juliet." Sophie rolled her eyes as she walked into Juliet's booth. "I've got Georgia's paperwork, anyway. Go take a break or something."

"Fine." Juliet pushed away from the counter, vacating her seat for Sophie, who had graduated the year before us. "Nice to see you, Georgia." She flashed a saccharine-sweet smile in my direction.

"You too." I offered her the practiced smile that had served as my glue for the past few years, holding me together while everything else disintegrated.

"Sorry about that." Sophie cringed, scrunching her nose and adjusting her glasses. "She's... Well, she hasn't changed much. Anyway, everything appears to be in order." She handed back the papers my lawyer had given me yesterday afternoon with my new social security card, and I slid them inside the envelope. How ironic that while my life had fallen apart, the physical manifestation of that dissolution was held together by a perfect, forty-five-degree staple. "I didn't read the settlement or anything," she said softly.

"It was in *Celebrity Weekly*!" Juliet sang from the back.

"Not all of us read that tabloid trash!" Sophie retorted over her shoulder, then gave me a sympathetic smile. "Everyone here was really proud of the way you held your head up through... everything."

"Thanks, Sophie," I replied, swallowing the lump in my throat. The only thing worse than failing at the marriage everyone had warned me about was having my heartbreak and humiliation published by every website and magazine catering to the gossip lovers who devoured personal tragedy in the name of a guilty pleasure. Holding my head up and keeping my mouth shut when cameras were thrust in my face was exactly what had earned me the nickname "The Ice Queen" over the last six months, but if that was the cost of keeping whatever was left of my dignity, so be it.

"So, should I say welcome home? Or are you just visiting?" She handed me a little printed paper that would serve as my temporary driver's license until the new one came in the mail.

"I'm home for good." My answer may as well have been broadcast from the radio station. Juliet would make sure everyone in Poplar Grove knew before dinner.

"Well, then welcome home!" She smiled brightly. "Rumor has it your mom is in town, too."

My stomach twisted.

"Really? I...uh...haven't been over there yet." *Rumor has it* meant Mom had been spotted in either one of our two grocery stores or the local bar. The second possibility was much higher. Then again, maybe it was a good—

Don't finish that.

Even thinking Mom might be here to help me would only end in crushing disappointment. She wanted something.

I cleared my throat. "How is your dad doing?"

"He's good! They think they got it all this time." Her face fell. "I really am sorry about what happened to you, Georgia. I can't even imagine if my husband..." She shook her head. "Anyway, you didn't deserve that."

"Thank you." I looked away, spotting her wedding ring. "Say hi to Dan for me."

"Will do."

I stepped into the afternoon light that painted Main Street with a comforting, Rockwellian glow, and sighed in relief. I had my name back, and the town looked exactly how I remembered. Families strolled by, enjoying the summer weather, and friends chatted against the picturesque rocky mountain backdrop. Poplar Grove had a population smaller than the altitude, big enough to demand half a dozen stoplights, and was so tight-knit that privacy was a rare commodity. Oh, and we had an excellent bookstore.

Gran had seen to that.

I tossed my paperwork on the front seat of my rental car, then paused. Mom was probably at the house right now—I'd never demanded she give back her key after the funeral. Suddenly, I wasn't so eager to head home. The last few months had sucked out my compassion, strength, and even hope. I wasn't sure I could handle Mom when all I had left was anger.

But I was home now, where I could recharge until I was whole again.

Recharge. That was exactly what I needed before seeing Mom. I headed across the street to The Sidetable, the very store Gran had helped start with one of her closest friends. According to the will she'd left, I was now the silent partner. I was…everything.

My chest tightened at the sight of the for sale sign on what used to be Mr. Navarro's pet store. It had been a year since Gran told me he'd passed on, and that was prime real estate on Main Street. Why hadn't another business moved in? Was Poplar Grove struggling? The possibility sat in my stomach like sour milk as I entered the bookstore.

It smelled like parchment and tea, mixed with a little bit of dust and home. I'd never been able to find anything close to its soothing scent in any chain store while I'd lived in New York, and grief pricked at my eyes with my first breath. Gran had been gone six months, and I missed her so much, my chest felt like it might collapse from the hole she'd left behind.

"Georgia?" Mrs. Rivera's jaw dropped for a second before she smiled wide from behind the counter, balancing her phone between her ear and shoulder. "Hold on one second, Peggy."

"Hey, Mrs. Rivera." I grinned and waved at her welcomingly familiar face. "Don't hang up on my account. I'm just stopping in."

"Well, it's wonderful to see you!" She glanced toward the phone. "No, not you, Peggy. Georgia just walked in!" Her warm brown eyes found mine again. "Yes, *that* Georgia."

I waved once more as they continued their conversation, then walked back to the romance section, where Gran had an entire stack of shelves dedicated to the books she'd written. I picked up the last novel she'd published and opened the dust jacket so I could see her face. We had the same blue eyes, but she'd given up dyeing her once-black hair around her seventy-fifth birthday—the year after Mom had dumped me on her doorstep the first time.

Gran's headshot was all pearls and a silk blouse, while the woman herself had been a pair of overalls, dusty from the garden, and a sun hat wide enough to shade the county, but her smile was the same. I grabbed another, earlier book just to see a second version of that smile.

The door jingled, and a moment later, a man on a cell phone began to browse in the general fiction aisle just behind me.

"A modern-day Jane Austen," I whispered, reading the quote from the cover. It had never ceased to amaze me that Gran had been the most romantic soul I'd ever known, and yet she'd spent the overwhelming majority of her life alone, writing books about love when she'd only been allowed to experience it for a handful of years. Even when she'd married Grandpa Brian, they'd only had a decade before cancer took him. Maybe the women in my family were cursed when it came to our love lives.

"What the hell is this?" The man's voice rose.

My eyebrows flew upward, and I glanced over my shoulder. He held a Noah Harrison book, where—go figure—there were two people in the classic, nearly kissing position.

"Because I wasn't exactly checking my email in the middle of the Andes, so yes, it's the first time I'm seeing the new one." The guy practically seethed as he picked up another Harrison book and held them up, side by side. Two different couples, same exact pose.

I'd definitely stick with my selection, or anything else in this section.

"They look exactly the same, that's the problem. What was wrong with the old— Yes, I'm pissed off! I've been traveling for eighteen hours and in case you forgot, I cut my research trip short to be here. I'm telling you they look *exactly* the same. Hold on, I'll prove it. Miss?"

"Yes?" I twisted slightly and glanced up to find two book covers in my face. *Space much?*

"Do these look the same to you?"

"Yep. They're pretty interchangeable." I slid one of Gran's books back onto the shelf and mentally whispered a little goodbye, just like I did every time I visited one of her books in a store. Was missing her ever going to get easier?

"See? Because they're not supposed to look the same!" the guy snapped, hopefully at the poor soul on the other end of the phone, because it wasn't going to go well if he was using that tone with me.

"Well, in his defense, all his books read the same, too," I muttered. *Shit.* It slipped out before I could censor myself. Guess my filter was just as numbed out as my emotions. "Sorry—" I turned to face him, lifting my gaze until I found two dark brows raised in astonishment over equally dark eyes. *Whoa.*

My ruined heart jolted—just like every heroine in one of Gran's books. He was the most gorgeous man I'd ever seen, and as the now-ex-wife of a movie director, I'd seen my fair share.

Oh no, no, no. You're immune to good-looking men, the logical side of my brain warned, but I was too busy staring to listen.

"They do not read the—" He blinked. "I am going to have to call you back." He moved both books to one hand and hung up, pocketing his phone.

He looked about my age—late twenties, maybe early thirties—stood at least six feet tall, and his black, just-out-of-bed hair fell carelessly over tanned, olive skin before reaching those lifted, black brows and impossibly deep brown eyes. His nose was straight, his lips carved in lush lines that only served to remind me exactly how long I'd gone without being kissed, and his chin was shaded in a light shadow beard. He was all angular, sculpted lines, and, given the flex of muscle in his forearms, I'd have bet the store that he was pretty well acquainted with the inside of a gym...and probably a bedroom.

"Did you just say they all read the same?" he questioned slowly.

I blinked. *Right. The books.* I mentally slapped myself for losing my train of thought over a pretty face. I'd had my name back for all of twenty minutes, and men were off the menu for the foreseeable future. Besides, he wasn't even from around here. Eighteen hours of travel or not, his tailored slacks blatantly screamed designer, and the sleeves of his white linen shirt were rolled in that casually messy style that was anything but casual. Men in Poplar Grove didn't bother with thousand-dollar pants or have New York accents.

"Pretty much. Boy meets girl, they fall in love, tragedy strikes, someone dies." I shrugged, proud that I didn't feel any heat creeping up my cheeks to give me away. "Throw in some legal courtroom drama, a little unsatisfying but poetic sex, and maybe a beach scene, and you've pretty much got it. If that's your thing, you can't go wrong with either book."

"Unsatisfying?" Those eyebrows drew tight as he glanced between the books, then back to me. "Someone doesn't *always* die."

Guess he'd read a Harrison book or two. "Okay, eighty percent of the time. Go ahead and see for yourself," I suggested. "That's the reason he's shelved on this side"—I pointed to the general fiction sign—"and not on this side." I swung my finger toward the romance marker.

His jaw dropped for a millisecond. "Or maybe there's more to his stories than sex and unrealistic expectations." His attractiveness slipped a peg or two as he tapped one of my pet peeves right on the nose.

My hackles rose. "Romance isn't about unrealistic expectations and sex. It's about love and overcoming adversity through what can be considered a universal experience." That was what Gran and reading thousands of romance novels had taught me in my twenty-eight years.

"And, apparently, *satisfying* sex." He arched a brow.

I willed my skin not to flush at the way his lips seemed to caress that word.

"Hey, if you don't like sex, or you're uncomfortable with a woman embracing her sexuality, then that really says more about you than the genre, don't you think?" I tilted my head. "Or is it the happily-ever-after you object to?"

"I am all for sex, and women embracing their sexuality, and happily-ever-afters." His voice went all growly.

"Then those definitely aren't the books for you, because the only thing they embrace is universal misery, but if that's what does it for you, enjoy." *So much for leaving behind the Ice Queen.* Here I was, arguing with a complete stranger in a bookstore.

He shook his head. "They're love stories. It says so right here." He held up one of the covers that happened to have a quote by Gran. *The* quote. The one her publisher had begged Gran for so often that she'd finally relented, and they'd made do with what she had to say.

"No one writes love stories like Noah Harrison," I read, a slight smile tweaking my lips.

"I'd say that Scarlett Stanton is a pretty well-respected romance writer, wouldn't you?" A lethally sexy smirk played across his face. "If she says it's a love story, then it's a love story."

How could someone so devastatingly handsome annoy the

shit out of me so thoroughly?

"I'd say that Scarlett Stanton was arguably the *most* respected romance writer of her generation." I shook my head, filed Gran's other book back where it belonged, and turned to walk away before I completely snapped at this guy throwing Gran's name around like he knew the first thing about her.

"So it's safe to take her recommendation, right? If a guy wants to read a love story. Or do you only approve of love stories written by women?" he called after me.

Seriously? I pivoted at the end of the aisle, my temper getting the best of me as I turned back to face him. "What you don't see in that quote is the rest of it."

"What do you mean?" Two lines appeared between his eyebrows.

"That wasn't the original quote." I glanced up at the ceiling, trying to remember her exact words. "What was it... 'No one writes painful, depressing fiction masquerading as love stories like Noah Harrison.' The publisher edited it for the blurb." *That was a step too far.* I could almost hear Gran's voice in my head.

"What?" It must have been the way he shifted under the fluorescent lights, but it looked like his skin paled.

"Look, it happens all the time." I sighed. "I'm not sure you noticed, but here in Poplar Grove, we all knew Scarlett Stanton pretty well, and she was never one to keep her opinions to herself." *Guess that's genetic.* "If I recall correctly, she did say that he wrote with a flair for description and was...fond of alliteration." That was the nicest thing she'd said. "It wasn't his writing she objected to—just his stories."

A muscle in his jaw ticked. "Well, I happen to like alliteration in my love stories." He walked by with both books, heading for the checkout. "Thank you for the recommendation, Miss..."

"Ellsworth," I responded automatically, flinching slightly as it left my lips. *Not anymore.* "Enjoy your books, Mr...."

"Morelli."

I nodded, then walked away, feeling his gaze follow me out the door as Mrs. Rivera rang up both books for him.

So much for getting some peace. Worst part of that whole little spat? Maybe he was right, and the books Gran wrote really were unrealistic. The sole happily-ever-after I knew of was my best friend, Hazel, and, since she was only on year five of her marriage, the verdict could hardly be determined.

Five minutes later, I drove onto our street, passing Grantham cottage, the closest of the rental properties Gran owned. It looked vacant, which was the first time since…ever. Only being a half hour or so out of Breckenridge meant rentals never stayed empty for long around here.

Shit. You didn't make the arrangements with the property manager. That was probably one of the dozens of unheard voicemails, or perhaps one of my thousand unread emails. At least the voicemail box had stopped accepting new messages, but the emails continued to pile up. I needed to pull myself together. The rest of the world didn't care that Damian had broken my heart.

I pulled into the driveway of the house I'd grown up in and parked. There was already a rental car at the apex of the semicircular drive.

Mom must be here. That ever-present exhaustion swelled, sweeping over me.

I left my suitcases for later but grabbed my purse before heading toward the front door of the seventy-year-old colonial. *The flowers are missing.* Perennials popped up here and there, all rather desiccated, but there were no bright splashes of color in the beds that usually lined the drive this time of the season.

The last few years—when she'd been too fragile to spend that much time kneeling—I'd flown out to help Gran plant. It wasn't like Damian had missed me…though now I knew why.

"Hello?" I called as I walked into the entry hall. My stomach churned at the stale scent of ash in the air. Had she been *smoking* in Gran's house? The hardwood looked like it hadn't been mopped since winter, and there was a thick layer of dust on the foyer table. Gran would have shit bricks to see her house like this. What had happened to Lydia? I'd asked Gran's accountant to keep her housekeeper on payroll.

The doors to the sitting room pushed open, and Mom came through, dressed for company. Her megawatt smile slipped when she saw me, then widened.

"Gigi!" She opened her arms and gave me the two-second, back-pat hug that had pretty much defined our relationship.

God, I hated that nickname.

"Mom? What are you doing here?" I asked the question gently, not wanting to send her into a meltdown.

She tensed, then pulled back, her smile faltering. "Well…I've actually been waiting for you, honey. I know losing Gran was a major blow, and now that you've lost your husband, I figured you might need a soft place to land." Her expression dripped with sympathy as she looked me up and down, grasping my shoulders lightly, ending her perusal with a slightly raised eyebrow. "You definitely *look* heartbroken. I know it's hard right now, but I swear the next time will be easier."

"I didn't want there to be a next time," I admitted quietly.

"We never do." Her eyes softened in a way they never had toward me.

My shoulders fell, and the thick defenses I'd built over the years cracked. Maybe Mom was turning over a new leaf, starting a new chapter. It had been years since we'd spent any real time together, and maybe we'd finally reached a point where we could—

"Georgia?" a man asked through the opening of the French doors. "Is he here?"

My eyebrows hit the ceiling.

"Christopher, if I could have a second? My daughter just arrived home." Mom flashed him the million-dollar smile that had snared her first four husbands, then took my hand and tugged me toward the kitchen before I could see into the sitting room.

"Mom, what is going on? And don't bother lying to me." *Please, just be real.*

Her expression flickered, reminding me that her ability to change plans on the fly was second only to her emotional unavailability. She excelled at both. "I'm concluding a business deal," she said slowly, looking like she was considering her words. "Nothing to worry about, Gigi."

"Don't call me that. You know I hate it." Gigi was a little girl who spent too much time looking out the window at taillights, and I'd grown up. "A business deal?" My gaze narrowed.

"It all came together while I've been waiting for you to come home. Is that so hard to believe? Sue me for trying to be a good mother." She lifted her chin and blinked rapidly, her lips pursing slightly like I'd hurt her.

I wasn't buying it.

"How did he know my name?" Something wasn't right here.

"Everyone knows your name, thanks to Damian." Mom swallowed and patted her perfect ebony French twist—her tell. She was lying. "I know you're hurt, but I really think there's a chance you could get him back if we play our cards right."

She was trying to distract me. I swept past Mom and into the living room with a smile.

Two men jumped to their feet. Both were in suits, but the one who had peeked through the open door looked to be a good twenty years older than the other.

"Sorry to be so rude. I'm Georgia Ells—" *Damn it.* I cleared my throat. "Georgia Stanton."

"Georgia?" The older one paled. "Christopher Charles," he said slowly, his gaze darting toward the door, where my mother had made her entrance.

Recognition flared at the name. Gran's publisher. He'd been the editorial director of her imprint when she'd written her last book about ten years ago at the age of ninety-one.

"Adam Feinhold. It's nice to meet you, Ms. Stanton," the other, younger one said. Both looked positively ashen as they glanced between my mother and me.

"And now that everyone's been introduced, Gigi, aren't you thirsty? Let's get you a drink." Mom rushed toward me with an outstretched hand.

I ignored her and took over the large wingback chair at the head of the seating arrangement, sinking into its familiar comfort. "And what exactly would my great-grandmother's publisher be doing all the way in Poplar Grove, Colorado?"

"They're here for a simple book deal, of course." Mom sat gingerly on the edge of the couch closest to me and arranged her dress.

"What book?" I asked Christopher and Adam directly. Mom had a lot of talents, but writing wasn't one of them, and I'd seen enough book deals to know publishers didn't just hop on planes for fun.

Christopher and Adam glanced at each other in confusion, so I repeated my question.

"What. Book?"

"I believe it's untitled," Christopher answered slowly.

Every muscle in my body locked. There was only *one* book Gran hadn't titled or sold that I was aware of. *Mom wouldn't dare...would she?*

He swallowed, then glanced toward my mother. "We're just finishing up some signatures and picking up the manuscript. You know Scarlett wasn't fond of computers, and we didn't want to chance something as precious as the only existing original copy to the gods of shipping."

They shared an awkward laugh, and Mom joined in.

"What book?" This time I asked Mom, my stomach pitching.

"Her first...and last." The plea in her eyes was unmistakable, and I loathed the way it managed to slice into my heart. "The one about Grandpa Jameson."

I was going to puke. Right there on the Persian rug Gran had loved. "It isn't finished."

"Of course not, dear. But I've made sure they hired the best of the best to see it through to completion," Mom said with a syrupy tone that did nothing to settle my nausea. "Don't you think Grandma Scarlett would want to have her final words published?" Then she gave me *the smile*. The one that looked open and well-meaning to outsiders but held pure threat of private retribution if I dared to publicly embarrass her.

She'd taught me well enough that I gave her one of my own. "Well, Mom, I think if Gran had wanted that book to be published, she would have finished writing it." How could she do this? Broker a deal for *that* book behind my back?

"I don't agree." Mom raised her eyebrows. "She called that book her legacy, Gigi. She was never able to handle the emotions of finishing it, and I think it's only fitting that we do it for her. Don't you?"

"No. And, since I'm the only beneficiary of her will, the executor of her literary trust, what I think is all that matters." I laid out the truth as unemotionally as I could.

She dropped the facade and stared at me in pure shock. "Georgia, surely you wouldn't deny—"

"So you're both named Georgia?" Adam asked, his voice pitching upward.

I blinked as the pieces clicked into place, and then I laughed. "This is rich." She wasn't just brokering a deal behind my back—she was posing as me.

"Gigi..." Mom begged.

"She told you she was Georgia Stanton?" I guessed, giving the suits all my attention.

"Ellsworth, but yes." Christopher nodded, his face reddening as he caught on.

"She's not. She's Ava Stanton-Thomas-Brown-O'Malley...or is it still Nelson? I can't remember if you changed it back." I lifted my brows in Mom's direction.

Mom flew to her feet and glowered. "Kitchen. Now."

"If you'll excuse us for one second." I flashed a quick smile at the duped publishers, then headed for the kitchen, because I wanted her explanation.

"You will not blow this for me!" she hissed as we reached the room where Gran had baked every Saturday.

Dishes lay scattered on the counter, and the odor of spoiled food lingered in the air.

"What happened to Lydia?" I asked, motioning to the mess.

"I fired her. She was nosy." Mom shrugged.

"How long have you been living here?"

"Since the funeral. I was waiting for you—"

"Let it go. You fired Lydia because you knew she'd tell me you were hunting for the book." Pure anger raced through my veins, tightening my jaw. "How could you?"

Her shoulders slackened. "Gigi—"

"I've hated that nickname since I was eight years old. Again: stop using it," I snapped. "Did you really think you'd get away with pretending to be me? They have lawyers, Mom! Eventually you would have had to hand over identification."

"Well, it was working until you walked in."

"What about Helen?" I scoffed. "Tell me you didn't offer up the manuscript without Gran's agent."

"I was going to bring her in as soon as they made an official offer. I promise. They're just here to get the book for a read-through."

I shook my head at her sheer... I didn't even have a word for it.

She sighed like I'd been the one to break her heart, and tears welled in her eyes. "I'm so sorry, Georgia. I was desperate. Please do this for me. The advance would help me get on my feet—"

"Really?" My eyes flashed toward hers. "This is about money?"

"Really!" She slammed her hands on the granite. "My own grandmother cut me out of her will for *you*. You got *everything*, and I was left with nothing!"

Guilt pricked unprotected slivers of my heart, the tiny shards that lived in denial, never quite getting the message that not all mothers wanted to be moms, and mine was among them. Gran had cut her out—but it wasn't because of me. "There is nothing to give here, Mom. She never finished the book and you know why. She said she only wrote it for family."

"She wrote it for *my* father! And I'm family! Please, Georgia." She gestured around us. "You have all this. Give me just *one* thing, and I swear I'll even split it with you."

"It's not about the money." Even I hadn't read the book, and she wanted to hand it off?

"Says the girl who has millions."

I gripped the edge of the island's counter and took deep breaths, trying to steady my heart, to bring logic into a situation that had none. Was I financially stable? Yes. But Gran's millions were earmarked for charity—just as she'd wished, and Mom wasn't a charity case.

But she *was* my last living family.

"Please, honey. Just listen to the terms they're offering. That's all I ask. Can't you at least give me that?" Her voice wavered. "Tim left me. I'm...broke."

Her confession hit me straight in my freshly divorced soul. Our eyes met, identical shades of what Gran had called *Stanton blue*. She was all I had, and it didn't matter how many years or therapists had come and gone, I'd never managed to wipe out the urge to please her. To prove my worth.

Money hadn't been the catalyst I'd envisioned.

But that was a statement of *her* character—not mine.

"I'll listen, but that's all."

"That's all I'm asking." Mom nodded with a grateful smile. "I really did stay for you," she whispered. "I just happened to find the book."

"Let's go." *Before I start to believe you.*

The men had a slight tinge of desperation in their tone as they explained the terms they'd offered my mother. I could see it in their eyes—the knowledge that the gold mine that was the very last Scarlett Stanton book was slipping through their fingers, because they'd never really had it.

"I'll have to give Helen a call. I'm sure you remember Gran's agent," I said after they finished. "And the performance rights are off the table. You know how she felt about that." Gran hated movie adaptations.

Christopher's face tightened.

"And where is Ann Lowell?" She'd been Gran's editor for more than twenty years.

"She retired last year," Christopher answered. "Adam here is the best editor we have on staff, and he's brought in his best writer to finish up what we're told is going to be about a third of the book?" He glanced at Mom.

She nodded.

She'd read it? The bitter taste of jealousy coated my tongue.

"He's the best," Adam gushed, glancing at his watch. "Millions of sales, phenomenal writing, critically acclaimed, and even better—a die-hard Scarlett Stanton fan. He's read everything she's written at least twice, and he's cleared the next six months for this project so we can push it out fast." He tried to give me a reassuring smile.

He failed.

My eyes narrowed. "You hired a man to finish Gran's book?"

Adam swallowed. "He really is the best, I swear. And your mom wanted to interview him to make sure he was the correct choice, so he's actually here."

I blinked, surprised that Mom had been that thorough, and shocked that the writer— *No.*

"I can't even remember the last time he had to pitch himself." Christopher chuckled.

My thoughts tripped, falling down a rabbit hole like a line

of dominos. *Impossible.*

"He's here right now?" Mom asked, glancing toward the door and smoothing her skirt.

"He just pulled up." Adam motioned to his Apple Watch.

"Georgia, you sit. I'll show our guest in." Mom sprung out of her chair and rushed for the door, leaving the three of us in an awkward silence broken only by the steady tick of the grandfather clock.

"So I met your husband at a gala last year," Christopher said with a tight smile.

"My ex-husband," I corrected him.

"Right." He winced. "I thought his last movie was overrated."

Just about every movie—besides Gran's—Damian had directed was overrated, but I wasn't going there.

A deep, rumbling laugh sounded from the foyer, and the hair on the back of my neck stood up.

"He's here!" Mom announced joyfully, swinging open the glass doors.

I stood as he walked in with my mother, and I somehow managed to keep my balance as he came into full view.

His flirtatious smile fell, and he looked at me like he'd seen a ghost.

My stomach hit the floor.

"Georgia Stanton, meet—" Christopher started.

"Noah Harrison," I guessed.

Noah—the stranger from the bookstore—nodded.

I didn't care how sinfully gorgeous the man was. The only way he'd get his hands on Gran's book was over my dead body.

CHAPTER TWO

Noah

Scarlett, my Scarlett,

Hopefully you don't find this until you're halfway across the Atlantic—too far gone to change your stubborn, beautiful mind. I know we agreed, but the thought of not seeing you for months, or years, ruins me. The only thing holding me together is knowing that you'll be safe. Tonight, before I crept from our bed to write this, I tried to memorize everything about you. The scent of your hair and the feel of your skin. The light in your smile and the way your lips purse when you tease. Your eyes— those beautiful blue eyes—bring me to my knees every time, and I can't wait to see them against the Colorado sky. You are strong, my love, and braver than I ever could be. I could never undertake what you now face. I love you, Scarlett Stanton. I have loved you since our first dance, and I will love you the rest of my life. Hold on to that while we are an ocean apart. Kiss William for me. Keep him safe, hold him close, and before you even have time to miss me, I'll be home with you, where there are no more air-raid sirens, no more bombings, no more missions, no more war—only our love.

I'll see you soon,

Jameson

*S*tanton. The beautiful, infuriating woman from the bookstore was Georgia-fucking-Stanton.

For the first time in years, I was speechless.

I'd never had that moment I'd so often written about, the one where someone takes a look at a total stranger and simply *knows*.

Then she'd turned around, holding a book by my favorite author, staring like it had the answers for the sadness in her eyes, and suddenly that moment was me...until it blew apart as I realized what she was saying.

No one writes painful, depressing fiction masquerading as love stories like Noah Harrison. Her earlier statement etched itself into my brain with all the blister and agony of a branding iron.

"Noah?" Chris prompted, gesturing to the last empty seat in what looked like an intervention.

"Of course," I muttered, but moved toward Georgia. "It's nice to officially meet you, Georgia."

Her handshake was warm, unlike her crystal-sharp blue eyes. There was no kicking that feeling, that hit of instant attraction, even knowing who she really was. I couldn't help it. Her words had left me uncharacteristically stumbling over my tongue in the store, and here I was, choking again.

She was stunning—exquisite, really. Her hair fell in waves so black, there was an almost blue shine to it, and the contrast with her delicate ivory skin brought to mind about a million different Snow White references. *Not for you, Morelli. This one wants nothing to do with you.*

But I wanted *her.* I was supposed to know this woman—I felt it with every fiber of my being.

"You seriously bought your own books?" she asked, arching a brow as I let go of her hand.

My jaw ticked. Of course that's what she'd remember. "Was I supposed to put them back and let you think your opinion had swayed me?"

"I commend you for the follow-through." A corner of her incredibly kissable mouth lifted. "But it might have made this moment a tad less awkward."

"I think that ship sailed the moment you said all my books read the same." *And called the sex unsatisfying.* All I needed was one night and I'd show her exactly how *satisfying* it could be.

"They do."

Had to give it to her; she'd doubled down. Guess I wasn't the only stubborn one here.

The other woman in the room gasped, and both Chris and Adam murmured, reminding me that this wasn't a social call.

"Noah Harrison." I shook the older woman's hand, taking in her features and coloring. This had to be Georgia's...mother?

"Ava Stanton," she replied with a blindingly white smile. "I'm Georgia's mother."

"Though they could easily pass for sisters," Chris added in with a little chuckle.

I controlled the urge to roll my eyes.

Georgia didn't, which made me bite back a smile.

We all took our seats, and mine was directly across from Georgia. She leaned back in her chair and crossed her legs, somehow managing to look both relaxed and regal in a pair of jeans and a fitted black shirt.

Wait. Recognition tingled in the back of my brain. I'd seen her somewhere—not just the bookstore. Images of her at a black-tie event flashed through my brain. Had we ever crossed paths?

"So, Noah, why don't you go ahead and tell Georgia—and Ava, of course—why they should trust you with Scarlett Stanton's unfinished masterpiece," Chris urged.

I blinked. "I'm sorry?" I was here to take delivery of the manuscript. Period. That had been the only condition of me nearly jumping out of my skin to say yes. I wanted to be the first to read it.

Adam cleared his throat and sent me a pleading look.

Was he serious?

"Noah?" His gaze darted meaningfully toward the women.

Guess so. I was caught somewhere between laughing my ass off and scoffing. "Because I promise not to lose it?" My voice pitched up at the end, turning my obvious statement into a question.

"Comforting," Georgia remarked.

My eyes narrowed.

"Noah, let's step out into the foyer," Adam suggested.

"I'll get everyone some drinks!" Ava offered, rising quickly.

Georgia looked away as I followed Adam through the French doors of the drawing room and into the vaulted entryway.

The house was modest for what I knew of Stanton's estate, but the craftmanship in the woodwork of the crown molding and the banister of the curved staircase spoke for both the quality of the build and taste of its previous owner. Just like her impeccable, captivating writing had been detailed without falling into frilly, the house felt feminine without stumbling into the floral-print-from-hell category. It was understated and elegant...reminding me of Georgia, minus the temper.

"We have a problem." Adam ran his hands over his dark blond hair and gave me a look I'd only seen once before—when they'd found a typo on one of my covers that had already gone to print.

"I'm listening." I folded my arms across my chest. Adam was one of my closest friends and as level-headed as they came in New York publishing, so if he thought we had a problem, we did.

"The mother led us to believe that she was the daughter," he blurted.

"In what way?" Sure, both women were beautiful, but Ava was easily a decade or two older.

"In the who-has-the-rights-to-this-book way."

My stomach threatened to heave up my lunch. Now it made sense—the mother wanted me on the book...*not* Georgia. *Holy shit.*

"Are you telling me that the contract we've spent weeks negotiating is about to fall apart?" My jaw clenched. I hadn't just made time for this project, I'd canceled my entire *life* for it, come home from Peru for it. I wanted this damn book, and the thought of it slipping through my fingers was inconceivable.

"If you can't convince Georgia Stanton that you're the perfect author to finish the book, then that's exactly what I'm telling you."

"Fuck." I lived for challenges, spent my free time pushing my mind and body to the limit through rock climbing and writing, and this book was my mental Everest—something to push me outside my comfort zone. Mastering another author's voice, especially one as beloved as Scarlett Stanton, wouldn't just be a professional feat, either. There were personal stakes for me here, too.

"Pretty much," Adam agreed.

"I met her earlier today. She hates my books." Which didn't bode well for me.

"I gathered that. Please tell me you weren't your usual asshole self?" His eyes narrowed slightly.

"Eh, 'asshole' is a relative term."

"Awesome." His tone dripped sarcasm.

I rubbed the skin between my eyebrows as my mind raced, thinking of some way to change the mind of a woman who'd obviously sealed her opinion of my writing long before we'd met. I couldn't remember the last time hard work or a little charm hadn't gotten me something I wanted this badly, and it wasn't in my nature to back down or concede defeat.

"How about I give you a minute or two to gather your thoughts, and then you come back in with a miracle?" He slapped my shoulder and left me standing in the entry while Ava puttered in the kitchen.

I slid my phone from my back pocket and dialed the only person I knew would give me unbiased advice.

"What do you want, Noah?" Adrienne's voice came in over the cacophony of her kids in the background.

"How do I convince someone who hates my books that I'm not a shit writer?" I asked quietly, turning toward the office doors.

"Did you really just call so I could stoke your ego?"

"I'm not kidding."

"You've never cared what people thought before. What's going on?" Her voice softened.

"It's ridiculously complicated and I have about two minutes to figure out the answer."

"Okay. Well, first, you're not a shit writer, and you have the adoration of millions to prove it." The background noise quieted, as if she'd closed a door.

"You have to say that—you're my sister."

"And I've hated at least eleven of your books," she responded cheerfully.

I huffed a laugh. "That's an oddly specific number."

"Nothing odd about it. I can tell you exactly which ones—"

"Not helping, Adrienne." I studied the small collection of photographs on the table, mixed in with a variety of glass vases. The one shaped like an ocean wave looked to be hand-blown, and it sat beside the picture of a young boy probably taken in the late forties. There was another shot that looked to be a debutante ball...Ava's, maybe? And another of a child who had to be Georgia in a garden. Even as a kid, she'd looked serious and a little sad, like the world had already let her down. "I somehow don't think telling Georgia Stanton that my own sister doesn't like my books is going to get me far."

"What I'm saying is that I hated your plots, not your writ—" Adrienne paused. "Wait, did you say Georgia Stanton?"

"Yes."

"Holy shit," she muttered.

"I'm probably down to thirty seconds over here." I felt every heartbeat like it was a countdown. How had this gone so wrong so quickly?

"What the hell are you doing with Scarlett Stanton's great-granddaughter?"

"Remember the whole *complicated* part of this conversation? And how do you know who Georgia Stanton is?"

"How do you *not* know?"

Ava waltzed through the entry, carrying a small tray with

what looked to be glasses of lemonade on it. She shot me a smile, then slipped through the slightly open doors.

Time was running out. "Look. Scarlett Stanton left an unfinished manuscript, and Georgia—who hates my books—is the one to decide if I get to finish it."

My sister gasped.

"Say something."

"Okay, okay." She went quiet, and I could almost see the gears turning in her quick mind. "You tell Georgia that under no circumstances will Damian Ellsworth be allowed to direct, produce, or sniff around the story."

My brow furrowed. "This has nothing to do with movie rights." The guy was a shitty director anyway. I'd already shot him down on more than one of my options.

"Oh, come on, if this is a Scarlett Stanton finished by *you*, it's going to be huge."

I didn't argue with that. Scarlett hadn't missed hitting the *New York Times* with a release in forty years. "What does Damian Ellsworth have to do with the Stantons?"

"Huh. I really do know something you don't. How odd..." she mused.

"Adrienne," I growled.

"Let me savor it for just a moment," she sang.

"I'm going to lose this contract."

"When you put it that way." I envisioned her rolling her eyes. "Ellsworth is—as of this week—Georgia's ex-husband. He was directing *The Winter Bride*—"

"The Stanton book? The one about the guy trapped in the loveless marriage?"

"That's the one. Anyway, he got caught having an affair with Paige Parker—ironic, right? The proof is due any day now. Don't you ever shop at a grocery store? Georgia's been on the front page of every tabloid for the last six months. They call her the Ice Queen because she didn't show a lot of emotion, and, you know, the movie."

"Are you serious?" It was a clever but cruel play on the haughty first wife in that book, who, if I remembered correctly, died before the hero and heroine found their happy ending. *Talk about life imitating art.*

"It's sad, really." Her voice drifted. "She usually avoided the media to begin with, but now...well, it's everywhere."

"Ah, shit." I gritted my teeth. No woman deserved that. My father taught me a man was only as good as his word, and that's what vows were, the ultimate word. There was a reason I'd never married. I didn't make promises I couldn't keep, and I'd never been with a woman I was ready to forsake all others for. "Okay. Thanks, Adrienne." I crossed to the drawing room doors.

"Good luck. Wait—Noah?"

"Yeah?" I paused with my fingers on the brass handle.

"Agree with her."

"I'm sorry?"

"This isn't about you; it's about her great-grandmother. Check your massive ego at the door."

"I don't have a—"

"Yeah, you do."

I scoffed. There was no shame in knowing you were the best at what you did, but romance wasn't what I usually wrote. "Anything else?" I asked sarcastically. Leave it to my sister to shine a light on every flaw.

"Hmmm. You should tell her about Mom."

"No." That wasn't happening.

"Noah, I'm telling you, girls are a sucker for a guy who loves his mom enough to read to her. It will win her over. Trust me, but don't try to flirt your way through, either."

"I'm not flirting—"

She laughed. "I know you *way* too well, and I love you, but I've seen pictures of Georgia Stanton, and she is *way* out of your league."

I couldn't disagree with her there. "Nice. Thanks, and I love you, too. See you next weekend."

"Nothing extravagant!"

"What I buy my niece for her birthday is between her and me. See you then." I hung up with my sister and walked into the living room. Every face but Georgia's swung my way, each of them more hopeful than the last.

I took my time as I made my way back to my seat, pausing to examine the photograph that had captured Georgia's attention.

It was Scarlett Stanton, sitting at a massive desk, her glasses perched on her nose as she typed on the same old-school typewriter she'd written all of her books on, and sitting with her back against the side of the desk, reading on the floor, was Georgia. She looked to be about ten.

She had the rights to her great-grandmother's book...not her mother, who was Scarlett's granddaughter, which meant there were family dynamics here far beyond my understanding.

Instead of sitting, I stood behind my assigned chair, gripping the sides lightly with my back to the fireplace as I studied Georgia like I would a cliff I was determined to climb, searching for the right route, the best path. "Here's the thing," I said directly to Georgia, ignoring everyone else in the room. "You don't like my books."

She lifted an eyebrow, her head tilting slightly.

"That's okay, because I happen to *love* Scarlett Stanton's books. All of them. Every single one. I'm not the romance hater you think I am. I've read them all twice, some of them more than that. She had a unique voice, incredible, visceral writing, and a way of evoking emotion that blows me out of the water when it comes to romance." I shrugged.

"In that, we agree," Georgia said, but there was no bite in her tone.

"There is no one who compares to your great-grandmother in this genre, but I wouldn't trust anyone else with her book, and

I know more than a few other writers. I am the one you need. I am the one who will do this book justice. Everyone else at the level this book demands will want to twist it their way, or put their own mark on it. I don't," I promised.

"You don't?" She shifted in her chair.

"If you let me finish this book, it will be *her* book. I will work tirelessly to make sure it reads as if she wrote the last half herself. You won't be able to tell where she stops writing and I start."

"Last third," Ava corrected.

"Whatever it needs." My eyes didn't stray from Georgia's steadfast gaze. What the hell had Ellsworth been thinking? She was achingly, traffic-stopping beautiful, with curves for miles and a mind sharp enough to match her tongue. No man in his right mind would cheat on a woman like her. "I know you have doubts, but I'll work until I win you over."

Keep your mind on the business.

"Because you're *that* good," she said with a heavy note of sarcasm.

I bit back a smile. "Because I'm just that damn good."

She studied me carefully as the grandfather clock ticked by the seconds beside us, then shook her head. "No."

"No?" My eyes flared and my jaw locked.

"No. This book is incredibly personal to this family—"

"It's personal to me, too." *Shit.* I might actually lose this one.

I let go of the chair and rubbed the back of my neck. "Look, my mom was in a bad car accident when I was sixteen, and…I spent that summer by her bedside, reading your great-grandmother's books to her." I left out that it had been part of the penance my father had demanded. "Even the *satisfying* parts." My lips quirked upward with her eyebrows. "It's personal."

Her gaze shifted, softening for a moment before she lifted her chin. "Would you be willing to take your name off the book?"

My stomach lurched. Damn, she went straight for the kill, didn't she?

Check your ego. Adrienne had always been the more rational of our duo, but heeding her advice in this instant was about as painless as raking my soul over a cheese grater.

Was it the dream of a lifetime to have my name next to Scarlett Stanton's? Sure. But it was about way more than that. It wasn't a lie—the woman had been one of my idols and was, to this day, still my mother's favorite author...and that included me.

"If taking my name off this manuscript is what it takes to assure you I'm here for the book and not the credit, I'll do it." I answered slowly, making sure she knew I meant it.

Her eyes flared with surprise, and her lips parted. "You sure about that?"

"Yes." My jaw flexed once. Twice. This was no different than not documenting a climb, right? I would know I'd done it, even if no one else did. At least I'd be the first one to get my hands on the manuscript, even before Adam or Chris. "But I would like permission to tell my family, since I already did."

A sparkle of laughter lit up her face, but she quickly schooled her features. "If, and that's *if*, I agree to let you finish it, I would demand to have final approval over the manuscript."

My grip tightened, digging into the fabric of the chair.

Adam sputtered.

Chris mumbled a swear word.

Ava's attention swung from her daughter's face to mine like we were a tennis match.

Even with all that going on, it somehow felt like Georgia and I were the only people in the room. There was a charge between us—a connection. I'd felt it in the bookstore, and it was stronger now. Whether it was the challenge, the attraction, the possibility of the manuscript, or something else, I wasn't sure, but it was there, as tangible as an electrical current.

"We can definitely discuss editorial input, but Noah has had final manuscript approval in his contract for his last twenty books," Adam countered softly, knowing it was one of my hard limits. Once I knew where a story was going, I let the characters take me there, come hell or editorial high water.

But this wasn't my story, was it? This was her great-grandmother's legacy.

"Fine. I'll agree to being second-in-command of the ship." It went against every bone in my body, but I'd do it.

Both Chris and Adam gawked at me.

"This once," I added, glancing toward my publishing team. My agent would lose his shit if I set a precedent here.

Slowly, very slowly, Georgia leaned back in her chair. "I have to read it first, then talk to Helen—Gran's agent."

I mentally cursed but nodded. So much for being first. "I'm staying at the Roaring Creek Bed and Breakfast, and I'll leave the address—"

"I know where it is."

"Right. I'll stay through the end of the week. If we work out a contract before then, I'll take the manuscript and the letters back to New York with me and get started." Good thing I liked rock climbing, because there was plenty of that to do around here while she decided. As much as I hated to admit it, this deal was now out of my hands.

"Agreed." She nodded. "And you can put your name on it."

My heart leaped. Guess I'd passed her test.

Chris, Adam, and Ava let out a collective sigh.

Georgia's eyes flew wide, and her head snapped toward her mother. "Wait."

Every muscle in my body locked.

"What letters?"

CHAPTER THREE

July 1940

Middle Wallop, England

Well, this was a problem she should have foreseen. Scarlett's gaze swept the platform, searching one last time just to be sure, her sister beside her doing the same. The train station was rather empty for a Sunday afternoon, making it obvious that Mary had forgotten to pick them up as promised. Disappointing, yet predictable.

"Surely she'll be along in a minute," Constance suggested, flashing a forced smile. Her sister had always been the more optimistic of them.

"Let's check outside," Scarlett suggested, looping her arm through Constance's as they carried their small luggage cases off the platform. Their leave had only been for two days, but time always seemed to crawl for Scarlett when they were home.

Leave was hard to come by—especially at their rank—in the Women's Auxiliary Air Force, but as usual, their father had pulled strings that neither of them had appreciated. Strings he liked to pull often, as if she and Constance were his personal puppets.

In a way, they still were.

When Baron and Lady Wright requested their presence, their daughters were expected to attend them, uniform or not. But those same strings were the ones he'd pulled to assure his daughters would be stationed together, and for that, Scarlett was immeasurably thankful. Besides, a weekend of listening to her mother attempt to plan her life out was well worth it when it meant Constance was able to see Edward. Her sister had fallen in love with the son of a family friend years ago. They'd all grown up together during their summers at Ashby, and she couldn't have been happier for her sister. At least one of them would get to be happy.

Her hat shielded her eyes from the sun as they left the station, but there wasn't much to be done about the stifling late July heat, especially in uniform.

"Honestly, I keep hoping she'll be a bit more punctual," Constance remarked quietly as people passed by on the pavement. Constance may have been noted as the more publicly reserved of the two of them, but she never withheld her opinion from Scarlett.

Her mother, on the other hand, thought Constance simply didn't have opinions.

"There was a dance last night." She gave Constance a knowing look and sighed. "We'd better get walking if we want to sign in on time." There was nothing else to be done about it.

"Right."

They grasped the handles of their luggage and began the long walk toward their station. Thankfully, they'd both packed light, because they hadn't even made it to the corner, and Scarlett was already exhausted, weighed down by the news her mother had delivered.

"I'm not going to marry him," she announced with a jerk of her chin as they made their way down the pavement.

"Feel better now?" Constance asked, lifting her dark eyebrows. "You've been holding that in all day. I think that might have been the quietest train ride we've ever had."

"I'm not going to marry him," she repeated, snapping every word. Just the thought of it made her stomach churn.

An older woman passing by shot her a reproachful stare.

"Of course not," Constance replied, but they both knew better. These were the only years either of them would belong to themselves, and only because they were in the middle of a war. Otherwise, she would have been married off to the highest bidder by now if her parents had their way.

"He's horrendous." She shook her head. Of all the things her parents had asked of her in her twenty years, this was the worst.

"He is," Constance agreed. "I can't believe he stayed all weekend. Did you see how much he ate? His father was even worse. There are rations for a reason."

His size wasn't as much of a concern to Scarlett as what he did with it. Marrying Henry Wadsworth would be the death of her. Not because he was a widely known philanderer or the embarrassment would do her in—that was to be expected. But even her scandal-managing mother couldn't hide Alice, their housekeeper's daughter, away fast enough to miss seeing the bruises on the young woman's body this morning.

Not only had her father ignored the blatant abuse, but he then sat Scarlett right next to Henry at breakfast.

No wonder she hadn't eaten a thing.

"I don't care if the bloody title is sold out from under them, I'm not marrying him." Her grip tightened on her luggage. They couldn't make her—not legally. But they threw around the word "duty," as if marrying that ogre would save the king himself from the grasp of the Nazis.

Even then, her love of king and country was enough to risk her life for the greater good, but this wasn't about king or country.

It was about money.

"All he wants is the title," Scarlett fumed as they made their way out of the village and started down the road that led to RAF Middle Wallop. "He thinks he can buy his way in."

"He's right." Constance's nose wrinkled. "But he hasn't asked you yet, so perhaps he'll find himself another title to buy while scrambling his pudgy arse up the social ladder."

Scarlett laughed at the thought of him scrambling up anything without hoisting his pants back up to his belly, but the sound died as quickly as it came. "None of it seems to matter right now, does it? Planning for a time that may never arrive." They'd have to live through *this* period first.

Constance shook her head, the sunlight glimmering off the shiny raven locks. "It doesn't. But one day, it will matter very much."

"Or maybe...it won't," she mused. "Maybe it will all be different." Scarlett glanced at the uniform she'd worn for the last year. In that time, nearly everything about her life had changed. As hot and uncomfortable as she was, she wouldn't have traded the material for anything.

"How?" Constance nudged her shoulder with a bright smile. "Come on. Entertain me with one of your stories."

"Now?" She rolled her eyes, already knowing she'd give in. There wasn't anything she'd deny Constance.

"What better time?" Constance gestured to the open, dusty road ahead of them. "We've got at least forty minutes on our hands."

"You could tell *me* a story," Scarlett teased.

"Yours are always so much better than mine."

"That's not true!" Before she could relent, a car slowed as it approached, giving Scarlett enough time to glance at the insignia before it pulled alongside them: 11 Group Fighter Command.

One of ours.

"Can I give you ladies a lift?" the driver asked.

American. Her head snapped toward the man, her brows arched high in surprise. She'd known there were a few Americans with the 609, but she'd never encountered one— *Oh my God.*

She tripped slightly, Constance catching her elbow before she could make an utter fool of herself.

Get a grip. You'd think you'd never seen a good-looking man. In her defense, he was a step beyond that description, and it wasn't just his light brown hair or that single strand that fell across his forehead, begging to be brushed back. It wasn't even that carved chin or the slight bump on his nose from what had to have been a previous break. What had her off-balance was the smile that curved his lips and the spark in his moss-green eyes as he tilted his head...as if he knew what his very appearance was doing to her pulse.

She sucked in a breath, but it was as if she'd swallowed lightning, the electricity turning her mouth dry then somersaulting in her stomach as her heart thundered. "We're all right, thank you," she managed to answer, whipping her gaze forward.

She wasn't putting her sister into a car with a strange man, no matter what the insignia said...right? The last thing she needed was to lose her wits over something as fleeting as attraction. She'd seen it in just about every woman she served with—attraction, then affection, then grief. Even Mary had lost two sweethearts in the 609 over the past few months. No, thank you.

Constance elbowed her slightly but remained quiet.

"Come on, it's another three miles to the station, and what... another half mile to the women's barracks?" He leaned over the passenger seat, still keeping pace beside them. "You're melting out there."

A bead of sweat raced down Constance's cheek as if to make his point, and Scarlett wavered.

"There's two of you and only one of me. Hell, you can both sit in the back seat if that would make you more comfortable." Even his voice was appealing, low and rough like the coarse sand at the beach.

Constance elbowed her again.

"Ow!" Scarlett scowled at her sister, then noted the circles beneath her eyes her late night with Edward. She sighed, then offered what she hoped was a natural smile to the American. "Thank you. A ride to the women's barracks would be lovely."

He grinned, and her stomach flipped again. *Oh, no.* She was in trouble...at least for the next three and a half miles. After that, he could put some other girl in trouble for all she cared.

He pulled over properly, then stepped out of the car and came their way. He was tall, with broad shoulders that tapered nicely into the belted waist of an RAF uniform. God help her, those silver wings and rank said he was a pilot, and she knew more than enough about those boys to take a little heed. According to the other girls, they were reckless, passionate, transient, and often short-lived.

He lifted their luggage into the trunk. Scarlett blatantly ignored Constance's sly smile as she glanced from the American back to Scarlett.

"Don't even think about it," Scarlett whispered.

"Why not? You are, and you should." Constance smirked as the American shut the trunk.

"Ladies," he said, keeping his eyes on Scarlett as he opened the door.

Constance slid into the back seat first.

"Thank you, Lieutenant." Scarlett ducked her head and took the seat next to Constance.

"Stanton," he said, leaning in to extend his hand. "I figure you should know my name. Jameson Stanton."

Blinking, Scarlett offered her own. His grip was firm but gentle. "Assistant Section Officer Scarlett Wright, and my sister, Constance, who is also an Assistant Section Officer."

"Excellent," he said with a smile. "Nice to meet you both." His gaze lifted to Constance, and he gave her a nod and a smile before releasing Scarlett's hand.

She felt wildly off-center as he shut the door and took his place behind the wheel, his eyes meeting hers in the rearview mirror as he pulled out onto the road.

He wasn't sure what to call that color of blue, but her eyes were stunning, and he was, well, stunned. They were the same shade as the water near some of the Florida beaches he'd seen on vacation. Bluer than the skies of his beloved Colorado. They were…going to get them into an accident if he didn't watch the road. He cleared his throat and focused on driving.

"You didn't seem surprised to hear that we're sisters," Constance remarked.

"Is anyone ever surprised to hear you're sisters?" he joked. Constance was maybe an inch shorter than Scarlett and had the same piercing blue eyes, but hers lacked the fire that kept his gaze darting back in the rearview.

"Our father, I suppose," Constance answered.

Jameson laughed.

"Guess which of us is older," Constance suggested.

"Scarlett," he answered without pausing to think it over.

"Why would you say that?" Scarlett challenged with a slight tilt to her head.

"You're protective of her."

Her eyes flared with surprise and her lips tugged upward.

"She's only eleven months older, but she acts as if it's eleven years," Constance teased.

That earned a full smile from Scarlett, accompanied by a shake of her head. Damn, she was a knockout. Who the hell left a woman like that to walk down the street? His brow puckered. "So what happened to your ride? I'm guessing you hadn't planned on walking all the way back to the station."

"She probably lost track of time," Scarlett answered in a tone that made him exceptionally glad he wasn't the one who'd forgotten.

Not a man, then. He filed that fact.

"We appeared to have overestimated a friend's ability to remember appointments," Constance added. "Your accent is lovely. Where are you from?"

"Colorado," he answered as a pang of homesickness stabbed quick and deep. "Haven't seen her in over a year, but she's still home." He missed the mountains and the crisp lines they cut against the sky. He missed the way the air felt in his lungs, light and clear. He missed his parents and Sunday dinners. But none of that would exist for long if they didn't win this thing.

"You're with the 609?" Scarlett asked with the same accent her sister had, the one that screamed money and education.

"For a few months now." He'd gotten to France only to be told that he was needed in England, and he wasn't the only one. There were a few of them in the 609, and the Brits had welcomed them with open arms once they'd shown their skills in the sky. "What about you two?"

He fought the urge to drive slower, to make the trip last a little longer just so he could see Scarlett smile again, even though he knew stopping had already put him in danger of being late to the flight line. His gut tightened as their eyes met in the mirror for another flash of a second before she looked away.

"We're both clerks in sector operations." Constance lifted her eyebrows at Scarlett.

"We've been in for about a year now," Scarlett added.

Two sisters. Both officers. Same position. Stationed together. Jameson was willing to bet that Daddy had money or influence. Most likely both. *Wait…sector operations?* He'd raise that bet to his whole month's pay that they were plotters. "You move a lot of flags over there?"

Scarlett arched a brow, and his entire body tightened.

"You honestly think we pilots don't know?" They were saving his ass, that was for sure. Plotters tracked all aircraft movement in the sky with the help of radio operators and RDF—Range and Direction Finding, creating the very map he flew by when the raids came. They were also top secret.

"I wouldn't presume to guess what you know," Scarlett responded with a faint smile.

Not only was she gorgeous but smart, too, and the fact that she didn't let on that he was right—when he now knew he was—earned his respect. He was intrigued. He was attracted. He was in a damnable mess because he only had a few more minutes with her.

The minute they passed through the gate, a pit formed in his stomach, and the odometer ticked like a countdown. He'd been stationed here nearly a month and he'd never seen her. What were the chances he'd ever see her again?

Ask her out.

The idea nagged at him as he pulled up in front of the women's barracks—the Brits called them huts. The entire station was still under construction, but at least these were done.

The girls climbed out before he could open their door, which didn't surprise him. The English girls he'd met since landing in country had learned to do a lot for themselves in the last year the UK had been at war.

He took their bags from the trunk but held on to Scarlett's as she reached for it.

Their fingers brushed.

His heart jolted.

She startled but didn't pull back.

"Can I take you to dinner?" he asked before he lost the nerve, which wasn't something he'd particularly had to worry about lately, but something about Scarlett had him tongue-tied.

Her eyes flared wide, and her cheeks flushed with heat. "Oh. Well…" Her gaze darted toward her sister, who was doing a poor job of hiding a smile.

Scarlett didn't let go of her luggage. Neither did he.

"Is that a yes?" he asked with a grin that just about took her knees out of service.

Trouble. For the first time in her life, she didn't want to avoid it.

"Stanton!" another pilot called out as he walked over with

Mary tucked beneath his arm and her lipstick smudging his face. At least that question was answered.

Mary gasped, then cringed. "Oh no. I'm so sorry! I knew I was forgetting something today!"

"Don't worry about it. Seems to have worked out for everyone involved," Constance responded with a cheeky little smile, her engagement ring winking in the sun.

Scarlett narrowed her eyes at her sister before a tiny tug reminded her that she still stood on the pavement with her luggage suspended between herself and Jameson. What kind of name was Jameson, anyway? Did he prefer it to James? Jamie, perhaps?

"I'm glad to see you, Stanton. Can I catch a ride with you to the flight line?" the other pilot asked as he disengaged from Mary.

"Sure. As soon as she answers the question." Jameson looked her dead in the eye.

A nagging little feeling told her that he'd always be this forthright. It also told her not to let go.

"Scarlett," Constance urged.

"I'm sorry, what was the question?" Had he asked another while she was distracted by staring? Her cheeks caught fire.

"Will you please let me take you to dinner?" Jameson asked again. "Not tonight, since I'll be flying. But some night this week?"

Her lips parted. She hadn't agreed to a date since the war began.

"I'm quite sorry, but I don't see men like you socially," she managed to croak out.

Constance let loose a sigh of frustration strong enough to change the weather.

"Men like me?" Jameson questioned with a tease in his tone. "Americans?"

"Of course not." She scoffed. "I mean, not that I've ever been asked by an American, naturally."

"Naturally." And that grin was back, wobbling her knees again. He really was too handsome for his own good.

"I mean pilots." She nodded toward the wings on his uniform. "I don't see pilots." Out of every job in the Royal Air Force, pilots were the most nomadic in regard to where they slept, and geography wasn't the least of it. They also had a tendency to die with a frequency she couldn't stomach.

"Shame." He clicked his tongue.

She tugged on her luggage, and he released it.

"It is most assuredly my loss," she professed, the words ringing true in her own ears. She shouldn't go. That didn't mean she didn't *want* to. Longing resonated through her like a church bell, hitting hard and loud, only to come again in softer echoes the longer she stood there looking up at him.

Was every American as handsome as he was? Surely not.

"No, I mean it's a shame that I'll have to resign. I do love to fly." A corner of Jameson's mouth quirked a little higher. "Wonder if they need more officers over at Sector Command?"

The other pilot scoffed. "Stop flirting—we're going to be late."

Scarlett arched a singular eyebrow at Jameson.

"Let me take you to dinner," he asked again, this time softer.

"Stanton, we really have to go. We're already late."

"Give me a second here, Donaldson. Come on, Scarlett, live a little." Those eyes of his stayed locked on hers, unraveling her defenses.

"You really are insistent," she accused, straightening her spine.

"It's one of my finer qualities."

"It hardly argues that I should acquaint myself with your less-than-finer ones," she muttered.

"You'll like those, too." He winked.

Oh, lord. That single action nearly wiped out any and all reasoning she had left. She snapped her mouth shut to keep from sputtering and prayed the flaming heat in her cheeks didn't give her away. "You're honestly going to stand there until I agree to go to dinner with you?"

He seemed to ponder that for a second, and she fought the urge to lean closer to him. "Well, you're still standing here, too, so I figure you might actually *want* to have dinner with me."

She did, damn him. She wanted to see him smile again, but she might not survive that little wink twice.

"Stanton!" Donaldson shouted.

Jameson watched her like she was a play and he couldn't wait to see what happened next.

"Well, if you're not, then fine, I'll go—" Constance started, stepping forward and jarring Scarlett out of her staring contest.

"I'll go to dinner with you," Scarlett blurted, mentally cursing her sister's gleeful little smirk.

"Are you going to make me turn in my wings first?" He smiled, and her stomach filled with another zing of electricity.

"Would you?" she challenged.

His head tilted to the side. "If it got me a dinner with you...I just might."

"Stanton, get in the bloody car!"

"You'd better go," she urged, stifling a grin.

"For now," he agreed, his eyes dancing as he backed away. "But I'll be seeing you, Scarlett." He flashed her another smile and disappeared into the car.

They pulled away a heartbeat later, vanishing down the road toward the airfield.

"Thank you for the help, dear sister." She rolled her eyes at Constance as they headed into the hut.

"You're quite welcome," Constance answered unabashedly.

"You're supposed to be the shy one, remember?"

"Well, it had appeared that you had taken my role for the moment, so I assumed yours. It's rather fun to be the bold, outspoken one," she mused, smiling over her shoulder as she waltzed through the door.

Scarlett scoffed but followed her conniving little matchmaker of a sister.

I'll be seeing you, Scarlett. Trouble, indeed…if he survived tonight's patrol flights. Her chest tightened at the all-too-real possibility that he wouldn't. Cardiff had been bombed last week, and patrols were becoming increasingly dangerous with the Nazis' advance. This vise of worry was the precise reason she had a no-pilots rule, but there wasn't much she could do but head to work and wait to find out if she would ever see Jameson again.

CHAPTER FOUR

July 1940

Middle Wallop, England

Dappled sunlight filtered through the leaves of the giant oak tree and flickered over Scarlett as she lay below on a thick plaid blanket, thoroughly enjoying her first day off in almost a week. Not that she minded keeping busy. There was a certain rush to being at work that she found utterly addictive.

But there was something to be said for a miraculously cooler day, a stiff breeze, and a good book.

"I've just finished," Constance said, waving a folded piece of paper from her seat at the picnic table.

"Not interested," Scarlett responded, turning the page so she could sink further into the misadventures of *Emma*. Her choice in literature was yet another thing for her mother to pick apart, another example of failing to meet their impossible expectations.

"You're not interested in what Mummy has to say?"

"Not if it has anything to do with Lord Ladder Climber."

"Do you want me to read it to you?" Constance leaned toward her sister, bracing her hand on the bench so she didn't tumble off.

"Not particularly."

Constance sighed heavily, then turned on the bench. "Okay then."

Scarlett could practically taste her sister's disappointment in the air. "Why don't you tell me about the other one, instead, poppet?" She glanced over the cover of her book to see Constance's eyes light up.

"Edward says that he loved our time together, and that he's

hopeful he can coordinate his leave with ours again soon."

Scarlett propped herself up on her elbows. "You could always meet him at Ashby. I know you both love it up there." She loved the small estate, too, but her affection was nothing compared to how Constance felt about the place where she'd fallen in love with Edward.

"We do." Constance sighed, running her fingers over the envelope. "But it's not worth the time to travel. It's easier to meet him in London." She looked off into the distance, as if she could see Edward's brigade group from there. Then her eyes popped wide, and her gaze darted back to Scarlett's. "You look beautiful," she blurted. "Try to relax."

"I'm sorry?" Scarlett's brow furrowed, then deepened as her sister scrambled to collect what few things she'd brought out to the table.

"Your hair, your dress, it's all perfect!" Clutching her things to her chest, Constance swung her legs over the bench. "I'll be... somewhere else!"

"You'll what?"

"I think she's trying to give us a little privacy."

Scarlett's gaze whipped toward the deep voice she'd been dreaming about for the past week and found Jameson Stanton approaching the edge of her blanket.

Her heart sprung to a gallop. She'd checked the casualty list daily, but seeing him in person was a relief after Brighton had been bombed last night.

He was dressed for flying, minus the gloves and yellow survival vest, and that crisp breeze she was so fond of played in his hair. She pushed herself to a sitting position and fought the urge to smooth the lines of her dress.

It was a simple, blue-checked shirtwaist dress, belted around her middle, with a modest neckline and sleeves that nearly reached her elbow, but compared to the sturdy, serviceable uniform she'd had on when they met last, she felt all but naked.

At least she was wearing shoes.

"Lieutenant," she managed to say in greeting.

"Let me help you up." He held out his hand. "Or I can join you," he offered with a slow smile she felt in every line of her body.

Just the thought sent heat streaking up her cheeks. It was one thing to declare that she was a modern woman to her mother, but quite another to act.

"That won't be necessary." Her hand shook as she took his. He pulled her to her feet in one smooth motion, and she caught herself with a palm to his muscular chest. There was nothing soft or yielding under her fingertips.

"Thank you," she said, quickly stepping back and breaking their connection. "To what do I owe this honor?" She felt exposed, overwhelmed. Everything about him was too much. His eyes were too green, his smile too charming, his gaze too forthright. She fetched her book, holding it to her chest like it might offer a shred of protection.

"I was hoping you might have that dinner with me."

He didn't take a step, but the air between them was charged with enough current that she felt as though they were both moving closer, and if she wasn't careful, they would collide.

"Tonight?" she squeaked.

"Tonight," he said, doing his best to keep his eyes on her face and not the curves of her body. Scarlett in uniform was breathtaking, but finding her lounging under a tree in that dress? She blew him right out of the sky. Her hair was pinned but loose, just as shiny and dark as it had been last week but without the service hat to cover it. Her eyes were wide and even bluer than he'd remembered as she blinked up at him. "Right now, actually." He smiled, simply because he couldn't help it. She seemed to have that effect on him. He'd been smiling all week, planning this dinner, hoping that Mary—Donaldson's current girl—hadn't been wrong, and Scarlett would be free.

Her soft lips parted in surprise. "You'd like to go to dinner right now?"

"Right now," he assured her with a grin, his focus dropping to the book she held in a death grip. "Emma can come along, too, if you like."

"I…" Her gaze darted to the left, toward the women's housing.

"She's free!" Constance yelled back from the porch.

Scarlett's eyes narrowed, and Jameson pressed his lips between his teeth to keep from laughing.

"She's about to be otherwise engaged in the act of murdering her sister!" Scarlett fired back.

"Do you need help burying the body?" Jameson asked, smirking when Scarlett's gaze snapped toward him. "If you're intent on murdering your sister, that is. I'd rather take you to dinner, of course, but if you insist, I'm quite capable of digging if that's what it takes to spend time with you."

A slow, reluctant smile spread across Scarlett's face, and his stomach pitched like he was mid-dive.

"You want to go to dinner dressed like that?" She motioned to his flight suit.

"It's all part of the plan."

Her head tilted in curiosity. "Okay, my evening is yours, Lieutenant."

He barely kept from raising his arms in victory. Barely.

"You're out of your mind," Scarlett said as Jameson buckled her into the front seat of the biplane. His hands moved quickly, tightening the harness that had her dress bunched awkwardly around her, though he'd put her blanket over her thighs and knees. As proficiently as he moved his hands about her waist, she had the feeling he'd been around more than a few girls without that barrier.

"You're the one who got in," he argued, strapping the helmet under her chin.

"Because the idea was so preposterous that I was certain you were kidding!" This had to be a joke. At any moment, he'd pull her from the cockpit and tease her about her reaction.

"I never joke about flying. Okay, I have the radio set to the training frequency, so I'll be able to hear you and likewise. Everything good?"

"You're actually serious about this, aren't you?" Her eyebrows lifted.

He paused with his thumb on her chin and lost all pretense of humor. "Last chance to back out. If you want to get down, I'll unbuckle you."

"And if I don't?" she challenged, arching an eyebrow.

"Then I'll take you flying." His gaze dropped to her lips, and her cheeks heated.

Her heart clamored at the possibility. "I thought you were taking me to dinner?"

"That requires flying." His thumb grazed the skin just beneath her lip, sending a pleasant shiver down her spine.

"And what happens if we get caught?" she asked, knowing that Royal Air Force didn't loan their planes so pilots could take their girls out—not that she was his girl.

He shrugged with a devilish smirk that sent her heart skipping. "Then I guess they'll send me back to the U.S."

She scoffed. "And that would be so bad? Being sent home?"

His focus drifted for a breath of a second, and his expression slipped. "It is when I'm not sure they'd let me back in."

"Why wouldn't they?" Her spirit of adventure flagged as her stomach sank.

"The whole treason thing." He motioned to the RAF patch on his shoulder. "And yes, being sent home would be a punishment. I'm here because I want to be, not because I have to be. Question is, are you?" His voice softened.

"I am exactly where I want to be." She'd forgotten that the Yanks who flew with them risked their own citizenship.

What a luxury it would be to choose war, yet Jameson did.

"Then let's get going before someone sees." He gave her a heart-stopping grin, then disappeared into the seat behind her.

Moments later, the engine turned over, the propeller began to spin, and every bone in her body vibrated as they pulled out from their spot in the line of planes, headed for the runway. Thank God the engine was loud enough to block the sound of her pounding heart.

Next to joining the WAAF against her parents' wishes, this was the most illicit thing she'd ever done. *It might be the most illicit thing you'll* ever *do.* She held the thought close to her chest, where her hands currently gripped the harness. They turned to the right.

"You ready?" he asked through her radio.

She nodded, pressing her lips into a nervous line. She was really going to do this, fly off into the unknown with an American pilot she'd met last week. If that wasn't the definition of reckless, she wasn't sure what was.

The hum of the engine pitched higher as the plane hurtled down the bumpy runway, gaining speed just like her heart rate, and though she could see the fields rush by on either side of her, she couldn't determine where the pavement ended. This was exhilarating, terrifying madness. The wind pricked her eyes and she blinked furiously, pulling the goggles down as the ground fell away.

Everything but her stomach leaped into the sky. *That*, she was certain, had remained on the ground. It settled as they gained altitude and she forced her breathing to steady and her muscles to ease, to relax long enough to take it all in.

It consumed her senses. The roar of the engine was dulled but not muted by her helmet, and the wind chilled her skin, but it was the view that took her breath away. The sun still clung to the sky, but she knew it would sink below the horizon soon. It was as if everything beneath them had become miniature...or they were giants. Either way, it was astonishing. She tried to carve every sensation into her memory so she could write it all down later, so she'd never be in danger of forgetting it, but just as she'd finished thinking of every word she would use to describe the landscape beneath, they were landing.

"Hold on for me," Jameson said through the radio, and her heart raced. He handled the airplane like it was part of him, like flying through the air was as simple as raising his hand.

The ground rushed up beneath them, and he landed, jostling her on the bumpy terrain. The field wasn't one she was familiar with, but it had seen its fair share of airplanes, if the tracks through the grass were any indication.

The plane rumbled as the engine died. Jameson appeared on her left, wearing a flush of wind on his cheeks and shoving his fingers through his hair.

"Can I help you out of that?" he asked, motioning to her harness.

"If I say no, will you feed me in the plane?" she teased, her lips curving upward.

"Yes." The answer was instant.

She swallowed, her throat suddenly dry at the intensity in his eyes. "Please do. Help me, that is." She tugged at her helmet first.

"Allow me." His fingers brushed hers aside gently, and she tilted her chin to give him better access. He undid the helmet with a few quick motions, and she pulled it off as he started on the harness.

"My hair is all over the place," she mused with a laugh, her hands rising to her abused curls. Her mother would have died of shock.

"You're gorgeous."

An ache unfurled in her chest, and their eyes locked as the last clasp of her harness came free. He meant it.

That ache sharpened. Oh God, what was this? Longing saturated the air, filling her lungs with every breath.

"Hungry?" he asked, breaking the silence but not the tension.

"Starved," she replied.

His chest tightened at the look in her eyes, but he turned away and held out his hand, letting her adjust her harness-wrinkled dress with what privacy he could give her. He helped her out of the cockpit when she was ready, then jumped the last few feet off the back of the wing and offered his hands.

"I'll catch you," he promised.

"You'd better." She smiled as she made her way down the wing, keeping one hand on the fuselage. Then she walked right into his arms, bracing her hands on the tops of his shoulders.

He gripped the curves of her hips as he slowly lowered her to the grass. He managed to keep his eyes on hers and not the dips and hollows of her frame, but his pulse kicked up at the feel of how perfect she felt under his hands, soft and warm, trim but not frail. This moment alone was worth the flight, the hours of preparation.

"Thank you," she said as he released her, a slight catch in her breath.

Her hair was windswept and had been bullied in places by her helmet, and those slight imperfections made her seem touchable. Attainable. Gone was the polished officer who'd caught his eye, and here was a woman who very well might catch his heart.

He blinked at that thought—he wasn't really a love-at-first-sight kind of guy, but he believed in attraction, chemistry, and even that little thing known as fate, and this felt like all three.

"Where are we?" she asked as he led her along the beaten-down path.

"Just a little north of the village." He led her to the small clearing they'd made with the truck yesterday.

She gasped, covering her hands with her mouth, and he smiled. There was a small table with three chairs, set for an early dinner. He'd even managed to scrounge up a real tablecloth. The look on her face right now? The pure delight in her eyes made it worth every single favor he now owed to a half dozen guys in the 609.

"How did you do this?" She wandered toward the table.

"Magic."

She tossed him a look over her shoulder, and he laughed.

"I might owe some of the guys a few favors. A lot of favors." He tilted his head as she turned at the first chair. "I might not have a night off for a while."

"And you did this all for me?" she asked as he pulled out her chair.

"Well, I had a couple other girls on the list just in case you turned me down," he joked.

"I'd certainly hate to see it go to waste," she deadpanned, pursing her lips. "Perhaps Mary would have obliged you."

He paused with his hand on the chair, gauging her tone. He'd been flying with the Brits for months now, but he never could guess if they were joking or not.

"Oh, your face is priceless." She laughed, and the sound was just as beautiful as she was. "Now tell me, are we expecting company?" She motioned toward the third chair.

"I invited Glenn Miller," he answered, pulling back the chair to reveal his most prized possession.

"You have a phonograph?" Her jaw dropped.

"I do." He popped the lid and started the little portable up, filling the quiet with The Glenn Miller Orchestra.

She studied him with a look on her face that he was hesitant to call wonder, but he sure liked it. So much for playing it smooth, because his heart took off like a thousand horses as he sat in the chair across from her.

He'd never been so nervous about a date in his life.

He'd also never had to repeatedly ask for one.

"Now, don't get excited; it's a picnic dinner." He reached for the basket at the center of the table.

"Really? Couldn't you have put a little more effort into this evening?" Her lips pursed, but he was on to her tell, so he just grinned and served them both.

It was all cold cuts, cheese, and one very expensive bottle of wine that he definitely hadn't had a ration card for.

"This really is lovely," she whispered.

"You make it lovely. The rest is just a little preparation," he countered as they began to eat.

She'd been to parties, and even out on a few dates before the war, but nothing that came close to this. The sheer effort he'd gone to was incredible. It had given her a second's pause when he'd teased about having a lineup waiting, but she refused to dwell on it and spoil the night.

There was no use looking for a parachute, since she'd already jumped.

"So how many favors do you owe for the phonograph?" she asked. Portables were hard to come by, not to mention ungodly expensive, and she knew what RAF officers made.

"I have to come back alive." He said it so matter-of-factly that she almost missed it.

"I'm sorry?"

"My mother gave it to me when I left last year." His voice dropped slightly. "She said she'd had a little tucked aside for when I got married, but then I announced rather suddenly—she was quite clear about that point—that I was off on what my father called a 'fool's errand.'"

Her heart plummeted at the shadow she saw flicker across his eyes. "He didn't approve?"

"He didn't approve when Uncle Vernon taught me how to fly. He absolutely loathed my decision to use those skills here. He thought I was looking for a fight." He shrugged.

"Were you?" The breeze rustled across the tops of the grass, pulling another strand of her hair free, and she quickly tucked it behind her ear.

"Partially," Jameson admitted with a conciliatory flash of a smile. "But I figure this war is going to spread if we don't stop it, and I'll be damned if I was just going to sit there in Colorado and do nothing while it crept up onto our front porch."

His hand tensed on his fork, and she leaned across the small expanse of the table to rest her fingers over his. The contact sent a slight buzzing sensation down her body.

"I, for one, am thankful you decided to come," she said. That singular choice told her more about the content of his character than a thousand pretty words ever could have.

"I'm just glad you decided to come tonight," he said softly.

"Me too." Their gazes held, and his hand slipped away from hers with a caress.

"Tell me something about you. Anything."

Her forehead puckered, trying to think of something that would keep his interest now that she'd decided she wanted it. "I think one day, I would like to be a novelist."

"Then you should be," he said simply, as if it were just that easy. Perhaps to an American, it was. She envied him that.

"One can hope." Her voice softened. "My family is in disagreement, and there's an ongoing argument about who should get to decide my future."

"What does that mean?"

"Simply put, my father has a title and he doesn't want to let it go. He refuses to see that the world is changing."

"A title?" Two lines formed between his eyebrows. "Like a job title? Or one you inherit?"

"Inherit. I want nothing to do with it, but he has other plans. I'm hoping I can change them before the war is over." That didn't seem to work. He still looked worried. "It's not like there's much of anything left anyway. My parents have spent just about everything. It's minor—the title—and really doesn't matter, I promise. Can we change the subject?"

"Sure." He set his silverware on the plate, then changed the record to Billie Holiday and offered his hand as "The Very Thought of You" began to play. "Dance with me, Scarlett."

"All right." She couldn't resist. He was magnetic, sinfully gorgeous, and ridiculously charming.

His arms surrounded her as they swayed to the beat in the dying sunlight, and she melted when he pulled her in close. Her head rested perfectly in the hollow of his shoulder, and the rough canvas of his coveralls only served to remind her that this was very real.

How easy it would be to lose herself in this man for a while, to forget all that raged around them and would eventually come for them, to claim something—someone—for herself.

"Do you have someone waiting at home?" she questioned, hating the way her voice pitched toward the end.

"No one at home. No one here. Just my little record player." His chuckling voice rumbled against her ear. "And I do love music, but it's hardly a monogamous relationship."

"So you don't fly every girl to sunset dinners?" She tilted her head back slightly.

He lifted his hand, taking her chin between his thumb and forefinger. "Never. I knew I was a lucky bastard if I even got one shot with you, so I figured it had better be a good one."

Her gaze dropped to his lips. "It was. It is."

"Good." He nodded slowly. "Now I have everything set up for the next officer I find on the side of the road."

She scoffed, then pushed off his chest with a laugh, but he kept hold of her wrist and reeled her back in, bringing his mouth dangerously close to hers.

Yes. She wanted to kiss him, to know how he tasted, to feel his lips moving with hers.

"Are you ready?" His hand splayed on her lower back, pulling her closer.

"Ready?" she asked, rising on her toes.

"Well, you seem a little inexperienced," he whispered, dipping lower.

"I am." It came out as breathless as she felt. She'd only been kissed once, so she could hardly call that experience.

"It's okay; we'll go slow," he promised as his hand rose to cup her cheek. "I don't want you to be frightened when I turn the controls over."

She ignored whatever Americanism that was and arched her neck, but the man stepped back. *He. Backed. Away?* She stood there like a fish with her mouth open as he grinned.

"Let's go, trainee, let's make this little flight legitimate." He held out his hand.

She blinked rapidly. "Trainee?" Was she getting her vernacular confused?

He drew her against him, caressing her neck and tunneling his hands through her hair as he lowered his lips to what had to be only centimeters above her own.

"You have no idea how badly I want to kiss you right now, Scarlett."

And there went her knees.

Good, then they were on the same page.

"But if we don't leave right this second, we'll lose the horizon, and that will make it three times harder to keep the airplane level while you're flying it."

She gasped, and he brushed his lips over hers, taunting her with the promise of a kiss before leaving her wanting.

"Wait. Flying it?" she exclaimed.

"Well, yeah, what do you think training flights are for?" He took her hand and tugged her gently. "Come on, you're going to love it. It's addictive."

"And deadly."

He turned, then lifted her in his arms so he could place her on the wing. Everywhere their bodies connected hummed.

"I won't let anything happen to you," he promised. "You just have to trust me."

She nodded slowly. "Okay. I can do that."

CHAPTER FIVE

Georgia

Dear Constance,

Leaving you today was the hardest thing I've ever done. If it were only me, I never would have left. I would have stayed by your side and seen this war through, just as we promised. But we both know this was never about me. My heart screams for all that we've lost in the past few days—at the injustice of it all. I promised you once that I would never allow our father to get his hands on William, and I won't.

I wish I could keep you safe as well. Our lives have turned out so very differently than we planned. I wish you were with me, that we had taken this journey together. You have been my compass all these years, and I'm not sure I'll be able to find my way without you, but as I promised this morning as we said our goodbyes, I will do my best. I carry you with me in my heart, always. I see you in William's blue eyes—our eyes—and his sweet smile. You were always meant for happiness, Constance, and I'm so sorry that my choices robbed you of so many chances to find it. There will always be a place for you with me.

I love you with all my heart,
Scarlett

"**A**nd then it just…ends," I said to Hazel as we sat on her back patio, watching her toddlers splash around in the baby pool at our feet. "And as a reader, it's the darkest moment, so you know there has to be a third act, right? But as her great-granddaughter—" I shook my head. "I understand why she could never write it."

I'd finished the manuscript at six a.m. but waited until the clock chimed seven before calling Hazel, and it was a respectable noon before I'd shown up at her place after a quick cat nap. She'd been my best friend since kindergarten—the year Mom left me on Gran's doorstep for the second time—and our friendship had survived despite the vastly different paths our lives had taken.

"So the book is based on her own life?" She leaned forward and wiggled her finger at her son in the blow-up pool in front of us. "No, no, Colin, you can't take your sister's ball. Give it back."

The mischievous little blond who happened to look just like his mother reluctantly returned the beach ball to his younger sister.

"Yep. The manuscript stops right before she left for the States, at least that's what the letters indicate. And the letters…" I blew my breath out slowly, trying to exhale the ache in my chest. That love, it wasn't what I'd had with Damian, and it started to make sense why Gran had been so against my marrying him. "They loved each other so much. Can you believe my mother found an entire box of Gran's correspondence from the war and never even told me?" I stretched my legs out in front of me, resting one bare foot on the side of the pool.

"Well…" Hazel grimaced. "It's your mom." She quickly sipped at her iced tea.

"True." I felt my sigh in the depths of my bones. Hazel did her best not to go negative when it came to Mom, and truthfully, she was probably the only one I'd allow to, since she'd been around through the worst of it. That was the thing about Mom—I could criticize her, but no one else was allowed to.

"How is it? Being home?" she asked. "Not that I'm not personally psyched that you're here, because I am."

"You're just happy to have someone else around you trust to babysit," I teased.

"Guilty. But seriously, how is it?"

"Complicated." I watched her children splash in the mid-shin water and contemplated my answer. "If I close my eyes, I can pretend the last six years never happened. I never fell for Damian.

I never met Damian's...fiancée—"

"Noooo!" Hazel gasped, her mouth dropping open. "He's engaged?"

"He is, according to the seventeen text messages I've gotten today. Thank God for do-not-disturb." The future Mrs. Damian Ellsworth was now a twenty-two-year-old blonde with much bigger breasts than the ones filling my healthy C cup. I shrugged. "I expected it, seeing as she's due any minute now." Didn't make it hurt any less, but it wasn't like I could change anything that had happened.

"I'm sorry," Hazel said quietly. "He never deserved you."

"You know that's not true, not at first anyway." I wiggled my ringless fingers at her two-year-old, Danielle, who gave me a toothy smile in return. "He wanted kids. I didn't give him kids. In the end, he found someone who could. Does it hurt like a bi—" I cringed but caught myself. Hazel would never let me live it down if her kids started swearing because of me. "That he didn't exactly wait for our marriage to end before hooking up with his lead? Or that it was on one of Gran's movies? Sure, but we both know she wasn't the first girl in his trailer, and she won't be the last. I don't envy her that." I'd been the launchpad for his career. I just hadn't admitted it until the last few years. "Besides, we both know the love was long gone." It had died little by little with Damian's affairs that I'd pretended hadn't happened, hollowing me out until all I had left to hold on to was my pride.

"Fine, you can be all zen about it. I'll hate him enough for the both of us." She shook her head. "If Owen ever did something like that..." Her expression fell.

"He never would," I assured her. "Your husband is wild about you."

"He might not be too wild about the twenty pounds I'm still hauling around from Danielle." She jiggled her belly, and I rolled my eyes. "But in my defense, he's working up to a dad bod, so we're even. A sexy dentist dad bod." She smirked.

I laughed. "Well, I think you look great, and the learning center turned out phenomenal! I passed it on the way into town."

She grinned. "That's been a labor of love made possible by a very generous donor." She sipped her tea and looked over her sunglasses at me.

"We need more Darcys in the world," I answered with a little shrug.

"Says the woman with a thing for Hemingway."

"I have a thing for the broody creatives."

"Speaking of broody creatives, you didn't tell me that Noah Harrison is drop-your-panties gorgeous!" She swatted my shoulder with the back of her hand. "I shouldn't have to web search him to know that! Details!"

He was *exactly* that gorgeous. My lips parted, remembering the intensity in those dark eyes. I'd probably spontaneously combust if he ever touched me...not that touching was even a remote possibility. I'd heard more than enough from Damian over the years to know Noah was also a cocky jackass.

"I was a little busy absorbing the fact that my mother tried to sell the manuscript behind my back," I argued. "And honestly, that man is an arrogant know-it-all who specializes in emotional sadism. Damian tried more than once to buy the rights to a few of his books." Though I should have probably started questioning anything Damian had told me at this point.

"Fine," she grumbled. "Can we at least agree that he's a *hot* emotional sadist?"

A corner of my mouth lifted. "We can, because he is. So hot." Heat crept up my neck just thinking about how good-looking that man was. "Add that to his career, and his ego is almost too big to fit through the door—you should have heard him in the bookstore—but yes, ungodly, impossible levels of hotness." I wasn't even starting in on the intensity with which he looked at me. The guy had the smoldering gaze down to a fine art.

"Excellent. Are you going to give him the goods?" She raised her eyebrows. "Because I'd give him whatever he asked for."

I rolled my eyes. "If by *goods* you mean the manuscript and the letters, I haven't decided yet." I rubbed my forehead as a lump formed in my throat. "I wish I could ask her what she wanted, but I feel like I already know. If she'd wanted the book finished, she would have done it herself."

"Why didn't she?"

"She told me once that it was kinder to the characters to leave them with their possibilities, but she didn't talk about it much, and I never pushed her."

"Then why are you considering this?" she asked softly.

"Because it's something Mom wants that I can give her." I smiled when Danielle dumped a cup of water over my toes.

"If that's not a loaded statement…" Hazel muttered with a sigh. "You're going to do it, aren't you?" There was no judgment in her tone, merely curiosity.

"Yeah, I think I am."

"I get why. Gran would get it, too."

"I miss her." My voice broke as my throat constricted. "There have been so many times I've needed her over the last six months. And it's like she knew it, too. She set up all those little packages and flower deliveries for me." The first had come on my birthday, then Valentine's Day, and so on. "But everything has fallen apart since she died—my marriage, the production company, my charity work…all of it." The production company had been hard, since Damian and I had started it together, but leaving it behind had been the only way to move forward. Losing the charity work, the foundation, now that made it blatantly obvious that I needed to find something to fill my days. A job, volunteering…something. There were only so many times I could clean the house, especially since Lydia had come back to help.

"Hey," Hazel snapped, forcing my gaze to meet hers before she softened. "I get leaving the production company. You hated all the movie stuff, but the charity was more than his connections.

The blood, the sweat, and the tears that went into it? Those were all yours, and now your future is yours to do whatever you want with it. Go back to sculpting. Blow some glass. Be happy."

"The lawyers are drawing up papers so I can start putting that money to work." The only caveat in her will when it came to her fortune was that I give it away to what charities I saw fit. "And it's been...years since I did anything with glass art." My fingers curled in my lap. God, I missed the heat, the magic that came from taking something at its melted, most vulnerable state and reshaping it into something uniquely beautiful. But I'd given all that up to start the production company when I got married.

"I'm just saying that I know Gran didn't throw away your tweezers—"

"They're called jacks."

"See, it hasn't been *that* long. Where's the girl who spent a summer in Murano, who got into her first-choice art school and put on her own show in New York?"

"One show." I held up a finger. "My favorite piece sold that night. It was right before the wedding, remember? The one that took me months." It was still in the lobby of an office building in Manhattan. "Did I ever tell you that I used to visit it? Not often, just on days I felt like Damian's life had swallowed mine. I'd sit on the bench and just stare at it, trying to remember how all that passion felt."

"So go make another one. Make a hundred of them. You're the only person who gets to put demands on your time now, though I wouldn't argue if you ever want to come volunteer at the center."

"I don't exactly have a furnace, or a block, or a studio—" I paused, remembering that Mr. Navarro's shop had been up for sale, then shaking my head. "I could definitely volunteer with the reading program, though. Just let me know when."

"Deal. You know Noah Harrison is going to turn that book

into a pain fest, right?" she asked, quirking an eyebrow.

"I'm counting on it." It couldn't end any other way.

Three days later, the doorbell rang, and I nearly jumped out of my skin. It was time.

"I'll get it!" Mom called, already clicking her way to the door—which was fine with me, since dread had my butt anchored to Gran's office chair, debating my choice for the thousandth time since telling Helen to send the final contract.

Three days. That was all it had taken them to hammer out the details. Helen had assured me it was more than fair, and we didn't give up anything Gran wouldn't have, including the performance rights—those, she'd only ever sold to Damian, and he sure as hell wasn't getting any more. In fact, it was the best contract of Gran's career, which was one of the reasons my stomach churned.

The other reason had just walked into the house.

I heard his voice through the door—deep and sure, tinged with excitement. The more I'd thought about this deal, the more I'd realized that he really was the only one who could do it. His ego was earned in this department. He was a specialist in gut-wrenching endings, and this story surely had one.

"She's in Gran's office," Mom said as she opened one of the massive cherry double doors that had closed Gran off from the world while she wrote.

Noah Harrison filled the doorway, but it felt like he consumed the room. He had that kind of presence—the kind that other men paid thousands of dollars in acting classes to try to pull off for Damian's films. The kind those actors had to have because they were playing roles Gran had written in her books.

"Ms. Stanton," he said quietly, sliding his hands into his pockets, his eyes seeing far more than I wanted them to.

I looked away, tucked a piece of my hair behind my ear, and silenced the part of my brain that nearly corrected him. *You're not Mrs. Ellsworth anymore. Get used to it.*

"I think if you're going to be writing Gran's story, you can call me Georgia." I brought my gaze to meet his and noted, to his credit, that he wasn't staring at the shelves of rare books or even the infamous typewriter that Gran had sworn by in the middle of the desk. His eyes were still on me.

Me. As if I were something just as rare and valuable as the treasures that filled this room.

"Georgia," he said slowly, as if tasting my name. "Then you'll have to call me Noah."

"It's really Morelli, right?" I already knew the answer, along with just about everything regarding his career up to this point. Whatever I hadn't known at the time of our unfortunate run-in at the bookstore, I'd been schooled on by Helen. Hazel had taken over when it came to the revolving door of women in his life.

"It's Morelli. Harrison is a pen name," he admitted with a slight tilt of his lips.

Drop-your-panties gorgeous. Hazel's description echoed through my brain as my cheeks flamed. How long had it been since I'd felt real, true attraction to a man? And why the hell did it have to be *this* man?

"Well, have a seat, Noah Morelli; I'm just waiting for them to send the contract." I motioned to both of the leather, winged-back chairs across from the one I sat in.

"I signed my portion before driving over, so they're probably accepting it right now." He chose the one on the right.

"Would either of you like a drink?" Mom offered from the doorway in her best hostess voice. God bless her, the woman had been on her best behavior since Monday. Attentive. Caring. I almost didn't recognize her. She'd even promised to stay through Christmas, swearing that I was what brought her back to Poplar Grove in the first place.

"Be careful—all she knows how to make are sodas and martinis," I whispered loudly.

"I heard that, Georgia Constance Stanton," Mom lectured with a mock scowl.

"I'm not sure about that. Last time she poured a mean lemonade." Noah laughed lightly, revealing straight, white—but not fake white—even teeth. Had to admit, I was looking for any imperfection at this point. Even his inability to see a romance through to a happily-ever-after was a mark in his favor at this point, which meant I was looking *hard*.

"And I can do it again," Mom said.

Ten years ago, I would have said Mom's chipper, maternal attitude was everything I'd ever wanted. Now it only served to remind me how hard we both had to try to even *act* normal around the other.

"That would be great, Ava," Noah answered, never looking away.

"Me too, Mom. Thanks." I flashed a quick smile that left as soon as Mom shut the door.

"I couldn't really care less about the lemonade, but you looked like you were about to grind your teeth into dust." He crossed his ankle over his knee and sank back into the chair, resting his chin between his thumb and forefinger as he leaned on his elbow. "You always this tense around your mom? Or is it the deal?"

He was observant, just like Gran had been. Maybe it was a writer thing.

"It's been…a week." It had been a year, if I was honest. From Gran's diagnosis to her refusal of treatment, to the burial, to finding Damian with— "So, it's Morelli," I said, halting the ever-present downward spiral of my thoughts that threatened to pull me under. "I like that better," I admitted. It suited him.

"So do I, honestly." He flashed that public smile, the one everyone in New York wore to functions they didn't actually want to attend but needed to be seen at.

Those pretty smiles were just one of the many reasons I left that city—they usually melted into ugly gossip the minute your back was turned.

His expression softened, as if he'd noticed my defenses rising. "But my first agent thought Harrison sounded more…"

"Generically American?" I tapped the touch pad on my laptop, willing the contract to appear in my email before either of us had the chance to get snarky like we had in the bookstore.

"Sellable." He shifted, leaning forward. "And I'm not going to lie, anonymity can be a lifesaver sometimes."

I cringed. "Or it can lead to arguments in a bookstore."

"Is that an apology?" That was definitely a smirk.

"Hardly." I scoffed. "I stand by every word I said. I just wouldn't have offered my opinion quite so freely had I known to whom I was speaking."

Delight flickered in his eyes. "Honesty. Now that's refreshing."

"I've always been honest." I hit refresh again. "The only people who ever bothered to listen are dead, and everyone else hears what they want to, anyway. Oh look, it's here." I sighed in relief and clicked open the email.

I'd gotten pretty good at these since Gran had put all her rights into a literary trust and named me as executor about five years ago, so it only took a few minutes to scan through everything that wasn't boilerplate. There weren't any changes from the one Helen had sent over for approval earlier.

When I reached the signature box beneath Noah's, I gripped the stylus, then paused. I wasn't just handing over one of her works—I was giving him her life.

"Did you know that she wrote seventy-three novels?" I asked.

Noah's eyebrows rose. "Yes, and all but one were on that typewriter," he added, nodding toward the World War II-era hunk of metal consuming the left side of the desk. When I tilted my head, he continued. "It broke in 1973 while she was writing *The Strength of Two*, so she used the closest model she could find while that one was sent back to England for repair."

My mouth dropped.

"I can nail all of your trivia, Georgia. I told you," he said, resting his chin on the tips of his fingers with a half smile more dangerously attractive than the flashier one had been. "I'm a fan."

"Right."

My heart thundered as I stared at the stylus. In this moment, the choice was still mine, but the second I signed on that line, her story became his.

You still have final approval.

"I know the worth of what you're giving me," he said quietly, his voice low and serious.

My gaze jumped to his.

"I also know you don't like me, but don't worry, I've made it my personal mission in life to win you over." A self-deprecating grin materialized for the length of a heartbeat before he wiped it away, rubbing his fingers over his lips as he looked down at the desk with open admiration.

The energy in the room shifted, easing some of my tension from my shoulders as he slowly brought those dark eyes back to mine.

"I will do this right," he promised. "And if I don't, then you pull it. You have the final say." Only the slight tick of his jaw gave away his nervousness.

"And you have an out in the contract, too, if you read it and decide you're just not up for the challenge." I'd have bet that he was a hell of a poker player, but I'd learned to spot a bluff a mile away when I was eight. Lucky for him, he was telling the truth. He honestly believed that he could finish the book.

"I won't use it. When I commit, I commit."

Just this once, I allowed myself to be comforted by someone else's confidence. *Arrogance. Whatever.*

I glanced at the lone photo Gran kept on her desk, right next to the paperweight I'd made her in Murano. It was of her and

Grandpa Jameson, both in uniform, so lost in each other that my chest ached for what they'd had...and lost. I'd never loved Damian like that. I wasn't even sure Gran had loved Grandpa Brian like that, either.

That was the real stuff, right there.

I signed my name on the contract and clicked enter, sending it off to the publisher as Mom walked in with the drinks, smiling from ear to ear.

She handed us our lemonade, and I retrieved two coasters from the desk drawer—not that there was much condensation to be had up here at eight thousand feet. But still. I wasn't risking this desk to anything.

"Did you sign it?" Mom's tone was calm, but she was white-knuckling her own hands.

I nodded.

Her shoulders relaxed. "Oh. Good. It's all done, then?"

"Publisher has to sign it, but yes," I answered.

"Thank you, Georgia." Her lower lip trembled slightly as she gripped my shoulder, caressing me with her thumb before letting go with two pats.

"Of course, Mom." My throat tightened.

"I hope you don't mind, but I'd like to wait a few more minutes," Noah said. "Charles told me they'd sign it immediately, and I'd much rather the deal be finalized before I take the manuscript off your hands."

"Naturally," Mom answered as she moved toward the door. "I will say, Noah—you look good at Gran's desk. It's nice to have your kind of creative genius in here again."

Your kind of creative genius? My stomach twisted.

"Well, it's an honor to be in Scarlett Stanton's office," he said over his shoulder. "I'm sure you've both gotten a lot of inspiration from this place."

Mom's brow puckered. "Funny you should mention it, but Georgia actually did go to some art school on the east coast. Not that she uses her degree, but we're all very proud."

Heat rushed up my neck, setting my cheeks on fire as my twisting stomach plummeted to the floor.

"It wasn't just any art school, Mom. It was the Rhode Island School of Design. It's the Harvard of art schools," I reminded her. "And I might not have used my studio major, but my concentration in media and technology definitely helped get my production company off the ground." Holy shit, was I five years old again? Because it sure felt like it.

"Oh, I didn't mean anything by it. I just thought you gave away money for a living." She gave me a reassuring smile.

I pressed my lips together and nodded. This wasn't the time or place for this fight. *I ran a twenty-million-dollar charity, for fuck's sake, but okay.*

She shut the door behind her, and Noah raised his eyebrows at me. "Do I want to know?"

"Nope." I clicked refresh on my inbox a little harder than necessary and avoided his eyes at all costs. "Feel free to look around the room and get a feel for her," I offered, clicking again.

"Thanks." He moved around Gran's office in silence for the next ten minutes while I hit the refresh button so often, my mouse sounded like morse code.

"You're in a lot of these pictures," he noted, leaning in toward Gran's photo gallery.

"She raised me." That was the simplest explanation to both the question he'd asked and the one he hadn't.

He studied me for an awkward moment, then moved on.

"Oh, thank God," I muttered, opening the notification that the contract had been accepted. I took the thumb drive I'd spent the last few days preparing and walked it over to him. "It's here. Deal is done."

"What's this?" His brow furrowed.

"It's the manuscript, the letters, and a few pictures." I pressed it into his palm. "Now you have everything."

His fingers wrapped around the drive, but his entire frame tensed. "I want the actual manuscript."

"Good, because it's here." I gestured to his palm. "I scanned everything in, and before you argue, the chances of you walking out that door with my gran's originals are zero and zero. Even she used to make a copy before sending it to her editor."

"But I'm not the editor. I'm now the writer who is finishing the original manuscript." His jaw ticked, and I got the feeling he wasn't used to losing. Ever.

"Were you planning on typing it out on this thing, too?" I nodded toward Gran's typewriter. "Just to keep it authentic?"

His eyes narrowed.

"Just checking. Originals stay. Period. Or hey, feel free to use that out." Originals never left the house, and he wasn't the exception just because he was pretty. Our eyes warred in a silent argument, but eventually he nodded.

"I'll begin reading tonight and will call you with my thoughts when I'm finished. Once we agree on the direction of the plot, I'll start writing."

I walked him to the door, unable to kick the nervousness tightening my chest. "You said you know the worth of what I just handed to you."

"I do."

Our gazes collided, the electricity—chemistry, attraction, whatever it was—coursing between us enough to raise goose bumps on my arm. "Earn it."

His dark eyes flared at the challenge. "I'll give them the happily-ever-after they deserve."

My hand tightened on the doorknob. "Oh, no. That's the one thing you *can't* do."

CHAPTER SIX

August 1940

Middle Wallop, England

Scarlett's heart clenched as she watched Jameson whirl Constance around the small dance floor of the local pub. He took so much care with Constance because he knew how precious she was to Scarlett, which only made her like him more.

Too much, too soon, too fast…it was all of that and then some, but she couldn't bring herself to slow it down.

"You're falling for him, aren't you?" one of his American friends—Howard Reed, if she remembered correctly—asked from across their table, his arm wrapped around Christine, another filter officer who bunked in the same hut as Scarlett.

Christine glanced over the top of the newspaper she was reading. The headlines were more than enough to convince Scarlett to look away.

"I…couldn't say," Scarlett answered, even as heat bloomed in her cheeks, giving her away. She was with Jameson every free moment they had, and between his flight hours and her schedule, there weren't a lot of moments to be had between them.

She'd only known him for three weeks, and yet she couldn't remember what the world had felt like before. There were now two eras in her life—before Jameson, and now.

She filed the *after Jameson* in the same category as *after the war*. Both were obscure enough concepts that she refused to waste her time examining either of them, especially now. Since the Battle of Britain, as Churchill had called it, had begun a few weeks ago, and the Germans had begun bombing various airfields around Britain, their time together had taken on the sharp, undeniable taste of desperation—an urgency to grasp on to what they could while they had it.

Work had picked up, too. Their schedule was grueling, and she found herself placing flags for Jameson's own patrols on the map, marking his current location and holding her breath as the news came in minute by minute from the radio operators. She noticed every time a 609 flag moved, even if it wasn't on her section of the board.

"Yeah, well, he's sweet on you, too," Howard remarked with a grin.

The song came to an end, but there was no band to clap for, just a record to be changed.

Jameson escorted Constance through the sea of uniforms and back to the table.

"Dance with me, Scarlett," he said, offering his hand and a smile that stripped away her defenses.

"Of course." She traded places with her sister, then slid into Jameson's arms as a slower tune started up.

"I'm glad I got to see you tonight," he said into her hair.

"I hate that it's only for a few hours." She rested her cheek on his chest and breathed him in. He always smelled like soap, aftershave lotion, and the tang of metal that seemed to cling to his skin even between patrols.

"I'll take a few hours with you on a Wednesday night whenever I get the chance," he promised softly.

His heartbeat was strong and steady as they swayed. Here was the only place she felt safe or certain about anything lately. There was nothing in this world that compared to the feel of his arms around her.

"I wish I could stay here, just like this," she said softly, her fingers making lazy circles on the shoulder of his uniform.

"We can." His hand splayed on her lower back without venturing into more southern territory, unlike many of the other soldiers around them with their partners.

Jameson was respectful to the level of complete and utter frustration. He hadn't so much as kissed her—not really, though he'd often move just close enough to spike her heart rate before pressing his lips to her forehead.

"For another fifteen minutes," she muttered. "Then you have to leave for patrol."

"And you have work, if I'm not mistaken."

She sighed, then looked away from the couple next to them as dancing became a fully involved kiss.

"Why haven't you kissed me?" Scarlett asked him softly.

His rhythm broke for a breath of a second, and he took her chin between his thumb and finger, tilting her face gently toward his. "Yet."

Her brow furrowed.

"Why haven't I kissed you *yet*," he clarified.

"Don't play with words."

"I'm not." He caressed her lower lip with his thumb. "I'm just making sure you know it's a *yet*."

She rolled her eyes. "Fine, then why haven't you kissed me *yet*?" All around them, the world changed so fast, she barely knew what to expect in the next minute. Bombs fell and planes crashed, yet he acted like they had years—when she wasn't sure they even had days.

He glanced toward the couple at their left. No wonder she was questioning his less than speedy timing. "Because you're not just another girl in a pub," he said as they began to sway again, his hand cupping her face gently. "Because we've only been alone once, and kissing you for the first time isn't something I want to happen in front of an audience." Not if he kissed her like he wanted to.

"Oh." Her eyebrows shot up.

"Oh." A slow smile spread across his face. If she knew half the thoughts that went through his head when it came to her, she would have put in for a transfer. "I also know your world has a hell of a lot more rules than mine, so I'm trying my best not to break any of them."

"Not so many, really." She tugged her lower lip between her teeth, as though she needed to think it over.

"Sweetheart, you're an actual aristocrat under this uniform." From what he'd been able to piece together between what little she told him about her family and the details Constance was more than willing to part with, the life Scarlett led as a WAAF officer was so different from her pre-war lifestyle that the two couldn't be compared.

She blinked. "My parents are."

He laughed. "And the difference is?"

"Well, I don't have any brothers, so the title will go into abeyance once my father passes," she answered with a shrug. "Constance and I are seen as equal under the law, so unless one of us declines the title, neither of us will inherit it. We've both decided not to decline, which is rather brilliant when you think about it." A corner of her mouth lifted in a secretive smile, making him wish they were alone and far from in public.

"You've decided to fight for it?" English peerage was so far beyond his area of expertise that he didn't pretend to understand.

"No." Her hand slid up his shoulder and over the collar of his uniform until she cupped the back of his neck. He felt her touch in every nerve of his body. "We decided *not* to fight for it by simply not declining it. Neither of us wants it. Constance is engaged to Edward, who will inherit his own, so our parents are pleased, and I want nothing to do with it." She shook her head. "We made a vow when we were younger. See?" She lifted her hand, showing a faint line of a scar down her palm. "It was all very dramatic."

His head tilted slightly as he absorbed her words. "And what *do* you want, Scarlett?"

The record changed, and the tempo picked up, but they stayed at the same, gentle sway at the edge of the floor, carving out their own little ballad.

"Right now, I want to dance with you," she answered, stroking her fingers down his neck.

"I can give you that." Man, it was those eyes that just about knocked him on his ass every time. She could have asked for the moon, and he would have flown his Spitfire into the stratosphere just to get her to look at him like she was right now.

When that song ended, they reluctantly left the floor, holding hands as they approached the table.

"Seven fifteen," Constance noted with a small grimace. "It's about time we get going, isn't it?" She stood and handed Scarlett her hat.

"It is," Scarlett agreed. "Especially since we'll need to drop by the airfield for Jameson and Howard." She turned to Christine, who was still consumed by the newspaper. "Christine?"

She startled. "Oh, I'm sorry. I was just reading about the bombing in Sussex."

Well, that certainly sobered the mood. Jameson's fingers tightened slightly around Scarlett's. "Well, I guess I'll drive and you read," he offered with a tight smile.

Christine nodded, and they all made their way to the car. Tonight, neither he nor Howard had been able to secure their company's car, but Scarlett had.

"You don't mind dropping us by the airfield?" he asked as he held the front passenger door open for her.

"Not at all," she promised, her hand skimming along his waist as she slid into the seat. "It will give me another ten minutes with you, and who knows when I'll get that again."

He nodded, then shut the door once she was in, wishing

she'd have preferred Constance, Christine, or even Howard drove instead of him so he could have tucked her in tight against him in the back seat. Instead, he took the wheel and began the drive to the airfield. This was always when the mood shifted between them, when they both mentally prepared for what their nights had in store while they'd be apart.

The sun was starting to set earlier now that they were in the middle of August, but he'd still have a healthy amount of light for takeoff in an hour.

"How about some music?" Constance asked, breaking the silence.

"The radio in this one is broken," Scarlett said. "Looks like one of us will have to sing."

Jameson smiled, shaking his head. The girl had a dry sense of humor, and he couldn't get enough of it.

"Here, I'll read. May I?" Howard asked, and Jameson heard the paper shifting hands. "I have five dollars that says I can get everyone to sleep before we reach the airfield with this thing." Howard's eyebrows shot up in the rearview. "Except you, Stanton. You'd better stay awake."

"On it," Jameson responded as they pulled onto the station. Once they were through the gate, he took Scarlett's hand, shaking his head at the mundane tone Howard used to read an article about supply shortages.

"He really might put me to sleep," Scarlett whispered.

Jameson squeezed her hand.

"Coming to the aid of our troops is none other than the head of Wadsworth Shipping, George Wadsworth—" Howard continued.

Scarlett stiffened at his side.

"—who has more than one merger to celebrate with a confirmed source stating that his oldest son, Henry, is to be engaged to the oldest daughter of Baron and Lady Wright..."

Scarlett gasped, covering her mouth with the hand he *wasn't* holding.

"Oh God," Constance muttered.

Jameson felt the earth beneath him shift, and his stomach bottomed out. *It can't be.*

Howard's solemn gaze met his in the rearview, and he knew it was.

"Well, surely there's more than one *Wright* in the country," Christine muttered, yanking the paper back from Howard. "Henry is to be engaged to the oldest daughter of Baron and Lady Wright, Scarlett..." Christine fell quiet as she glanced toward Scarlett.

"Please, read the rest," Jameson snapped. What the hell? Had she played him for a fool? Or had he been a fool all along?

"Um...Scarlett," she continued to read, "who is currently serving in His Majesties' Women's Auxiliary Air Force. Both of Wright's daughters joined the fight last year and were commissioned as officers." The paper crinkled. "The rest is about the munitions," she finished softly, just in time for him to park the car at the edge of the lot that faced the narrow end of all three hangers.

"Looks like you lost that five dollars, Howard, because we're all wide awake." Jameson killed the engine and threw open the door. She was already in a relationship and about to be *engaged*. While he'd been falling in love with her, she'd been using him for what? A little entertainment? He glanced to the runway at his left, ready to launch, to leave the ground behind for a few hours.

Jameson slammed the door, and the sound jarred Scarlett from her shock. She flew out of the car, but he was halfway down the pavement to the hangar by the time she caught up with him. "Jameson! Wait!"

How could they do this? How could they inform the *Daily*

that she and Henry were going to be engaged when she'd firmly told her mother she wouldn't do it? It was *them* behind this, not just George. This reeked of her parents' interference, and she'd be damned if it cost her Jameson.

"Wait for what, Scarlett?" he snapped as he strode away, those warm, dark eyes of his going cold and taking her heart with them. "Wait for you to marry some rich society-type? Was that why you wanted to know why I hadn't kissed you yet? Were you worried about running out of time to pull one over on me?" He never broke stride, those long legs carrying him farther away from her with every step.

"That's not what's going on! I'm not engaged!" she argued, racing to get ahead of him. "Listen to me!" She put her hands on his chest and stopped, forcing him to pause or run her over.

He halted, but the look he gave crushed her all the same.

"Are you *getting* engaged?"

"No!" She shook her head emphatically. "My parents want me to marry Henry, but I won't do it. They're trying to force my hand." She would never forgive them for this. Not ever.

"Force your hand?" His jaw ticked, and her mind scrambled for a way to make him understand.

"Yes!" She didn't bother to check if they were being overheard or where the others from the car were. She didn't care who heard what she said as long as he did. "It's not true."

"It's in the paper!" He stepped back from her and laced his fingers over his hat.

"Because they think publishing it as fact will force me to agree out of embarrassment or duty!" she fired back.

"Will it?" he challenged.

"No!" Her chest tightened, facing the possibility that he might not believe her.

He looked away, clearly torn, and she couldn't blame him. Her parents and the Wadsworths had dumped her in a damnable mess.

"Jameson, please. I swear I'm not marrying Henry Wadsworth."
Death was preferable.

"But your parents want you to?"

She nodded.

"And this Wadsworth guy wants you to?"

"Henry's father believes the title—and the seat in the House
of Lords—will fall to Henry if we marry, and if not Henry, then
our firstborn son, which it won't because—"

"*Your* firstborn son?" His eyes narrowed. "Now you're having
future kids with this guy?"

Apparently, that was *not* the thing to say to get him to understand.

"Of course not! None of it matters, because I'm not going
to marry him!" A dull buzzing sounded in her head, as though
her own mind were shutting down to spare her what felt like
impending heartbreak. "If you believe this stunt, you let them
win. I will not."

"It's easy to lose a fight you don't know you're in." At least
he was looking at her again, but the accusation in his eyes nearly
brought tears to hers. He looked as though he'd been betrayed,
and in a way, he had.

"I should have told you," she whispered.

"Yes, you should have," he agreed. "What kind of parents
try to force their daughter into a marriage she doesn't want?"
His hands slid to the back of his neck, as if he needed to keep
those hands busy.

"The kind who have sold off nearly all the land and spent
themselves into financial ruin." Her arms fell to her sides as
Jameson's eyes widened. "Titles don't necessarily mean lavish
bank accounts." The buzzing grew louder.

"Stanton! Reed! We have to go!" someone shouted from
behind them.

"Financial ruin." Jameson shook his head. "You mean to tell
me that your parents are what? Selling you off?"

"Trying to, yes." There was the ugly truth of it, and his face showed it. She bristled. "Don't look at me like that. You Americans think you've escaped the system of inherited wealth, but instead of the king and the peerage, you have the Astors and the Rockefellers."

"We don't sell off our daughters." His eyebrows shot high.

"I could name at least three American heiresses who have married into the peerage in the last decade alone." Scarlett folded her arms across her chest.

"So now you're defending this?" Jameson shot back as Howard ran by, turning to jog in reverse.

"Stanton! Now!" Howard shouted, waving his arm.

"No, that's not what I mean!" Scarlett sputtered. The buzzing noise shifted, the tone deepening. *Approaching aircraft.* The patrol before Jameson's was returning, which meant she had precious seconds. "Jameson, I'm not marrying Henry. I swear it."

"Why not?" he questioned, then snapped his gaze skyward, his eyes narrowing before she could even answer.

"Among other reasons, because I want you, you daft Yank!" God, she'd really lost it, arguing in public like this, but she couldn't bring herself to stop, and the man wasn't even *listening* anymore.

"Are those ours?" Howard pointed in the same direction Jameson's attention was already focused.

The squadron broke through the low-hanging clouds, and her stomach curdled. Those were not Spitfires.

The air-raid sirens wailed out the warning, but it was too late.

The end of the runway blew apart with a deafening blast she felt throughout her body. Smoke and debris filled the air as the next one hit within a heartbeat, louder and closer.

"Get down!" Jameson tugged her into the curve of his body, turning his back on the blasts and pulling her to the ground. Her knees collided with the pavement.

The hanger fifty yards in front of them exploded.

CHAPTER SEVEN

Noah

Dear Scarlett,

    I miss you, my love. The sound of your voice over the telephone doesn't compare to holding you in my arms. It's only been a few weeks, yet it feels like forever since I was reposted. Good news, I think I've been able to secure us a house close by. I know the moving has been hell on you, and if you decide you'd rather stay near Constance, then we can adjust our plans. You've given up so much for me already, and yet here I am, asking you to do it all over again. I promise when this war is over, I will make it up to you. I swear I'll never put you in the position to sacrifice for me again.

    God, I miss the feel of your skin against mine in the morning and the sight of that beautiful smile when I walk through the door at night. Right now, it's only Howard welcoming me, though he's not here much since meeting a local girl. Before you ask, no, there are no local girls for me. There's only a blue-eyed beauty who holds my heart and my future, and I'd hardly call her local, since she's hours away.

    I can't wait to hold you in my arms again.

Love,

Jameson

The rhythm pounding through my earbuds matched the beat of my feet against the pathways through Central Park as I wove in and out of the meandering tourists. Friday of Labor Day weekend had them out in full force, fanny packs and all. It was humid today, the air sticky and thick, but at least it was full of sea-level oxygen.

My mile time had sucked the entire week I'd been in Colorado. I'd mostly stayed around seven thousand feet while researching in Peru, minus the times I'd gone climbing, but Poplar Grove's elevation had been twenty-five hundred feet higher. Had to admit, though, despite the brutal lack of oxygen, the Rocky Mountain air had felt lighter, easier to move in, too. Not that Colorado beat New York in any other department. Sure, the mountains were beautiful, but so was the Manhattan skyline, and besides, nothing could compare to living in the very heartbeat of the world. This was home.

Only problem was, my head wasn't here, and hadn't been since I'd flown back more than two weeks ago. It was split down the middle between World War II Britain and modern-day Poplar Grove, Colorado, even sans oxygen. The manuscript ended at a crucial turning point in the plot, where the story could either descend into cataclysmic heartbreak or rally back from the depths of doubt to reach a love-conquers-all climax that would turn even the surliest bastard into a romantic.

And while I was normally content to play the surly part, Georgia had stepped in and stolen my role, leaving me the uncharacteristic romantic. And damn, did this story demand it. The letters between Scarlett and Jameson did, too. In the middle of a war, they'd found the real thing. They couldn't even bear to be separated for longer than a few weeks. I wasn't sure I'd ever been *with* a woman for more than a few weeks at a time. I liked my space.

I hit mile six and was no closer to understanding Georgia's asinine demand than I was when I'd left her house two weeks ago or understanding the woman herself. Usually, I ran until my thoughts worked themselves out or a plot point came to me, but just like every other day for the past two weeks, I slowed to a walk and ripped out my earbuds in pure frustration.

"Oh, thank God. I thought you—" Adam gasped. "Were

going. For a seventh, and I. Was going to. Have to drop out," he managed to say between heaving breaths as he caught up beside me.

"She doesn't want it to have a happy ending," I growled, killing the music pumping through my phone.

"So you've said," Adam noted, lifting his hands to the top of his head. "As a matter of fact, I think you've mentioned that almost every day since you got back."

"I'm going to keep saying it until I can wrap my head around it." We reached a bench near a fork in the path and stopped to briefly stretch, as was our routine.

"Great. I look forward to reading it once you do." He braced his hands on his knees and leaned over, drawing in gulps of air.

"I told you we should run more often." He only joined me once a week.

"And I told you that you're not my only writer. Now when are you sending the Stanton portion of the manuscript? This thing is a tight turnaround."

"As soon as I finish it." A corner of my mouth lifted. "Don't worry, you'll have it by the deadline."

"Really? You're going to make me wait three months? Cruel. I'm wounded." He slapped a hand over his heart.

"I know I sound like a kid, but I want to see if you're able to tell where Scarlett's writing leaves off and mine begins." I hadn't felt this excited about a book in the last three years, and I'd written six during that time. But this one…I had that *feeling*, and Georgia was tying one hand behind my back. "She's wrong, you know."

"Georgia?"

"She doesn't understand what her great-grandmother's branding was. Scarlett Stanton is a guaranteed happy ending. Her readers expect it. Georgia isn't a writer. She doesn't get it, and she's wrong." One thing I'd learned over the last twelve years was not to screw with readers' expectations.

"And you're so certain you're right because what? You're infallible?" There was more than a hint of sarcasm there.

"When it comes to plotting? Yes. I'm comfortable saying I'm pretty fucking infallible, and don't start on me about my ego. I can back it up, so it's more like confidence." I leaned into a stretch and smiled.

"Hate to check your *confidence,* but if that was the case, you wouldn't need your editor, would you? But you do need me, so you're not."

I ignored the obvious truth in his argument. "At least you read my book before suggesting changes. She won't even let me tell her my idea."

"Well, does *she* have one?"

I blinked.

"Did you ask her?" He lifted his brows. "I mean, I'd be happy to offer some suggestions but, since you haven't even shown me the existing portion yet..."

"Why would I ask her? I never ask for input before something is finished." It ruined the process, and my gut instincts hadn't failed me yet, anyway. "I cannot believe I actually signed a contract giving someone who's not even in the industry final approval." And yet I'd do it again just for the challenge.

"For having dated as much as you have, you really don't understand women, do you?" He shook his head.

"I understand women just fine, trust me. And besides, you've had what? One relationship in the past decade?"

"Because I married her, jackass." He flashed his wedding ring. "Screwing your way through New York isn't what I'm talking about. The milk in my fridge is older than the length of your average relationship, and it's not even close to the expiration date. It is harder to truly know and understand one woman than it is to charm your way through a thousand nights of a thousand different women. More rewarding, too." He checked his watch. "I need to get back to the office."

The thought made me shift uncomfortably.

"That's not true. The relationship part." Fine, the longest relationship I'd had was six months, involved a lot of personal space, and had dissolved the way it had begun—with mutual affection and an understanding that we weren't going the distance. I saw no reason to emotionally entangle myself with someone I couldn't see a future with.

"Okay, let's clarify. I don't think you understand Georgia Stanton." Adam smirked, leaning into a calf stretch. "Have to admit, it's fun watching you struggle over a woman who doesn't automatically fall at your feet."

"Women don't fall at my feet." I was just lucky that the ones I was interested in usually felt the same way. "And what's not to get? From where I stand, this is a case of publishing royalty becomes wife of a Hollywood elite only to be thrown over for the younger, newer, pregnant model and goes home with her millions to sign another deal that makes more millions." Was she mouth-wateringly gorgeous? Absolutely. But it also felt like she was being difficult just for the fun of it. I was starting to see that dealing with Georgia might be more challenging than getting the book actually written.

"Wow. You're so far off the mark, it's almost funny." He finished stretching and stood, waiting for me to do the same. "You know much about her ex?" he asked with a head tilt and poignant stare.

"Sure. Damian Ellsworth, the *acclaimed* director, and resident of Soho, if I'm not mistaken." I stopped at a food cart and bought us two bottles of water. "Always given me a slimy, creepy vibe." I was confident, but that guy was a pompous prick.

"And what's he most known for?" Adam questioned after he'd thanked me and twisted the top off his.

"Probably *The Wings of Autumn*," I guessed as we continued our trek, freezing as it hit me.

Adam looked over his shoulder, then paused. "There it is.

Come on." He motioned me forward, and I found my footing.

"Scarlett never sold her movie rights," I said slowly. "Not until six years ago."

"Bingo. And then she only sold ten books' worth of rights for almost no money to a brand-new, no-name production company that's owned by..."

"Damian Ellsworth. Fuck me."

"No thanks, you're not my type. But do you get it now?" We reached the edge of the park and threw our empty bottles into the recycling before merging onto the crowded sidewalk.

Ellsworth was more than a decade older than Georgia but had only managed to get his foot through the Hollywood door... *Shit.* It had been right around the time they'd gotten married.

"He used his marriage to Georgia to get to Scarlett." *Asshole.*

"Seems like it." Adam nodded. "Those rights rolled out the red carpet for him, and he still has five of those movies left to make. He's set. And once it was clear the trips to the fertility clinic weren't working out, he found someone else."

My head snapped toward Adam as my stomach soured. "They were struggling to have kids and he knocked up someone else?"

"According to *Celebrity Weekly.* Don't look at me like that. Carmen likes to read it, and I get bored when I'm soaking my legs in the bathtub. Legs you continually put through the ringer, I might add."

Damn. That was a whole other layer of screwed up. She'd started the man's career and he hadn't just cheated; he'd emotionally, publicly annihilated her. "It's becoming clear why she isn't about the happy endings right now."

"And the worst part was that she was part owner of the production company, but she signed it all over in the divorce," Adam continued as we crossed the street. "She gave everything to him."

My brow furrowed. That was a shit-ton of money. "Everything? But he's at fault." How was that fair?

Adam shrugged. "They were married in Colorado. It's a no-fault state, and she gave it up willingly, or so I read."

"Who does that?"

"Someone who wants out as quickly as possible," he noted. We crossed the final street, bringing us to the block my publisher's building was on, but Adam stopped in front of the one next door. "And, since all but a sliver of Scarlett's estate goes into a literary trust earmarked for charity work, those millions you mentioned aren't exactly Georgia's. I know you like your research trips, but you should Google more often."

"Holy shit." My stomach dropped at just how wrong my assumption had been.

He clapped my back. "Feel like an ass now, don't you?" he asked with a grin.

"Maybe," I admitted.

"Wait until you realize that the book you're finishing isn't listed in the literary trust—"

My gaze whipped over to his.

"—and she still asked Accounting to wire that entire advance to her mother's account," he finished with a smirk.

"Okay, *now* I feel like a jackass." I ran my hands down my face. She wasn't even getting paid for this deal.

"Excellent. How about one more? Follow me." He walked us inside the office building. The foyer was vaulted to at least the second floor, and escalators lined the edges before the elevator banks began, leaving the center open to display a massive vertical glass sculpture.

It started deep blue on bottom, reaching out in wisps of waves that bubbled at the edges as though breaking on an unseen beach. Rising higher, the blue morphed into aqua before the edges lost their rough, foam-like texture. Then aqua became dozens of shades of green as the glass reached out with swirls—branches, narrowing as the sculpture grew taller, until it peaked at twice my height.

"What do you think?" Adam asked with a shit-eating grin on his face.

"It's spectacular. The lighting is ingenious, too. Shows off the color and artistry." I glanced sideways at him, knowing this little detour had to mean something.

"Look at the placard." That grin was still going strong.

I moved forward and read the tag, my eyes widening. "Georgia Stan— What the hell?" *Georgia* did this? I looked up at it with fresh eyes, and even I could admit my jaw dropped a little.

"Just because she's not a writer doesn't mean she's not creative. Humbled? Just a little?" Adam moved to stand at my side.

"Just a little," I said slowly. "Maybe a lot." My attention dropped to the placard again, noting the date. *Six years ago.* Coincidence or pattern?

"Good. My work here is done."

She hadn't just gone to art school. She was an artist. "She won't listen to me, Adam. She's hung up on me both times I've called. I'm trying to get this thing plotted out so I can dig into it, but the second I start in about the ending, it's dead on the other end. She doesn't want to collaborate; she just wants it her way."

"Sounds like someone else I know. How much listening have *you* done?" he challenged. "It's not just your book this time, buddy; it's hers, too, and for someone who loves primary sources, you're ignoring the one right in front of your face. She's your resident expert on all things Scarlett Stanton."

"Good point."

"Come on, Noah. I've never known you to shy away from a challenge. Hell, you seek them out. Pick up the phone and use that legendary charm to get your foot in the proverbial door. Then get to listening, buddy. Now, I have to shower before a meeting." He headed toward the revolving door.

"I've already tried the charm!" And it got me exactly nowhere, which was professionally annoying and personally... well, frustrating, especially considering the way I was still drawn to her from more than a thousand miles away.

"Not if you've only called twice, you haven't."

"How did you even know this was here?" I called across the foyer.

"Google!" He gave me a two-fingered salute and disappeared out of the building, leaving me with the proof that I hadn't been the only creative genius in Scarlett's office that day.

Then I started my research—not on the Battle of Britain but on Georgia Stanton.

I glanced between my phone—which lay harmlessly in the middle of my desk—and the phone number I'd scrawled on the notepad beside it. I was a week closer to my deadline, and though I'd plotted out what I felt was the right path for the characters, I hadn't started writing. There was no point if Georgia was just going to demand that I change it all.

Use that legendary charm…

I dialed the number, then turned to stand at the massive windows lining my home office, looking down at Manhattan as the phone rang. Was she going to answer? That particular worry was a first for me when calling a woman, not because picking up was a given but because I'd never really cared.

Ask about her grandmother. Ask about her. Stop yelling in her general direction and start treating her like a partner. Just pretend she's one of your college friends and not someone from work or someone you're interested in. That had been Adrienne's advice, followed by a sarcastic quip that I'd never had a partner in my life because I was a control freak.

I hated when she was right.

"Noah, to what do I owe the honor?" Georgia answered.

"I saw your sculpture." *Way to ease into it.*

"I'm sorry?"

"The one of the tree rising out of the ocean. I saw it. It's stunning." My grip tightened on my phone. According to the internet, it was also the last one she'd done.

"Oh." There was a pause. "Thank you."

"I didn't know you were a sculptor."

"Uh...yeah. I was. A long time ago. _Was_ being the operative word there." She forced a laugh. "Now I spend my days in Gran's office, sorting through a mountain of paperwork."

Subject closed. _Noted._ I resisted the urge to dig—for now.

"Ah, paperwork. My favorite way to spend the evening," I joked.

"Well, you'd be in heaven, because it's a hot mess. There's. So. Much. Paperwork," she groaned.

"Ooh, I love it when you talk dirty to me." _Fuck._ I winced and mentally calculated how much I was about to pay in a sexual harassment lawsuit. What the hell was wrong with me? "Shit. Sorry, I don't know where that came from." So much for treating her like a friend from college.

"It's okay." She laughed, and the sound hit me like a freight train to the chest. Her laugh was beautiful and left me smiling for the first time in days. "Well, now that I know what turns you on," she teased, and I heard a creak in the background that I recognized. She'd leaned back in the chair. "Honestly, it's fine, I promise," she managed as her laughter simmered. "But really, did you need something? Because the minute you say the words _happy ending_, I'm going back to my paperwork."

I cringed, then swiped my glasses from my face and started to spin them by the handle. "Uh. We can get to that later," I offered. "I was just trying to add some personal details, and I was wondering if your gran had a favorite flower?" My eyes shut tightly. _You are the dorkiest of the dorks, Morelli._

"Oh." Her voice softened. "Yeah, she loved roses. She has a massive garden out behind the house full of English tea roses.

Well, I guess she *had* a garden. Sorry, still getting used to that."

"It takes a while." I stopped spinning the glasses and set them on the desk. "Took me about a year when my dad died, and honestly, it creeps out from time to time when I forget he's gone. Besides, the garden is still there; it's just yours now." I glanced at the photo of Dad and me standing beside the 1965 Jaguar we'd spent a year restoring: it would always be Dad's, even if it was now in my name.

"True. I didn't know your dad died; I'm sorry."

"Thanks." I cleared my throat and turned my attention back to the skyline. "It was a few years ago, and I did my best to keep it from becoming a thing in the press. Everyone's always digging up my backstory to see if there's a reason all my stories have..." *Don't say it.* "Poignant endings."

"And is there a reason?" she asked quietly.

I'd been asked the question at least a hundred times over the years, and I usually responded with something like *I think books should reflect real life*, but this time I took a second.

"No tragedy, if that's what you're asking." A smile tugged at my lips. "Typical middle-class family. Dad was a mechanic. Mom still is a teacher. Grew up with barbecues, Mets games, and an annoying sister I've grown to appreciate. Disappointed?" Most people were. They figured I had to have been orphaned or something else equally horrific.

"Not at all. Sounds pretty perfect, actually." Her voice dropped off.

"With the writing, I step into a story and the first thing I see about a character is their flaw. The second thing I see is how that flaw will lead to redemption...or destruction. I can't help it. The story plays out in my head, and that's what goes down on the page." I moved back and leaned against the edge of my desk. "Tragic, heartwarming, poignant...it just is what it is."

"Hmm." I could almost see her considering my statement with that little tilt of her head. Her eyes would narrow slightly, and then she'd nod if she'd accepted my thought. "Gran used to say she saw the characters as fully fleshed-out people with complicated pasts, set on a collision course. She saw their flaws as something to overcome."

I nodded like she could see me. "Right. She usually used whatever their flaw was to humble them while proving their devotion in the most unexpected way possible. God, she was the *best* at that." It was a skill I had yet to master—the successful grovel. The grand gesture. My stories always came just shy of it before the chance was yanked away by the bitch we called fate.

"She was. She loved...love."

My eyebrows rose. "Right, which is why this story needs to preserve that," I blurted, then grimaced. A breath passed, then two. "Georgia? Are you still there?" The click was coming any second now.

"It does," she said. There was no anger in her tone, but no flexibility, either. "This story is about love at the heart of it, but it's not a romance. That's the whole reason I gave it to you, Noah. You don't write romance, remember?"

I blinked, finally seeing how big the divide between us was. "But I told you I would write *this* as a romance."

"No, you told me Gran was better than you at writing romance," she countered. "You promised you would get it right. I knew it needed a *poignant* ending, so I agreed that you were the man for the job. I thought you'd come the closest to capturing what she really went through after the war."

"Holy shit." This wasn't Everest, this was the moon, and the whole situation was caused by crossed wires. Our goals had never been the same.

"Noah, don't you think if I wanted this book to be a romance, I would have told Christopher to find me one of his romance writers?"

"Why didn't you tell me that in Colorado?" I asked through gritted teeth.

"I did!" she snapped defensively. "In my foyer, I told you that the one thing you couldn't do was give them a happy ending, and you didn't listen. You just tossed back a cocky 'watch me' comment and walked out."

"Because I thought you were challenging me!"

"Well, I wasn't!"

"I know that *now*!" I pinched the bridge of my nose, searching for a way forward when it looked like we were at an impasse. "Do you honestly want your gran's story to be sad and mournful?"

"She wasn't sad. And this isn't a romance!"

"It should be. We can give it the ending she deserves."

"With what, Noah? You want to end her real-life story with some happy piece of fiction where they're running toward each other in an empty field with their arms outstretched?"

"Not exactly." *Here we go.* This was my chance. "Picture her walking a long, winding dirt road lined with pine trees, calling back to the way they met, and the second he sees her—" I saw it all play out in my head.

"Holy mother of all that's cliché."

"Cliché?" I nearly choked on the word. Even being thought of as an asshole was better than *cliché*. "I know what I'm doing. Just let me do it!"

"Do you know why I keep hanging up on you?"

"Enlighten me."

"Because nothing I say matters to you, and it keeps us both from wasting our time."

Click.

"Damn it!" I snapped, carefully setting down my phone so I didn't throw it.

It *did* matter what she said. I was just doing a piss-poor job of letting her go first, which, again, was a problem I only seemed to have with this particular woman.

Writing was so much easier than dealing with actual people. Maybe people didn't finish my books—hung up on me in a literature sense—but I never knew if someone stopped reading before they got the point, because I'd already had the chance to make it. Even if they slammed it shut in disgust, it wasn't in person.

I raked my hands over my face and let out a hiss of pure irritation. I'd finally met someone with bigger control issues than I had.

"Any advice, Jameson?" I asked the pages of the manuscript and correspondence I'd printed out. "Sure, you somehow managed to keep communicating through a war zone, but you sure as hell didn't have to knock down Scarlett's walls over the telephone, did you?"

I gave myself a moment to fall into the story, to really theorize what Georgia was asking of me, but picturing Scarlett learning to let go and move on, fictionally condemning her to what had to have been a half-life felt too heavy, even for me.

Three months. That was all I had to not only convince Georgia that Scarlett and Jameson needed to end this story blissfully together but write the damned thing in another author's style and voice. Then I glanced at the calendar and realized it was actually less than three months and cursed. Loudly.

I had to change tactics or there was a very real possibility that I was going to blow a deadline for the first time in my career.

CHAPTER EIGHT

August 1940

Middle Wallop, England

Heat blasted Jameson's face as hanger two went up in flames. The explosion tossed them backward like they were nothing more than paper, but he managed to keep his arms around Scarlett. His back took the brunt of the impact, forcing the air from his lungs as Scarlett landed on top of him.

He rolled, trying to shelter her with his body as much as he could as bomb after bomb fell in the span of a few thunderous heartbeats. He'd seen at least two dozen pilots go down in the last few months, their deaths nothing more than another photo pinned on the wall.

Not Scarlett. Not Scarlett.

He cursed. The war had finally done the very thing he'd traveled all the way to Europe to stop—it had come for someone he cared about. He'd never wanted to shoot down an enemy aircraft more in his entire life.

His ears rang as he propped himself up on his elbows and searched the crystal-blue eyes beneath him as what he hoped was the last of the bombs fell in the not-so-far-off distance. "Are you okay?"

There was a good chance they'd try another pass, especially since both hangers one and three still stood.

She blinked and nodded. "You have to go!"

Now he was the one nodding.

"Then go!" she urged.

He could do far more to protect her in the air than acting as her shield on the ground, so he scrambled to his feet, then pulled her to hers. A shape moved off to the left, and relief flooded his system as Howard rose to his knees, then stood.

The man still had his hat on.

"Get to hanger one!" Jameson shouted.

Howard nodded and took off at a run.

Jameson cradled Scarlett's face in his hands. There was so much to say and no time to say it.

"Be careful, Jameson!" Scarlett demanded, the plea echoing in her eyes.

He pressed his lips to her forehead in a fierce kiss, squeezing his eyes shut. Then he glanced over her head to make sure the car hadn't been hit and breathed another ounce easier as he saw Constance behind the wheel, Christine at her side.

"*You* be careful," he ordered Scarlett, looking into her eyes one last time before tearing himself away and running for hanger one before he could question her safety.

Scarlett's knees trembled as she watched Jameson sprint past the fire that used to be hanger two. Her fear for his safety outweighed the concern for her own but rivaled that for her sister. *Oh God, Constance.*

Scarlett turned and sprinted for the car, nearly losing her footing once or twice on the scattered debris.

Constance beckoned her forward, motioning wildly with her hands while glancing toward the sky. She was alive. Jameson was alive.

That was all she could rely on for right now.

Scarlett yanked the door open and threw herself into the back seat, shutting the door quickly behind her.

Constance didn't need any instructions; she already had

the car in reverse. "Tell me you're okay!" she shouted over her shoulder as she whipped the car around, then threw it into drive.

"I'm fine. You two?" Scarlett asked as her hands began to shake. She gripped her knees, then hissed. Her palms came away bloody.

"We're steady as can be!" Christine answered with a trembling smile.

"Good," Scarlett answered. Seeing that the bottom of her skirt already bore bloodstains, Scarlett muttered a curse and wiped her hands clean on the fabric of her uniform. "Drive faster, Constance. Jameson's going to be on the board."

Scarlett wasn't tired after one watch, so she took a second, replacing another filter officer who hadn't come in. Constance refused to leave her side, but her exhaustion was palpable, so Scarlett set her up on a cot in the break room so she could rest. In four hours, they'd both be on again.

Then she headed back to the board.

Their board was covered in markers tracking the raids currently assaulting RAF airfields all over Britain, including the one that had taken place at their own. The hectic, quick movements of the plotters happened in silence while the control officers overhead in the galley made movement decisions, relayed orders, and talked to pilots directly.

For hours, she listened to the voice in her headset, plotting the markers.

Code number.
Estimated size of raid.
Height.
Coordinates.
Arrow.

Every five minutes, the locations were updated and a new arrow marked the direction of the raid, changing with the color designation on the clock.

Red. Blue. Yellow.

Red. Blue. Yellow.

Red. Blue. Yellow.

She kept her mind on task, knowing if she let herself wander, she couldn't fulfill her duty. Without her and the women around her, the control officers couldn't relay coordinates to the pilots in the air.

Without her, Jameson was flying blind. She'd tried to watch for the 609 yellow flags on top of the raid markers, signaling which raids they'd engaged, but there was no time for any section of the board but her own.

On hour four, she should have taken a break, but her replacement hadn't arrived. She tried to not think of possible reasons why.

On hour eight, that break would have been over. Four hours on, four hours off—that was the rule.

On hour nine, Constance took over the section to her right.

At hour ten, Constance pushed a marker into Scarlett's section, as she'd done countless times before as flights moved across the map. But this time she took the scant seconds to make eye contact with her sister.

The marker had a 609 flag.

Jameson.

Scarlett's heart lurched. She hadn't spoken to him since the hangar. She'd hoped like hell that he'd flown and returned and might have been resting, but the pit in her stomach told her he was with his squadron, engaged against an estimated thirty German aircraft.

Every five minutes, she returned to that marker, moving it across the coastline and swapping out the arrow for the next color. Every five minutes, she allowed herself one fervent prayer that he would make it through the night.

Even if he chose not to believe her about Henry.

Even if she never saw him again.

She needed to know that he was all right.

Thank God she hadn't been assigned with the control officer, where she could hear the voices of the pilots come through the radio. It would have driven her mad to hear the losses reported.

By hour twelve, her arms trembled with exhaustion. The 609 flag had disappeared from her section as the board slowed. No doubt it would fill again by nightfall. The raids came in waves, each one taking a little more than they could afford to lose.

Two more Radio Direction Finding stations had been lost.

She'd lost count of how many RAF bases they'd bombed.

How many more hits could the airfields sustain? How many more fighters could they lose? How many more pilots—

"You ready?" Constance asked as they passed through the doorway of the operations room.

"Yes," she answered, her voice thick with lack of use.

"Your poor knees." Constance's brows knit.

Scarlett glanced down at the clean skirt her Section Officer had insisted she change into, since hers had been ruined by rips and blood, and glimpsed her scabbed-over knees. "It's nothing."

"Let's get you into a bath." Constance offered her a shaky smile and linked their elbows. "Christine, would you mind driving?"

"Not at all."

"Assistant Section Officer Wright?" a high, feminine voice called across the small lobby.

Both women turned to see their section officer stride forward.

"Scarlett," she clarified, beckoning her with a hand.

Scarlett gave her sister a pat on the shoulder, then met Section Officer Gibson in the middle of the small lobby. "Ma'am?"

"I wanted to commend you for keeping your wits about you tonight. There aren't many girls who could perform for

twelve straight hours, and even fewer who could do so after...
experiencing a raid." Her lips were tight, but the older woman's
eyes were soft.

"Just doing my job, ma'am," Scarlett answered. There were
men doing far more than she was in far worse circumstances.
Doing her best was the least she owed them.

"Indeed." She dismissed her with a nod, but there was a hint
of a smile before she turned to walk away.

She joined Constance at the door, and then the pair walked
into the morning sunlight. Scarlett blinked, the light stinging
her eyes despite her hat. Eight in the morning had never felt
quite so brutal.

Her breath caught, and she gasped at the tall figure standing
in the middle of the pavement in service uniform.

"Jameson," she whispered, her knees nearly giving out in
relief.

He covered the distance between them, eating her alive with
his eyes. She was okay. He'd flown two missions last night,
breaking only to refuel and eat before launching again, and he'd
worried about her the entire time.

"The thing about you working Special Duties is there's no
one who will confirm that you made it to work." His voice came
out sandpaper rough, and he didn't care.

"Right. They wouldn't." Her gaze raked over him, as if she
needed the same reassurance he did—they were both alive.

Her sister glanced between them. "I'll wait for you in the car."

"I'll take her home," Jameson offered, unable to look away
from Scarlett. "That is, if you'd like me to."

Scarlett nodded, and Constance slipped away.

Only feet separated them, and he knew his next words would

either narrow or widen that gap, so he chose them carefully. He took her hand and led her from the sidewalk, through the short grass, until they were hidden from view and shaded by the heavy limbs of a giant oak tree.

There was worry in those blue eyes as she looked up at him. Worry, and relief, and the same longing he felt every time he looked at her.

Maybe the right words weren't words.

He cradled her head in his hands and kissed her.

*F*inally. She felt as though she'd been waiting a lifetime for this man, this kiss, this moment, and it was finally here. There was no hesitation on her part, no gasp of surprise as he stroked his lips across hers, kissing her softly.

She slid her hands up his chest, resting them just above his heart. Then she kissed him back, rising on her toes to press her mouth to his. It was as though he'd set a match to a pile of tinder—she went up in flames.

He deepened the kiss, gliding his tongue across her lower lip before drawing it between his. *Yes.* She wanted more of that. When she opened to him, his tongue swept inside, stroking hers as he learned the curves of her mouth.

He was *good* at this.

Heat licked its way down her spine, igniting her skin and singeing her common sense into a hasty retreat. Her hands fisted in his uniform, and she threw herself into the kiss, yanking him closer even as she felt them moving backward. Her back hit the tree, and she barely blinked. He tasted like apples and something deeper, darker. More. She wanted more.

She wanted to kiss Jameson every day for the rest of her life.

She felt his groan throughout her body when she explored

his mouth the way he had hers, finally drawing his lower lip between her teeth lightly.

"Scarlett." He swore against her lips, then took her mouth over and over, moving his hand to her waist to pull her closer.

Nothing was close enough. She wanted to feel his every breath, every heartbeat, wanted to live inside that kiss where there were no bombs, no raids, nothing that would pry him from her arms.

She lifted her hands to his neck and arched against him as his lips slid to the curve of her jaw. Pure, insistent need unfurled in her belly, and her fingernails bit into his skin as she gasped at the sensation. He worked his lips down her neck in hot, open-mouthed kisses, and she tilted to give him better access.

He reached the collar of her uniform and, with a groan, brought his mouth back to hers. The kiss spiraled, taking her with it. She'd never felt so consumed by another person in her life, never willingly given this much of herself. In the midst of letting go, she stumbled onto the truth she'd been too hesitant, too cautious to admit until now: Jameson was the only one she would ever want like this.

He gripped her hips with strong hands, then slowed the kiss until it was nothing more than soft brushes of his lips against hers.

"Jameson," she whispered as he rested his forehead on hers.

"When I saw those explosions coming for us, I didn't know how to protect you." His grip tightened.

"You can't," she said softly. "There's nothing either of us can do to keep the other alive." Her fingers caressed the nape of his neck.

"I know, and it's killing me."

Her stomach tightened. "I'm not marrying him. I need you to know that. I spent all night watching the waves of the raids, and the thought of losing you—of you up there, thinking God knows what..." She shook her head. "I'm not marrying him."

"I know." He kissed her again, light and soft. "I should have let you explain. The shock just about ripped me apart."

"There will be more," she warned him. "If my parents went this far, they'll go further. There will be more rumors, more articles, more pressure. As long as you know the truth of it, I can handle them."

He nodded and swallowed, a pained look crossing his face before he brought his gaze back to hers. The intensity she found there stole her breath. "I'm in love with you, Scarlett Wright. I've done everything I can to fight it, to take it slower, to give you what time and space you need. But this war isn't going to give us that time, and after last night, I'm not hiding it anymore. I'm in love with you."

A sweet ache began to throb in her chest. "I'm in love with you, too." What was the point of avoiding it, of not giving in, when neither of them knew if they'd be alive tomorrow?

The smile that lit his face was echoed on hers, and for the first time in what felt like forever, she allowed herself to feel that happiness radiate, to sink into every fiber of her being. But now that they'd admitted it, what were they going to do with it?

"There's talk of the Americans getting their own squadron," she whispered. Another squadron meant a transfer.

"I've heard." A muscle ticked in his jaw.

"What are we going to do?" Her voice broke on the last word.

"We're going to face it all head-on. Your parents, the war, the whole Royal Air Force," he said with a flash of a smile. "We'll do it together. You are mine, Scarlett Wright, and I am yours, and from this second on, we don't keep secrets."

She nodded, then kissed him sweetly. "Okay. Now take me home before we do something that gets us both court-martialed."

He grinned. "Yes, ma'am."

She knew that what was coming for them might very well crush this new, fierce feeling that filled her chest, but for this moment, they were safe, they were together, and they were in love.

CHAPTER NINE

Georgia

Dearest Jameson,

Here we are again, writing letters. I would give anything to reach through this paper, to stretch across the long miles between us just to touch you, to feel your heartbeat. How many more times can this war separate us before we're simply allowed to be happy? I know we're lucky, that we've been stationed together longer than most, but I am greedy when it comes to you, and there is no replacement for feeling your arms around me. But don't worry, my arms only hold the other Mr. Stanton, and he makes every day we're apart just a little brighter...

I glared down at my phone for what felt like the billionth time that week. Just when I thought Noah might understand, that he might actually grasp the simple fact that I wasn't backing down, he'd call again and suggest some cheesy conclusion to Gran's story, and each was worse than the last.

Like right now.

"I'm sorry...did you just say he pops out of a Christmas present?" I pulled the phone away from my ear and glanced at the screen, making sure that was actually Noah on the other end. Yep, that was his number, his low—and I could admit, begrudgingly—sexy voice, spinning an absolutely ludicrous tale.

"Exactly. Just picture it—"

"You have lost your mind, and you might just be driving me to lose mine in the proce—" That was it. My eyes narrowed. "That isn't your real ending, is it? None of these are."

"I have no idea what you're talking about. That is a joy-ful celebration of love and hope." He was good. He even sounded offended.

"Uh-huh. You're giving me blatantly bad, corny endings to wear me down so I won't dismiss your actual idea, aren't you?" I finished pouring my sweet tea and headed for Gran's office—my office.

"Actually, I had a more...poignant idea, too." There was a sound like a soft crash, like he'd thrown himself onto his couch—or bed.

Not that I was thinking about his bed, because I wasn't.

"Okay. Please, do tell." I set the tea on the coaster and fired up my computer. I'd put off everything possible during the divorce, which meant I had six months of estate work for Gran to dig out of, but I was almost through it.

"So there they are on a passenger ship halfway across the Atlantic, thinking they've made it out, and *bam*! A U-boat sinks them."

My mouth dropped open. "Well, that's...dark." But at least he was giving my stance some real thought, right?

"Just wait. So as the ship goes down, he gets them to a lifeboat, but there's just not enough room, and Scarlett is torn between taking that remaining seat for William's safety and fighting the panicked crowd for another boat."

My brow furrowed. *Wait a second.*

"Throw in some action to keep the reader on the edge of their seat, but in the end, it's just them in the water, Jameson pushing Scarlett up onto what's left of the wreckage—"

"Oh my *God*, I know you are not giving me the ending to *Titanic*!" My voice pitched high enough that I winced.

"Hey, you wanted sad."

"Unbelievable. Are you always this hard to work with?"

"I wouldn't know, because I don't work with anyone but Adam, who can't even start editing this novel until I get it done." His tone sharpened. "So are you ready to discuss actual options here?"

"Like what? He flies in and lands on the street in front of

their house? Or wait, I know, he chases her through the port in a mad dash to catch her before she boards a boat in a reimagined rom-com from hell scene with a forties twist?" I hammered the keys of my laptop with my password. "None of that is happening."

"I was actually thinking more of a puppy with a little key on its collar—" He'd slipped into sarcasm.

"Ugh!" I hung up.

Mom popped through the door with a smile. "Everything okay?"

"Yep. Just dealing with—" My phone rang again. "Noah," I said in sheer exasperation as his name appeared on my screen. "What?" I snapped into the phone.

"Do you have any idea how childish it is to keep hanging up on someone you agreed to partner with?" he asked with a voice so smooth and unbothered, it only irked me more.

"The satisfaction it brings me is more than worth what could be seen as a lack of maturity." Or maybe I was simply reveling in the fact that I *could* hang up. That I wasn't at anyone's beck and call for the first time in six years.

"On that note, how about we end in a beautiful orchard, where they're picnicking—"

"Noah," I warned.

"Only to have Jameson stung by a bee—no, dozens of bees, and he's allergic—"

"It isn't *My Girl*!"

Mom's eyebrows hit the ceiling.

"You're right, so let's talk about how to really give them a happy ending readers can root for."

"Goodbye, Noah." I hung up.

"Georgia!" Mom gasped.

"What?" I shrugged. "I said goodbye. Don't worry. He'll call back tomorrow, and we'll start all over again." We'd been going round and round for weeks now.

"Is everything okay with the book?" Mom asked, sitting in the same chair Noah had. Things between us were still awkward—but I figured they always would be, and I had to admit, it was more than nice having her here. Knowing she planned to stay through Christmas had eased the tension and even given me a little hope that we might find some real footing. After all, we only really had each other now that Gran was gone.

I rubbed the skin between my eyes. "He's still fighting me on the ending."

"Is that what's holding everything up?"

Opening my eyes, I found her staring at a framed picture of Gran and Grandpa William when he was in his twenties. I'd never known him—he'd died when Mom was sixteen.

I'd been born less than a year later.

"Well, it's certainly holding him up, since he refuses to actually start it until we agree what should happen in the end." I'd never been so grateful for a contract clause in my life. "If he had his way, it would be all hearts and rainbows."

Mom's forehead puckered as she looked back to me. "Like the rest of her books."

"Pretty much." A quick glance at my watch told me I had twenty minutes before my scheduled call with the lawyers.

"And you think that's a bad thing?"

I swiveled in the wheeled armchair and grabbed the two-inch-thick binder my legal team had overnighted last week. "I think it's wrong for this story."

"But isn't he..." Mom pressed her lips in a tight line.

"Say it." I flipped the binder open.

"Well, he's the expert, Gigi. You're...not."

I paused mid-page-flip at the use of that name. "He very well might be the expert at crafting his own story, but if it's between Noah Harrison and myself, when it comes to Gran, then I'd say I'm the expert." Page flipped.

"I just think it's a little ridiculous to hold up the entire contract because you're having creative differences. Don't you?"

She crossed her legs as her forehead puckered in concern. "Isn't it best to just get this all over with so you can really dig in to your life here?"

"Mom, the contract is done. It has been for about a month now." It was all over the news, too—so much for keeping it quiet. Helen was fielding dozens of calls about sub rights. I'd never been so glad to be out of New York City in my life. At least here, I could forward emails or refuse calls from people I knew only wanted access to the manuscript.

In New York, it had been impossible to go to the bathroom at a cocktail party without someone in the industry approaching me about Gran. Then again, I'd always been with Damian, so maybe I'd simply been attending the wrong parties.

"So this little...quarrel you're having with Noah Harrison isn't holding it up?" She leaned forward.

"Nope. It's a done deal."

"Then why hasn't the advance been delivered?"

My gaze snapped to hers. "What?"

She fidgeted, her face lining with worry. "I thought the publisher was supposed to pay the advance once you signed."

"Right, but it's not all deliverable at once. It takes time on their end." My stomach churned, but I ignored it. Mom was doing her best, and I had to give her a chance. Jumping to the wrong conclusion would only serve to set our relationship back.

"What do you mean it's not deliverable all at once?"

Alarm bells chimed in my head, but there was nothing in her gaze except pure curiosity. Maybe she was finally taking an interest? "It's split in thirds. Signing, delivering, publishing."

"Thirds." Mom's eyebrows shot up. "Interesting. Is it always like that?"

"Just depends on the contract." I shrugged. "The first part should be in your account any day now, so be sure to watch for it. If it doesn't show up, let me know and I'll ask Helen to check up on it."

"I'll watch for it," she promised, rising to her feet. "You look like you're about ready to work, so I'll get out of your hair and see what Lydia left us for dinner."

I shifted in my chair uneasily. "Mom?"

"Hmm?" She turned at the doorway.

"I'm glad you're here." I swallowed, hoping to dislodge the lump in my throat.

"Of course, Gi—" She winced. "Georgia. You know, it helped to be around family after my first divorce." Her smile faltered. "That one took something precious from me, and it was your gran who put me back on my emotional feet and reminded me who I am. A Stanton. That was the last time I didn't hyphenate, I'll tell you." Her knuckles whitened on the door handle. "Don't ever give away your name again, Georgia. There's power in being a Stanton."

My phone lit up with an incoming call. *The legal team.*

"Your name?" I guessed. "That's what the first one took?" *Say me. Say it cost you me.*

"No. I was the naive one who gave that away, but I was twenty. He took my hope." She motioned to my phone. "You'd better get that." A little wave of her fingers, and she was gone.

Right.

I swiped to answer the call and lifted it to my ear. "Georgia Stanton."

Two days later, Hazel and I walked out of the Poplar Pub after grabbing some lunch that I'd mostly picked at. Nothing tasted good anymore. It was all just sustenance, anyway.

"So how many times does that make it?" Hazel asked as we headed down the sidewalk along Main Street. With the tourist season in its fall lull and the kids back to school, there was peaceful quietness that wouldn't be found again until the ski season melted away for those few weeks before summer vacation.

"I'm not exactly keeping count." Noah called. Noah argued. I hung up. It was just that simple.

"You barely touched your lunch," she noted, looking over her sunglasses at me and tucking a curl behind her ear.

"I wasn't very hungry."

"Hmm." Her eyes narrowed. "So I was thinking of heading to Margot's for a pedicure, since you helped me get all the new workbooks organized at the center in record time and Owen's mom has the kids for the afternoon. What do you say?"

"You absolutely should. You deserve a little pampering." I moved to the right so Mrs. Taylor and her husband could pass, offering them a smile. I'd missed that—the simple act of recognizing someone on the street. New York was always bustling, pedestrian traffic moving in a steady, purposeful current of strangers.

"So do you."

"Oh." We passed my favorite creamery, and the Grove Goods Bakery, which smelled like heaven—Thursday cinnamon rolls. My car was only another block down.

"Georgia..." She sighed, gripping my elbow as we stopped in front of the bookstore. "You're off a little more than normal today."

There was no use hiding anything from Hazel. "I'm fine when I'm busy, and I have been until now. Moving, cleaning, everything with the book, digging through the estate paperwork kept me focused on what's right in front of me, but now..." I sighed and glanced around the town I adored. "Everything about this place is the same. It looks the same, smells the same—"

"Is that a good thing?" Hazel pushed her sunglasses to the top of her head.

"It's a *great* thing. It's just that *I'm* not the same anymore, so I need to figure out where I fit. It's hard to explain...it's like

I'm itchy, restless."

"You know what would help?" Mischief lit her smile.

"So help me God, if you say a pedicure—"

"You should jump Noah Harrison."

I snorted. "Yeah, okay." My temperature rose just thinking about— *Stop it.*

"I'm serious! Fly to New York for the weekend, hash out the book details, and get laid." She smiled when Peggy Richardson dropped her jaw, clearly having heard us as she walked by. "It's basically multitasking. Nice to see you, Peggy!" Hazel even waved.

Peggy adjusted the strap of her purse and continued down the street.

"You're unbelievable." I rolled my eyes.

"Oh, come on. If you won't do it for you, do it for *me*. Did you see that shot of him at the beach I sent you yesterday? You can do laundry on that man's stomach." She hooked her arm through my elbow, and we started back down the street at a thoroughly indulgent, slow pace.

"I've seen all three dozen of the pictures you've sent me." The man had abs for *days*, and the skin that stretched across the muscles of his torso and back was deliciously inked, too. According to the article she'd sent, he had one for every book he'd written.

"And you still don't want to jump him? Because if not, I'm totally adding him to my hall-pass list. I'll even bump Scott Eastwood for that man."

"I never said I didn't want to—" I grimaced, slamming my eyes shut. "Look, even if Noah wanted to, I've never been a fling kind of girl, and I'm not going to rebound with the guy finishing Gran's book. Period."

Her eyes sparkled. "But you want to. And of course he would—you're hot. You're divorced, and don't forget I'm well aware that Damian wasn't doing it for you."

"Hazel!" I hissed, my eyes darting over my shoulder, but no one was there.

"It's true, and I'm just looking out for you here. I know you have a thing for the broody, creative types. Did you see those tattoos? Classic bad-boy vibe, and how many bad-boy authors do you know?"

"There are plenty of *bad-boy* authors in the world."

"Like whom?"

I blinked. "Uh. Hemingway?" Bad choice.

"He's dead. Fitzgerald, too. Shame." She rolled her eyes.

"I'll get a pedicure right now if you drop it."

"Fine." She grinned. "For now, but I still think you should jump him."

I shook my head at her ridiculously bad idea and saw Dan Allen through the glass windows of Mr. Navarro's shop. "Is Dan still a real estate agent?" *He must have it listed.*

"Yep. He helped us find our house last year," Hazel answered, then waved as Dan caught us staring.

"Do you mind if we take a few minutes before pedis?" I looked again at the bay display windows that flanked the door, imagining how the light would hit them in a few hours with the afternoon sun.

"No problem."

I opened the heavy glass door and stepped into the shop. There were no more giant aquariums or bales of hamster bedding. Even the shelves were gone. The space was empty except for Dan, who greeted us with a charismatic smile that hadn't changed since high school.

"Georgia, it's been forever! Sophie mentioned she saw you when you got into town." He stepped forward and shook my hand, then did the same with Hazel.

"Hey, Dan," I looked around his lanky frame to the space at the back of the store. "Sorry to bust in. I was just curious about the shop."

"Oh, are you in the market for some commercial space?" he asked.

"Just...curious." Was I in the market? Was it even practical?

"She's curious." Hazel grinned.

He launched into real estate mode, telling us all about the ample square footage while he led us past the only fixture that remained, the glass display counter where I'd paid for my first goldfish.

"So why hasn't it sold?" I asked as he opened the back door that led to what had to be storage. "Mr. Navarro's been gone for what? A year?"

"It's been on the market for about six months, but the storage room, well, here, I'll show you." He flipped on a light, and we followed him into the massive, unfinished space.

"Whoa." There were two large garage doors, a cement floor and walls, and a few rows of fluorescent lights hanging from the high ceilings.

"There's more storage than shop, which Mr. Navarro had liked, since it kept his classic car hobby out of Mrs. Navarro's driveway."

There. That was the perfect spot for the furnace. Maybe just a day furnace, though. And a reheating one, of course. The alcove was perfect for an annealing oven, too. I studied the ceiling next. High, but some good-size vents wouldn't hurt.

"I know that look," Hazel said from behind me.

"There's no look," I replied, already picturing the best place for a bench and block.

"How much do they want for it?" Hazel asked.

The price made my eyes pop. Add the startup costs and I'd wipe out just about everything I had in savings. It was naive to even think about it, yet here I was, doing exactly that. After asking Dan to call me if he got an offer, we headed out for pedicures.

Hazel fired off a text at her mom to join us, and I did the same with mine, but she didn't answer. Then again, she'd been napping a lot lately.

My toenails were Summer Coral pink as I parked in the garage, the logical side of my brain already at war with the creative, listing every reason I shouldn't even dream of buying the shop. It had been years since I'd been in a studio. It was risky to start a business. What if I failed at that as spectacularly as I had my marriage? *At least no one would put it in the tabloids.*

My keys jingled as I tossed them onto the kitchen counter.

"Is that you, Gigi?" Mom called from the entry.

I rolled my eyes at the nickname and headed in her direction. "It's me. I have the wildest idea. Oh, and I texted earlier about a pedicure—"

Mom smiled, her hair and makeup perfectly done, her suitcases at her side in the entry, lined up like little ducks in a row. Her designer purse was slung over her shoulder. "Oh, good! I was hoping I'd get to see you before I had to go."

"Go where?" I folded my arms across my chest and rubbed the skin of my arms to ward off the chills as goose bumps rose on my skin. There wasn't a cure for the instant hit of nausea.

"Well, Ian called, and it turns out he got himself into a little snag, so I'm just going to pop up to Seattle and help him out." She fished her phone from her pocket.

Ian. Husband number four. The one who liked to gamble.

Pieces clicked into a puzzle that I'd willingly kept myself from seeing. "The advance came in, didn't it?" I sounded small... I felt small, too.

"I'm glad you asked, because it did!" Mom beamed. "Now, I didn't want you to worry about a thing, so I told Lydia to make sure the house was stocked with groceries."

Groceries. Right.

"When will you be back?" Ridiculous question, but I had to ask.

She yanked her gaze from her phone, meeting mine in a flash of guilt.

"You're not." It was a statement, not a question.

Hurt flashed in Mom's eyes. "Well, that was mean."

"Are you?"

"Well, not right away. Ian is going to need a little looking after, and this could really be our chance to rekindle things. There's always been that zing between us. It's never faded." She fumbled with her phone. "I called an Uber. They take forever around here."

"It's a small town." I glanced around the entry, from the French doors that led to the living room to the framed pictures on the walls. Anything to keep from looking right at her. Bile rose in my throat, and my heart screamed as the fragile stitches I'd thoughtlessly sewn there popped one at a time.

"Don't I know it." She shook her head.

"What happened to Christmas?"

"Plans change, honey. But you have your feet under you now, and as soon as you feel like you're ready to face the rest of the world, you get back to New York City, Gigi. You'll go stagnant here. Everyone does." She scrolled through her apps. "Oh, good. Seven minutes."

"Don't call me that."

Her face snapped to mine. "What?"

"I told you, I hate that nickname. Stop using it."

"Well, pardon me. I'm just your mother." Her eyes widened in sarcasm.

"You know he's just going to drain your account and dump you again, right?" That's exactly what he'd done the first time, which was when Gran had cut her out of the will.

Mom's eyes reduced to slits. "You don't know that. You don't know him."

"But *you* should." My jaw ticked, and I embraced the anger that filled my chest, wrapping it like Kevlar around my hemorrhaging heart. I'd believed her like a naive five-year-old, believed that she'd stick around for me this time, even if it was just for the next few months.

"I don't know why you're being so nasty." She shook her head like *I* was the one delivering the blows here. "I stayed for you, took care of you, and now I deserve to be happy, just like you."

"Just like me?" I ran my hands down my face. "I'm *nothing* like you."

Her expression softened. "Oh, my little heart. You took off for college, and what did you find? A lonely, older man to take care of you. You may have graduated, but don't lie to yourself—you weren't there for an education; you were husband hunting, just like I was at that age."

"I wasn't," I fired back. "I met Damian on campus while he was researching filming locations."

Pity...God, that was pity in her eyes. "Oh, honey, and you don't think the fact that your last name was Stanton had *anything* to do with it?"

I lifted my chin in the air. "He didn't know. Not when we met."

"You keep believing that." She checked her phone again.

"It's true!" It had to be. The last eight years of my life were a lie if it wasn't.

Mom sucked in a deep breath and rolled her eyes heavenward, like she was praying for patience. "Dear, dear Georgia. The sooner you come to grips with the truth, the happier you'll be."

Color flashed through the window beside the door. Her ride was here.

"And what truth is that, Mom?" She was leaving again. How many times was this? I'd stopped keeping count when I was thirteen.

"When you have someone like your gran in the family, it's nearly impossible to get out from under that kind of shadow." She tilted her head. "He knew. They all know. You have to learn to use it to your advantage." Her soft tone was at odds with her harsh words.

"I'm not you," I repeated.

"Maybe not yet," she admitted, grabbing the first suitcase. "But you will be."

"Leave your key." Never again. This was the last time she'd blow into my life and leave once she got what she wanted.

She gasped. "Leave my key? To my grandmother's house? My *father's* house? You are a lot of things, Georgia, but cruel isn't one of them."

"I'm not kidding."

"Do you know how that makes me feel?" Her hand flew to her chest.

"Leave. Your. Key."

She blinked back tears as she pried the key from the ring, then dropped it into the crystal vase on the entry table. "Happy now?"

"No," I said softly, shaking my head. I wasn't sure I'd ever be happy again.

I stood there frozen in the same entry hall she'd left me in so many times before and watched her struggle with her suitcases without offering to help.

"I love you," she said, waiting in the doorway for my reply.

"Have a safe flight, Mom."

She bristled and closed the door.

Then the house was quiet.

I didn't know how long I stood there, watching a door I knew from experience would only open again when it was convenient for her. Knowing I was never what she'd wanted and cursing myself for letting my guard down and believing otherwise. The grandfather clock ticked steadily from the living room, somehow steadying my heartbeat. It was a hundred-year-old pacemaker.

Every other time she'd walked out, I'd had Gran's arms around me.

Alone wasn't a harsh-enough word for whatever this was.

I pulled myself together and turned back to head for the kitchen, only to be stopped by a knock at the door.

I may have been naive, but I wasn't green. Mom had forgotten something, and it wasn't me. She hadn't abandoned her plans.

Hadn't had a change of heart.

But still, that damnable kernel of hope flickered in my chest as I opened the door.

A set of darker-than-sin eyes stared down at me under a cocked brow as his mouth slowly curved into a wry smile.

Noah Harrison was on my porch.

"Try to hang up on me now, Georgia."

I slammed the door in his gorgeous, smug, romance-minded little face.

CHAPTER TEN

September 1940

Middle Wallop, England

Jameson had been born to fly the Spitfire. It was agile, responsive, and moved like it was an extension of his body, which was just about the only advantage he had in combat.

Was Great Britain cranking out planes at an unprecedented rate? Yes. But what they needed were pilots with more than twelve hours in the cockpit heading into a dogfight.

The German pilots were more experienced, with more hours, more aces, and more confirmed kills in general. Thank God the Nazi long-range capabilities were shit, or the RAF would have lost the Battle of Britain more than a month ago.

But they were still in it.

Today had been the hardest yet. He'd barely rested between launches, and that had been at airfields that weren't his own. London was under attack. Hell, the whole island was. It had been for the last week, but today the skies were heavy with smoke and aircraft. The Nazi assault seemed endless. They were pummeled by wave after wave of bombers and their fighter escorts.

Adrenaline sang through his body as he zeroed in on an enemy aircraft somewhere to the southeast of London, coming up on the fighter's tail nice and close. Closer made it easier to hit his target. It also made it easier to go down with them. The enemy began a steep climb, taking them nearly vertical as Jameson chased him through a heavy layer of clouds. His stomach pitched.

He had a few seconds, no more.

Already his engine sputtered, losing power.

If he went fully inverted, he'd lose the whole thing. Unlike that Messerschmitt, he didn't have fuel injection under his hood. The carburetor of his little Spitfire had a very real chance of being his doom.

"Stanton!" Howard shouted through the radio.

"Come on, come on," Jameson growled as his thumb hovered over the trigger. The instant the fighter appeared in his crosshairs, Jameson fired.

"Yes! Got him!" he shouted as smoke streamed from the Messerschmitt, his own engine gasping its final warning.

He banked hard left, narrowly missing the plummeting fuselage of the enemy fighter. Gasping, he leveled out, then descended through the clouds, letting the engine and his heartbeat steady itself. One more second, and he would have flooded the engine and joined the Messerschmitt as a crater in the English countryside.

Two confirmed kills. Three more, and he'd be an ace.

An aircraft pulled alongside him, and he glanced left to see Howard shaking his head.

"I'm telling Scarlett you did that," he warned over the radio.

"Don't you dare," Jameson snapped, glancing at the photograph he'd wedged in the framework of the altimeter. It was Scarlett, mid-laugh, captured just after the sisters had joined the WAAF. Constance had given it to him after Scarlett refused, saying he knew exactly what she looked like without carrying her picture into battle. Of course he knew what she looked like. That was why he liked looking at her so much.

"Then don't pull that again," Howard warned.

Jameson scoffed, knowing they'd have words about it at beer call. Scarlett had enough on her shoulders to worry about without throwing his flying habits into the mix. As long as he came home to her, how he did it was a moot point as far as he was concerned.

Especially since he was due to leave RAF Church Fenton in a few days and had yet to think of a way to bring her with him.

The Eagle Squadron, composed of other American pilots serving in the RAF, was actually happening.

He was being transferred.

"Sorbo leader," the call came over the radio, "this is fighter command. We have forty-five plus on approach at Kinley at angels thirteen. Vector 270."

"Received," their wing commander answered.

They were headed back into the thick of battle.

Two days. That's how long it had been since Scarlett had word of Jameson. She knew the squadron had refueled elsewhere during what had been the longest two days of her life. The air raids from the fifteenth had worn her to the bone, both in the operations room and in her heart.

She knew of at least two dozen fighters who'd carried their pilots to their graves.

The blitz of bombings yesterday saw much of her day in the air-raid shelter when she was not on watch. All she'd thought about was Jameson. Where was he? Was he safe? Had he been injured...or worse?

Today she was waiting for him, and she wasn't alone. There were perhaps a dozen women in their little group, all sweethearts of the pilots, all gathered on the stretch of pavement between the parked cars and the two remaining hangars on the airfield. It was approximately the same spot where she and Jameson had been when the now-demolished hangar had been done in a month ago.

The hum of engines filled the air, and her heartbeat skyrocketed.

They were here.

She squared her shoulders as the Spitfires landed, wishing

she'd worn her uniform instead of her blue-checkered dress. A woman in uniform was required to keep herself together, and at this moment, she felt anything but. Her nerves were simply shot.

It was easily another twenty minutes before the first pilots made their way down the pavement, still wearing their flight suits. A few she recognized, especially the three other Americans who would be leaving with Jameson in two short days. She should have been prepared for his transfer orders—God knew the RAF was the most mobile force in Britain—but it had still hit her like a blow.

Her stomach clenched as more and more pilots appeared.

Then she saw him.

She ran, cutting through the grass to bypass the foot traffic.

He spotted her and stepped clear of the crowd just before she reached him, catching her easily as she threw herself into his arms.

"Scarlett, my Scarlett," he said into her neck, his arms wrapped around her waist, holding her as her feet dangled far above the ground.

"I love you." Her arms shook slightly as she held tight, the full measure of her relief coursing through her in a shock wave of emotion.

"God, I love you." With one arm locked tight around her back, he cupped her face with the other, pulling back enough to lock their gazes.

"I was terrified for you." The truth spilled from her lips so easily, even after she'd withheld those very words from her sister over the last two days.

"There was no reason to be." He smiled and pressed a kiss to her lips.

She melted against him, kissing him back despite the very public audience. Today, she couldn't bring herself to care if the king himself were watching.

He held her carefully but kissed her passionately for a long, hard moment, then eventually, he brushed his mouth over hers and drew back. Much to her delight, he didn't put her down. He was the only person who managed to make her feel delicate without making her feel small.

"Marry me," he said, his eyes dancing with happiness.

She startled. "I'm sorry?"

"Marry me." His eyebrows lifted with the corners of his mouth. "I've spent the entirety of the last week trying to think of how to keep us together, and that's how. Marry me, Scarlett."

Wait, had he just proposed? No matter how much she loved him, it was too soon, too reckless, and entirely too much like a business deal. Her mouth opened and shut a few times, but she couldn't quite make the words come out for a few embarrassing seconds. "Put. Me. Down." There they were.

He held her tighter. "I can't live without you."

"You've only lived with me for two months." Her mouth tightened as she lectured her foolish heart to keep quiet.

"I *wish* I'd lived with you for two months," he whispered, his voice dropping to that low, growly tone that turned her insides to mush.

"Oh, you know what I mean." She laced her fingers behind his neck, more than aware that he had yet to do as she'd asked and lower her.

"We could live together for the rest of our lives," he said softly. "One home. One dining room table…one bed."

"You can't seriously be suggesting that we rush into marriage because you'd like to get me into bed." She arched an eyebrow. Not that she hadn't thought about Jameson that way. She had. Frequently. Too frequently according to her morals and not frequently enough, according to the ladies she lived with.

His eyes flared with humor. "Well, no, but I love which piece of furniture you focused on. If I just wanted to get you into bed, you'd know it by now." His gaze dropped to her lips. "I want to marry you because it's a foregone conclusion. It doesn't matter if we date another year, Scarlett, we're going to end up married eventually."

"Jameson." Her cheeks flushed, even though she resented how good it felt to hear those words.

"If we do it now, we won't be separated."

"It's not that simple." Her heart warred with her head. There was something utterly romantic about running off to marry a man you were head over heels in love with and had only known two months. There was also something naive about it.

"It is," he assured her.

"Says the man who won't lose *his* job." There were about a dozen reasons flitting through her mind about why this was a horrid suggestion, but that one shouted the loudest.

He blinked in sheer confusion, then slowly lowered her to the ground. "What do you mean?"

She took his hand, and they started toward the car. "There's no place for me at RAF Church Fenton. Believe me, I've inquired, and *if* I marry you"—a small smile lifted her lips—"I can't guarantee I'd be reposted. We'd still be apart unless I left the WAAF for family reasons."

His face fell. "The only part I liked about what you just said was 'if I marry you.'"

"I know." She had to admit, she liked that, too.

Their situation was damnable. Even if she thought she could do something so reckless, she could never abandon Constance. They'd agreed to see out this war together. But if Constance was willing to seek a transfer—

"You love your job, don't you?" he asked, as though admitting defeat.

"I do. It's meaningful."

"It is," he agreed. "So what do we do?" he asked, lifting her hand and pressing a kiss to the back of it. "In two days, I'm going to be on the other side of England."

"Then I guess we enjoy what time we have." Her chest ached, both with how much she loved him and the agony of what was coming.

"I'm not letting you go." He turned and lifted her into his arms. "I might not be here physically, but that doesn't mean we're not together. Understand?"

She nodded. "Then I hope we're both very good at writing letters."

Of all the places she would have loved to go on leave—such as Church Fenton—spending the weekend at her parents' London house was last on the list. To be honest, it didn't even *make* the list.

The only reason she'd agreed to come at all was because they'd promised to stop feeding nonsense stories to the press, and it was her mother's birthday.

The more she came home, the more she realized she wasn't the same girl who'd left it. Perhaps the dutiful, biddable daughter she'd been at the start of this war had been simply another casualty in the Battle for Britain.

They'd won, and the Germans had halted their all-out assault after those horrifying mid-September days, though bombing raids were still terrifyingly common.

Jameson had been gone more than a month, and though he wrote twice a week, she missed him with a ferocity that escaped words. Every part of her ached when she thought about him. Logically, she'd made the right choice. But life was so...uncertain, and there were parts of herself that cursed logic and demanded she get on a train.

Meet me in London next month. We'll get separate rooms. I don't care where we sleep as long as I get to see you. I'm dying here, Scarlett. The words from his latest letter echoed through her head.

"You miss him," Constance noted as they descended the staircase.

"Unbearably," she admitted.

"You should have said yes. You should have run off and married him. In fact, you could go now. Right now." Constance lifted her eyebrows.

"And leave you?" Scarlett questioned, linking elbows with her sister. "Never."

"I would marry Edward if I could, but after Dunkirk...well, he still wants to wait until the war is over, and besides, I'd rather see you happy."

"I will be very happy next month, when I will use my forty-eight hours to meet him here in London," she whispered. The excitement was nearly too much to keep in. "Well, not *here*. I don't think our parents would approve."

"What?" Constance's eyes widened with her smile. "That's brilliant!"

"And what about you? Wasn't that another letter from Edward I saw?" Scarlett raised her eyebrows and bumped her sister's hip.

"It was!"

"Girls, do sit down," their mother prompted as they entered the dining room, which was dimly lit. All their windows were covered tightly to block out any light that might shine through at night, as the blackout dictated, but it also served to make the daytimes equally dreary.

"Yes, Mother," they answered in time, each taking their place at the obscenely long table.

Her father walked in, dressed in an immaculately pressed suit, and smiled at each of his daughters, then his wife, before taking his seat at the head. It was quiet, as always, the discussion kept to pleasantries.

"Are you girls enjoying your leave?" their father asked as they finished the main course. The chicken had been an unexpected treat, given the state of rationing.

"Absolutely," Constance answered with a grin.

"Definitely," Scarlett chimed in as the girls shared a secretive smile. Her parents didn't know about Jameson. She'd need to tell them eventually, but not on her mother's birthday.

"I wish you were home more," her mother noted, her smile failing to hide the sadness in her tone. "But at least we'll see you again next month."

"Actually, we might not be able to visit quite so often," Scarlett admitted. From now on, she'd spend every bit of leave she was given to see Jameson.

Her mother's gaze snapped to hers. "Oh, but you must. We have so many arrangements to make before the summer."

Scarlett's stomach turned over, but she managed to lift her water and sip. *Don't jump to conclusions.* "Arrangements?" she questioned.

Her mother drew back slightly, as though surprised. "Weddings take arranging, Scarlett. They don't just happen. It took Lady Vincent a year to plan her daughter's wedding."

Scarlett's eyes flickered toward Constance. Had she told them about Jameson's proposal?

Constance subtly shook her head, already shrinking back in her chair.

Good God. Were her parents still intending to push the match with Henry? "And who is getting married?" Scarlett asked, straightening her spine.

Her parents shared a telling look, and Scarlett's heart plummeted.

Her father cleared his throat. "Look, we've let you have your fun. You've fulfilled your duty to king and country, and even though you know my thoughts on this war, I respected your choice."

"Appeasement was not the solution to the German hostility!" Scarlett snapped.

"Had they just negotiated an acceptable—" Her father shook his head, then took a deep breath, his jaw ticking. "It's time to do your duty to your family, Scarlett." His voice left no room for misinterpretation or argument.

Icy rage seeped into her veins. "Just to be clear, Father, you associate my duty to this family with marriage?" Their whole way of thinking was *ancient.*

"Naturally. What else could I possibly mean?" Her father lifted his silver eyebrows at her.

Constance swallowed and put her hands in her lap.

"It's for the best, dear," her mother urged. "You'll want for nothing once the Wadsworths—"

No.

"I would want for *love.*" Scarlett took her napkin from her lap and placed it on the table. "I thought I made it clear back in August when I asked you to stop feeding the paper lies."

"It may have been premature, but it certainly wasn't a lie." Her mother drew back as if insulted.

"Allow me to clarify: I will not marry that monster. I refuse."

"You what?" Her mother's jaw dropped. "You are getting married this summer!"

"Well, it won't be to Henry Wadsworth." Even the name tasted vile in her mouth.

"You have someone else in mind?" her father quipped sarcastically.

"I do." She lifted her chin. Birthday be damned, this couldn't wait. They could not continue to plan her life. "I'm in love with a pilot, an American, and if I choose to marry, it will be *him.* You will have to find your income infusion elsewhere."

"A Yank?"

"Yes."

"Absolutely not!" Dishes clanged as her father slammed his hands on the table, but Scarlett didn't flinch.

Constance did.

"I will do as I please. I am a full-grown woman"—Scarlett stood—"and an officer in the Women's Auxiliary Air Force. I am no longer a child for you to order about."

"You would do this? Ruin us?" Her mother's voice broke. "Generations of sacrifices have been made, but you will not?"

She knew exactly where to hit her daughters hardest, but Scarlett pushed the guilt aside. Marrying Henry would only delay the inevitable. The way of life her parents clung to was disintegrating. There was nothing she could do to stop that.

"If there is ruining to be done, I'm quite comfortable saying that I am not the cause." She took a deep breath, hoping there was something she could salvage here, a way to make them see. "I love Jameson. He is a good man. An honorable man—"

"I'll be damned if I see this title, this family's legacy, given to the spawn of a bloody Yank!" her father shouted, coming to his feet.

Scarlett kept her head high and her shoulders square, thankful that she'd spent the last year working in the most stressful environment imaginable, perfecting the art of remaining calm during a tempest. "You make the mistake of assuming I want anything to do with your *title*. I do not aspire to wealth or politics. You cling to something I have no interest in." Her voice was soft yet steel.

Her father's face pinkened, then deepened to a purely red hue as his eyes bulged. "So help me God, Scarlett, if you marry without my permission, I will no longer acknowledge you as my daughter."

"No," her mother gasped.

"I mean it. You won't inherit a thing." He jabbed his finger toward her. "Not Ashby. Not this house. Nothing."

Her heart didn't break—that would have been too simple. It ripped, straining, then tearing at the fibers of her soul. She truly meant that little to him. "Then we agree," she said softly. "I am free to do as I wish, as long as I willingly accept your

mother lifted her chin. "We've cut the staff. We've sold most of the land at Ashby. We've economized the last few years. We all make sacrifices."

"But in this case, you'd like to sacrifice *me*, and I'll not have it. Goodbye, Mother." She walked out of the townhouse and sucked in a shaky breath.

Constance followed her, shutting the door behind her. "So I guess we'll need to purchase new train tickets, seeing as ours were for tomorrow."

She did not deserve her sister, but she hugged her anyway. "How do you feel about applying for a transfer?"

CHAPTER ELEVEN

Noah

Scarlett, my Scarlett,

Tonight, I miss you more than my words can possibly convey. I wish I could fly to you, even if just for a few hours. The only thought that keeps me going here is knowing you'll be with me soon. On nights like tonight, I escape by picturing us in the Rockies, at home and at peace. I'll teach William how to camp and fish. You'll be able to write—to do whatever you want. And we'll be happy. So happy. We're due a little tranquility, don't you think? Not that I regret volunteering for this war. After all, it brought me to you...

She slammed the door in my face.

She actually slammed the door in my *face*.

I sucked in a deep breath, noting the particular burn in my lungs that always accompanied the high altitude. Of all the outcomes I pictured during the flight, this hadn't been one of them.

The solution had come to me while I'd been rereading Scarlett's and Jameson's letters. He'd been able to break down Scarlett's walls because he'd been *there*, holding on to that suitcase in Middle Wallop, so I'd packed mine and gotten on a plane.

I steadied my temper, lifted my hand, and knocked again. To my surprise, she answered.

"As I was saying, hang up on me—" My words froze in my throat.

There was something very wrong here. Georgia looked...off,

as though she had just been delivered the kind of news you had to sit down to hear. Not that she wasn't as beautiful as always, but her skin was bloodless, her face slack, and her eyes—those exquisite blue eyes—were empty.

"Is everything okay?" I asked softly, my chest tightening.

She looked right through me for a second. "What do you want, Noah?"

Something was definitely wrong.

"Can I come in? I promise not to talk about the book." My chest tightened with an immediate, overwhelming urge to fix whatever had gone wrong.

Georgia's brow knit, but she nodded and opened the door for me.

"Come on, let's get you something to drink." Did this have to do with Damian?

She nodded again, then led us down the hall and into an expansive kitchen. It was all I could do to keep my hand off the small of her back or offer her a hug. *A hug?*

I'd never been this far inside the house before, but the kitchen fit what I had already seen. It was a Tuscan theme, with tawny-colored cabinetry and darker granite countertops. The woodwork was ornate but not overdone. The appliances were professional grade. The only thing that seemed out of place were slightly discolored pieces of artwork pinned to a bulletin board on the wall.

"Why don't you sit down," I suggested, gesturing to the stools that lined the kitchen island.

"Isn't that supposed to be my line?" she asked, averting her gaze.

"Let's just pretend our roles are fluid for the moment." I moved to the stove, noting the teakettle on the back corner burner. To my relief, Georgia sat down, resting her forearms on the granite.

I dropped the keys to my rental car into my right pocket, filled the teakettle with water, and set it back on the stove, igniting the gas burner. Then I began my hunt.

I opened three cabinets before I found the one I was looking for. "Do you have a favorite?"

Georgia looked past me to the carefully organized tea supply. "Earl Grey," she responded.

There was a squeezable honey bear next to the tea, and on instinct, I brought that to the countertop, too.

"You're not having any?" Georgia glanced toward the singular packet of tea.

"I'm more of a hot chocolate kind of guy," I admitted.

"But you're making tea."

"You look like you need it."

Two lines appear between her eyes. "But why would you..." She shook her head.

"Why would I what?" I braced my palms on the island across from where she sat.

"Never mind."

"Why would I *what*?" I asked again. "Why would I take care of you?" I guessed.

Her gaze flickered my way.

"Because, contrary to popular belief, I'm not that big of an asshole, and you look like your dog just died." I tilted my head. "And both my mother and sister would kick my ass if I didn't." I shrugged.

Surprise flared in her eyes. "But they'd never know."

"I try to live *most* of my life like my mother will always find out what I've done." Corner of my mouth tugged upward. "In reality, she usually does anyway, and the lectures last for hours. *Hours.* And as for the other parts...well, she *never* needs to know." My brow puckered as the overwhelming silence of the house hit me. "Where is your mother? Usually she's the one making sure you're hydrated."

She scoffed. "She was making sure *you* were hydrated. She's well aware that I can fend for myself." She laced her fingers in front of her, and her knuckles turned white. "Besides, she's probably halfway to the airport by now."

My stomach sank. Given the tone with which she'd said that, my bets were on Ava being the reason Georgia looked shell-shocked. "Was it a planned trip?"

Georgia laughed, but there was nothing happy about the sound. "Yeah, I'd say it was planned *well* in advance."

Before I could question her, the teakettle whistled. I removed it from the burner, only to realize I hadn't looked for a cup.

"Cabinet to the left, second shelf," Georgia said.

"Thanks." I grabbed a mug, then set the tea to steep.

"I should be the one thanking you."

I arched a brow. "Fluid roles, remember?"

She offered me a smile. It was barely there, lasting only a flash of a second, but it was genuine.

"Do you take it with milk, too?" I asked as I slid the mug and honey across the island to her.

"God no." She tilted the honey bear on its head and squeezed a dollop of the amber liquid into her tea. "Gran would tell you that's sacrilege."

"Would she?" I asked, hoping she would elaborate.

Georgia nodded and slid off her stool, coming around the island to open the drawer directly behind me. "She would." She took the spoon from the drawer and returned to her seat before stirring her tea. "She actually preferred sugar, though. The honey was always just for me. It didn't matter how long I'd been away; she always kept it for me, kept a place for me." A wistful look crossed her face.

"You must miss her."

"Every day. Do you miss your dad?"

"Absolutely. It's gotten better with time, but I'd give anything to have him back." Come to think of it, I'd only ever heard about the Stanton women. "What about your dad?"

"I don't have one." She said it so matter-of-factly that I

blinked. "I have one, or *had* one, of course. I'm not the product of immaculate conception or anything," she said as she took her spoon to the dishwasher and put it in. "I've just never met him. He and my mom were both in high school when I was born, and she never gave up his name."

Another piece of the puzzle that was Georgia Stanton clicked into place. She never knew her father. Scarlett raised her. So what did that make Ava?

"Are you sure you don't want anything to drink?" she asked. "It feels a little weird not getting you something when you made tea for me." She looked at me expectantly.

"Not everything is quid pro quo," I said softly.

Her spine straightened, and she turned her back on me, heading for the refrigerator. "In my experience, it's always quid pro quo." She took a bottle of water from the refrigerator, then shut the door. "In fact, there are very few people who don't want something from me." She set the bottle of water down on the counter in front of me and returned to her seat. "So please, drink up. After all, you didn't fly all the way to Colorado because your Spidey senses told you I needed a cup of tea."

You want something, too.

Her eyes said it even if her mouth didn't, and damn it, she was right. My stomach fell into what felt like a bottomless pit.

I nodded once, and then we both drank.

"Why are you here? Not that I'm not thankful for the tea, or the distraction, because I am. I just wasn't expecting you." She leaned forward, warming her hands on the mug.

"I promised I wouldn't talk about the book." Book or not, I was glad to be here, glad to see her in a way that had zero to do with anything professional. The woman had been on my mind in one way or another for the past month.

"You always keep your promises?" Her eyes narrowed in speculation.

"I do. Otherwise, I wouldn't make the promise." It had been

an expensive lesson.

"Even to the women in your life?" She tilted her head. "I've seen quite a few pictures."

"Checking up on me?" *Please say yes.* God knew my browser history was full of Georgia Stanton.

"My best friend keeps sending me pictures and articles. She thinks I should jump you." She shrugged.

She what? I squeezed my water bottle so hard, I crushed it. "Really?" My voice dropped, pushing every single image that sentence brought to mind far out of my head, or at least trying to.

"Funny, right? Especially given the parade of women you keep your *promises* to." She gave me a sugar-sweet smile and batted her lashes.

I laughed, then shook my head. "Georgia, the only promises I make to women are what time I'll pick them up and what they can expect while they're with me. Days. Nights. Weeks. I find it saves a lot of misunderstandings and a lot of drama if everyone knows what they're getting up front, and despite your thoughts on my writing, I've never had an *unsatisfied* complaint." I twisted the top back onto my empty water bottle, keeping my thoughts *far* away from the things I wanted to *promise* her.

"So romantic." She rolled her eyes, but color flushed her cheeks.

"I never claimed to be, remember?" I smirked, leaning back against the counter.

"Ah yes, the bookstore. Noted. So you've never broken a promise?" Her voice pitched in disbelief.

My face fell.

"Not since I was sixteen and I forgot to take my little sister, Adrienne, for ice cream after I said I would." I winced, remembering the sound of the beeping hospital monitors. "My mom took her and got into the accident I told you about."

Georgia's eyes widened.

"Adrienne—my sister—was fine, but Mom...well, there were

a lot of surgeries. After that, I made it a point to never commit myself unless I was sure I could follow through." I'd also drafted my very first book the following summer.

"You've never missed a deadline?"

"Nope." Though that might change if she didn't start communicating with me about this particular book.

Curiosity sparkled in those crystal blue eyes. I could have written an entire novel dedicated to them. In a way, I guess I already was, given that she and Scarlett had the same ones.

"Never blown a New Year's resolution?"

I grinned. "I never make them," I admitted like it was a dirty little secret.

She tugged her bottom lip between her teeth.

Shit. I wanted to suck it free. The bottle crinkled in my hand.

"Never stood a woman up for a date?"

"I always say that I'll do my best to make it, and I do. I never *promise* a woman I'll meet her unless I'm already there." Anyone who went out with me knew that if I was sucked into a story, chances were, they were getting a cancellation text. Granted, I'd send it hours in advance, but the story came first. Always. "I'm not exactly the guy you depend on during a deadline. Unless you're my publisher."

"So you're more about the semantics," she argued, sipping her tea.

I barely managed to keep from sputtering. "No, I'm more about defining expectations and either meeting or exceeding them." We locked eyes, and that tangible hit of electricity struck me again.

"Uh-huh." She clicked her tongue. "Do you still have dinner with your mother?"

"Once a week. Unless I'm on book tour, a research trip, vacation, that kind of thing." I gave it some thought. "Sometimes she makes me cut it to every other week." My lips tugged at the corners.

"*She* makes *you* cut it?"

"She does." I nodded. "She would prefer I spend less time at her house and more time finding a wife."

Georgia startled, nearly spit out her tea. "A wife." She set the mug on the counter. "And how is that going?"

"I'll let you know," I managed with a straight face.

"Please do. I'd hate not to be in the know when it comes to your love life."

I laughed and shook my head again. She was something else.

"Gran would have liked you," she mused quietly. "She wasn't a fan of your books, that's true. But you, she would have liked. You have just the right mix of arrogance and talent that she would have appreciated. Plus, it doesn't hurt that you're pretty. She liked pretty men." Georgia rubbed at the back of her neck. It was long and graceful, just like the rest of her.

"You think I'm pretty." I grinned, raising my eyebrows.

She rolled her eyes. "Out of all that, you dwell on *pretty.*"

"Well, if you'd said sexy, handsome, well-endowed, or body-like-a-god, I would have dwelled on those, but you didn't, so I'm just making do with what content I have." I tossed my water bottle in the recycling bin at the end of the island.

Her cheeks turned a deeper shade of pink.

Mission accomplished. She'd been so pale there for a while that I was starting to wonder if I'd get to see that fire again.

"I can hardly testify to those last two." She took her mug to the dishwasher.

"Guess your friend didn't show you *every* article," I teased. I liked that she was neat. Not that I had any business liking anything about her, to include the way her shorts clung to her very nice ass, but there I was, doing it anyway. How had that ass escaped my attention last time I was here? Or those mile-long legs? *You had other, more important things on your mind.* "So the first two are in?" My eyes trailed down the nape of her neck as she returned to her seat.

"Depends on how much you're pissing me off at the moment." She lifted a shoulder.

"And right now?"

Her gaze swept over me from head to toe and back up again, taking in my cargo shorts and NYU shirt. *I would have worn the Armani had I known there'd be a test.*

"I'd say you're a solid seven." Again, she pulled it off straight-faced.

Nice. I lifted a single brow. "And when I'm pissing you off?"

"You slide right off the scale into the negatives."

I laughed. Damn, how long had it been since a woman had made me laugh so many times in just a few minutes?

She folded her hands on the island, and her energy shifted. "Tell me why you're really here, Noah."

"I promised—"

"So, what? You're just going to stand in my kitchen and make me tea?" Her chin lifted. "I know you're here about the book."

I studied her carefully, taking in the rise of color in her cheeks and the spark in her eyes. She was mostly back to what I'd consider *normal,* but in all honesty, I didn't have a baseline when it came to Georgia Stanton. I was flying blind.

"You want to get out of here?" I asked.

"What do you have in mind?" She looked more than skeptical.

"How's your life insurance?"

"No," she said a half hour later as she stared up at the rock face that stretched a hundred feet above us.

"It's fun," I argued, gesturing to a couple of guys who were all grins as they packed up their equipment. "See, they think it's fun."

"You have lost your mind if you think I'm climbing that." She lifted her sunglasses to the top of her head so I could see just how serious she was.

"I didn't say you had to climb the whole thing," I argued. "There's a less challenging path right over there." That one was only thirty-or-so feet, and my niece could easily do it, not that I was about to say *that* to Georgia.

"Are you trying to kill me?" she whispered as the other climbers walked past on the trail.

"We have equipment." I gave the shoulder strap of my backpack a pat. "I brought an extra harness." I eyed her footwear. "Your shoes aren't exactly what I'd recommend, but they'll do until we can get you some good ones."

Her eyes narrowed. "When you said, *throw on some active wear and let's go for a hike*, I assumed, shockingly, that we were *hiking*." She gestured to her Lululemon-covered body.

"We did hike," I argued. "It was half a mile to get up here from the trailhead."

"Semantics, again!" she snapped, putting her hands on her very nice hips.

Stop looking at her fucking hips.

"What are you afraid of?" I turned my Mets cap backward and shoved my glasses to the top of my head.

"Falling off the mountain!" She pointed to the rock face. "It's a pretty realistic fear when you think about *climbing* it."

"Think of it as vertical hiking." I shrugged.

"Unreal." She jabbed her finger in my direction.

"I was only kidding about the life insurance comment. I won't let you fall." *Ever.* She'd already been let down too many times.

She scoffed. "Okay. Right. And how exactly are you going to prevent it?" She lifted her eyebrows.

"I'll be your belay partner and control the rope in case you fall. See, we put the harness on—"

"Why the hell do you even *have* an extra harness? Do you just fly around the United States, hoping to pick up women climbers?" She folded her arms across her chest.

"No." Though I couldn't help but wonder if that thought was spurring her on or not. Sure, it made me an ass, but the thought of Georgia getting all worked up out of jealousy was pretty fucking hot. "It's *my* extra harness in case *mine* breaks. I like to climb, therefore, I bring my equipment when I'm going somewhere with mountains...you know, like *Colorado*."

"How did you even know about this place, anyway?" she asked, still downright hostile.

"I found it the last time I was here."

She tilted her head.

"During the days I was waiting for you to decide if I was good enough to—"

"You promised!" And the finger was back again.

I pressed my lips in a tight line and breathed in through my nose for a count of three. "Georgia, I'm not going to force you up that rock face—"

"As if you could."

"—but I am promising that if you choose to climb, I will not let you fall off the mountain." I lowered my face to hers, making sure she knew I was serious.

My best friend thinks I should jump you. My brain was pretty much a broken record after hearing that.

"Because you control gravity?" She blinked.

I had never met a more frustrating woman in my life.

"Because I'm going to—"

She lifted that brow again.

I sighed. "If you *wanted* to climb, I would go first and hook the rope up. I scouted it the first time I was here."

Her brows lowered. "And what would keep *you* from falling off?"

I swung the backpack from my shoulders and shook it lightly. "I'd clip in. We're not talking about Yosemite here. It's pretty well-traveled. Then as you climbed, I'd have you on belay, so if you *did* slip off, you'd just hang there dangling until you found your footing."

Her jaw dropped. "You what?"

I lifted the backpack slightly. "You would be attached to one end of the rope, and I would have the other."

She drew back.

"You'd be safe," I promised.

She shook her head, her mouth tightening.

A thought dawned on me. "Georgia, if you don't want to climb because you're scared of heights, or you don't want to scrape up your hands, or you just flat don't want to, that's fine."

"I know that." Her eyes said she *hadn't* known that. What? Like I was going to shove her up the mountain while she begged me not to?

"Right." My chest ached. "But if you don't want to climb because you think I'll drop you, then that's a whole other matter. I promise you that I will not drop you." I kept my voice even and low, hoping she'd hear the truth in my words. "I'm really good at this."

She swallowed, then glanced at the bag. "I barely know you."

"See? More articles your best friend missed out on. You can run a google search on my climbing history if we've got service up here. It's pretty well documented that I'm an avid climber, and I don't just mean the easy stuff."

Her forehead puckered. "I never said you weren't."

My stomach lurched. "So it's not my skill level you're worried about," I said slowly.

She averted her gaze and shifted her weight. "You could be a serial killer," she suggested, sarcasm dripping from her tone as she lifted her hands.

Deflecting. She uses humor to deflect.

"I'm not."

"You kill off a lot of people in your books. Just saying." She looked up the rock face, tilting her head back.

"Not through homicide, and now who's talking about books?"

A smile tugged at her lips.

"Besides, there are three other climbers right there." I pointed to a group midway up the face. "Pretty sure they'd rat me out if I murdered you in broad daylight."

She stared at the other climbers silently.

"You're not going to climb, are you?" I asked quietly.

She shook her head, her lips pursing as she watched the other climbers.

Her refusal stung. It shouldn't have, and I knew it, but it still did. "Want to hike up the rest of the trail?"

Her head snapped my way in surprise. "You can climb. I'm happy to watch."

"I didn't come up here for me." I'd brought her in hopes that the fresh air would help clear out whatever had taken her down earlier.

She winced. "I'd still hate to make you miss out. Go ahead. I'm fine." She nodded, plastering on a smile so fake, it was almost comical.

"I'd rather hike with you. Come on." I nodded back toward the trail and slipped my pack over my shoulders.

"You're sure?" She narrowed her eyes.

"Absolutely."

"It's not you." She sucked in a breath, then glanced back up at the rock wall. "The last man who promised to keep me safe screwed his lead and dropped me on my ass," she said softly. "But I'm sure you already know that. Everyone knows that."

If I'd been the serial killer she'd joked about, Damian Ellsworth would have been my first victim.

"And after today..." She shook her head, the edges of her mouth trembling. "Today just isn't a good day for the whole trust fall thing. So let's get going." She forced another smile, then took off up the trail.

She doesn't trust you. I swore under my breath as I realized that was the same reason she wouldn't let me finish the book how I wanted.

It all came down to trust.

I steadied myself before striding after her, cursing at the irony. I'd spent the majority of my life making sure I lived by my word, and now it was being questioned by a woman so jaded even I couldn't dig out of the hole someone else had dug.

Guess it was good that I was an expert climber.

"So how long are you here for?" she asked as we continued the hike.

"Until I finish the book." My lungs burned as we pushed up the trail. "And, since my deadline is in two and a half months, I'd guess I'll be here about that long."

"What? Really?"

"Really."

Two little lines appeared between her brows. "So where are you staying?"

"I rented a little place down the road," I replied, a smug smile quirking at my lips.

"Oh?"

"Yep. It's called Grantham Cottage."

She stopped in the middle of the trail, so I turned around and kept walking backward, savoring the surprise and horror on her face. "Like I said, hang up on me now, *neighbor*."

The look on her face made the hassle of tracking down a rental entirely worth it.

CHAPTER TWELVE

November 1940

Kirton-in-Lindsey

It was different being surrounded by other Americans now that Jameson was in the 71st Eagle Squadron. Almost like being back home, except they weren't anywhere near it.

"They're all so young," Howard muttered as they watched the new recruits at their first beer call. It was an English tradition he'd been all too glad to keep, seeing as it wasn't just about the camaraderie. This was where they had it out when disputes needed to be settled.

"Most of them are the same age we are," Andy countered, leaning back against the walls of their newly acquired rest room. They'd been lucky enough to fall in on a collection of armchairs to mix in with the harsh wicker ones that sat scattered around the space, but the three of them stood apart in more than the physical sense.

"Not really," Jameson said. "Not in the way that matters." The three of them had seen combat. War was no longer something romantic, something to glorify. These new kids were just that, kids. They'd all been freshly delivered via Canada, having smuggled themselves out of the States in hopes of joining The Eagles.

Overnight, those—like Jameson—who had considered themselves rookies throughout the Battle of Britain were now the veterans. The new Americans were all pilots, but most of them were commercial. They'd flown supplies or even people. They'd dusted crops. They'd showboated in front of crowds.

They'd never shot another man out of the sky.

There were a few who had, and they'd already lost one back to 64 squadron. Not that Jameson blamed him. They'd been plucked from daily missions and tossed into training now for six weeks, and the frustration over their uselessness was mounting. They were needed in the sky.

This was bullshit.

"Maybe Art was right to leave," Howard grumbled before draining half his beer.

"You read my mind." Jameson looked down at his full glass. It wasn't as satisfying as it had been when they'd done this after a mission. It felt...fake, like they were playing at being fighter pilots.

At least the unit had been moved to Kirton-in-Lindsey last week. That was one step closer to being operational. Unfortunately, they'd transferred the Buffaloes with them.

The American aircraft didn't perform well at high altitude, and that was the least of its problems. The engine overheated regularly, the cockpit controls weren't dependable, and it lacked the armament they'd come to depend on. Sure, the new men liked the open, airy cockpit, but they'd never flown a Spitfire.

Jameson missed his Spitfire almost as much as he missed Scarlett.

God, he missed Scarlett. It had been nearly two months since he'd seen her, and he was slowly going out of his mind. If not for the unit move, he would have made the trip to Middle Wallop already— he was that desperate to look into those blue eyes. She'd spent her October leave with her parents, which was understandable, but according to her letter, it hadn't gone well. He hated the pressure that loving him put her under. It wasn't fair that she was forced to choose between her family and Jameson, but he'd be lying if he didn't admit his happiness at being the one chosen.

Without flying combat missions, he had more downtime, which meant she was never far from his mind. His letters increased from twice a week to three times, and sometimes even four. He wrote the letters as though he were talking to her, as though she were there with him, hearing how much he missed her. How much he longed for her. He told her stories from his childhood and did his best to paint a picture of life in his tiny hometown.

Even now he smiled, just thinking about taking her to Poplar Grove. His mother would love her. Scarlett always said exactly what she meant. She never minced words or played games. She wasn't coy or flirtatious, either. She guarded her emotions the same way she protected her sister—someone was only given access once they'd proven their worth.

Sometimes he felt like he was still proving his.

"Hey, Stanton!" One of the men called over with a distinctly Boston accent. "Is it true you've got an English sweetie?"

"It is." Jameson's grip tightened on his glass.

"Well, where do you find one?" He lifted his eyebrows, and some of the new guys laughed.

"Don't let him get to you," Howard said under his breath.

"I picked her up on the side of the road," Jameson answered in a deadpan.

"She have any friends?" the rookie prodded. "We could all use a little friendly company, if you get my meaning."

"Okay, now you can let it get to you." Howard whacked Jameson's shoulder.

"How is Christine, anyway?" Jameson asked with a slight tilt to his lips.

"Far away. Very far away."

"She does have friends," Jameson said loudly, so this jerk could hear him. "None of them would be interested in meeting you, but she does have them."

"Oh!" The men howled.

The man flushed. "Well, her standards couldn't be too high if she's with you, Stanton."

Right, these guys are still in the whip-it-out-and-measure stage. Andy rolled his eyes, and Howard finished off his beer.

"She is definitely out of my league, boys." Jameson nodded thoughtfully. "But she'd chew you up and spit you out before you even got close, Boston."

Howard lurched, spraying beer through his lips onto the floor in front of them. Every head turned toward him as he wiped the remains of his drink from his chin and pointed toward the door on the far end of the room. "She's also here."

Jameson's head whipped toward the entry, and his heart stopped.

Scarlett stood in the doorway, her jacket folded over an arm. She looked like *heaven*.

Her glossy black hair was pinned back, barely brushing the collar of her uniform. Her cheeks were pink, her lips curved in a barely contained smile, and damn, he could see the blue of her eyes from here. She was here. At his base. In his rest room. She was *here*.

He was halfway across the room before he'd even thought to move, abandoning his beer on the nearest table as he went. A few short strides and he was home, sucking in his breath at the warmth of her skin as one of his hands cupped the back of her neck and the other palmed her waist.

"You're here," he whispered, awestruck as she smiled up at him. This wasn't a dream. She was real.

"I'm here," she answered just as softly.

His gaze dropped to her mouth, and his grip tightened at the hunger that threatened to consume him. He needed her kiss more than he needed his next breath, but he wasn't about to do it here. Not in front of the jackass who'd implied he needed *company*.

"For how long?" he asked, his stomach pitching at the knowledge that it was most likely only a few hours. He would have met her halfway if she'd told him. He wanted as much time as he could get with her.

"About that..." Her grin turned playful. "Do you have a minute?"

"I have a lifetime." Which he'd offered her...and she'd refused, but he was trying incredibly hard not to think about that part.

"Brilliant." She smiled and stepped out of his arms, taking his hand in hers. Then she looked back across the room. "Boston, is it?" she asked.

"Uh. Yeah." He stood, rubbing the back of his neck as he flushed red.

"Ah. Well, let's all hope that the WAAF isn't ever integrated into His Majesty's forces. It would be a shame for me to officially outrank you, Pilot Officer." She offered him a polite smile, which Jameson knew well enough to recognize as her go-to-hell face, and he failed to stifle his laugh. Her smile shifted to a genuine one when she spotted Howard. "Lovely to see you, Howie."

"You too, Scarlett."

Jameson led her down the hall, then opened the door to the empty briefing room. He tugged her inside, shut and locked the door, then tossed her coat on the nearest desk and proceeded to kiss her senseless.

Scarlett didn't melt; she came alive under his touch. She wound her arms around his neck and arched, seeking as much contact as she could get as his tongue twined with hers. He groaned into her mouth and kissed her deeper, wiping out the agonizing weeks of separation with every stroke of his tongue and scrape of his teeth.

Only with Jameson did Scarlett allow herself to simply *feel*. The need, the longing, the pain, the overwhelming ache of love in her heart—she surrendered to it all. Every other part of her life was managed and controlled. Jameson shredded the rules she'd been raised under and brought her into a world of emotion just as vibrant and colorful as he was.

Urgent need beat at her. *More. Closer. Deeper.*

"How long would you like me?" Her grip tightened on his neck.

"Forever." His hands flexed on her waist as he skimmed his teeth along the delicate flesh of her earlobe.

Lord, he made it hard to think when he did that.

"Good, because I've been reposted here," she managed.

Jameson froze, then slowly drew back, his eyes wide with disbelief.

"Are you displeased?" she asked, her chest clenching at the possibility. Had she been a fool? What if the letters hadn't meant anything to him? What if he'd already moved on but hadn't had the heart to tell her? Every girl back at Middle Wallop had made it clear they'd be happy to take her place, and she knew it had to be the same here.

"You're here...as in here, here?" His eyes searched hers.

"Yes." She nodded. "Constance and I asked to be reposted, and it was granted just a few days ago. I didn't want to get your hopes up in case it was denied, and when it wasn't, I figured I'd be here before a letter would even reach you. Are you disappointed?" She repeated the question, her voice hitching at the end.

"God, no!" He smiled, and the tension in her chest evaporated. "I'm...surprised, but it's a great surprise!" He kissed her soundly. "I love you, Scarlett."

"And I love you. Thank goodness, because I can't just go and ask to be reposted back to Middle Wallop." She tried to keep a straight face, but she simply couldn't. Had she ever been this happy in her life? She didn't think so.

"I don't know how long the 71st will be here," he admitted, stroking his thumbs over her cheeks. "Squadrons move all the time, and there's already talk that we'll be reposted elsewhere." Just the thought of it made his stomach curdle. Her reposting here was a temporary bandage on a hemorrhaging wound, but he was so damned grateful for whatever time they'd have.

"I know." She turned in to his hand and kissed his palm. "I'm prepared for that."

"I'm not. These months have been unbearable without you."
He leaned his forehead against hers. "I didn't know how much
I loved you until I had to wake up, day after day, knowing there
was no chance I'd see you smile or hear you laugh, or hell, hear
you shout at me." He'd been incomplete, always thinking of her
no matter what he'd been doing.

He'd been so distracted, he was surprised he hadn't pranged
an aircraft, not that he couldn't fly one of those Buffaloes with
his eyes closed.

"It's been awful," she admitted, dropping her gaze to his
lips, then down the lines of his uniform. "I missed your arms
around me, and the way my heart leaps whenever I see you." She
brushed her fingers over his lips. "I missed your kisses, and even
the way you tease."

"Someone has to make you laugh." He nipped at the pad of
her thumb.

"You do that quite well." Her smile faltered. "I don't want to
spend another month like that, let alone two."

His face tightened. "How are we going to avoid it in another
few months when they decide the 71st is needed somewhere else?"

"Well, I've had a thought about that." Her eyes narrowed in
speculation. "But it would require you telling me *your* thoughts
again." She pressed her lips between her teeth.

He blinked. "My thoughts? I asked you to m—" His jaw
dropped. "Scarlett, are you saying…" His eyes frantically searched
hers.

"I'm not saying anything until you ask." Her chest tightened,
praying he hadn't changed his mind, that she hadn't gambled
her entire happiness and dragged her sister across England to
be refused.

His eyes flared. "Wait right here." He stepped back, holding
his pointer finger in the air. "Don't move a muscle." Then he ran
from the room.

Scarlett swallowed and set her knees together, rearranging

her skirt. Surely he hadn't meant *those* muscles. God knew anyone could have waltzed in.

The mechanical ticks of the clock were her only company in the silence, and she did what she could to steady her heart.

Jameson slid back into the room, his hand gripping the doorframe to make the turn. Then he recovered his balance and shut the door behind him before approaching her.

"Better now?" she asked.

He nodded, nervously jamming his fingers through his hair before dropping to one knee before her and holding a ring between his thumb and forefinger.

She sucked in a breath.

"I know I'm not what you pictured when you thought of marriage. I don't have a title, or even a country right now." He grimaced. "But what I do have is yours, Scarlett. My heart, my name, my very being—it's all yours. And I promise I will spend every day of my life earning the privilege of your love if you let me. Will you do me the honor of being my wife?" His brows knit slightly, but there was so much hope in his eyes that it was nearly painful for her to see it, to know she'd made him question what her answer would be.

"I will," she said, her lips trembling as she smiled. "I will!" she repeated with an excited nod. She now knew what her life looked like without him in it, and she never wanted to feel that loss again. Her job, her family, this war—they'd deal with whatever came together.

"Thank you, God." He stood and swept her into his arms. "Scarlett, my Scarlett," he said against her cheek.

She held on tight, letting herself absorb this moment. Somehow, they'd make it last.

He set her down and slipped the ring onto her left finger. It was beautiful, with a solitaire diamond set in gold filigree, and it fit her finger perfectly. "Jameson, it's gorgeous. Thank you."

"I'm so glad you like it. I picked it up when we were at Church-

Fenton, hoping I could get you to change your mind." He kissed her softly, then took her hand. "We can still catch the commander if we're quick."

"What?" she asked as Jameson gathered her coat, then guided her into the hallway.

"We have to get the commander's permission. Chaplain's, too." His eyes were bright with excitement.

"Well, there's plenty of time for that." She laughed.

"Oh no. I'm not risking that you'll change your mind again. Wait here for just a second." He dipped into another room, leaving her in the hallway, struggling not to sputter. Within a moment he was back with his own jacket and hat.

"We are not getting married tonight," she said quickly. That would be complete and utter madness.

"Why not?" His face fell.

She cupped his cheek with her hand. "Because I'd like to unpack the dress I bought. It's not much, but I'd like to wear it."

"Oh. Right." He nodded, considering her words. "Of course you would. And your family?"

Heat rose in her cheeks. "Constance is now the only family I have."

"Not for long." He pulled her gently against him. "You'll have me, my mom and dad, and my uncle, too."

"And that's all I need. Besides, we'll need to find accommodations. I'm certainly not spending my wedding night with the 71st sleeping beside us." She gave him a pointed look.

He blanched. "Hell no. We can see the commander and the Chaplain tomorrow, if that works for you."

She nodded. "I'll unpack my dress but not much more." A hum of anticipation vibrated through her whole body.

"I'll find us a place of our own." He touched his forehead to hers.

"And then we'll get married," she whispered.

"Then we'll get married."

CHAPTER THIRTEEN

Georgia

Dearest Jameson,

I miss you. I need you. Nothing here is the same without you. Constance thinks we might be able to move the rosebush, but I'm not sure we should. Why uproot something that is happy right where it is? Unlike me. I'm wilting here without you. Keeping busy, of course, but you're never far from my mind. Please stay safe, my love. I cannot breathe in this world without you. Be careful. Before you know it, we'll be together again.

All my heart,
Scarlett

"What do you mean he just *showed up*?" Hazel's eyebrows flew sky-high, her green eyes flaring wide.

"Out of everything I told you happened yesterday, *that* is what surprises you?" I looked pointedly over my coffee at her.

"As much as I love you, Ava rolling out the minute the advance hit is pretty much her MO. Was I hoping she'd keep her promise and stay? Of course. I was rooting for her to turn over a new leaf, but she might need to turn over a whole tree at this point. I just thought you would have called me when— Colin, honey, don't touch that." She scurried to my breakfast nook where her children sat playing, and she shut the first cabinet door.

"It's fine," I assured her. "Gran always kept those cabinets full of toys for exactly that." Most of those toys were older than I was.

"I know, but I don't want them to—" She caught the look I was leveling on her. "Right. This cabinet is fine, but let's leave Aunt Georgia's other cabinets alone, okay?" She swung open the door and walked back to the island, taking the stool beside mine. "I swear, I just wanted to stop by and check on you, not ransack your house."

"Please." I rolled my eyes. "I'm glad you did. It's not like I have a whole lot going on." A smile tugged at my lips as I leaned back slightly and watched them play.

"So he's...here?" Hazel asked, lifting her coffee mug.

"He rented Grantham Cottage."

"He what?" Her mug clicked against the granite as she set it down, forgetting to drink.

"You heard me." I took another fortifying swallow. All the caffeine in the world wouldn't help me today, but I was willing to give it a try.

"That's like..." She leaned in as if someone might hear us. "Next door."

"Yes." I nodded. "I even called the trust attorney last night, who confirmed that the property manager rented it out as I instructed." I scrunched my nose. "Then I may have asked if I could revoke the lease, and he told me that not liking Noah wasn't a legal reason."

Hazel gawked at me.

"Would you please say something?" I asked when the silence became painfully awkward.

"Right. Sorry." She shook her head and glanced at the kids.

"Relax, they aren't going anywhere."

"You have no idea how fast they move. I swear I clocked Dani at a three-minute mile yesterday." She crossed her legs and studied me. "So, the hottie is next door."

"The writer is...well, if you can even call the cottage 'next door.'" It was basically *on* the property—that's how close it was, which was one of the reasons Gran had never sold it. She said it was better to pick and choose your neighbors than get saddled with a nosy Nellie.

Hazel's eyes narrowed.

"In fact, he's supposed to be here any minute so we can get

down to the super fun business of arguing. He literally *moved* here so he could argue with me. Who does that?" I took another sip of my coffee.

"Someone who recognizes you for the stubborn—"

"Hey now," I warned.

"You know it's true. If anything, he gets points for getting on a plane instead of hitting redial." She shrugged. "Plus, it makes my earlier suggestion of *working out* your frustration with him *on* him easier."

Traitor.

"Whose side are you on?"

"Yours. Always yours. I didn't even add the man to my hall pass."

"Good. Then he doesn't get points. There are no points to be had." I finished off my coffee and took the mug to the sink. When I turned around, Hazel's head was tilted as she studied me. "What?"

"You like him." She sipped her coffee.

"I'm s-sorry?" I sputtered, my stomach twisting.

"I said what I said."

"Take it back!" I snapped, like we were seven years old again.

"You're wearing real clothes. Jeans, a shirt you had to iron, and your hair is down. You like him." A smile spread across her face.

"I'm starting to regret letting you through the door." My phone buzzed, and I snatched it from the counter before Hazel could see the screen. It was a text message from Noah.

Noah: Headed up. Need anything?

It would have been childish to respond that I needed him to take his gorgeous, insistent ass back to New York. I thought about doing it, anyway.

"I do *not* like him," I fired back at Hazel, then tapped out a text message.

Georgia: Come on in. The door is unlocked.

"And he's on his way," I added, leaning my hip against the counter. Just because I'd woken up and felt...human didn't mean I liked him. It meant I was preparing for a business meeting. My phone buzzed again.

"Kids, we need to pack it up. Aunt Georgia has a friend coming over," Hazel called over to Oliver and Dani.

Noah: You can't just leave your doors unlocked. It's not safe.

I scoffed. Unsafe, my ass.

Georgia: Says the man who climbs mountains.

I set my phone on the counter and sighed at my best friend. "I don't like him," I repeated.

"All right," she said with a soft nod, taking her coffee mug to the sink. "But you need to know that it's okay if you do."

I flinched. It wasn't, though.

"Give it back!" Oliver wailed.

"It's mine!" Danielle shrieked.

Both Hazel and I spun, but Danielle raced right past us, Oliver on her heels.

"For fuck's sake," Hazel muttered to the heavens, already moving.

"You cannot leave your door—oomph!" Noah's voice bellowed from the entry.

Before we could make it out of the kitchen, Noah was already rounding the corner, a giggling kid under each arm. I didn't notice the sheer size of those biceps. Nope. I didn't. I also didn't pay attention to the curve of his mouth or the straight-up sex appeal in his smile. It was inhuman to look that good this early in the morning.

"See what happens when you leave your door unlocked?" he asked, bouncing the kids slightly. "All sorts of wild creatures get in."

Dani roared, which only made Noah smile wider.

No. No. No. No melting, no sighing, nothing. Nada.

"Hey, you're not supposed to be nice to strangers," I groaned.

"Isn't he your friend, Aunt Georgia?" Oliver argued.

Lord save me from small towns. The kids hadn't ever met a stranger.

"Yeah, Aunt Georgia, are you saying we're not friends?" Noah challenged with mockingly wide eyes. I rolled mine as he set the kids on their feet and offered his hand out to Hazel. "Hi. Noah Morelli. I'm guessing the cute kids are yours." He laid the charm on thick, and it worked, given Hazel's grin.

He gave her his real name.

"Hi, Noah. I'm Hazel, Georgia's best friend." She shook his hand and let go. "You're good with kids." Her eyebrows lifted.

"Only thanks to my sister. Best friend, huh?" He shot me a devious smile. "The one with the articles?"

Kill me right now.

"Guilty." Her grin only widened.

"So, can you give me tips on getting a word in edgewise with that one?" He motioned toward me.

"Oh sure! You just have to let her—" She caught my glare and straightened her spine. "Sorry, no-points Noah, I'm team Georgia. Kids, we have to go right now." *Sorry*, she mouthed at me as she hurried to the kids in the breakfast room.

"Don't worry about the mess," I said over my shoulder. She had enough on her plate without picking up my house. It wasn't like I had much else to do today, and she needed the break. "Besides, don't you have to open the center?"

"I hate to— Oh my God, I'm going to be so late!" She scooped a kid into each arm, then nearly skidded by, stopping to kiss my cheek. "Thanks for the coffee."

"Have a good day at work, dear," I sang, dropping a banana in her oversize purse.

"It was nice to meet you, Noah!" she yelled back as she raced out the door.

"You too!"

The door shut with an audible *wham*.

"A banana?" he asked, lifting his eyebrows.

"She always remembers to feed her kids breakfast, but she gets too busy to eat for herself," I answered with a shrug as my phone buzzed.

Hazel: He gets about a dozen points for that maneuver with the kids.

"Traitor," I muttered, sticking my phone in my back pocket without responding.

"So," Noah said, tucking his hands into his front pockets.

"So," I responded. "I've never scheduled a fight before." The air between us could have crackled with all the anticipatory electricity flying about.

"Is that what you'd call this?" He smirked.

"What would *you* call it?" I put the coffee mugs in the dishwasher.

He gave it a moment's thought. "A premeditated walk for the purpose of discovering a mutually beneficial path so we might navigate our personal and professional differences to attain a singular goal," he mused. "If I had to call it something off the cuff."

"Writers," I muttered. "Then let's *walk* ourselves back to the office."

His eyes flared with delight. "I have a better idea. Let's walk along the creek."

I arched an eyebrow at him.

He put his hands up. "No climbing. I'm talking about the creek in your backyard—the one in the letters, right? I think better on my feet. Plus it takes breakable objects out of the equation if you want to throw something at me."

I rolled my eyes. "Fine. I'll get my shoes."

By the time I got back to the kitchen, now wearing hiking boots and a much more sensible T-shirt, he'd cleaned up the mess Hazel's kids had left, and even I had to reluctantly admit he was scoring points.

Broody writer? Check.

Hot as hell? Check.

Good with kids? Double check.

My chest went all tight on me. This was *so* not good.

"You didn't have to, but thank you," I told him as we headed out the kitchen door and onto the patio.

"I didn't mind—whoa." He came up short, staring at the expanse of garden that Gran had loved.

"It's an English-style garden, naturally," I explained as we started down the path between the trimmed hedges. Fall had set in, bringing out the oranges and golds everywhere but the greenhouse.

"Naturally," he said, taking it all in, his attention darting to one plant, then another.

"Are you memorizing it?" I asked.

"What do you mean?"

"Gran used to tell me that she was memorizing a place. The way it looked and smelled, the sounds she heard, the smaller details she could drop into a story that would make the reader feel like they were there. Is that what you do?"

"I never thought about it that way, but yeah." He nodded. "This is beautiful."

"Thank you. She loved it, even when she was complaining that she couldn't get some of her favorite plants to live at altitude." We reached the back gate, where an evergreen hedge separated us from the Colorado wilderness. I turned the wrought iron handle and walked us through. "She said it made her feel closer to her sister."

"Constance taught her, right?"

"Yep." It was weird, but comforting that someone else had read Gran's manuscript, knew that part of her life as intimately as I did.

"Well, damn. This is beautiful, too," he said toward the aspens ahead of us.

"It's home." I took a deep breath, feeling my soul settle the way it always did at this particular view. We were nestled in a valley of the Elks, which rose up high before us, their crowns already tipped with the first snow.

The meadow behind Gran's house was colored in shades of burnished gold, both from the knee-high grass that had surrendered to the cycle of fall and the leaves of the aspen trees that flanked both sides.

"This is my favorite time of year. Not that I don't miss fall in New York, because I do. But here there's no riot of color. No war between the trees as to whose leaves will be the brightest. Here, the mountains turn gold, as if they all agreed. It's peaceful." I walked us along the path that had been worn into the meadow long before I was born.

"I can see why you'd want to come back," Noah admitted. "I'm a sucker for autumn in New York, though."

"And yet, here you are, living just down the road." We reached the creek that ran through Gran's property—my property now. It wasn't much by East Coast standards. Maybe ten feet wide and two feet deep at the most, but water was different in the Rockies. It didn't flow steadily, and it wasn't smooth or predictable. Here, it could slow to a trickle, and when you least expected it, send a wall of water in a flash flood that would destroy everything in its path. It was like everything else in the mountains—dangerously beautiful.

"I did what I had to." He shrugged, and we turned to walk along the creek. "Do you miss New York?"

"No."

"Quick answer."

"Easy question." I tucked my thumbs into my back pockets. "I guess this is when we start the book fight?"

"I'm not the one saying it has to be a fight. Let's start out easy. Ask me a personal question. Anything you want." He pushed up his sleeves as we walked, revealing a line of ink down one forearm that looked like the tip of a sword. "I'll answer one if you do."

That seemed easy enough.

"Anything?"

"Anything."

"What's the story behind that tattoo?" I motioned toward his forearm.

He followed my line of sight. "Ah, that one was actually my first." He pushed up his sleeve as far as the material would let him go, revealing the blade of a sword that served as the needle for a compass. I'd seen enough pictures to know it covered his shoulder, though I could only see the base of it right now. "I got it the week before *Avalon Waning* published. I wove a King Arthur parable into this guy's search for—"

"His lost love. I've read it." I nearly tripped as he gave me a slow smile, and I jerked my gaze back to the path. "Do you have tattoos for all your books?"

"One, that's *two* questions, and yes, but the other ones are smaller. When *Avalon* published, I thought it might be my only book. My turn."

"It's only fair." *Here comes the question about the last affair...*

"Why did you quit sculpting?"

What? My pace slowed, but he matched it. "Damian asked me to put it on pause and help him get Ellsworth Productions off the ground, which made sense. We were newlyweds and I thought I was helping to build our future. It was still art, just *his* form of art, right?" I shrugged at the naive thoughts of a twenty-two-year-old girl. "And then pause became more of a stop, and that part of me just..." The right words had always failed me in this topic. "...dimmed. It went out like a fire I'd forgotten to tend. The flames dwindled so slowly that I didn't notice until they were nothing but embers, and by that time it was the rest of my life that had gone up in flames. There's not a lot of room for creativity when you're focused on breathing." I could feel his stare, but I couldn't meet it. Instead, I sucked in a breath and

forced a smile. "I think it's coming back, though. Little by little."
I thought about Mr. Navarro's shop, then the cost of actually
doing something about it. "Anyway, that's one question, and I
owe you another, so ask away."

"Why don't you trust me with the story?"

My spine straightened. "I don't trust anyone with it, and
neither did Gran. It's not easy, knowing someone is about to
fictionalize what actually happened to your family. It's not just
some story to me."

"Then why sell it at all? Just to make your mother happy?" His
dark brows lowered. "Is that really the only reason you agreed?"

Was it? I watched the creek rush past, giving his question
some thought. He earned another point by not prodding for an
answer. "It was fifty-fifty," I finally said. "I wanted to make my
mother happy. I wanted to be able to give her something she
wanted, since...it doesn't happen often."

He shot me a quizzical look.

"We have a complicated relationship. Let's just say that while
you eat with your family once a month, Mom and I have dinner
maybe once a *year*." That was putting it lightly, but this wasn't a
therapy session. "The other part of me watched Gran work on
that book off and on up to the winter I got married."

"Did she stop then?"

"I'm not sure, since I moved to New York, but I came home
every couple of months, and I never caught her working on it
again." I shook my head. "William—my grandfather—was the
only person she ever let read it, and that was back in the sixties
before she wrote the last few chapters. After he died—car
accident," I said in quick explanation, "she didn't touch it for a
decade. But it was important to her, so eventually she took it out
again. She wanted to get it right."

"Let me get it right." His voice lowered as we neared the
bend in the creek.

"I hoped you would, but then you started spewing all the

happily-ever-after—"

"Because that's her brand!" His posture stiffened beside me. "Authors have a contract with their readers once they get to the point your gran was at. She wrote seventy-three novels that gave her readers that joyful payoff of a happy ending. You honestly think she was going to flip the script for this one?"

"Yes." I nodded emphatically. "I think the truth of what happened was too painful for her to write, and the fantasy you want to create was even more so, because it only reminded her of what she couldn't have. Even the years she spent married to Grandpa Brian weren't...well, you've read what she had with Grandpa Jameson. It was rare. So rare that it comes around maybe what? Once a generation?"

"Maybe," he admitted softly. "That's the kind of love that stories are written about, Georgia. The kind that makes people believe it has to be out there for them, too."

"Then you ask Grandpa Jameson how it ends. She said only he would know, and he's kind of hard to get ahold of." I looked back toward the path. The creek began its gentle curve, following the geography of my backyard. "Have you thought about where it would be shelved?" I asked, trying a different avenue to bring him to my point of view.

His eyebrows lifted. "What do you mean?"

"Is it going under your name or hers?" I stopped walking, and he turned to face me. The sunlight caught in his hair, making it shine in places.

"Both, like you said. Do you want to know the marketing budget, too?" he teased.

I shot him a glare. "Are you really willing to forsake general fiction and be shelved in the—*gasp*—romance section? Because the guy I met in the bookstore last month definitely wasn't."

He blinked, drawing back slightly.

"Hmm. Hadn't made it past the new release table in your mind, had you?"

"Does it matter?" he countered, rubbing his hands down his stubble in obvious frustration.

"Yes. What I'm asking you to do keeps you in the section that isn't for—" I cocked my head to the side. "What was it you said again? Sex and unrealistic expectations?"

A muttered curse slipped from his lips. "I'm never going to live that down, am I?" He turned away, looking into the trees, then muttered something that sounded like *unsatisfying*.

"Nope. Want to keep telling me all about that romance ending? Because that's where they'll shelve you if you write it. Her name overpowers yours. You might be hot shit, but you're no Scarlett Stanton."

"I don't give a shit where the book gets shelved." Our eyes locked for a tense moment.

"I don't believe you."

He lowered his head. "You don't know me."

My cheeks heated, my heart rate spiked, and more than anything, I wanted to have this argument over the phone so I could end it and stomp out the infuriating flickers of emotion Noah never failed to ignite within me.

I liked it numb. Numb was safe.

Noah was a lot of things, but safe wasn't one of them.

I ripped my eyes away from his.

"What is that?" He leaned slightly, his eyes narrowing.

I followed his line of sight. "The gazebo." The breeze whipped by, and I tucked my hair behind my ears as I marched past Noah, heading into the aspen grove. Space. I needed space.

The crunching footsteps behind me implied that he followed, so I kept going. About fifty feet in, dead center in the grove, was a gazebo fashioned entirely from the trunks of aspen trees. I walked up the steps, trailing my fingers lovingly over the railings, which had been sanded smooth and replaced over the years, just like the floor and roof. But the supports were the originals.

Noah came up beside me, turning slowly so he could see

all of the space. It was roughly the size of our dining room but shaped in a circle. I watched him carefully, preparing myself for what would no doubt be a judgment of the rustic little space I'd favored as a kid.

"This is phenomenal." His voice dropped as he walked to one of the railings and looked over the edge. "How long has it been here?"

"Gran built it in the forties with Grandpa Jameson's dad and uncle. They finished it before VE day." I leaned back against one of the trunks. "Every summer Gran would have a desk brought out so she could write here, and I'd play while she worked." I smiled at the memory.

When he turned toward me, his expression had softened, sadness filling his eyes. "This is where she waited for him."

I wrapped my arms around my middle and nodded. "I used to think their love was built into it. That's why she always had it repaired, never rebuilt."

"You don't anymore?" He moved close enough to my side that I felt the heat of him against my shoulder.

"No. I think she built her sorrow, her longing into it. Which makes sense now that I'm older. Love doesn't last, not like this place." My gaze slid from trunk to trunk to trunk as a million memories played through my mind. "It's too delicate, too fragile."

"Then it's infatuation, not love." His voice lowered, and yet another flicker of emotion—longing this time—flared into a flame that centered in my chest.

"Whatever it is, it never quite measures up to the ideal, does it? We just pretend it does, lapping up the sand when we come across the mirage. But this place? It's sturdy. Solid. The sorrow, the longing, the ache that eats you up after the missed chance… those make fine supports. Those are the emotions that last the test of time."

I felt his stare again but still couldn't meet it, not with all the word vomit I'd just spewed all over him.

"I'm sorry he didn't love you the way you deserve."

I flinched. "Don't believe everything you read in the tabloids."

"I don't read tabloids. I know what wedding vows mean, and I've learned enough about you to know that you took them seriously."

"It doesn't matter." I tucked my hair again before I could stop my hands, his gaze warming my skin like a physical touch.

"Did you know that our brains are biologically programmed to remember painful memories better?" he asked.

I shook my head as a shiver of cold swept over me now that we were shaded. Noah closed the inches between us, giving me his heat. The man was a furnace, if his arm was any indication.

"It's true," he continued. "It's our way of protecting ourselves, to remember something painful so we don't repeat the same mistake."

"A defense mechanism," I mused.

"Exactly." He turned his head to look at me. "Doesn't mean we shouldn't do whatever it was again. Just means we have to push past the pain our brains won't let go of."

"What do they say about the definition of insanity?" I asked, tilting my face so I could meet his eyes. "Doing the same thing over and over, expecting a different outcome?"

"It's never the same. There are a million variations of any situation. No two people are alike. The tiniest change to any encounter could leave us with very different results. I like to think of the possibilities as a tree. Maybe you start with the one path—" He tapped the nearest trunk. "But fate throws all the branches out and what seems like a tiny choice, left or right, becomes another and another, until the possibilities of what could have been are endless."

"Like if I hadn't found out Damian was cheating, I'd still be with him? Well, maybe if there wasn't a baby." My voice dropped off, and I shut that line of thinking down.

"Maybe. But you're on a different branch now because you

did. And maybe that other branch exists in the fictional realm of possibilities, but in this one, you're here with me." His gaze dropped to my lips and back. "I'm sorry that he fucked up but not sorry you know about it. You deserve better."

"Gran never wanted me to marry him." I shifted my weight but left us connected. "She wanted what she had with Grandpa Jameson for me. Not that she didn't love Grandpa Brian, because she did."

"It took her forty years to move on. Was she finally happy?"

I nodded. "She really was, from what she's said. I never really pushed her to talk about it, though. It always seemed too painful. Damian did once or twice, but he was always a nosy ass. Still, even while she was married to Grandpa Brian, she wrote out here, like she was still waiting for Jameson all those years later."

"She was the ultimate romantic. Look at this place..." He studied the gazebo. "Can't you feel them here? Can't you see them happy in some other fictional realm of possibility? Some other branch where the war doesn't rip them to shreds?"

I swallowed, thinking of Gran—not the way I remembered her, but the way she looked in the photograph, wildly, recklessly in love.

"I can," Noah went on. "I see them cutting a little landing strip into the meadow so he could fly, and I see them with half a dozen kids. I see the way he looks at her, like she's the reason the seasons change and the sun rises until they're a hundred and one years old."

That was one year more than Gran had lived, and though I knew it was greedy, I wanted it. Out of every year I'd been alive, this was the one I'd needed her the most.

Noah pivoted, consuming the space in front of me, looking at me with such intensity that I had to fight not to look away. He saw too much, made me feel too exposed. But my body certainly didn't mind how close he was. My heart thundered, my breath hitched, my blood warmed.

"I see them walking hand in hand at sunset to get a few minutes away—after they put the kids to bed, of course. I see her looking up from her typewriter to watch him walk by, knowing if she gets her work done for the day, he'll be waiting. I see them laughing, and living, and fighting—always passionate but fair. They're careful with each other because they know what they have, they know how rare it is, how lucky they were to survive it all with that love intact. They're still magnetic, still make love like they'll never get enough, still open, bluntly honest, yet tender." His hand rose to cup my cheek, warm and steady. My breath caught, my pulse leaping at the touch. "Georgia, can't you see it? It's in every line of this place. This isn't a mausoleum, it's a promise, a shrine to that love."

"It's a beautiful story," I whispered, wishing that had been their fate...or mine.

"Then let them have it."

I sidestepped out of his reach, then walked across the gazebo to get some perspective. He wove his words into a world I wanted to live in, but that was his talent, his job. It wasn't real.

"It wasn't what she wanted, or she would have written it that way, ended it like all her other books," I said. "You still think it's a story, with characters who speak to you and choose their own branches. It's not. It's the closest she came to an autobiography, and you can't change the past." The tightness in my chest transformed to an ache. "What you described is why you're so good at what you do, but it's not what she wanted." I walked to the split in the railing and down the stairs, staring up at the tops of the trees.

"What she wanted or what *you* want, Georgia?" he asked from the top of the steps, frustration cutting lines on his forehead.

My eyes slid shut, and I took a steadying breath, then another before turning back to him. "What I want has only ever mattered to one person, and she's dead. This is all I can give her, Noah. The gift of honoring what she went through—what they lost."

CHAPTER FOURTEEN

November 1940

Kirton-in-Lindsey, England

The pub was jammed full of uniforms from bar to door. It had taken Jameson a week to secure a house nearby but, for a rather healthy chunk of his pay, as of yesterday, they now had a place of their very own. At least for as long as the 71st stayed in Kirton.

As of this afternoon, Scarlett was his wife.

Wife. It wasn't that she wasn't aware of just how reckless they'd been to marry so quickly—it was simply that she didn't care. That beautiful man with the bright smile and undeniable charm was now her husband.

Her breath hitched as their eyes locked across the crowded room. *Husband.* She glanced at the clock and wondered exactly how much longer they'd have to stay at their wedding breakfast, because the only hunger she had was for him.

And they were finally married.

"I'm so very happy for you," Constance said, squeezing her sister's hand lightly under the table.

"Thank you." Scarlett's smile was a mile wide, just as it had been since they'd come to Kirton. "It's a far cry from what we pictured as girls, but now I couldn't imagine having it any other way." The wedding that afternoon had been small, attended only by their closest friends and a few of the pilots from the 71st, but had been perfectly lovely. Constance had procured a small bouquet, and though Scarlett's dress wasn't the family heirloom she had always assumed she would wear, the way Jameson looked at her told her she looked beautiful, nonetheless.

"Me either," Constance agreed. "But I could say that about everything in our life. Nothing is how I pictured it two years ago."

"It isn't, but maybe in some small ways it's better." Scarlett understood her sister all too well, and though she longed for the days before the war, before the bombings, and the rationing, and the commonplace death, she couldn't regret any of her decisions that brought her to Jameson.

Somehow, she'd found a miracle in the middle of the maelstrom, and it may have taken her a moment to realize what she had, but now that she did, she would fight with everything she had to keep it—to keep him.

"I am sorry Mother and Father didn't come," Constance whispered. "I held out hope until the very last moment."

Scarlett's smile slipped, but not much. She'd known that her letter would go unanswered. "Oh Constance, ever the romantic. It should have been you to elope, not me." Scarlett stared across the pub, marveling that Jameson was hers. How ironic that the more practical of the two of them had been the one to run off and be married. She could barely believe it herself, yet here she was celebrating her wedding—in a pub, of all places.

True, it was nothing like she pictured as a child, yet it was all the better for it. And besides, who was she to deny fate, when it had taken a million and one separate events to bring her to Jameson?

"Maybe I am an idealist." Constance shrugged. "I just can't believe they wouldn't want to see you happy. I'd always thought their threats were just that, idle threats."

"Don't be angry with them," Scarlett said gently. "They're fighting for the only way of life they know. They're not unlike a wounded animal when you think about it. And I refuse to be sad today. It is their loss."

"It really is," Constance agreed. "I've never seen you look so happy, so beautiful. Love looks good on you."

"Will you be all right?" Scarlett turned slightly in her chair, facing her sister. "Our home is only a few minutes from the airfield, but—"

"Stop." Constance lifted her eyebrows. "I will be perfectly fine."

"I know. I just can't remember the last time we were separated for any length of time." Perhaps a few days here or there, but not much else.

"We'll still see each other at work."

"That's not what I meant," Scarlett said softly. Now that she was married, she'd follow Jameson when the 71st inevitably left Kirton. Training the new pilots couldn't last forever.

"Well, we'll handle that when the time comes. For now, the only thing that's changing is where you sleep..." She tilted her head. "Oh, and where you eat, and spend your free time, and of course who you'll be *sleeping* with." Her eyes danced.

Scarlett rolled her eyes but felt her cheeks heat as Jameson came toward them in his dress uniform. She spun her new ring around her finger with her thumb, assuring herself that this wasn't a dream. They'd made it happen.

"That was the last of them," Jameson said with a smile, his gaze skimming down the long line of Scarlett's neck to the simple, classy dress she'd chosen. He would have married her in her uniform or even her bathrobe—he didn't care. He'd take this woman any way he could get her. "I swear I've been holding the same pint for the last hour and a half, hoping no one will notice." He put the glass on the table.

"You could have had more than one. I think it's expected." Scarlett's own glass was still full.

"I wanted to have a clear head." His lips tugged upward. He

wasn't about to be drunk the first time he got his hands on her. Hell, he'd nearly carried her over his shoulder to their new house last night, but waiting was better. The anticipation of it was killing him in the sweetest way imaginable.

"Did you?" Lord, that smile of hers nearly took him out at the knees.

"What do you say I take you home, Mrs. Stanton?" He held out his hand for hers.

"Mrs. Stanton," Scarlett replied with a spark of joy in her eyes as her fingers brushed his.

"You sure as hell are." Just hearing her say it sent his heart skyrocketing.

They made their farewells, and it was only a matter of minutes before Jameson parked one of the squadron cars in front of what was now their home.

He swept her off her feet, lifting her into his arms at the edge of the sidewalk. "You're mine."

"And you're mine," she replied, lacing her fingers behind his neck.

He kissed her softly, brushing his lips over hers as he walked them up the sidewalk, only lifting his head when they came to the steps.

"My trunk—" she started.

"I'll get it later," he promised. "I want you to see the house." She'd been on watch when he'd found it yesterday. His stomach dipped. "It's not what you're used to." He'd learned enough about her family to know this little place of theirs would probably fit in one of the Wrights' dining rooms.

She kissed him in reply. "Unless you're asking me to share it with eleven other women, it's far better than anything I've had over the last year."

"God, I love you."

"Good, because you're stuck with me now."

He laughed, then somehow managed to unlock the door and

push it open without dropping her as he carried her over the threshold. "Welcome home, Mrs. Stanton," he said as he set her feet on the floor.

Mrs. Stanton. He was never going to tire of saying it.

Scarlett's gaze made a quick sweep of the interior. The house opened into a modest living room that, thankfully, had come furnished. A staircase divided the space, with the dining room to the right, including a small table and chairs, and the kitchen lay just beyond it to the back of the house.

"It's lovely," Scarlett said as she took it all in. "Quite perfect, really." She ran her hand over the dining room table as she walked, and Jameson followed her into the kitchen.

She paled, her smile vanishing as her gaze jumped from the oven to the small table, and over the counters. Horror emanated from every line of her face.

"What's wrong?" His stomach pitched. Was it missing something? Shit. He should have waited for something better.

She turned to face him, then met his gaze with wide eyes. "This might not be the most opportune time to tell you, but I can't cook."

He blinked. "You can't cook," he repeated slowly, just to be sure he'd heard her right.

She shook her head. "Not a thing. I'm sure I could figure out how to turn the stove on, but not much else."

"Okay. But the kitchen is acceptable?" He tried to equate the angst in her eyes to her confession and came up short.

"Of course!" She nodded. "It's lovely. I'm just not sure what to do with it. I never learned to cook at home, and it's been the officers' mess since then." She tugged her lower lip between her teeth.

The relief was so sharp and sweet that he couldn't help but laugh as he wrapped his arms around her. "Oh, Scarlett, my Scarlett." He kissed the top of her head and breathed in her scent. "I'm not saying I can put on a five-course meal, but if I can fry up eggs and bacon over a campfire, I think I'll be able to keep us fed while we figure it out."

"If we could even get real eggs," she muttered as her arms wrapped around his waist.

"Very true." As a pilot, a diet of eggs and bacon bettered his chances of surviving a water landing and were shoved at him with such regularity that he'd nearly forgotten how rare they were.

"I've learned to press my own clothing over the last year, and do some wash, but not much else in the domestic sense of things," she said into his chest. "I'm afraid you may have gotten a bad deal by marrying me."

He tilted her chin and kissed her gently. "I got more than I could have dreamed of by marrying you. We'll figure everything else out together."

Together. Her chest ached with how much she loved him. "Show me the rest of the house."

He took her hand and led her up the small staircase to the second floor. "The bathroom," he said as he motioned through the open doorway to the functional space, then opened the door to the right of it. "The landlord called this a box room, but I'm not really sure what he meant, since it's more of a rectangle."

Scarlett laughed, taking in the smaller, vacant bedroom. "It's just a second, smaller bedroom." The space would only accommodate a single bed and dresser...or a crib. "It's for a child..." Her voice trailed off.

Jameson's eyes locked with hers, flaring slightly. "Do you want that? Children?"

Her heart stuttered. "I hadn't..." She cleared her throat and tried again. "If you're asking if I want children now, the answer is no. There are too many uncertainties at the moment, and they would be coming into a world where we couldn't guarantee their safety." Children had been evacuated from nearly every military target—including London—and just the thought of losing a child to a bombing raid was more than she could bear.

"I agree." His thumb caressed the back of her hand reassuringly, but worry lined the space between his eyebrows.

She lifted her hand to his cheek. "But if you're asking if I want your children someday, then my answer is emphatically yes." There would be nothing better than a green-eyed little girl, or a boy with his smile when this was all said and done.

"After the war." He tilted his head and kissed the center of her palm, sending a tingling jolt of pleasure down her arm.

"After the war," she whispered, adding it to the ever-growing list of things to be accomplished at a later date she wasn't sure would ever come.

"But you know there's always a chance, right?" The muscle in his jaw flexed.

"I do." Her fingers trailed down his neck. "It's a risk I'm willing to take if it means I get to touch you." She followed the line of his collar past his knotted tie and down to the first button of his jacket.

His eyes darkened as he palmed her waist, tugging her closer. "I've been waiting my entire life to touch you."

"There's one more room to show me," she murmured. The bedroom. *Their* bedroom.

Her heart thundered, and her body heated against his. She may have been a virgin, but the stories she'd heard from the girls she'd served with over the last year were enough to more than educate her about what was going to happen tonight.

She felt as though she'd been waiting her entire life for this moment, this night, this man. He was her reward for waiting, for ignoring every other flyer with a proposition and a cocky smile. Perhaps she'd argued that it was her morality that kept her from crossing that line, but staring up at Jameson, she knew she'd simply been waiting for him.

"There is." His gaze dropped to her lips. "I want you to know that this only goes as far as you want. I may be dying to get my hands on you, but not until you're comfortable. I don't want you scared, and the only trembling I want to feel beneath my fingertips will be from your desire, not your fear—"

Fear was the furthest thing from what she felt as she rose on her toes and kissed him, stopping his words with her mouth. They had waited long enough. "I'm not scared. I know you would never hurt me. I want you," she finished in a whisper, lacing her fingers behind his neck.

He kissed her deeply, stroking and sliding his tongue against hers in a thorough, lazy exploration of her mouth that left her clutching at him for more. He took her mouth like he had all night and no other goal, as if this kiss was the culmination and not the preamble.

Every time she tried to quicken the pace, he slowed the kiss down, holding her tight against him with steady, sure hands.

"Jameson." She flicked the first of his buttons open.

"Impatient?" He grinned against her mouth, lifting his hand to cradle the back of her head, threading his fingers through her hair.

"Very." She opened the next button.

"I'm trying to take it slow for you," he said between sipping kisses that left her arching up for the deeper ones as she tugged at the belt of his dress uniform.

"Stop." She put her lips to his neck.

He groaned and kissed her hard, locking his arm around her waist and lifting her against him, all pretense of teasing a distant memory. This kiss was openly carnal, blatantly possessive, and everything she'd been craving since she'd faced him in front of the chaplain.

They kissed their way down the short hallway and into their bedroom, where he set her down with a long slide along his body.

"If there's anything you want to change—" He motioned to the room.

She gave it a glance. Serviceable furniture, light blue curtains that matched the clean bedding spread over a large bed. "It's perfect." She barely finished the words before she was kissing him again.

He got the message and stripped off his jacket. It landed somewhere, but she didn't bother to look. Her hands were already busy with his tie, making swift work of the fabric the way she did daily with her own uniform.

The fingers in her hair gripped lightly, tugging her head back and exposing her neck to his mouth. Heat rushed through her, building hotter with every caress of his lips. By the time he reached the neckline of her dress—just above her collarbone—her breath was no longer steady.

She started to undo his shirt as he found the trail of buttons down her back, never lifting his mouth from hers as he undid them one by one. Then he turned her gently and kissed a path down her spine, caressing every inch of skin he exposed. He reached the base of her spine, then guided her to face him again.

She found him on his knees, his shirt unbuttoned to his waist, looking up at her with eyes glazed with the same desire coursing through her veins. Her nerves almost got the best of her, but she pushed them aside as she slipped one arm from her dress, then the other, holding the fabric just above her breasts for the length of several heartbeats before she found the courage to drop it.

The dress slid off in a flutter of satin, leaving her standing in nothing but the underwear and silk stockings she'd saved two months of pay to acquire. The look on his face made it more than worth the sacrifice.

"You..." His gaze was hot enough to warm her skin as he took her in. "You are so exquisitely beautiful, Scarlett." He looked stunned, astonished really, and...hungry.

She smiled, and he gripped her hips and tugged her forward, kissing the sensitive skin of her stomach. After a year of wearing issued garments that made her just another identical cog in a large piece of machinery, she felt completely and utterly feminine. She speared her fingers through his hair to hold her steady as his mouth journeyed up her body.

He stood, then shed both his collared shirt and the soft cotton one underneath.

Her mouth watered at the sight of his bare torso, the soft skin that stretched over ropes of hard muscle. His stomach tensed when she traced the lines that ran down either side with her fingertips, memorizing the planes and hollows.

She brought her eyes to meet his questioning gaze—as if this man had anything to worry about. He was just as carved as any of the statues she'd seen, but so very warm under her hands.

"Well?" he asked, raising an eyebrow.

"You'll do," she deadpanned, fighting the purse of her lips.

He huffed a laugh, then kissed every thought from her head. They were a flurry of questing hands as their remaining clothes fell to the floor with every step toward the bed. She gasped as he palmed her breast, then melted when he swept his thumb over the stiff peak.

"Perfect," he murmured against her lips, then lowered her to their bed. She devoured him with her eyes as he rose above her, his hair falling forward to brush along his eyebrow. Every single part of him was flawless. He was so much bigger than she was and infinitely stronger, but she'd never felt more cherished.

"I love you, Jameson." She brushed those locks back just to watch them fall again. Out of every sensation bombarding her body, from the feel of his strong thighs inside of her much smaller ones, to the wisp of cool air across her exposed breasts, the swell of love—of unfettered joy—in her chest flared the brightest.

"I love you, too," he promised. "More than my own life."

She arched up and kissed him, inhaling sharply as their bodies came in full contact. He brushed his lips over the patch of skin just beneath her ear, then moved down her body, slowly, methodically exploring her curves with lips and hands.

He sucked the peak of her breast into his mouth. Her fingers tightened in his hair as his tongue unraveled her. Everywhere he touched seemed to catch fire—the curve of her waist, the swell of her hips, the tops of her thighs. He turned her into a living flame, stoked a hunger she hadn't known she was capable of. His hands felt so good, her entire body began to ache with it.

He brought his mouth to hers again, and she poured everything she felt into the kiss when words failed her. Her hands stroked down the broad lines of his back, and he deepened the kiss, groaning into her mouth before yanking his away, his breath coming in the same quick pants her own did.

"I forget my name when you touch me," he said, bracing his weight on an elbow as his other hand traveled down her belly.

"It's the same for me." There was a slight tremble in her fingers as she lifted them to the back of his neck.

"Good." He kept his eyes locked with hers as he reached between her thighs, gently cupping her. "You okay?"

Her breath hitched and she nodded, her hips rolling against him, seeking pressure, friction, anything that would relieve the ache.

The muscles of his shoulders went tight for a breath, and then his fingers were *there*, sliding through her, stroking from her entrance to where that ache centered. The first touch sent a jolt of pleasure so intense, she felt it all the way to her fingertips. The second was even better.

"Jameson!" she cried out, her nails digging into his skin as he returned to that spot again and again, swirling and teasing, overwhelming her senses.

"You're incredible." He kissed her once. "Are you ready for more?"

"Yes." If everything he did felt like this, she'd always want more.

His fingers slipped to her entrance as his thumb kept her on edge, building the tension inside her to a breaking point. Then he slid one digit inside her. Her muscles locked around him as she whimpered, her hips rocking slightly with need.

"Okay?" he asked, the lines on his face taut with worry and restraint.

"More." She kissed him.

He groaned and a second finger joined the first, stretching her. The pleasure more than made up for the slight burn as her body accommodated him. Then those fingers moved within her, stroking and gliding as his thumb moved faster, driving her higher, until she felt so tight she knew she'd snap or shatter if he stopped.

"I...I..." Her thighs locked as that tension within her rose like a wave.

"Yes, right there. God, you're so beautiful, Scarlett." His voice somehow grounded her even as she lost complete control over her body.

He changed the pressure, curled his fingers, and the wave crested and fractured her into a million shimmering pieces. She flew, calling his name, the pleasure so blindingly sweet that the world around them faded as it washed over her again and again, until her muscles liquified and she went limp beneath him.

Her entire body hummed with satisfaction as he withdrew his hand and shifted so the head of him pressed at her entrance.

"That..." She struggled to find an adequate description. "That was extraordinary."

"We're just getting started." He grinned, but the strain was evident in the rigid set of his jaw.

Right. She lifted her knees so he could settle deeper into the cradle of her thighs.

He gripped her hip but held completely still above her, watching her intently.

"I'm okay," she assured him. She was better than okay.

He relaxed slightly, then kissed her breathless, using his hand to build that fire again, flicking over her nipple, teasing her waist, finding the hypersensitive spot between her thighs. That same spiraling need built within her again as she kissed him back, stroking his shoulders and chest.

When she rolled against him, he sucked in a breath through his teeth.

"Tell me if I hurt you," he demanded, resting his forehead on hers.

"I can take it," she promised, her fingers sliding down his ribs and past his waist to his hips and the firm curve of his backside where she held firm, pulling him tighter against her. "Make love to me."

"Scarlett," he growled, his muscles clenching beneath her fingers.

"I love you, Jameson."

"God, I love you." His hips flexed, and he pushed inside her, taking her inch by inch in rolling thrusts until he filled her completely, then moved once more, stretching her to a point near pain to hold him completely.

Their breathing was ragged as he stilled, giving her body time to adjust.

"Are you okay?" His voice was rougher than gravel.

"I'm great," she promised, her smile shaky as the burn lessened and her muscles relaxed.

"You feel like heaven, but better. Hotter," he said through gritted teeth.

She moved slightly, testing the feel of him inside her.

"God. Scarlett. Don't do that." His brow furrowed like he was in pain. "Give yourself a moment."

"I'm fine." She smiled up at him and did it again.

He groaned, withdrawing slowly and sliding back in. The burn was still there, but it was nothing compared to the indescribable pleasure of him moving inside her.

"Again," she demanded.

A wicked smile lifted his lips as he did exactly as she ordered, making both of them moan this time. Then he set a rhythm, taking her with slow, deep thrusts that drove that tension within her a little higher each time. Every stroke felt better than the last.

They moved together like one soul stretched between two bodies, seamless as they shared the same space, the same air, the same heart.

"Jameson." She felt that wave building again, and she tightened, her hips rising to meet his as he thrust faster, harder.

"Yes," he said against her lips, working his hand between them and pushing her right over that edge, hurling her into a kaleidoscope of bliss and color as she came apart in his arms again.

She was still swimming in the throes of her climax as she felt him drive into her with abandon, keeping her with him as he tensed above her, shouting her name as he found his release.

They were a tangle of sweaty limbs and complete euphoria as he rolled to his side, taking her with him as they struggled to steady their breathing. He traced lazy circles on her back as her heartbeat calmed.

She felt spent and utterly, completely sated as her lips curved upward. "If I'd known you were capable of *that*, we wouldn't have waited."

He laughed, the sound rumbling through his chest into hers. "I'm glad we did. This has been the best day of my life, Mrs. Stanton."

"Mine too." Her heart leaped at her new name. She was well and truly his. "I just wish we had time for a honeymoon." As it was, they were both on duty in the morning.

"Every night of our lives will be our honeymoon." He caressed her cheek. "I'm going to spend the rest of my life making you deliciously, wonderfully happy."

"You already do." She glanced at her fingers as they trailed over the defined muscles of his arm. "When can we do that again?" The craving for him had only grown.

"Are you sore?" Concern filled his eyes.

"No." Tender a bit, but not sore.

"Then right now." He kissed her and started all over again.

CHAPTER FIFTEEN

Noah

Scarlett, my Scarlett,

How are you, my heart? Do you think you could bring the roses here? I hate to think you and Constance put in all that work just to leave it behind. I promise you, when we get to Colorado, I'll build you a garden you never have to move from and a shady place to sit and write on sunny days. I'll build your happiness with my own two hands. God, I miss you. Hopefully I'll find us some digs in the next few days, because I'm losing my mind here without you. Kiss our sweet boy for me.

I love you with my entire soul,

Jameson

*U*se the opt-out.

That wasn't going to happen. I signed a contract that I'd complete the book, and I would. But keeping my word meant getting closer to the only woman who made me want to kiss the shit out of her as she drove me up a wall.

This was dangerous territory, but I couldn't bring myself to care. Georgia had me just as knotted up about her as I was the damned book. The two were so closely intertwined that I couldn't separate them. She was just as stubborn as Scarlett had been the first time Jameson met her, but unlike Jameson, I didn't have a Constance to help me out.

Unlike Scarlett, Georgia had already had her trust and heart broken.

I was zero for two when it came to Georgia, and at an impasse when it came to the book.

Georgia was right. Scarlett wasn't a character; she was a real person who had really loved Georgia. Given what I'd seen from her mother and the asshole ex, she might have been the only person in the world who had truly, unconditionally loved Georgia.

That's what I kept in mind as I stood on Georgia's front porch with one last pitch and an armful of what I hoped would be goodwill. I'd been in Colorado for two weeks, climbed two easy fourteeners, and as of yesterday, I had two plot lines ready to write. In a few days, I'd only have two months until my deadline.

"Hey," she said with an awkward smile as she opened the door.

"Thanks for seeing me." One day I would get used to those eyes knocking me off my feet, but today was not that day. Her hair was up, too, revealing the long line of her neck. I wanted to run my lips along the column, then— *Knock it off.*

"No problem, come on in." She stepped back, and I walked through the door.

"This is for you." I handed over the muslin-covered root ball carefully so she didn't prick herself on the thorns of the plant above. "It's an English tea rose, aptly named Scarlett Knight. I thought you might like it for the garden." It was quite possibly the most awkward gift I'd ever given, but here I was giving it, because I somehow sensed that even a tiny blue box wouldn't move this woman.

"Oh! Thank you." She smiled, real and true as she took the plant, appraising it with a gardener's eye. I knew that eye well. My mother had it. "It's lovely."

"You're welcome." My gaze skipped over the table in the entry, catching on the vase. The edges of the glass wave had the same frothy texture as the piece in New York. "You made this, didn't you?"

Her attention shifted from the rosebush to the vase. "Yes. Right after I got back from Murano. I spent a summer apprenticing there after freshman year."

"Wow. It's remarkable." How did someone capable of doing

that just stop? And what kind of man married a woman with that kind of fire and then systematically snuffed it out?

"Thanks. I love that one." A wistful look crossed her face.

"Do you miss it? Sculpting?"

"Lately." She nodded. "I found the perfect space for a studio, but I can't justify the cost."

"You should. I'm sure you'd have no trouble selling pieces. Hell, I'd be your first customer."

Her gaze jumped to mine, and there it was again, the indescribable connection that kept me up at night, thinking about her. "I should put this in the greenhouse."

"I'll come with," I offered, swallowing back the ball of nerves that had worked its way up my throat like I was sixteen again.

"Okay." She led me through the kitchen and out the back door, but instead of heading straight into the garden, she turned left, walking me along the patio to the greenhouse.

The blast of humidity was almost enough to make me homesick as I followed her into the glass building. Both the size and variety of flowers in here were impressive. The floor was cobblestoned moss rock, and there was even a small fountain in the center, blocking out any potential noises from the outside world with the steady trickle of water.

"Do you maintain this yourself?" I asked as she carried the rosebush to a potting bench.

"God, no." She snorted. "I might know a thing or two about plants, but Gran was the gardener. I hired a professional about five years ago when she finally started to slow down."

"At ninety-five," I added.

"She was pretty unstoppable." Her smile was instant and had the added bonus of acting like a vise around my chest. "She got so mad at me, too. Said I was making assumptions about her health. I argued that I was simply freeing up the time it took her to water."

"You were making assumptions about her health." The

corners of my lips tugged upward.

"She was ninety-five; can you blame me?" She set the rosebush down on the bench. "I'll pot it later."

"I don't mind waiting." Or delaying what I was about to offer her. Somehow Georgia had mastered what college and deadlines had failed to do: she'd turned me into a procrastinator.

"You sure?"

"Positive. And I'm the last person to tell you about rosebushes, but I thought this guy was more of an outdoor one?" At least that was what the picture online had shown.

"Well, yeah, usually. But it's almost October. I'd hate to stick him in the ground and hope for the best when his little root system wouldn't have had a chance to develop before the first frost." She opened the large cabinet next to the shed and hauled out a container and a various assortment of small bags.

"So you're saying it's a bad gift?" I half teased. *Shit.* Why hadn't I thought of that?

Her cheeks pinkened. "No, I'm saying it has to live in the greenhouse until spring."

"Can I help?"

"You don't mind getting dirty?" She took in my athletic pants and long-sleeved Mets tee.

"I prefer dirty." I shrugged with a grin.

"Grab the potting soil." She rolled her eyes as she rolled up her sleeves.

I pushed my sleeves up and walked over to the cabinet, which was much deeper than it initially looked. There were at least three different bags along the bottom.

"Which one?"

"The one that says 'potting soil.'"

"They all say 'potting soil.'" I met her teasing gaze with a raised eyebrow.

She leaned around my side, brushing against my arm as she pointed to the blue bag on the left. "That one, please."

We locked eyes, and the inches between us charged. She was close enough to kiss—not that I was going to do something that reckless, but damn did I want to.

"Got it." My gaze dropped to her lips.

"Thanks." She stepped away as color flushed from her neck to her cheeks. She wasn't immune to me, either, but I'd known that from the second our eyes met in the bookstore. It didn't mean she wanted to act on it.

I grabbed the right bag, then ripped the top open and poured it into the container when she told me to.

"That's perfect." She stepped in and added handfuls from the various smaller bags, then mixed it all together.

"This feels very complicated." It was fascinating to watch her pick and choose from the soil amendments.

"It's not," she said with a shrug, using her bare hands to plant the rosebush. "Plants are way easier than people. If you know what plant you're working with, then you know what pH it likes the soil to be. If it likes it well drained, or saturated. If it prefers nitrogen or needs a calcium boost. Does it like full sun? Part sun? Shade? Plants tell you what they need right off the bat, and if you give it to them, they grow. They're predicable that way." She leveled the soil out carefully, then washed her hands at the potting bench sink.

"People can be predictable, too." I hefted the now half-empty bag back to the shed. "If you know how someone was damaged, you have a good idea of how they'll react in a situation."

"True, but how often do you know someone's damage before you start that relationship? It's not like we all walk around with warning labels on our foreheads."

I leaned back against the bench as she filled the watering can. "I like that idea. Warning—narcissist. Warning—impulsive. Warning—listens to Nickelback."

She laughed, and an ache flared in my chest, demanding to hear the sound again. "What would yours read?" she asked.

"You first."

"Hmm…" She shut off the faucet, then lifted and tipped the watering can over the rosebush. "Warning—trust issues." She lifted a brow at me.

That made perfect sense.

"Warning—always right."

She scoffed, finishing up with the can.

"I'm serious. I have a really hard time admitting I'm wrong, even to myself. I'm also a control freak."

"Well, you're wearing a Mets shirt, so at least you chose the right New York team." She smiled and put the can back on the bench.

"I grew up in the Bronx. There is no other team. I keep forgetting that you lived in New York." The pictures I'd seen of her from the net showed a glossed and polished Georgia, not the gardener with a messy bun and ripped jeans. Not that I should have been looking at her jeans or the way her ass filled them out…but I was.

"From the day I got married until the day I met you, actually." Her smile faded and she crossed her arms over her chest. "So what exactly did you want to talk to me about? Because I know you didn't go to the trouble of ordering that rosebush just to deliver it. I saw the label."

Here went nothing.

"Right." I scratched the back of my neck. "I want to make a deal."

"What kind of deal?" Her eyes narrowed. That was quick.

"The kind where I ultimately get more than you do, admittedly." My lips flattened.

Her eyes flared with surprise. "Well, at least you admit it. Okay, shoot."

"I think we both need to get out of our comfort zones when it comes to dealing with each other and this book. I'm not used to having someone dictate my endings, let alone an entire story, since two-thirds of it is already written, and you don't trust me farther than you can throw me."

Her head tilted slightly, not bothering to deny it. "What do you have in mind?"

"I will spend some time getting to know Scarlett—not just the character she wrote herself as in the book, but the real woman, and then I'll write two endings. One will be the one I want, and the other will be what I'm known for—what you want. You can choose between the two." I grabbed my ego in a choke hold to keep the asshole quiet.

"And I have to..." She lifted her brow.

"Go rock climbing. With me. It's a trust thing." *Smooth. Real smooth.*

"You want me to put my life in your hands." She shifted her weight, clearly uncomfortable.

"I want you to put Scarlett's life in my hands, which I think starts with yours." Because she valued Scarlett's more. That's what the trip to the gazebo and the internet had taught me. She was ruthlessly protective of her great-grandmother, while she'd allowed her husband out of their marriage with little to no consequence.

"And the final decision is still mine?" she clarified, her forehead crinkling.

"One hundred percent, but you have to agree to read both endings before you decide." I'd win her over one way or another. I just had to get her to read it my way.

"Deal."

CHAPTER SIXTEEN

February 1941

Kirton-in-Lindsey, England

"**G**ood morning!" Scarlett said to Constance as she arrived for her morning watch.

"So loud." Eloise, who had only been posted to Kirton for the last month, winced as she stirred a mug of cocoa.

"Someone stayed out with the boys a bit too long last night," Constance explained as she handed Scarlett a steaming mug of coffee.

That could probably be said for most of the 71st and the WAAFs this morning, as well as a healthy percentage of the single, civilian girls from Kirton. Scarlett was among the sleepless, too, but for much...different reasons. After what they'd both considered an acceptable amount of time, Jameson had taken her home for their own celebration, though there had been a sharper, more desperate edge to his lovemaking.

As of yesterday, the 71st was officially ready for defensive duties. Training, and the blissful months of relative safety, were over. The only thing to celebrate in her mind was that the unit had finally been outfitted with Hurricanes, rather than the cumbersome Buffaloes Jameson hated so very much, but he still missed his Spitfire.

Scarlett offered Eloise a compassionate smile. "More water, less cocoa." She finished putting her things away and looped her arm through Constance's elbow as they headed for the door. "How late did you stay out, poppet?"

"Just long enough to see some of the girls home." She sent

a meaningful look toward Eloise, who followed close behind.

"Which was totally unnecessary," the pretty little blonde added. "Did I enjoy myself? Certainly. But it's not like I'm silly enough to end up in any of the dark alcoves with a flyer. I'm not about to have my heart broken when—" She winced. "Not that you're silly, of course, Scarlett. You're married."

Scarlett shrugged. "Yes, and that was still silly of me. We both know there are no guarantees. I worry every time Jameson flies—and he's only been training these last few months, but now..." Her heart plummeted, but she forced a smile.

"He'll be fine." Constance gave her a squeeze, and they walked toward the briefing room.

Scarlett nodded, but her stomach hollowed out. She plotted aircraft every day that had lost their radar and ended up crashing simply because they couldn't see how close they were to safety. She plotted the raids, the losses, and changed the numbers, all the while knowing that it would soon be Jameson back in combat.

"And don't worry about this one," Eloise said, nudging Constance. "She's head over heels for that little army captain of hers. She spends most nights penning letter after letter."

Pink rose in Constance's cheeks.

"When exactly does Edward get leave again?" Scarlett grinned. Nothing would be better than seeing Constance as settled and happy as she was.

"In a few weeks," Constance answered wistfully, sighing at the threshold of the briefing room, which was already half full.

Scarlett's eyes flared with surprise as she spotted one of the occupants. "Mary?"

Mary's head whipped her way. "Scarlett? Constance?"

Both Scarlett and Constance scurried around the long table to embrace their friend. It had been four months since they'd seen each other at Middle Wallop, and yet it seemed like an entire lifetime had passed.

"You both look wonderful!" Mary exclaimed, her eyes

sweeping over her friends.

"Thank you," Scarlett responded. "You do as well." It wasn't a lie, but there was something...off about Mary. The spark in her eyes had dimmed, and she could do with a few nights' rest. A weight settled in her chest. Whatever had sent their friend here wasn't good.

"She should practically be glowing, since she's married now." Constance nudged her sister. "Show her!"

"Oh, all right." Scarlett rolled her eyes but held out her left hand with as little fuss as possible, keeping her focus on Mary.

"My God." Mary's gaze flickered from the ring to Scarlett's eyes. "Married? To whom?" She'd barely asked the question before her eyes widened. "Stanton? Eagle Squadron is still here, right?"

"Yes and yes," Scarlett answered, unable to keep her lips from twitching upward.

Mary softened. "I'm happy for you. You two really are perfect for each other."

"Thank you," she replied gently, still sensing there was a reason for Mary's appearance. "Now what on earth are you doing here?"

Mary's face fell. "Oh. Michael...he was a pilot I'd been seeing since you were reposted..." She blinked rapidly and tilted her chin up. "He went down during a raid last week." Her mouth trembled.

"Oh no, Mary, I'm so sorry." Constance lifted her hand to Mary's shoulder.

Scarlett swallowed painfully past the lump in her throat. That made three lovers Mary had lost in the last— She stiffened. "They didn't..." She shook her head. Surely they wouldn't be so cruel.

"Label me a jinx and repost me?" Mary flashed a brittle smile, then cleared her throat. "What else were they going to do?"

"Anything but that," Constance snapped, shaking her head. "It's not your fault."

"Of course it isn't," Scarlett added, guiding her to an empty chair at the table. "They're too bloody superstitious. I'm so sorry you lost him."

"Risks we take falling in love with them, right?" Mary folded her hands in her lap and stared straight ahead as Scarlett took the seat next to her, Constance on her left.

"Right," Scarlett muttered.

"Good morning, ladies. Let's get started," Section Officer Cartwright announced as she swept into the room with her immaculately pressed uniform. "Take your seats."

Chairs squeaked across the floor as the women gathered around the conference table. At Middle Wallop, Scarlett would have known most, if not all, of them. But living with Jameson meant she had met only a few of the ladies here at Kirton. There was no more hut gossip, no more flurries of excitement before a dance, no more late-night chats.

She was still part of them, yet oddly separate. She wouldn't give up Jameson—not for the world—but there was part of her that sorely missed the company of other women.

"Mail," Cartwright ordered, and a young clerk stood at the head of the conference table, calling names and sliding envelopes down the long, polished expanse.

"Wright."

Both Constance's and Scarlett's attention whipped toward the clerk as a letter came spinning their way.

Stanton, not Wright. Scarlett reminded herself when she saw the letter was addressed to Constance. Not that anyone would be sending her mail, anyway. Her parents still hadn't deigned to respond when she wrote to them after her marriage, though Constance still received regular missives from their mother.

They never asked after Scarlett.

Constance's shoulders fell a fraction of an inch as she opened the envelope as quietly as possible. "It's from Mother."

Scarlett offered her hand a brief squeeze. "Perhaps there

will be one tomorrow." She knew all too well how it felt to wait for a letter from the man you loved.

Constance nodded, then lowered the envelope beneath the table.

Scarlett adjusted her seat slightly, blocking Constance from Cartwright's hawklike gaze so she wouldn't be caught reading during the briefing.

"Now that's been handled," Cartwright began. "You should have all read through the new standards provided to you at last week's briefing. I'm pleased to say that we haven't had a single WAAF late for her watch since the half-hour policy was enacted. Well done. Are there any questions about last week's policy changes?"

"Is it true the 71st is to be reposted?" a girl from down the table asked.

Scarlett's heart stopped. *No. Not so soon.* Her head spun with every possibility. They hadn't had enough time yet, and there were only so many favors she could call in to be reposted with Jameson—if they were even headed to a station that had an ops center.

Section Officer Cartwright sighed in obvious frustration. "Aircraftwoman Hensley, I hardly see how that has anything to do with last week's policy change."

The younger woman blushed. "It would...change where the aircraft originate from on the board?"

There was a collective groan.

"Excellent attempt, but no." Cartwright glanced down the table, pausing briefly on Scarlett. "While I understand that many of you have formed emotional attachments—against advisement—to members of the Eagle Squadron, I'll remind you that it is, quite frankly, none of our business where the unit will be sent now that they're fully operational."

A dozen forlorn sighs filled the conference room, but Scarlett's wasn't one of them. She was too busy conquering the emotional devastation to sigh as though she suffered from nothing but a crush.

"Girls," Cartwright groaned. "While I could use this as an opportunity to remind you of your responsibility regarding virtuous behavior, I won't." And yet with that line, she surely had.

"What I will say is that rumors are rumors. If we believed or got caught up in every piece of *maybe* that landed in our ears, we'd be halfway to Berlin by now, and I expect you—"

Constance began to hyperventilate at Scarlett's side, clutching the letter so hard, she expected to see her sister's nails pop through the paper.

"Constance?" Scarlett whispered, her breath catching at the horror in her sister's eyes.

Constance's scream filled the room, the sound tearing through Scarlett's ribcage and gripping her heart with an icy fist.

Scarlett reached for Constance's wrist, but the scream had already morphed into a mournful wail, stuttering with gut-wrenching sobs that shook her shoulders.

"Poppet?" she asked quietly, gently turning Constance's face toward hers. Tears didn't just streak down her face—they ran in a continuous line, as though her eyes couldn't be bothered to fill, then empty.

"He's. Dead." Constance's words came between heaving cries. "Edward. Is dead. There was a. Bombing raid—" Her chin sank as the sobs came faster and harder.

Edward. Scarlett's eyes fluttered shut for a moment. How could the blue-eyed boy who'd grown up with them be gone? He'd been as much a fixture of their lives growing up as her own parents.

He was Constance's soul mate.

Scarlett tugged Constance into her arms. "I'm so sorry, love. So, so sorry."

"Assistant Section Officer Stanton, do you need to remove

your sister from the room, or can she control herself?" Cartwright snapped.

"I'll care for her privately if we can be excused." Scarlett bristled, but the insensitive wretch was right. A display like this wouldn't be tolerated, no matter how justified. Constance would be labeled hysterical, undependable. Girls had been reposted, never seen again after failing to stifle their emotions.

Cartwright narrowed her eyes but nodded.

"Hold on for just a second longer," Scarlett begged her sister in a whisper, wrapping her arm around Constance's shoulder and tugging her to her feet. "Walk with me." Another whisper.

As quickly as she could manage without tripping them both, Scarlett led Constance from the briefing room. The hallway was mercifully quiet, but still not private enough.

She opened a door to a smaller room—the supply depot— then pulled her sister inside and shut them in before leaning against the only empty wall and holding Constance tight. When her knees buckled, Scarlett slid to the floor with her, rocking slightly as Constance sobbed with ugly, gasping breaths against her shoulder.

"I've got you," she murmured against her sister's hair. If there was anything she could have done to take away her pain, she would have done so. Why her? Why Constance, when it was Scarlett's love who risked his life every day? Her vision went blurry.

This was something she couldn't protect Constance from. There was nothing she could do but hold her. Tears toppled from her lids, leaving wet, chilled streaks in their wake.

Eventually, Constance's breathing evened out enough to manage speech. "His mother told ours," she explained, the letter still clutched and crumpled in her hand. "It happened the day after he wrote last. He's been dead for almost a week!" Her shoulders caved in as she burrowed farther in to Scarlett. "I can't..." She shook her head.

A loud knock sounded at the door.

"Stay here," Scarlett ordered her sister, standing quickly and swiping at her cheeks as she hurried to the door. She raised her chin as she found Section Officer Cartwright on the other side, then moved into the hallway, shutting the door to give Constance as much privacy as possible.

"Who died?" Cartwright asked in that blunt way the military prized.

"Her fiancé." She took every emotion clawing at her throat and shoved it down. Later, she could feel it. Later, she could curl up in Jameson's arms and cry for the friend she'd lost—the love her sister had been denied. Later…but not now.

"I'm sorry for her loss." Cartwright swallowed, then looked down the hall and back, as though she, too, needed to compose herself, then lifted her chin. "While the circumstances of your birth afford you both certain…leniencies, I would be remiss in my duties if I did not warn you that she cannot afford another such outburst."

"I understand." She didn't, but she'd seen enough lectures about emotional stability to know they weren't being singled out. It simply was.

"Ever." Cartwright raised her brows and spoke softly.

"It won't happen again," she promised.

"Good. You have to be of steady hands and stout hearts to stand at that board, Assistant Section Officer. Men's lives are at risk. We cannot afford to lose one because we are distraught over one already lost. Should the Senior Section—"

"It. Won't. Happen. Again." Scarlett squared her shoulders and stared her superior in the eye.

"Good." Her gaze drifted toward the door, where Constance's soft cries were still making their way through the heavy wood. "Take her to her quarters—or better yet, your home. I'll have Clarke and Gibbons cover your watches. Make sure she's calm before you bring her through the halls." It was as much compassion as Scarlett had seen Cartwright give to anyone, and though it wasn't enough, Scarlett saw it for what it was—a lifeline.

"Yes, ma'am."

"She'll find another. We always do." She turned on her heel and strode down the hall.

Scarlett slipped back into the supply room, closing the door and sinking to the floor to gather her sister in her arms.

"What am I going to do?" Constance broke her heart a little more with every sob. Every tear.

"Breathe," Scarlett answered as she swept her hand up and down Constance's back. "For the next few minutes, you're going to breathe. That's all." If she'd lost Jameson— *Don't think like that. You can't afford to let that in.*

"And then what?" Constance cried. "I love him. How am I supposed to live without him? It hurts too much."

Scarlett's face twisted as she fought for control, for the strength Constance would need. "I don't know. But for these minutes, we breathe. Once that's done, we'll take on the next."

Maybe by then, she'd have the answer.

"Is it true?" Scarlett asked as she flung her coat over a chair in the kitchen more than a month later.

"Nice to see you, too, dear," Jameson answered with a smile as he flipped the potatoes in the pan.

"I'm being serious." She crossed her arms over her chest.

He had half a mind to tell the potatoes to go to hell and eat his wife for dinner instead, but the narrowing of her eyes gave him pause. It wasn't just another rumor she was questioning. She knew. He muttered a curse. Damn, news traveled fast.

"Can I take that as a yes?" she questioned, her eyes sparked with so much anger, he half expected to see flames shoot out of them at any moment.

He moved the potatoes off the burner, then faced his beautiful, furious wife. "Kiss me first."

"I beg your pardon?" She arched a brow.

He wrapped his arms around her and tugged her close, savoring the feel of her body against his. They'd been married five months. Five incredibly happy, almost normal months—if there was such a thing in the middle of a war—and everything was about to change. Everything but the way he felt about her.

He loved Scarlett more than he had the day he married her. She was thoughtful, strong, smart as a whip, and when he put his hands on her, they both went up in flames. But this...this he'd been desperately clinging to this new normal they'd carved out for themselves.

"Kiss me," he ordered again, lowering his face. "I've barely seen you in the last few days. We haven't eaten dinner together for a week because of our schedules. Love me first."

"I love you always." Her eyes softened, and she brought her lips to his, kissing him gently.

His heart jolted, just like it did every time. He kissed her slowly, thoroughly, but kept himself in check. He wasn't trying to distract her with sex—not that she'd fall for it anyway. One more moment—that was all he needed.

He pulled back gently, lifting his head so he could see her eyes. "We're being reposted to Martlesham-Heath."

Those crystal-blue eyes he loved flared with disbelief. "But that's..."

"Eleven group," he finished for her. "We're operational. They need us there." Where the majority of the action took place. He cradled her face in his hands and fought the rending sensation in his heart—it was too similar to the one he'd felt back at Middle Wallop when they'd been forced to part. "We'll figure it out."

"Mary told me Howard said you were being reposted, but..." She shook her head, coming alive, and backed out of his grasp, leaving him holding air.

Damn it, Howard.

"Scarlett, honey—"

"We'll 'figure it out?'" She gripped the back of the kitchen chair and took a deep breath. "When?"

"A matter of weeks," he answered, lowering his arms.

"No, when did *you* find out?" Her eyes narrowed.

"Just this morning." He mentally cursed Howard for telling Mary before he'd even seen Scarlett. "I know it's complicated, but I looked into married quarters on station before my flight—"

"What?" Her voice rose, which was as good as a Mayday when it came to her temper. The woman barely—if ever—lost that calm, collected cool of hers.

"I know it's a jump to assume you'd be willing to ask for another transfer, especially with Constance..." *Barely breathing.* His sister-in-law had become a veritable ghost since losing Edward, and there was no chance Scarlett would leave her, no guarantee, either, that Constance would want to go. "Anyway, housing is full, so we'd have to live off-station like we are now, but I can start looking for digs."

"*Willing to ask for another transfer,*" Scarlett repeated, her eyes catching fire. "What makes you think I *can* transfer there, Jameson? There's not...I can't..." She rubbed the bridge of her nose.

She couldn't tell him because her job required more clearance than his. Of course he knew what she did—he wasn't born yesterday—but that didn't mean she came home and divulged where the other filter rooms were, or the radar stations. Too much knowledge was dangerous for a pilot who could easily crash into enemy hands. And sure, it was fine to know where she currently worked; sector operations were— *Holy shit, that's it.* "There's no sector operations at Martlesham," he guessed quietly.

She shook her head in answer. "What Constance and I do, the training involved..." She met his gaze, and the pain he saw there dug its claws into his soul. "Command isn't exactly going to let us go become drivers or mechanics. We are what we are." She was as—if not more—essential to the mission as he was.

"You're remarkable." His stomach churned, knowing this meant an already difficult situation was about to become impossible. Just the thought of waking up without her, of not laughing together as they burned whatever they'd been trying to cook, of falling asleep without her in his arms for weeks on end was enough to make his heart scream in protest. What the hell would it be like in actuality?

"Hardly," she blew him off. "Just highly trained and nimble-fingered, neither of which is working in our favor at the moment. Martlesham is hours away. They've cut practically all our leave, and you won't be getting much, either. We'll never see each other." Her shoulders hunched as she tucked her chin.

His heart damn near broke as he crossed the distance between them and pulled her against his chest. "We'll figure it out. My love for you didn't fade when half of England separated us. A few hours is nothing."

But it was everything. Forget a Living Out pass; it was too far to get a Sleeping Out pass unless he took forty-eight hours, and she was right, their days of easily attained leave were a thing of the past. It could be months between visits, depending on how the war went.

He uttered another curse word under his breath. They'd come so close to losing each other during that raid at Middle Wallop, and if something happened to her now… Bile rose in his throat. "You could always go to Colorado."

She stiffened in his arms, then looked up at him like he'd lost his mind.

"I know you won't," he said softly, tucking a strand of her hair that had come loose from the pinks. "I know your sense of duty won't allow it, and you won't leave Constance anyway, but I'd be a shit husband if I didn't at least ask you to go, to be safe."

"I'm not sure if you've noticed, but I'm not American." She raised her hands to his T-shirt-covered chest—neither of them ever cooked in full uniform. They'd learned that lesson early in their marriage to the detriment of two otherwise perfectly good jackets.

"I'm not sure you've noticed, but you're not exactly British anymore, either." Thank God the WAAF had no problem taking foreign nationals. "We both seem to be in between countries at the moment."

She huffed a small laugh. "And how exactly are you hoping to get me into your country? Fly, then push me out over Colorado?" she teased, pressing a kiss on his chin.

"Now that you mention it..." He grinned, loving that she could always find the levity in a situation.

"Seriously, though, let's scrap that as a possibility, because it isn't one. You can't even get into your own country without being arrested right now."

"Actually..." He tilted his head as his thoughts raced. "I never renounced my citizenship. Never swore loyalty to the king, either, so I'm not treasonous. Did I break neutrality laws? Yes. Would I be sent to jail if I headed home? Probably. But I'm still American." He glanced at his uniform jacket as it hung over a kitchen chair, the eagle bright on the right shoulder. "You didn't break any laws, and you're my wife. You're entitled to American citizenship. We'd just have to get you a visa." A spark of hope glimmered in his chest. He had a way to get her out of this war—to ensure she lived through it.

She flat out laughed and pushed out of his arms. "Right, and that takes a year, if not longer, from what I've read in the papers. The war might very well be over by the time that happened. And besides, you're right. I won't leave my country—even if it's technically not mine anymore—when it needs me, and I won't abandon Constance. We swore to see this through together, and we will." She took his hand and placed a kiss on his wedding band. "And I'll never leave you, Jameson. Not if I can help it. A few hours are nothing compared to thousands of miles across an ocean."

"But you'd be safe—" he started.

"No. We can discuss this again when the war is over or our circumstances have drastically changed. Until then, my answer is no."

Jameson sighed. "Of course I had to fall for the obstinate girl." Yet he wouldn't have loved her had she been anyone else.

"*Obstinate, headstrong girl*," she corrected him with a small smile. "If you're going to quote Austen, do it correctly." She pressed her lips in a firm line. "What's the farthest you can live from the station and still have a Living Out pass?"

"It depends on the station commander." Some were compassionate and believed that the air crew tended to be more reliable if they lived on- or off-station with their families. Others didn't give a shit—or passes. "What about you?"

"I'm barely allowed a pass as it is. All the other women live in the huts or are billeted in the old married quarters." Her brow puckered.

"None of the other women are married to someone posted at the same station," he noted. Soon, she'd be just like the few others with wedding rings—married but forced to live apart.

She gnawed on her lower lip, clearly thinking something over.

"What's going on in that remarkable brain of yours, Scarlett Stanton?"

Her gaze jumped to meet his. "I can't go with you, but there's a slight chance I might be able to get reposted closer than where we are now."

He tried like hell not to hope but failed. "I'll take even the slightest chance over the possibility of going months without seeing you."

"If only postings were up to you, my husband, and as I am not currently recognized as my father's daughter, I can't pull the strings I did to get here." She laced her fingers behind his neck. "But I'll try."

Relief loosened the knot in his throat but didn't dispel it completely. "God, I love you."

"If I can't get reposted and all we have are weeks, then we'd better make them count." She nodded toward the stove and its forgotten contents. "Skip dinner and take me to bed."

"We don't need a bed." He lifted her to the kitchen table and sank into her kiss. She was right—if they only had weeks, he wasn't wasting a second of it.

CHAPTER SEVENTEEN

Georgia

Jameson,

Oh, love. I could never regret choosing you. You're the very breath in my lungs and the beat of my heart. You were my choice before I even knew there was one to make. Please don't worry. Close your eyes and picture us in that spot you've told me about—where the creek bends. We'll be there soon, and even sooner I'll be in your arms again. Until then, we'll be waiting here for you. Always waiting. Always yours.

Scarlett

"This was the worst idea in the history of ideas!" I shouted down at Noah from fifteen feet above him, clinging to a wall I had no business being on. He'd waited a week before forcing me to hold up my end of the deal, but that didn't make it any easier.

"So you've told me every five minutes since you started climbing," he called up. "Now look to your left at that purple hand-hold."

"I hate you," I snapped, but reached for the hold. He'd taken me to a climbing gym a half hour away, so it wasn't like I was dangling off the side of a mountain, but still. I might have been tied into the harness, but he held the other end of the rope. "You think you'd be better at metaphors, being a writer and all. Put your life in my hands, Georgia," I did my best Noah impression. "Look at my superior climbing abilities and pretty face, Georgia."

"Well, at least you still think I'm pretty."

"You suck!" My arms trembled as I stepped up to the next foothold. The bell about thirty feet above me was only second on my shit list to Noah. I hated heights. Hated the weakness in my own body since I'd stopped taking care of it. I *really* hated the impossibly gorgeous guy beneath me with the rope.

"If it's easier, I can grab Zach to belay you instead, then climb up and guide you myself," Noah offered.

"What?" I glared down at him and the climbing gym attendant. "I don't know *Zach*. He looks like he's in high school!"

"Taking a gap year, actually," the employee answered, waving up at me.

"You're not helping," Noah said quietly, but I still heard him. "But Zach is employed here, and you dying would probably really mess up his job, so I think you can trust that he's a professional."

"You move and I swear I'll kick off my shoes so they hit you in the head, Morelli!" I shut my eyes for a second and stared straight ahead at the textured, gray rock of the climbing wall. Looking down made it even worse.

"Well, at least I rate higher than someone," Noah joked.

"Barely!" I reached for the green handhold just above my right hand, then secured my foot on the next logical hold and pulled myself up the wall. "This only makes me hate you more," I said as I gripped the next hold.

"But you're climbing," he countered.

Again, I reached for the next handhold, placed my feet, and continued upward. "I guess I just don't see how this is going to help solve our plotting issues, considering I'm going to kill you as soon as I get down from here." I was only a few feet away from the accursed bell. As soon as I rang that sucker, I was home free.

"I'll take my chances," he called up. I couldn't help but notice how tight he kept the line. It was comforting, seeing I had to be a good twenty-five feet above him now. "You know, if you honestly hate it that much, I'm not gonna hold you to the bargain. This is really about trusting me, not hating me."

I kept my eyes on the prize and hoisted myself another foot, then two. "The hell with that," I called down. "I'm almost there."

"You sure are." I heard the pride in his voice and glanced down to see the same as he smiled up at me.

I was far from happy, but even I could admit I felt empowered. Capable. Strong.

Well, maybe not that strong. My arms and legs shook with fatigue as I made that last handhold and climbed the last twelve inches by sheer willpower alone.

Ring. Ring. Ring.

"Yes!" Noah shouted.

I felt the bell's vibrations from the depths of my soul. They were strong enough to break apart my own preconceived notions that this was impossible. Strong enough to wake parts of me that had been sleeping since long before Damian's latest indiscretion.

Perhaps even before I met him.

Just because I could, I rang the bell again just once. This time it wasn't in desperation to be let down, to be set free of the bargain I made for myself, or to be validated by the person who had set me on this task.

It was in victory.

Logically, I knew it wasn't Everest. I was maybe forty feet up a climbing wall in a professional environment, secured with ropes, a harness, and a liability policy.

But my chest swelled, filling with a ferocious sense of pride nonetheless.

I could still do hard things.

Gran was gone, Damian had betrayed me, and Mom had left yet again, but I was still here. Still climbing.

And though there was part of me that wanted to throttle Noah, I knew he was the only reason I was on this wall, climbing in the first place. He was the reason I'd started paying attention to my own life again. The reason I looked forward to waking up in the morning lately.

It wasn't that I was living for him, but that he simply made me want to live. To fight. To prove my point. To take a stand when I'd usually defer to someone else's emotions and take the path of least resistance.

Maybe my life had caught on fire, but that's where I shined, right at the melting point where I could take the molten remains and reshape them into something beautiful. I wanted to sculpt again. I wanted to bend glass to my will. I wanted another chance to be happy, which led me to glance in Noah's direction. I wanted...to get down because *whoa* was I high.

"Okay," I called to him. "How do I get down?"

"I'll lower you."

"You'll what?" I chanced another look in his direction. *Holy shit*—this actually *was* Everest. He looked a million miles away. So much for feeling empowered. I wanted off this thing *now*.

"I'll lower you," he repeated, slowing his words down, as if I'd misunderstood instead of balked.

"And how exactly does that work?" I gripped the handholds tighter, whitening my knuckles.

"Easy," he said. "You sit back in the harness, then walk your way down the wall as I lower you."

I blinked a few times, then looked down again. "I'm supposed to just lean back and trust that you won't drop me on my ass?"

"Exactly." He grinned shamelessly, and for the first time, I didn't find it all that charming.

"What if the rope breaks?"

His grin faded. "What if there's a massive earthquake?"

"Are we expecting one?" My biceps screamed in protest as I held myself there, perched on the damn wall like a lizard.

"Are you expecting me to drop you?" he challenged.

"It would make it easier on you to finish the book," I argued.

"There's some truth to that," he admitted. "And I'm sure the story behind the murder would really drive sales."

"Noah!" There was nothing funny about this, and yet there he was, teasing me.

"The chances of an earthquake are far more likely than those of me dropping you." There was an edge to his voice this time, but when I took another look at his face, there was only patience. "I'm not going to let anything happen to you, Georgia. You have to trust me. I've got you."

"Can't I just climb down?" It couldn't be that hard, could it?

"Sure, if that's what you want to do," he answered, his voice dropping.

"Yeah," I whispered to myself. "I'll just climb down." Surely it couldn't be any harder than climbing up here had been, right?

Muscles aching and plagued by tiny, incessant tremors, I lowered my foot to my previous foothold. "See? That wasn't so bad," I muttered. The line was tight, offering me support as I moved my hands and then my left foot down.

Then I shrieked, my voice high and loud, as my foot slipped and I fell. It was only a matter of inches before the rope caught my weight, and I hung suspended, parallel with the wall.

"Are you okay?" Noah asked, his voice pitching slightly.

I sucked in a full breath, then another, willing my heartbeat to settle at an acceptable, nondramatic level. The harness dug slightly into the skin just beneath the curve of my butt, but other than that, I was perfectly fine.

"A little embarrassed," I admitted reluctantly, heat flooding my already flushed cheeks. "But otherwise fine."

"Do you still want to climb down the rest of the way?" Noah asked without judgment.

I lifted my arms, raised my hands to the holds directly in front of me, cringing as they shook. The truth was, if he was going to drop me, he would have done it by now.

"So I'm just supposed to sit back in the harness?" I asked, silently praying that he wasn't an *I told you so* kind of guy.

"Put your feet against the wall," he ordered.

I lifted them slightly and did as he asked.

"Both hands on the rope." Another order.

I followed it.

"Good," he praised. "I'm going to lower you, and I want you to sit back into the harness and walk your way down the wall. Got it?" His voice was strong and steady, just like the man himself. What did it take to ruffle a guy like Noah? Sure, I'd pricked his temper a few times, but even through the most uncomfortable of our arguments, I'd never seen him actually lose it, at least not in the door-slamming, screaming way Damian often did when things hadn't gone his way.

"Got it," I called down, offering Noah a shaky smile.

"I don't want to startle you, so we'll go on three. Slow and steady."

I nodded.

"One, two, three," he counted us off and lowered me enough to fully sit back. "Good job. Now let's walk you down the wall."

Slowly, steadily, Noah let the rope out, lowering me down the climbing wall. A few seconds in and it wasn't half bad. Defying gravity came with a little adrenaline rush, especially when I boldly emulated another climber farther down the wall, taking fun little hops.

As I got closer to the ground, I glanced up at the bell I had just rung. It seemed so high, and yet I'd been there, all the way up at the top.

All because Noah had been determined to earn my trust— and he had.

I was all smiles when my feet met the earth. "That was amazing!" I threw my arms around Noah, and he held me tight, lifting me right back off my feet.

"You were amazing," he corrected me.

He held me so easily, as if I weighed nothing, and smelled so good it was all I could do to not put my nose to his neck and breathe deep. His scent was a unique combination of the sandalwood and cedar of his cologne mixed with soap and a little sweat. He smelled like a man was supposed to, all without faking it. Damian would have paid thousands of dollars to smell like Noah did effortlessly.

Stop comparing them.

I pulled back slightly, just enough to look in his eyes. "Thank you," I whispered.

His smile was slow and the sexiest I'd ever seen. "What are you thanking me for?" he asked as his gaze darted to my lips and back. "You're the one who did all the work."

Oh, shit. He really wasn't an *I told you so* kind of guy, and that only made me like him more. Made me want him more.

The energy between us shifted, pulling taut, as though we were connected by more than just this rope. There was something here, and it didn't matter how hard I fought it or how frequently we bashed heads about the book—it only grew.

His gaze heated and his grip tightened.

There were only inches between our lips—

"Are you guys done?" a small voice asked.

Blinking, I looked down at a girl who couldn't have been older than seven.

"I was hoping to do this one next, if that's okay?" she asked with hopeful eyes.

"Right, of course," I replied.

Noah set me down and unhooked my harness from the rope line with quick, efficient moves. *God, could his arms be any hotter?* The muscles of his biceps strained against the short sleeves of his athletic shirt. Good thing it stretched, or he probably would've busted through.

"Thank you," I said again as he unhooked from the line.

"That was all you. All I did was keep you safe." The low timbre of his voice warmed my entire body.

"On belay," another voice said. An older girl, probably in high school, had taken Noah's place, and the younger one had already tethered herself to the rope. "Climb on."

"Climbing," the little girl answered, and then scurried up the wall like she'd been bitten by a radioactive spider.

"You have to be kidding me," I muttered, watching the girl take only minutes to do what had taken me a half hour.

Noah huffed a soft laugh. "A few more times and you'll be just as good as she is," he assured me.

I shot him a look of pure skepticism.

"You didn't fall once on the way up," he remarked, reaching for my face slowly, giving me a chance to shy away. I didn't. "That's pretty amazing." He took a slightly sweaty lock of my hair that had escaped my ponytail and tucked it behind my ear.

"I've never had a problem reaching for things I want," I replied softly. "It's the falling that gets me into trouble."

And that's exactly what this was, I realized. It was one thing to joke with Hazel about a post-divorce rebound, but quite another to like more than just his body, even though it really was incredible. It would be all too easy to fall for Noah Morelli.

"I caught you." There was no smirky smile or flirtatious wiggle of his eyebrows, but that didn't matter. The truth was intoxicating enough.

He *had* caught me.

"You did," I answered softly.

"Want to do another one?" he asked, the corners of his mouth quirking up.

I laughed. "I don't think my arms would let me even if I wanted to. They feel like spaghetti noodles." I held them out as examples, as if he could see the exhaustion in my muscles.

"I'll rub them down later," he promised, and this time that sexy little smile of his reappeared.

My breath caught, imagining his hands on my skin.

"Want to learn how to belay?" he asked, halting my flash of fantasy.

"Spaghetti noodle arms, remember?"

"Don't worry, the harness does all the work."

"You trust me with your life?" I asked, peering up at him and doing my best not to stare at his long eyelashes or the curve of his lower lip.

"I trust you with my career, and that's pretty much the same thing to me, so yes." The intensity in his eyes was a clear challenge, and I felt it like a jolting shock to my heart, exceptionally painful yet life-affirming.

He really had risked it all for this book, hadn't he? He'd left the city he loved and moved his life here to see it through.

In that moment, I knew two things about Noah Morelli.

The first was that his priority was and would always be his career. Anything else he loved would take a back seat.

The second was he and I operated on complete opposites of the trust spectrum. He gave it first, then waited for the outcome. I withheld it until it was earned. And he had more than earned mine.

It was time I started trusting myself, too.

"Lead on."

Once he'd dropped me off at home, I pulled out my phone and called Dan. Within the hour, I'd put an offer in on Mr. Navarro's shop.

I was all in.

CHAPTER EIGHTEEN

May 1941

North Weald, England

It had been almost eight weeks and the light still hadn't returned to Constance's eyes. Scarlett couldn't push her, couldn't advise her, couldn't do anything but watch her sister grieve. And yet, she'd still asked her to transfer with her to North Weald. It was the most selfish thing she'd ever done, but she didn't know how to simultaneously be a wife and a sister, so now both suffered.

Though she may have been on the outs with her parents since marrying Jameson against their wishes, they'd apparently kept the rift private, since Scarlett and Constance's request to transfer to North Weald had been approved.

They'd been here for a month, and though Scarlett rented a house off-station for the nights Jameson could get a Sleeping Out pass, Constance had chosen to billet with the other WAAFs in the huts on the station.

For the first time in her life, there had been an entire week of Scarlett's life where she'd lived completely, utterly alone. No parents. No sister. No WAAFs. No Jameson. He was over an hour away at Martlesham-Heath but came...home—if that's what this was—whenever he could get a pass. Between her worry over Constance and her fear that something would happen to Jameson, she lived in a constant state of nausea.

"You really don't need to do this," Scarlett told her sister as they knelt on ground only recently thawed by spring. "It still might be a bit early."

"If it dies, it dies." Constance shrugged, then continued

digging with the small trowel, readying the space for a small rosebush she'd taken from their parents' garden while on leave that weekend. "It's better to try, right? Who knows how long we'll be at this station? Maybe Jameson gets reposted. Maybe we do. Maybe just I do. If I keep waiting for life to give me the most opportune circumstances to live it, I never will. So fine, if it freezes and dies, then at least we tried."

"Can I help?" Scarlett asked.

"No, I'm just about done. You'll have to remember to water it regularly, but not too much." She finished tilling the soil at the edge of the patio. "The plant will tell you. Just watch the leaves and cover her up if it gets too cold at night."

"You're so much better at this than I am."

"You're better at telling stories than I am," she noted. "Gardening is learned, just like mathematics or history."

"You write perfectly well," Scarlett argued. They'd always received similar marks in school.

"Grammar and essays, sure." She shrugged. "But story lines? Plots? You are far more talented. Now, if you truly want to help, you sit there and tell me one of your tales while I put this girl in." She formed a mound of dirt at the bottom of the hole, then placed the crown of roots over the mound, measuring the distance to the surface.

"Well, I guess that's easy enough." Scarlett sat back and crossed her ankles in front of her. "Which story and where were we?"

Constance paused in thought. "The one about the diplomat's daughter and the prince. I think she'd just discovered—"

"The note," Scarlett jumped in. "Right. The one where she thinks he's sending her father away." Her mind slipped back into that little world, the characters as real to her as Constance was sitting beside her.

Eventually, the two sisters lay on their backs, staring up at the clouds as Scarlett did her best to weave a story worthy of distracting Constance, if only for a few moments.

"Why wouldn't he simply tell her he's sorry and move on?" Constance asked, rolling to her side so she could face Scarlett. "Wouldn't that be the most straightforward answer?"

"It would," Scarlett agreed. "But then our heroine won't see his growth, can't really find him worthy of that second chance. The key to bringing them the ending they deserve is to pick at their flaws until they bleed, then make them conquer that flaw, that fear, in order to prove themselves to the one they love. Otherwise it's really just a story about falling in love." Scarlett laced her fingers behind her head. "Without the potential for disaster, would we ever really know what we have?"

"I didn't," Constance whispered.

Scarlett locked eyes with her sister. "You did. I know you loved Edward. He knew it, too."

"I should have married him the way you did Jameson," she said softly. "At least we would have had that before…" She drifted off, her eyes lifting toward the trees above them.

Before he died.

"I wish I could take your pain." It wasn't fair that Constance was in such misery while Scarlett counted the hours between Jameson's days off.

Constance swallowed. "It doesn't matter."

"It does." Scarlett sat up. "It matters."

Constance mirrored her but didn't meet her eyes. "It really doesn't. The other girls who move on, who see love affairs as temporary—I understand. I really do. Nothing here is guaranteed. Planes go down every day. Bombing raids happen. There's no point holding your heart back when there's a good chance you'll die tomorrow anyway. May as well live while you can." She glanced over the small garden. "But I know I'll never love anyone the way I did Edward—the way I still do. I'm not sure I'll ever have a heart to give. Seems safer to read about love in novels than it is to honestly experience it."

"Oh, Constance." Scarlett's heart broke yet again for what Constance had lost.

"It's fine." Constance hopped to her feet. "We'd better get ready, since we have watch in a little over an hour."

"I can make us something to eat first," Scarlett suggested. "I've gotten rather good at a couple quick things."

Constance looked at her sister with well-deserved skepticism. "I've got a better idea. Let's get dressed and run over to the officers' mess."

"You don't trust me!" Scarlett scoffed.

"I trust you implicitly. It's your cooking I doubt." Constance shrugged, but her teasing smile was genuine, which was more than enough for Scarlett.

Dressed and fed, the girls made it to watch in plenty of time. They left their coats in the cloak room, then headed for the filter room. As busy as their boards were in their small sector, it was hard to imagine what the ones at Group Headquarters looked like.

"Ah, Wright and Stanton, always the pair," Section Leader Robbins noted with a smile at the door. "Anything you ladies need before watch begins?"

"No, ma'am," Scarlett replied. Out of all her section leaders, Robbins was turning out to be her favorite.

"No, ma'am," Constance echoed. "Just show me to my section of the board."

"Excellent. And when you both have a moment, I'd like to talk to you about your responsibilities." The woman smiled, her eyes crinkling at the corners.

"Are we lacking?" Scarlett asked slowly.

"No, quite the opposite. I'd like you both to train as tellers. More pressure, but I would be willing to wager that you'd both make Section Officer by the end of the year." She glanced between the sisters, measuring their reactions.

"That would be wonderful!" Scarlett answered. "Thank you

so much for the opportunity; we would—"

"I need to think on it," Constance interjected, her voice dropping.

Scarlett blinked back her surprise.

"Naturally," Robbins said with a kind smile. "I hope you have an...uneventful night."

The sisters made their farewell, and before Scarlett could question Constance about her answer, her sister opened the door and disappeared into the always-silent filter room.

Scarlett followed her in, then put on her headset and relieved the WAAF at her corner of the board, taking a quick sweep over her section to familiarize herself with tonight's activities. There was a bomber raid coming across her quadrant, nearly to Constance's.

Would the raids *ever* end? Tens of thousands had been killed in London alone.

The radio operator's voice came through her headset, and she fell into the routine of work, letting the other worries wait until later.

Every so often she'd glance at Constance. On the outside, her sister appeared normal—her hands were steady and her moves efficient. This was where Constance thrived lately, where emotion couldn't reach her. Knowing the emptiness that swirled inside sent another wave of nausea rolling through her.

It wasn't fair that she'd been able to keep her love, when Constance hadn't.

Minutes ticked by as she moved the aircraft across the board, and then her stomach pitched for an altogether different reason.

The 71st was on the move, not toward the bombing raids but the sea. *Jameson.*

She moved the squadron across her quadrant in five-minute increments, noting the number of planes and the general direction, but soon they were no longer hers to keep watch over, and others took their place.

The hours flew, but she was too worried to eat during her break, too anxious to see the 71st return to do much else but hover over that board, because she knew he was flying tonight. When her fifteen minutes were up, she headed back into the filter room and took over her station once more.

She noted with no small sense of satisfaction that the number of bombers on their way out was smaller than coming in. They'd had a few victories tonight.

The radio operator's next plot came through her headpiece, and she reached for a new marker with a slight smile. The 71st was back in her quadrant.

She placed the marker at the appropriate coordinate, then froze as the radio operator updated the number of aircraft.

Fifteen.

Scarlett stared at the marker for precious seconds as her heart lurched into her throat. *She's wrong. She has to be wrong.* Scarlett hit the microphone switch on her headset.

"Could you give me the strength of the 71st again?" she said.

Every head in the room snapped her direction.

Plotters didn't talk. Ever.

"Fifteen strong," the operator repeated. "They lost one."

They lost one. They lost one. They lost one.

Scarlett's fingers trembled as she replaced the little flag on the marker to one that read fifteen. It wasn't Jameson. It couldn't be. She would know, wouldn't she? If the man she loved with all her heart had gone down—had died—she'd feel it. She'd have to. There was simply no way her heart could continue beating without his. It was an anatomical impossibility.

But Constance hadn't known...

The next plot came through her headset, and she moved the appropriate markers, changing out the arrows to the timed color groups.

Jameson. Jameson. Jameson. Her limbs moved by muscle memory as her mind swam and her belly churned, dinner curdling as the 71st got closer to Martlesham-Heath. Even after they were hangered and officially off the board, Scarlett couldn't kick the sick feeling in her stomach.

So far, the Eagle Squadron had been miraculously lucky—they hadn't lost a pilot. She'd almost become complacent in their luck, but that had ended tonight. Who was it? If it wasn't Jameson—*please, God, don't be Jameson*—then it was someone he knew. Howie? One of the newer Yanks?

She glanced at the clock. She had four more hours to go.

She wanted to ring Martlesham-Heath, to demand the call sign of the downed pilot, but if it was Jameson, she'd know soon enough. They'd no doubt already be waiting for her at home. Howie would never let her find out through the gossip mill.

The time passed in torturous five-minute blocks, ticking away as she moved the markers, changed the arrows, heard the orders called out from Group Headquarters. By the time their watch was over, Scarlett was a tangle of nerves with a rapid heartbeat and not much else.

"Let me drive you home. I know your bicycle is here, but I have the section car," Constance said after they gathered their things from the cloakroom.

"I'm fine." Scarlett shook her head as they walked toward their bicycles. The last thing Constance needed was to comfort *her*.

"He's okay," she said softly, touching Scarlett's wrist. "He has to be. I can't believe in a God so cruel as to take both our loves. He's okay."

"And if he's not?" Scarlett's voice was barely a whisper.

"He will be. Come on. Get in the car; no arguments. I'll tell the other girls to walk back to the hut." Constance led her to the car, then spoke to the other members of the watch before sliding behind the wheel.

The drive was short—only a few minutes off the station—but for the smallest of moments, Scarlett didn't want to turn the corner, didn't want to know. But they did.

There was a car parked outside her house.

"Oh God," Constance whispered.

Scarlett squared her shoulders and took in a deep breath. "Why don't you want to take the teller training?"

Constance glanced her way as she pulled up behind the car, which bore the 11 Group insignia. "Right now? You want to talk about that right now?"

"I just always thought you planned to advance." Her heart beat so fast, it almost blended into a steady thrum.

"Scarlett."

"There's more pressure, yes, but more pay with the promotion." Her hand gripped the handle like a vise.

"Scarlett!" Constance snapped.

She ripped her gaze away from the 11 Group insignia and looked at her sister.

"I promise I will come over tomorrow morning and talk to you about the training, but right now, you cannot stay in the car."

"Do you wish you'd never opened the letter?" Scarlett whispered.

"It would only have delayed the inevitable." Constance forced a shaky smile. "Come on, I'll walk you to the door."

Scarlett nodded, then pushed her door open and stepped out onto the pavement, readying herself for another set of doors opening.

The car doors didn't open. Her front door did.

"Hey, you." Jameson filled the doorway, and Scarlett's knees nearly gave out.

She broke into a run, and he met her halfway, swinging her into his arms with a hug so tight, she felt the pieces of her click back into place. He was okay. He was home. He was alive.

She buried her face in his neck, breathed in his scent, and held on for dear life, because that's exactly what he'd become — her life.

"I was so worried," she said against his skin, unwilling to draw back for even a moment.

"I knew you would be. That's why I got a pass and drove up." He kept one big hand splayed on her back and held the nape of her neck with the other. Holding Scarlett was all he'd thought about since the moment they'd lost Kolendorski. "I'm okay."

She just held on tighter.

Jameson looked over Scarlett's shoulder and nodded at Constance, who watched them with a wistful smile. She nodded back, then turned away, heading for the car she'd brought Scarlett home in.

"Who was it?" Scarlett asked.

"Kolendorski." He'd liked the guy. "Turned to intercept a bomber and got taken out by two fighters. We all saw him go down in the sea." No attempt to bail out. No Mayday. He went in vertically with enough force that if he hadn't been killed before, he'd been dead on impact. No one could survive that kind of crash.

"I'm so sorry," she said, easing her grip a little. "I'm just..." Her shoulders shook, and he gently pulled back so he could see his wife.

"It's okay. Everything is okay," he assured her, swiping away her tears with the pad of his thumb.

"I don't know why I'm being such a ninny." She forced a distorted smile through her tears. "I saw the strength number change, and I knew one of you was gone." She shook her head. "I love you."

"I love you, too." He kissed her forehead.

"No, that's not what I mean." She stepped out of his arms. "I love you so much that my heart feels like it beats within your body. I watched what losing Edward did to Constance, and I know that I'm not strong enough to lose you. I won't survive it."

"Scarlett," he whispered, wrapping his arms around her and pulling her close because there was nothing else he could do. They both knew that tomorrow it could be him. With the prevalence of the bombing raids, it could be her. Every goodbye kiss they shared held the bittersweet taste of desperation because they knew it could be their last.

And if it were her... He sucked in a steadying breath to quiet the unwelcome, impossible thoughts. There was nothing for him without Scarlett. She was the reason he ran a little faster when they scrambled to intercept a bombing raid. She was the reason he pushed the newer pilots harder. She was the reason he'd stay no matter how many letters his parents sent, telling him they were proud of him in the same line that they begged for him to come home. He didn't need to swear loyalty to the king—he'd sworn it to Scarlett, and she was his to protect.

"Come on." He took her hand and led her inside, but instead of carrying her to their bedroom and making love to her as he'd planned for every minute of his drive, he took her to the living room, where he put Billie Holiday on the record player. "Dance with me, Scarlett."

Her lips lifted, but it was too sad to be called a smile. She slid into his arms and laid her head against his chest as they swayed in small circles, steering clear of the coffee table.

This right here was where he lived. Everything else he did was to get him back safely for more of this—more of her. Living apart was a special kind of torture; knowing she was only an hour away, but he couldn't get to her, caused too many sleepless nights. He missed the feel of her skin against his in the morning, missed the scent of her hair when she'd fall asleep on his chest. He missed talking about their days, planning their future, kissing their way through yet another burned dinner. He missed everything about her.

"I have news for you," he said softly, brushing his lips over her temple.

"Hmm?" She lifted her head, apprehension filling her eyes.

"We're being reposted." He tried to keep a straight face, but his lips didn't obey.

"Already?" Her brow puckered and her lips flattened. "I don't—"

"Ask me where." Now he was grinning—so much for keeping it a surprise.

"Where?"

He lifted his brows.

"Jameson," she chastised. "Don't tease me. Whe—" She inhaled sharply, then narrowed her eyes. "You tell me right this very minute, because if you get my hopes up just to squash them like a bug, you'll be sleeping alone tonight."

"No, I won't," he said with a smile. "You like me too much for that."

"Not at this moment I don't."

"Fine, then you like what I do to your body too much for that," he teased, his gaze heating.

She arched a brow.

"Here," he finally said as the song wrapped up. "We're being reposted here. In a couple weeks we'll be in the same bed every night." He raised his hand to her cheek. "We'll be back to burning breakfasts and racing each other for the shower."

A grin spread across her beautiful face, and his chest tightened. Just like that, she turned an absolute shit day into something truly exceptional.

"I was asked to train to be a teller," she admitted quietly, as if someone could hear them. Joy flashed across her eyes. "It could mean I'd make Section Leader before the year is out."

"I'm proud of you." Now he was the one grinning.

"And I'm proud of you. Aren't we the pair?" She rose and brushed her mouth over his. "Now what were you saying about what you could do to my body?"

He had her upstairs before the next song started.

Scarlett stumbled into the kitchen the next morning to find Jameson at the stove, frying up breakfast. Her stomach flipped at the smell, then somersaulted.

"You okay?" Constance asked from the corner, where she was opening a jar of jam.

Right, they were supposed to talk about training this morning. She'd forgotten, which added another reason to be annoyed at herself.

"Fine," Scarlett lied, trying to swallow the nausea. "I didn't see you there. I'm so sorry I completely abandoned you last night."

Constance smiled, glancing between Scarlett and Jameson. "No need to explain. Just happy it all worked out." The light flickered from her eyes as she brought the jam to the table.

"What can I do to help?" Scarlett asked, putting her hand between Jameson's shoulder blades.

"Nothing, honey—" His brow lowered. "You look a little green."

"I'm fine," she said slowly, hoping they'd leave it be. Had she hoped the nerves would settle now that Jameson was due to be reposted here? Yes. Apparently her body hadn't gotten the memo.

Constance studied her carefully. "Do you want to chat later?"

"Of course not. I'm glad you're here."

Constance nodded, but there was an odd, firm set to her mouth. She looked...somehow older this morning.

Jameson brought the fried sausages and potatoes to the table while Scarlett sliced a loaf of bread. They tucked in, and Scarlett nearly sighed with relief as her stomach settled.

"Would you two like some privacy?" Jameson asked from his side of the square table, his gaze bouncing between the sisters.

"No," Constance answered, setting her fork on a half-empty plate. It wasn't like her to leave half her breakfast, but she hadn't exactly been normal the last two months. "You should hear this, too."

"What is it?" A weight settled on Scarlett's chest. Whatever her sister was about to say, it wasn't good.

"It would be a waste for me to take the teller training," she said, squaring her shoulders. "I'm not sure how long I'll be allowed to keep my commission."

Scarlett paled. There were very few reasons a woman would be forced to resign her commission. "What? Why?"

Constance fumbled her hands in her lap for a moment, then lifted her left hand to reveal a sparkling emerald ring. "Because I'll be married."

Scarlett's fork fell from her hand, clattering against the plate.

Jameson, to his credit, didn't move a muscle.

"Married?" Scarlett ignored the ring and locked eyes with her sister.

"Yes," Constance said, as though Scarlett had asked if she wanted more coffee. "Married. And my fiancé isn't exactly supportive of my role here, so I doubt I'll be encouraged to keep it once we're wed." There was no emotion in her voice. No excitement. Nothing.

Scarlett's mouth opened and shut twice. "I don't understand."

"I knew you wouldn't," Constance said softly.

"You have the same expression you wore the day our parents forbade you from marrying Edward until after the war." Dutiful—that was it. She looked resigned and dutiful. The nausea returned with a vehemence as that foreboding feeling slipped from Scarlett's chest to her belly. "Who are you marrying?"

"Henry Wadsworth." Constance lifted her chin.

No.

Silence filled the kitchen, sharper than any words could have been.

No. No. No. Scarlett reached for Jameson's hand under the table, needing an anchor.

"It's not up to you," Constance argued.

Scarlett blinked, realizing she'd spoken out loud. "You cannot. He's a monster. He'll ruin you."

Constance shrugged. "Then he ruins me."

If it dies, it dies. Her words as she planted the rose yesterday echoed in Scarlett's mind. "Why would you do this?" She'd been home this last weekend. "They're making you, aren't they?"

"No," Constance rebutted softly. "Mummy told me they're going to have to sell the rest of the land around the house at Ashby."

Not the London house…their home. Scarlett pushed past the pang of regret at the news.

"Then it is their fault for not managing their own finances. Please don't tell me you agreed to marry Wadsworth in an attempt to keep the land. Your happiness is worth far more than the property. Let them sell it." More importantly, Constance would never survive a marriage to Wadsworth. He'd beat her spirit to death and body close to it.

"Don't you see?" Pain flickered over Constance's features. "They'd sell off the pond. The gazebo. The little hunting cottage. All of it."

"Let them!" Scarlett snapped. "That man will destroy you." Her hand gripped Jameson's.

Constance stood, then pushed her chair under the table. "I knew you wouldn't understand, and you don't have to. It's my decision to make." She strode from the room, her shoulders back and her head high.

Scarlett raced after her. "I know you love them, and you want to please them, but you do not owe them your life."

Constance paused with her hand on the doorknob. "I have

no life left for myself. All I have are memories." She turned slowly, losing her polished facade and letting her anguish show.

The pond. The gazebo. The hunting cabin. Scarlett's eyes drifted shut for the length of a deep breath. "Poppet, owning those places will not bring him back."

"If you lost Jameson, and you had a chance to keep the first house you lived in at Kirton-in-Lindsey, even if only to walk through the rooms to talk to his ghost, would you?"

Scarlett wanted to argue that it wasn't the same. But she couldn't.

Jameson was her husband, her soul mate, the love of her life. But she'd loved him for less than a year. Constance had loved Edward since they were children, swimming in that pond, playing games in the gazebo, stealing kisses in the hunting cabin.

"There's no saying the land would even be there by the time you wed." Which hopefully wouldn't be this summer—only a few weeks away.

"He's purchasing them now, in good faith...as an engagement gift. It was all settled this weekend. I know you're disappointed in me—"

"No, never that. I'm frightened for you. I'm terrified that you're throwing away your life instead of—"

"Instead of what?" Constance cried. "I will never love again. My chance for happiness is gone, so what does it matter?" She opened the front door and stormed out, leaving Scarlett to scramble after her.

"You don't know that!" Scarlett yelled from the pavement, stopping her sister before she reached the street. "You do know what he'll do to you. We've seen it. Can you honestly give yourself to a man like that? You are worth so much more!"

"I do know!" Constance's face crumpled. "I know it in the same way you do. I saw your face last night. Had it been Howie at your door, telling you it was Jameson who'd been lost, you would have been decimated. Can you look me in the eye and tell me you'll ever love again if he dies?"

Bile rose in Scarlett's throat. "Please don't do this."

"I have the power to save our family, to keep our land, to perhaps teach my children to swim in that very pond. We are not the same, you and I. You had a reason to fight the match. I have a reason to accept it."

Scarlett's mouth watered, and her stomach convulsed. She hit her knees and lost her breakfast into one of the bushes that framed their doorway. She felt Jameson's hand at the nape of her neck, gathering her unpinned hair as she heaved, emptying her belly.

"Honey," he murmured, rubbing circles on her back.

The nausea subsided, gone as quickly as it had come.

Oh God. Her mind scurried, trying to trace an invisible calendar. She hadn't had a moment's peace since March. They'd moved in April…and it was May.

Scarlett stood slowly, her gaze meeting Constance's wide, compassionate one.

"Oh, Scarlett," she whispered. "Neither of us will be Section Leader by the end of the year, will we?"

"What is that supposed to mean?" Jameson asked, his hand steady when Scarlett felt like the slightest breeze might send her back to the ground.

Scarlett looked up at him, taking in those beautiful green eyes, the strong set of his chin, and the worried lines of his mouth. He was about to worry a lot more.

"I'm pregnant."

CHAPTER NINETEEN

Noah

Scarlett,

Here we are again, separated by miles that feel too long at night, waiting for our chance to be together again. You've given up so much for me, and here I am, asking for more, asking you to follow me once again. I promise you, once this war is over, I'll never let you regret choosing me. Not for one minute. I'll fill your days with joy and your nights with love. There is so much that waits for us if we can just hold on...

"I brought lunch," I called out to Georgia as I walked in the front door of her house. Had to admit, it was still a little weird to walk into Scarlett Stanton's house without knocking, but Georgia had insisted, since we'd started spending our afternoons together last week in what she called Stanton University.

"Thank God, because I'm famished," she called out from the office.

I walked through the open side of the French doors and stopped short. Georgia sat on the floor in front of her great-grandmother's desk, surrounded by photo albums and boxes. She'd even moved the large wingback chairs out of the way to make room.

"Wow."

She looked up at me and offered an enthusiastic smile. *Damn.* Just like that, my mind wasn't on her great-grandmother or the book I'd staked my career on. It was on Georgia, plain and simple.

Something had changed between us the day we'd gone rock-climbing. Not only did it feel like we were actually on the same consequence, which includes *not* inheriting the very things I do not want."

"Scarlett!" her mother called out, but Scarlett didn't lower her gaze or give an inch as her father attempted to stare her down.

"And if I have a son," she continued, "he, too, will be free of this anchor of obligation you treasure more than your daughter's happiness."

Her father's eyebrows shot up. The only thing he'd ever wanted was a son. She'd never give him hers.

"Scarlett, do not do this. You have to marry the Wadsworth boy," he demanded. "Any sons that come from *that* union will be the next Baron Wright."

He seemed to have forgotten that if Constance, too, had sons, it would not be so cut-and-dried.

"That sounds like an order." Scarlett pushed in her chair and gripped the back.

"It is. It has to be."

"I only take orders from my superior officers, and as I recall, you have elected not to serve in a war you have never approved of." The ice in her veins permeated her tone.

"This visit is over." He spoke through gritted teeth.

"I agree." She kissed her mother's cheek on the way out of the dining room. "Happy birthday, Mother. I'm so sorry I cannot give you what you want."

Then she removed herself to her room, where she quickly changed into her uniform and packed her dress into her suitcase.

As she came down the stairs, she found Constance waiting for her at the threshold, dressed identically, suitcase in hand.

"Do not do this to us," her mother begged, coming out of the drawing room.

"I will not marry Henry," Scarlett repeated. "How can you ask me to? You would see me marry a man I loathe? A known abuser of women, all to keep what?" Scarlett asked, softening her voice.

"It's what your father wants. What the family needs." Her

As if he sensed the hunger within her, or felt it himself, he grasped her backside and lifted her against him so they were eye level. Her fingers speared into his hair as he walked to the briefing table and sat her at the edge of it, all without breaking the kiss.

She'd never been more thankful for wearing a skirt, which made it easy for him to fit himself between her thighs, bringing them flush. She gasped at the contact, and he tilted her head, taking her mouth as though he needed to lay claim again, as though she might disappear at any moment.

"I missed you," he said against her mouth.

"I missed you, too." Her voice came out breathless as her heart pounded. Even if they'd only shared this moment, everything she'd done to get here would have been worth it.

His lips trailed down her neck, lightly sucking just above her collar. She inhaled sharply when he flicked his tongue against her. Mercy, that felt good. Shivers of pleasure darted down her spine, pooling low in her belly as she caught fire. He burned away the November chill that had clung to her skin since she'd arrived this morning. She could never be cold in Jameson's arms.

He flicked open the buttons of her uniform and slid his hands inside to caress her waist over the soft, white shirt. His thumbs stroked her ribs, teasing the inches just below her breasts, and she rocked against him, urging him on.

He kissed her again and pulled her closer.

She gasped, feeling the hardness of him through the layers of fabric that covered their bodies. He wanted her. Instead of shying away, she blatantly rolled her hips against his.

Anything could have happened to him in the last seven weeks—or to her. She had him now and she was done denying herself, done fighting the reckless speed or the intensity of their connection. She'd take him in whatever ways he wanted to give himself.

"How long do I have you for?" he asked, his breath tantalizing the shell of her ear just before his lips did.

"You're taking the easy way out, and that's not who you are!"

"What the hell makes you think you know me?" I fired back.

"You sculpted a tree coming straight out of the water!"

"And?" I folded my arms over my chest.

"Whether it's conscious or unconscious, there are pieces of me in every story I tell, and I bet it's the same for you with sculpting. That tree isn't anchored by earth. It shouldn't be able to grow, and yet there it is. And don't think I didn't notice the lighting. It shined straight through to highlight the roots. Why else would you call it *Indomitable Will*?"

He remembered the name of the piece? I shook my head. "This isn't about me. It's about her. About them. Wrapping this up with a bow, whether it's a tearful reunion at a train station or showing her rushing to his bedside, cheapens what she went through. The book ends here, Noah. Right at this gazebo, with Scarlett waiting for a man who never came back to her. Period."

He looked up to the sky like he was praying for patience, and the fire in his eyes had lowered to a simmer by the time he brought his gaze back to mine. "If you force this, it will earn inevitably shitty reviews and disappoint her fans who will burn me at the stake for fucking with Scarlett Stanton's legacy. That's what people will remember, not her love story, not the hundred other books I could write in my lifetime."

I bristled. *His career.* Of course. "Then use the opt-out and walk away." I did exactly that, not bothering to look back as I headed down the path.

I'd seen enough looks of disappointment in my life without adding his to the mix.

"The farthest I'm walking is back to my place. I'm here for the next two and a half months, remember?"

"Good luck crossing the creek in those shoes!" I called back over my shoulder.

team, but there was now a heightened awareness, as if someone
had started a countdown. I couldn't have written the sexual
tension any better. Every simple touch between us since then
was measured, careful, as if we were matches in the middle of a
fireworks cache, knowing too much friction would set the whole
place ablaze.

"Want to picnic?" she asked, gesturing to a vaguely open bit
of floor at her side.

"I'm game if you are." I picked my way across the spread of
memories to claim the spot at her side.

"Sorry," she said with a sheepish cringe, her wide-neck
sweatshirt slipping off her shoulder to reveal a lilac bra strap.
"I was looking for that one picture I told you about from Middle
Wallop and got kind of lost in this."

"Don't apologize." Not only did she look better than our
lunches, she'd unlocked a veritable treasure trove of family
history and laid it bare for me.

If that didn't say *opening up*, I wasn't sure what else could.
We'd come a long way from her hanging up on me. Everything
about the woman next to me was soft, from the sweep of her hair
into that knot on her head, to her bare, shorts-clad, mile-long
legs crossed beneath her. There was nothing icy about her.

"Once I found the pictures, I couldn't help myself." She smiled
down at the open photo album on her lap as I took the boxes of
takeout from the bag.

"No tomato," I said, handing hers over. I couldn't remember
if my last girlfriend liked her coffee sweet or black, yet here I
was, committing everything about Georgia Stanton to memory
without even trying. I had it bad.

"Thank you," she replied with a smile, taking the box before
pointing up to the desk behind us. "Iced tea, unsweetened."

"Thanks." Guess I wasn't the only one committing the details
to memory.

"I still think you're a weirdo for drinking it without sugar, but whatever floats your boat." She shrugged and flipped a page in the album.

"That you?" I brushed off her commentary and leaned over her shoulder slightly. Whether it was her shampoo or perfume, the light citrus scent I breathed in went straight to my head, along with other body parts I needed under firm control around Georgia.

"How can you tell?" She shot me a quizzical look. "You can't even see my face."

"I recognize Scarlett, and I highly doubt there was any other little girl dressed up as a princess Darth Vader." Scarlett's smile was proud, just like it was in every picture I saw of her and Georgia together.

"Fair point," Georgia admitted. "Guess I was feeling a little dark side that year."

"How old were you?"

"Seven." Her brow furrowed. "Mom had come to visit before marrying husband number two, if I remember correctly."

"How many husbands has she had?" It wasn't that I was judging, as much as the look on Georgia's face had me more than curious.

"Five marriages, four husbands." She flipped the page. "She married number three twice, but I think they're getting divorced, since she's currently back with number four. I honestly don't bother keeping track anymore."

It took a second to connect those dots.

"Anyway, you need the pictures from the forties, and these are mostly just me—" She moved to shut the album.

"I'd love to see them." Anything to help me understand her better.

She looked at me like I'd lost my mind.

"I mean, Scarlett's in them, too, right?" *Weak*.

"True. Okay. We can move to the older stuff next. Don't let it get cold." She motioned to the burger I had in front of me.

We ate and flipped through the album. Page after page was filled with pictures of Georgia's childhood, and though some of the pictures included Hazel or Scarlett, it was years—and my entire lunch—before Ava appeared again. Georgia looked like a happy child for the most part—huge smiles in the garden, the meadow, out by the creek. Book signings in Paris and Rome—

"No London?" I asked, turning the page back to make sure I hadn't missed one. Nope, just Scarlett and Georgia—who was missing two front teeth—at the Colosseum.

"She never stepped foot in England again," Georgia said softly. "This was the last book tour, too. She wrote for another ten years, though. Swore it kept her from going senile. What about you?"

"Me? Am I at risk for going senile?" My eyebrows shot up. "How old do you think I am?"

She laughed. "I know you're thirty-one. I meant, do you think you'll write until you're ninety?" she rephrased, elbowing me gently.

"Oh." I rubbed the back of my neck, trying to imagine a time I *wouldn't* write. "I'll probably write until I'm dead. Whether I choose to publish it or not is a different subject." Writing a book and going through the publishing process were two completely different beasts.

"I get that." As someone raised in the industry, she undoubtedly did.

Another page, another picture, another year. Georgia's smile was blindingly bright as she stood in front of a birthday cake—twelve, going by the decorations—with Ava at her side.

In the next picture, which looked to be a few weeks later, the light was gone from Georgia's eyes.

"You're not going to ask why my mother didn't raise me?" She peered at me sideways.

"You don't owe me an explanation."

"You really mean that, don't you?" she asked softly.

"I do." I knew enough of the bare bones to piece it together. Ava had become a mother in high school, but she wasn't cut out for being a mom. "Contrary to what experience you have with me because of our project here, I'm not in the habit of prying information out of women who don't want to give it." I studied the lines of her face as she looked anywhere but at me.

"Even if it helped you understand Gran?" She flipped the album page carelessly, as if the answer was inconsequential, but I knew better.

"I promise I'll never take anything you don't wholeheartedly want to give me, Georgia." My voice dropped.

She turned my way and our eyes met, our faces only a breath apart. Had she been any other woman, I would have kissed her. I would've acted on the blatant attraction that had grown way past any analogy I could've mustered. This was no longer a simple zing of electricity, and it had developed far beyond a shot of lust or a surge of overwhelming desire. The inches between us were thick with need, pure and primal. It was no longer a matter of if, but when. I saw the battle raging in her eyes that felt all-too-familiar, because I waged the same war against inevitability.

Her gaze traveled to my mouth. "And what if I wholeheartedly want to give it to you?" she whispered.

"Do you?" Every muscle in my body tightened, locking down the nearly uncontrollable impulse to discover how she tasted.

Her cheeks flushed, and her breath hitched as she looked away, back to the photo album. "I'll tell you whatever you want to know." She flipped through a chunk of the album, landing on her wedding pictures, not formal, but candid.

"You look beautiful." It was more than that. Wedding-Day Georgia wore a look so openly, honestly in love that a stab of irrational jealousy flooded me. That asshole hadn't been worthy of her heart, her trust.

"Thanks." She flipped to what was obviously the reception. "Funny, but now when I think about that day, I mostly remember

Damian schmoozing anyone he could in Gran's circle." She said it easily, as if it was the punch line to a joke.

My brow knitted. How long had it taken Ellsworth to dull her sparkle?

"What?" she asked, glancing my way.

"You don't look anything like the Ice Queen in these pictures," I said softly. "I don't understand how anyone could ever mistake you for cold."

"Ah, back when I was all hopeful and naive." Her head tilted as she turned the page yet again, this time revealing a shower of bubbles as the bride and groom made their way toward their honeymoon getaway car. "The nickname didn't come until later, but that first time I found out he was cheating on me, something..." She sighed and flipped again. "Something changed."

"Paige Parker?" I guessed.

She scoffed. "God, no."

My attention snapped to her face as she turned a chunk of pages—years.

"He wasn't that careless back then. Actresses get you caught, but eighteen-year-old assistants don't." She shrugged.

"How many—" The question was out of my mouth before I could stop myself. It was none of my business how incredibly hurtful Ellsworth was. If I were married to Georgia, I'd be far too busy keeping her happy in my bed to even *think* about someone else's.

"Too many," she responded quietly. "But I wasn't about to tell Gran that I didn't get that same epic love she did—not when all she wanted was to see me happy, and she'd just had that first heart attack. And I guess, admitting that I'd made the same mistake as my mom was...hard."

"So you stayed." My voice lowered as another piece of the Georgia puzzle clicked into place. *Indomitable will.*

"I adapted. It's not like I wasn't used to being left." She grazed her thumb over a picture, and I looked down to see a colorful autumn tree in a location I recognized well—Central Park. Georgia stood between Damian and Ava, her arms around both, her smile a dim shadow of the one just a few years before. "There's a warning, a sound your heart makes the first time it realizes it's no longer safe with the person you trusted."

My jaw flexed.

She turned another page, another black-tie affair. "It's not as clean or impersonal as a break or a shatter. Besides, those are easy to repair if you can find all the pieces. Truly crushing a soul—now *that* requires a certain level of...personal violence. Your ears fill with this desperate"—*flip*— "rasping"—*flip*—"gasp. Like you're fighting for air, suffocating in plain sight. Strangled by life and someone else's shitty, selfish decisions."

"Georgia," I whispered as my stomach turned, my chest pulling tight at the agony and anger in her words, pausing over a picture from the red-carpet premiere of *The Wings of Autumn*. Her smile was bright but her eyes flat as she posed at Damian's side like a trophy, both generations of Stanton women at her right. She was freezing over right in front of my eyes, each picture a little colder than the last.

"And the thing is," she continued with a little shake of her head and another mocking smile, "you don't always recognize that wet sound for what it is—an assassination. You don't register what's actually happening as the air disappears. You hear that gurgle, and it somehow convinces you that the next breath is coming—you're not broken. This is fixable, right? So you fight, holding on to whatever air there is." Her eyes filled with unshed tears, but she raised her chin and held them back as the pages flew by with every sentence. "You fight and you thrash because this fated, deep-rooted thing you called love refuses to go down with a single shot. That would be far too merciful. Real love has to be choked out, held under the water until it stops kicking. That's the only way to kill it."

She flipped again and again, the album a color-streaked

kaleidoscope of photos she'd obviously chosen with great care to send Scarlett, constructing the lie of a happy marriage.

"And once you finally get it, finally stop fighting, you're too far gone to get to the surface to save yourself. And the spectators tell you to keep swimming, that it's only a broken heart, but that little flicker that's left of your soul can't even float, let alone tread water. So you're left with a choice. You either let yourself die while they accuse you of being weak or you learn to breathe the goddamn water, and then they call you a monster for what you become. Ice Queen, indeed."

She stopped on the last picture—this one a mirror of the first premiere, taken only a couple months before Scarlett's death. The rest of the pages in the album were devastatingly blank.

My hands clenched. I had never wanted to beat the shit out of someone the way I did Damian Ellsworth. "I swear, I would never hurt you like he did." I ground out every word, hoping she registered my conviction.

"I never said he did," she whispered, two lines forming between her eyebrows as she glanced at me with confusion.

The doorbell rang, startling us both.

"I'll get it," I offered, pushing to my feet.

"I'm on it." She scrambled, the photo album sliding off her lap as she beat me to stand, barely pausing before she raced for the door, nimbly dodging the piles of photos.

I watched from the doorway as she signed for the package. If I hadn't been sitting next to her, I never would have guessed she'd just unloaded the way she had. Her polished smile was at the ready as she made polite small talk with the driver.

She took the substantial box and said her goodbyes, closing the door with her hip before setting the box on the entry hall table.

"It's from the lawyers," she said with a grin, and I wondered for a second if she'd lost her mind. No one was ever *that* happy to get a box from their attorneys. "Hold on a second; I need scissors."

"Here." I stepped forward, whipping my Gerber out of my pocket and opening the knife attachment so I could offer it to her. "I thought you didn't close on the new studio for another two weeks?" I couldn't wait to see what she created.

"Thanks." She took the tool, then ripped into the package with childlike glee. "It's not for the studio. She sends me something every month."

"Your lawyer?"

"No, Gran." Her smile was brighter than any I'd seen from her as she pried back the edge of the box. "She left directions and gifts. So far it's been about once a month, but I don't know how long she planned it out."

"That might be the coolest thing I've ever heard." I took the Gerber back, secured the blade, and slipped it into the pocket of my cargo pants.

"It really is," she agreed, ripping open a card. "Dearest Georgia, now that I'm gone, it's up to you to be the witch of the house, no matter where you are. I love you with all my heart, Gran."

My eyebrows shot up at the witch comment until Georgia laughed and pulled a witch's hat from the box.

"She always dressed up like a witch to hand out candy to the kids on Halloween." She plunked the hat on her head, right over her bun, and kept digging.

Right. Halloween was in two weeks. Time was flying, my deadline approaching, and I was still empty-handed. Worse than that, I only had six weeks left with Georgia if I turned the manuscript in on time, which I would.

"She sent you a witch hat and a case of king-size Snickers?" I asked, feeling oddly connected to Scarlett Stanton in that moment as I peered into the box.

Georgia nodded. "Want one?" She plucked a bar from the box and waved it.

"Absolutely." I wanted *Georgia*, but I'd settle for the bar.

"They were Gran's favorites," she said as we peeled our wrappers. "But she said they were called Marathon bars back in England. I can't even begin to tell you how many pages of her manuscripts had little chocolate fingerprints at the edges."

I bit into the bar, then chewed as I followed Georgia back into the office. "All on that typewriter."

"Yep." She peered at me with a tilted head, studying me carefully.

"Chocolate on my face?" I asked, taking another bite.

"You should write the rest of the book here."

"I am, remember? There's no way in hell I'm going back to New York without a finished manuscript. Pretty sure Adam wouldn't even let me off the plane." As it was, I was ducking his calls left and right. Pretty soon he'd be out here, too, if I didn't pick up.

"I mean...here, here," she said, motioning toward Scarlett's desk. "Gran's office, *here*. It's where she worked on it."

I blinked. "You want me to finish the book in here?" The words came out slowly, stumbling over my own confusion.

She took another bite and nodded, glancing around the room. "Mm-hmm."

"I don't always write on a typical schedule..." But I'd be close to Georgia every day.

"So? You have a key. I won't always be here, anyway, not with getting the studio set up. And if it's ever ridiculously late, you can crash in a guest bedroom." She shrugged and hopped over two piles of photos on her way to the desk. "The more I think about it, the more it fits." She walked behind the desk and pulled out the chair. "Come on—try it on for size."

I polished off the chocolate bar and tossed the wrapper in the trash can beside the massive cherry desk, hesitating. That was Scarlett's desk. Scarlett's typewriter. "You protect that thing like it's the Resolute desk, coasters and all."

"Oh, you still have to use coasters. That's nonnegotiable."

She tapped the high back of the chair and laughed. "Come on, it won't bite."

"Right." I rounded the corner and sank into the office chair, then pulled myself forward so I sat at the desk. Georgia's laptop lay closed to my right, but on my left sat the famed typewriter.

"If you're feeling bold…" Georgia ran her fingers over the keys.

"No, thank you. First, I'd probably break it, and second, I make way too many corrections as I go to ever think about using a typewriter. That's hard-core, even for me." My eyes caught on the shirt box on the edge of the desk. It was labeled "UNFINISHED" in thick, black marker. "Is that…"

"The originals? Yeah." She slid the box my way. "Go ahead, but I'm sticking to my guns on this one. Originals stay here."

"Noted." I flipped the top off, then lifted the stack of papers to the polished surface of the desk. She'd typed these pages herself, and here I was, getting ready to finish them. *Surreal.*

The manuscript was thick, but it wasn't only the word count that stacked up the pages but the pages themselves. I thumbed through quickly. "This is amazing."

"I've got another seventy-three boxes just like it," she teased, leaning back against the desk.

"You can actually *see* her write it, then revise. The pages are all in different stages of aging. See?" I held up two pages from Chapter Two, when Jameson had just approached Scarlett where she sat with Constance. "This page here has to be the original. It's aged, and the quality of the paper is lower. This page"—I waved it slightly, my lips tugging up at the smudge of chocolate at the edge—"can't be more than a decade old."

"Makes sense. She liked to revise, always added word count." She braced her hands on the edge of the desk. "Personally, I think she liked living there, between the pages with him. Always adding little bits of memory but never closing the door."

That was something I understood. Closing out a book meant I

said goodbye to those characters. But they weren't just characters to Scarlett. They'd been her sister. Her soul mate. I read a few sentences from the first page, then the second. "Damn, you can actually see her skill evolve."

"Really?" Georgia adjusted slightly, turning her head to see the pages.

"Yeah. Every writer has a particular flow to their sentence structure. See here," I pointed to a spot on the first page. "Slightly choppier. By here," I selected a different passage on the second, "she smoothed out." I'd bet my life that the first pages most closely resembled the style of her early works. I glanced up to find Georgia's eyes on me.

She failed at stifling a smile.

"What?" I asked, slipping the pages back into the manuscript where they belonged.

"Now you have chocolate on your face." She laughed softly.

"Awesome." I swiped my hand over the stubble closest to my mouth.

"Here." She slid along the desk, the bare skin of her legs brushing against mine.

I suddenly wished I'd worn shorts as I rolled back slightly, hoping she'd come closer.

She filled the space between my knees, cupped the side of my face, and brushed her thumb over the patch of skin just below the corner of my mouth. My pulse kicked up a notch, and my body went tight.

"There," she whispered, but didn't move her hand.

"Thanks." Her touch was warm, and it took everything I had not to lean in to it. Damn, I wanted her, and not just her body. I wanted inside her mind, past the walls even George R.R. Martin would be proud of. I wanted her trust simply so I could prove I was worthy of it.

She swept the tip of her tongue over her lower lip.

My self-control hung by a thread, and the look in her eyes

was slowly pulling at the edges of it, fraying the strands.

Still, she didn't move.

"Georgia." Her name came out as both a plea and a warning.

She moved closer. Not close enough.

My hands found the curves of her waist and I tugged, bringing her as close as the chair allowed.

Her breath caught in a tiny gasp that sent all the blood in my body straight to my dick. *Calm the hell down.* She slid her hand along my jaw and into my hair.

My grip tightened on her waist through the thick fabric of her sweatshirt.

"Noah," she whispered, lifting her other hand to hold the back of my neck.

"Do you want me to kiss you, Georgia?" My voice was rough, even to my own ears. There could be no mistake here. No mixed signals. There was too much riding on this, and for once, it wasn't my career I was thinking about.

"Do you want to kiss me?" she challenged.

"More than I want my next breath." My gaze dropped to that incredible mouth, and her lips parted.

"Good, because—"

Her phone rang.

You have got to be kidding me.

She shifted, leaning closer.

Another ring.

"Don't—" I started.

With a groan, she ripped her phone from her back pocket, then sucked in a breath as her eyes narrowed at her screen. She swiped violently, answering the call and lifting the device to her ear.

"—answer it," I finished with a sigh, letting my head fall back against the chair.

"What the hell do you want, Damian?"

CHAPTER TWENTY

July 1941

North Weald, England

"It's better, right?" Scarlett asked as she forced the buttons of her uniform jacket through the holes. She wasn't going to be able to hide it much longer. She wasn't sure she was even effectively hiding it *now*.

Jameson leaned against the doorframe to their bedroom, his mouth pressed in a firm line.

"I've taken out every spare quarter inch," Constance murmured, tugging the hem lightly. "Perhaps we could request a larger size?"

"Again?" Scarlett's eyebrows rose as she took in her reflection in the oval mirror that topped their dresser.

Constance winced. "True. The first time, the supply clerk looked at me as though I'd been stealing her rations."

The uniform was tight, straining at seams not only over her belly but also her hips and chest.

"I have an idea," Jameson said from the doorway, crossing his arms over his chest.

"Let's hear it," Scarlett responded, tugging the sides of her jacket together near the bottom, where there weren't any buttons.

"You could tell them you're five months pregnant."

She met his gaze in the mirror with an arched eyebrow.

He didn't smile.

Constance looked between the two of them. "Right. I'll just be…somewhere else!"

Jameson moved so she could slide by, and then he shut the

bedroom door, leaning against it. "I'm serious."

"I know," she said softly, running her hand over the swell of her belly. "But you know what they'll do."

He leaned his head back, thunking it against the door. "Scarlett, honey. I know your work is important, but can you honestly tell me that being on your feet for eight hours straight isn't killing you? The stress? The schedule?"

He was right. She was already exhausted every morning when she opened her eyes. It didn't matter how tired she was; there was no time to rest.

But if she came clean—resigned her commission—what would she be then?

"What would I do all day?" Scarlett asked, her fingers tracing the raised lines of the rank on her shoulder. "For the last two years I've had direction. I've had meaning and purpose. I've accomplished things and dedicated myself to the war effort. So what am I supposed to do? I've never been a housewife." She swallowed, hoping to dislodge the knot there. "I've certainly never been a mother. I don't know how to be either of those things."

Jameson crossed the room, then sat on the edge of the bed, gripped his wife's hips, and pulled her between his spread knees. "We'll figure it out together."

"We," she said softly, her face falling. "But nothing changes for you," she whispered. "You still go to work, still fly, still fight in this war."

"I know this isn't what you wanted—" His face fell.

"It's not that," she promised in a rush, lacing her fingers behind her husband's neck. "I was just hoping I'd be ready. I hoped the war would be over, that we wouldn't have to bring a child into a world where I worry if you'll come home every night or fear a bomb may fall on our house while he slept." She took his hands and covered the swell of her belly. "I want this baby, Jameson. I want our family. I just wanted to be ready, and I'm not."

Jameson's hands stroked over her stomach as they did every day when he said goodbye to their child as he headed off to fly. "I don't think anyone is ever ready. And no, this world isn't safe for *her*. Not yet. But she has two parents fighting like hell to change that. To make it safe for her." The corner of his lips twitched upward as he looked at his wife. "I'm incredibly proud of you, Scarlett. You've done everything you can. You can't change the regulations. All you can do is bring that fight home. I know you'll be a wonderful mother. I know my schedule is unpredictable, and that I never know when I'll actually make it home." *If he makes it home*, she thought. "I know the majority of this will fall on you, but I also know you're up for the challenge."

She cocked a brow. "There you go again, thinking our baby's a girl. Your son won't take kindly to that when he's born."

Jameson laughed. "And there you go again, thinking our daughter is a boy." He leaned forward and placed his mouth just above her belly. "You hear that, sunshine? Mommy thinks you're a boy."

"Mommy knows you're a boy," Scarlett challenged.

Jameson kissed her belly, then tugged Scarlett closer so he could brush a kiss over her lips. "I love you, Scarlett Stanton. I love every single thing about you. I can't wait to hold a piece of both of us, to see these gorgeous blue eyes in our child."

She ran her hands through his hair. "And what if he has your eyes?"

Jameson smiled. "Having seen both you and your sister, I'd say you might have some dominant genetics in the eye department." He kissed her again, slowly. "You have the most beautiful eyes I've ever seen. It would be a shame not to see them carried down. We'd call them Wright blue."

"Stanton blue," she corrected, something inside her shifting, preparing for the change she could no longer avoid through denial. "I still can't cook. Even after all these months, you're still better than I am. All I know how to do is throw an excellent party and plot aircraft for incoming raids. I don't want to fail."

"You won't. We won't. As much as you and I love each other, can you imagine how much we're going to love this kid?" His smile was brighter than ever and just as contagious.

"Only a few more months," she whispered.

"Only a few more months," he repeated. "Then we'll have a new adventure."

"Everything will change."

"Not the way I love you."

"You promise?" she asked, her fingers trailing the line of his collar. "You fell in love with a WAAF officer, which, from the fit of this uniform, won't be true in the next week. Hardly seems like you got the good end of this bargain." How was he going to love her if she wasn't even herself?

He pulled her even closer, so he could feel the curves of her body against his. "I love you in whatever role you play. Whatever uniform you want to wear. Whoever you want to be. I will love you."

That was a promise she would hold on to later that day as she faced Section Leader Robbins in her office, fidgeting with her cap after her watch.

"I was wondering when you'd come to see me," Robbins said, motioning to the chair in front of her desk.

Scarlett took it, adjusting her skirts as she sat.

"Honestly, I'm surprised you lasted this long." Robbins gave her an understanding smile. "I thought you'd be here a month ago."

"You knew?" Scarlett's hands flew to her belly.

Robbins lifted an eyebrow. "You threw up for two months straight. I knew. I just thought it best to let you come to this conclusion on your own, and selfishly, I wanted to keep you. You're one of my best girls. That being said, I was only giving you two more weeks before I said something myself." She opened a desk drawer and pulled out some papers. "I have your discharge papers ready. You just need to take them up to headquarters."

"I don't want to be discharged," Scarlett admitted quietly. "I want to do my job."

Robbins studied her carefully and sighed. "And I wish you could."

"There is nothing I can do?" Her heart lurched, feeling as though she was being cleaved in two.

"You can be a wonderful mother, Scarlett. Britain needs more babies." She slid the papers across the desktop. "You'll be sorely missed."

"Thank you." Scarlett squared her shoulders, then took her discharge papers.

Just like that, it was over.

There was a steady, dull hum in her ears as she turned in her discharge papers. It didn't fade until she stood in front of that same oval mirror in her bedroom, staring at a reflection that was no longer rightfully hers.

She took off her hat first and placed it on the dresser. The shoes came next. Then the stockings.

She raised her hands to the belt of her jacket twice before she managed to get it undone.

This uniform had given her freedom she never would have experienced without it. She never would have stood up to her parents without the confidence she'd earned over the long days and nights of watches. She never would have seen her worth as more than a pretty showpiece.

She never would have met Jameson.

Her fingers trembled at the first button. Once she took it off, that was it. There were no more watches. No more briefings. No more smiling as she walked down the street, proud that she was doing her part. They weren't just clothes—they were the physical manifestation of the woman she'd become, the sisterhood she belonged to.

She heard a shuffle behind her and lifted her eyes in the mirror to see Jameson standing exactly where he'd been that morning, leaning in the doorway, but instead of his pressed uniform, he still wore his flying suit.

His hands clenched with the need to hold her, but he kept his arms folded across his chest. He didn't say anything as he watched her struggle with the buttons of her jacket. His chest ached at the pain, the loss in her eyes as she finally got them undone. She must have told her section leader today. She wasn't just getting undressed; she was being unmade.

As much as he wanted to cross the room and ease her, this was something she had to do for herself, by herself. Besides, he was already responsible for taking so much from her that he couldn't bear to be a part of this, too.

Tears filled her eyes as she slid free of the jacket, folding it carefully before placing it on the dresser. Next came the tie, then the shirt, and finally she stepped out of the skirt. Her hands were steady as she placed it on the pile, standing in nothing but the civilian underwear she'd always insisted on.

She swallowed, then lifted her chin. "And that's…that."

"I'm so sorry." His words came out like they'd been scraped over broken bottles.

She walked to him, all lush curves and sad eyes, but when their gazes met, hers was steady. "I'm not."

"You're not?" He palmed her cheek, needing to touch her.

"I'm not sorry about anything that's led me to you."

He carried her to their bed and showed her with his body exactly how lucky he felt to have found her.

...

One month later, Scarlett marveled at the freedom the simple wrap dress afforded her as she and Jameson shopped in a small London store that specialized in children's clothes.

There were some parts of civilian life—such as not melting in her uniform in the August heat—that more than agreed with her.

"I wish we'd done this two months ago," Jameson muttered as they took in the scant racks of infant garments.

"It will be okay," she assured him. "He won't need much to start out with."

"She." Jameson grinned, then bent to kiss her temple.

As of June, clothing was now rationed, which meant she was going to need to get creative in a few months—and do a lot more wash. Blankets, gowns, and nappies—they had a lot to acquire before November.

"He," she argued with a shake of her head. "Let's get these to start with." She handed Jameson two gowns that would work for both a girl or a boy.

"Okay."

Her face puckered slightly as she stared at the small selection of nappies.

"What's wrong?" he asked.

"I've never put on a nappy before—a diaper," she clarified for him. "I know I need pins, but I don't have anyone I can ask." She still hadn't spoken to her parents, and it wasn't like her mother had done the child-rearing herself, anyway.

"You can always hire a nappy service," a young clerk with a quick smile suggested from the end of the aisle. "They're becoming quite popular."

Jameson nodded in consideration. "It would leave us with less laundry, and probably ease a little of your we're-never-going-to-be-able-to-buy-enough stress."

Scarlett rolled her eyes. "We can talk about it after dinner. I'm starving."

"Yes, ma'am." He gave her a smile and took their items to the counter.

Of all the things to talk about while he had a precious forty-eight hours of leave, nappies were not on her list.

A few moments later, they were out on the bustling street, walking hand in hand. The bombings had ceased...for now, but the evidence was everywhere she looked.

"Anywhere you want to eat?" Jameson asked, adjusting his hat with one hand.

Scarlett swore she saw at least three women swoon from the sight, not that she blamed them. Her husband was incredible from the top of his head to the tips of his toes. "Not particularly. Though I wouldn't mind going back to the hotel and having you for dinner." She kept her face as straight as she could manage.

He stopped in the middle of the pavement, forcing the crowd to flow around them. "I'll get a taxi right now." His smile was pure hedonism.

"Scarlett?"

Scarlett froze at the sound of her mother's voice, her grip tightening on Jameson's hand as she turned slowly to face her.

She wasn't alone. Scarlett's father stood at her side, looking as shocked as Scarlett felt for all of a heartbeat before he managed to school his features into the stone she knew so well.

"Jameson, these are my parents, Nigel and Margaret, but I'm sure they'd rather you call them Baron and Lady Wright." Finally, she had a real use for all the comportment lessons she'd been forced into.

• • •

"Sir." Jameson stepped forward, offering his hand to Nigel but losing Scarlett's in the process. So this was the infamous father his wife and her sister had such mixed feelings about. He was dressed in a neatly pressed suit, his pepper and silver hair slicked back with minimal fuss.

Her father looked at Jameson's hand, then brought his gaze back up. "You're the Yank."

"I'm American, yes." Jameson bristled but managed a smile as he lowered his hand, taking Scarlett's again. He couldn't imagine having this kind of rift with his own parents, and if he could ease the tension, he would. It's the least his mother would expect from him. "Ma'am, your daughters speak very highly of you."

Scarlett squeezed his fingers at his lie.

Margaret had the same dark hair and piercing blue eyes as her daughters. In fact, the resemblance was so close that he couldn't shake the feeling he was getting a glimpse at what Scarlett would look like in thirty years. Scarlett wouldn't have that cold, firm set to her mouth, though. His wife was far too warm for that.

"You're…going to have a child," her mother said quietly, her eyes round as they locked on Scarlett's stomach.

The irrational impulse to stand in front of his wife was instant.

"We are," Scarlett said, her voice firm and chin high. He'd always been in awe of her self-control, but this was an all-time high. "I understand you convinced Constance to throw her life away?" She asked the question with the same tone she'd used to request he pass the milk this morning.

Jameson blinked, realizing he'd entered an entirely different arena of warfare where he wasn't the expert—his wife was.

"Constance's choices are her own," Margaret said just as politely.

"Is it a boy?" Nigel asked, staring at Scarlett with a spark of something in his eyes that looked a little too close to desperation for Jameson's comfort.

"I could hardly know, as I am still pregnant." Scarlett tilted her head. "And if he is, that is none of your business."

This was the strangest family he'd ever encountered...and somehow he was a part of it.

Scarlett turned her attention back to her mother. "Constance's choices are her own, but you took advantage of her broken heart. You and I both know what he'll do to her. You willingly sent a lamb to the slaughter, and I will do everything in my power to convince her not to go through with it."

As shots across the bow went, that one was a direct hit.

"As far as I'm concerned, you made the choice for her when you refused him," her mother replied unemotionally.

And that one was an entire bombing raid.

Scarlett's sharp intake of breath was enough for him to know her mother's words had found their mark.

"It was nice to meet you both, but we're going to go now," Jameson said, tipping his hat.

"If that's a boy, he can be my heir," Nigel blurted.

Every muscle in Jameson's body tensed, preparing for the fight. "If our baby is a boy, he's *our* son," he said.

"He's not your anything," Scarlett said to her father through gritted teeth, her hand rising protectively over their child.

"If Constance doesn't marry Wadsworth—as you are hell-bent on stopping it," her father mused with a scheming gleam in his eyes, "and you have the only heir, the line is clear. If she does marry him, and they have children, that's a different matter."

"Unbelievable." Scarlett shook her head. "I'll sign over my claim right now. Here, in the middle of the street. I don't want it."

Nigel's gaze flickered between Scarlett and him, then narrowed on Scarlett. "What are you going to do when your Yank gets himself killed?"

Scarlett's spine stiffened.

Jameson couldn't argue against the possibility. The life expectancy of a pilot wasn't years, or even months. The odds weren't exactly in his favor, especially at the rate the 71st was flying missions. Since getting issued Spitfires a few weeks ago, they were one of the top squadrons for enemy kills.

He was one battle away from making ace...or crashing.

"You'll have a baby to support on a widow's stipend, since I'm assuming you no longer wear the uniform or have income of your own."

"She'll be fine," Jameson interjected. Changing his will already made sure Scarlett would inherit what land was his if he didn't make it home, but he wasn't telling her parents that.

"When that happens, you'll come home." Her father ignored Jameson entirely. "Think about it. You have no real skill. Can you honestly say you'd go to the factories? What would you do with your child?"

"Nigel," Margaret chastised softly.

"You'll come home. And not for you—you'd rather starve than give us the pleasure. But for your child?"

The color ran from Scarlett's face.

"We're leaving. Now." Jameson turned his back on her parents, cutting directly in front of them instead of letting Scarlett's hand go.

"She doesn't even have a country!" Nigel called after them.

"She'll be American soon enough!" Jameson said over his shoulder as they walked away.

Scarlett held her head high as Jameson stepped into the street, hailing a taxi. A black car pulled to the curb, and Jameson opened the door, ushering Scarlett in first. Rage raced through his veins, hot and thick.

"Where to?" the driver asked.

"The U.S. Embassy," Jameson replied.

"What?" Scarlett twisted in her seat as the cab lurched forward into traffic.

"You have to get a visa. You can't stay here. Our baby can't stay here." He shook his head. "You told me they were cold and monstrous, but that was..." His jaw flexed. "I don't have the words to describe what happened back there."

"So you're taking me to the embassy." She lifted a brow.

"Yes!"

"Love, we don't have our marriage records or any of my personal identification. They're not just going to give me a visa because you say so," she said, calmly stroking his hand.

"Shit!"

The driver glanced back at them but continued on.

"I know they're...upsetting. But they don't have any power over me anymore—over us. Jameson, look at me."

"If something happens to me, I need to know that you can get to Colorado." Just the thought of her going back to her *family* sent another hot pulse of anger through him. "We're not poor—at least not in land—and I've already changed my will. If I die, you have options, but going back to those two isn't one of them."

"I know." She nodded slowly. "I won't. Nothing will happen to you—"

"You don't know that."

"—but if it does, I'll never go back there. I promise."

His eyes searched hers. "Promise me we'll start the visa process."

"I'm not leaving you!"

"Promise. Me. If nothing else, you'd have it if I die." He wasn't giving on this one, wasn't being the sensible, sensitive husband. She had to belong *somewhere* if he went down.

"Okay. Fine. We'll start the process. But we can't do anything about it today. We have to get an appointment—"

He kissed her hard and quick, not giving a shit that they were in public or potentially scandalizing the cab driver.

"Thank you," he whispered, his forehead against hers.

"Can we go back to the hotel now?"

He gave the driver the destination change with a grin that didn't fade as they made their way to the hotel. It didn't even fade as they climbed the wide staircase up to their room or as he unlocked their door.

Even if he didn't survive this war, she would—their child would.

"What is that?" Scarlett asked, gesturing to a large box on the desk as they walked into the room. She was completely, utterly drained, not only from walking miles while they shopped but from the encounter with her parents on the street.

"I bought you a present while you were sleeping this morning and arranged to have it delivered. Go on." He motioned her toward the box.

"A present?" She put the bag with the baby clothes on their bed, then looked over her shoulder at him with skepticism. "What are you about?"

"Just open it." He shut the door, then came up beside her, half sitting on the desk to face her.

"It's not my birthday." She tugged one flap open.

"No, but it's the start of a new era for you."

She opened the next flap, and again, peering down into the wide box as it opened.

Then she gasped, her chest constricting at what she found.

"Jameson," she whispered.

"Do you like it?" he asked with a grin.

She ran her fingers lightly over the cool metal casing. "It's…" *Amazing. Wonderful. Thoughtful. Too much.*

"I thought maybe you could write down some of those stories you're always thinking up inside that beautiful brain of yours."

A joyful laugh burst from her throat, and she flung herself into his arms, holding him tight. "Thank you. Thank you. Thank you."

He'd bought her a typewriter.

CHAPTER TWENTY-ONE

Georgia

Jameson,

I miss you. How long has it been since we've written letters? Months? Even living in the same house, your flight schedule and my watches have us missing each other by minutes. It's the sweetest form of torture, sleeping next to your pillow, my head filled with your scent, knowing you're flying in the skies above me. I pray that you're safe, that you're reading this while I'm already at work, smiling as you fall asleep next to my pillow with my scent, wishing you were holding me. Sleep well, my love, and maybe I'll make it home this afternoon before you're due on the flight line. I love you.

Scarlett

"**Y**ou're sure?" Helen asked, her tone efficient as always. Gran's agent had always left minimal room for nonsense, which was why Gran had chosen her after the first had passed away twenty years into her career.

"Absolutely," I assured her, switching the phone to my other hand and crossing into the entry way. "I already told him when he called a couple of weeks ago, but Damian has all the Scarlett Stanton rights he's going to get. And you know how Gran felt about movies. I don't care what he's offering: the answer is no."

She chuckled. "I sure do. Okay, then, no manuscript for Ellsworth Productions."

My heart ached at the mention of the company I'd helped build, which only made me that much more determined not to give my ex another single thing.

"Thank you." I headed for the giant bowl of candy on the entry table and refilled it with a fresh stock of Snickers bars.

"Of course," Helen said. "And honestly, I'm looking forward to telling him to stick it. I think I'll give him a call when we're done. How is that manuscript coming, anyway?"

I paused at the foyer mirror, adjusting my witch hat while taking in the added bonus of seeing Noah in the reflection, typing at Gran's desk behind me. Lord, that man even made writing look sexy. His shirtsleeves were pushed up his forearms, and his brow was furrowed in concentration as his fingers flew over his keyboard.

"Georgia?" Helen prompted.

"It's coming." Which was more than I could say for me, since I'd dutifully kept my hands off the writer-in-residence. There wasn't a day I didn't think about that almost-kiss or contemplate climbing into his lap for a do-over so I could follow through with at least one of the daydreams I'd had about his mouth on mine. The doorbell rang for the millionth time that evening. "Gotta run, Helen; it's a madhouse around here tonight."

"Happy Halloween!"

We hung up, and I opened the front door, offering the kids a wide smile. Halloween was the best. For one night, you could be whomever you wanted—whatever you wanted. Witches, Ghostbusters, princesses, astronauts, the Black Knight from Monty Python, nothing was off the table.

"Trick or treat!" two kids said in unison, their parents bundled up behind them. Halloween snowstorms happened in Poplar Grove more often than not.

"What do we have here?" I asked, dropping to their eye level. "A firefighter and a..." Oh God help me, I was clueless. What was that costume?

"Raven!" the boy answered enthusiastically, muffled a bit by the scarf awkwardly wedged into his costume.

"Right!" I plunked a full-size Snickers bar into each bag.

"Whoa, nice Fortnite skin!" Noah said behind me, his voice alone sending a thrill down my spine. Of course he knew.

"Thanks!" The boy waved.

"Thank you!" his sister added.

The two raced back to their parents and started the walk down the drive, leaving footprints in the fresh inch of fallen snow.

"I didn't think you'd get so many trick-or-treaters, since you're so far out of town." Noah moved back so I could close the door.

"Gran always gave out full-size bars. Earned her quite the crowd." I put the candy on the table and turned to face him. "How's it going in there?"

"Finished for the day." He tilted the brim of my hat upward, drawing my eyes to meet his. "How about you? Feel like a badass after closing on the studio today? Because you are."

"Maybe a little." I couldn't help but smile. It was really happening. "Plus, I got both furnaces and the annealing oven ordered. Which ending are you working on?" I asked, willing my body not to heat, my cheeks not to flush. Not that it mattered— the look in those deep brown eyes told me Noah Morelli was more than aware of the effect he had on me. I recognized the same need in him, from the scalding hot gazes to the innocent touches that only lasted long enough to singe my skin and leave me craving more.

"Mine," he answered with a shameless grin.

"Hmmm."

"Don't worry, I'll write your sobfest next."

"Poignant," I reminded him.

"Whatever you want to call it. I'll win you over in the end." Oh yeah, that was a definite smirk.

"We'll see." After all these weeks, it was still my go-to answer, even though I was more certain than ever about the ending I'd pushed for. And as for him winning me over in real life? Okay, he had me there.

He glanced around the entry, then stepped into the sitting room.

"What are you looking for?" I asked.

"It just occurred to me. I've never seen the phonograph."

"You wouldn't," I said with a shrug. "Gran said it broke or something back in the late fifties."

"That's too bad." Disappointment flickered over his features. The doorbell rang again, and he took the candy bowl with a soft smile. "I've got this one."

Watching Noah hand out candy to another group of kids turned my insides to mush. Call it biology, or the result of hundreds of thousands of years of evolution, but being good with kids was…well, hot.

"Want me out of your hair?" he asked after he closed the door. There was no expectation in the question, which only made it that much more enticing. He was an audacious flirt, but never pushed for more, even after I'd almost kissed him in the office.

You should have kissed him in the office, you masochist. Look at him.

"Not at all." That was the problem. It didn't matter how much time I spent with Noah, I always wanted more. "Why don't you stick around?"

"Happy to." His voice lowered.

I nodded and yanked my gaze from his before he saw too much.

It was half past eight before the last trick-or-treaters had come and gone.

"There won't be any more," I said as the grandfather clock chimed.

"You can see the future?" Noah asked with a faint smile.

"I wish." I scoffed. If I could have seen the future, I would have known what the hell I was doing. As it was, I had no clue.

I wanted him. That was easy enough to justify. But this... Whatever this was, it was far beyond physical want. I liked him, enjoyed being around him, talking to him, figuring out what made him laugh. In that way, this was already so much more dangerous than chemistry. I'd already trusted him with my life and Gran's story. I was frighteningly close to trusting him as a friend...maybe a lover. "It's a town rule," I explained, taking off my witch hat. "Trick or treating ends at eight thirty."

"You actually have a rule about trick-or-treating?" His eyebrows rose.

"We do." I nodded. "It's right up there with awning covers, but we have it. Welcome to small-town life."

"Fascinating," he mused as his phone rang. He took it from his pocket and glanced at the screen. "Shit," he muttered. "It's my agent."

"You're welcome to take it in the office if you want," I offered.

His brow knit. "Are you sure? I don't want to tie you down if you have hot Halloween plans."

"Maybe I like being tied down," I said as evenly as I could manage.

He arched a single brow, and his eyes darkened.

"Go take your call." I stifled a grin. Guess he wasn't the only audacious flirt around here.

"Trouble. Georgia Stanton, you are pure trouble." He blew out a deep breath, then swiped to answer his call as he walked into Gran's office, which I really needed to stop thinking of as hers. "Hey, Lou. What's so important that you're calling me from Hawaii?"

He didn't shut the door, but I walked away to give him privacy. A stab of anxiety hit me square in the chest, knowing he was probably discussing his future. "Don't be ridiculous," I muttered to myself.

This wasn't Noah's only upcoming project, of course. He'd been putting out two books a year for the last eight years.

Eventually, he would finish this one. Eventually, he would start the next. Eventually, he would leave.

Every day he worked brought us closer to his inevitable departure. Two months ago, I would've relished in that knowledge, counted down the days until Noah was out of my life. Now the thought sent a jolt of panic straight through me.

I didn't want him to go.

I ditched the hat and stepped out the front door, welcoming the blast of icy air, then blew out the candles inside the two jack-o'-lanterns the English club from the high school had given me. They'd carved them for Gran the last decade. A quick check of the snow-covered driveway told me we didn't have any trick-or-treating stragglers, so I came back inside and closed the door.

"Ellsworth offered *what*? Just to see it?" I heard Noah's raised voice through the office door. "The manuscript isn't even done yet."

I froze, my heart lodging in my throat, and though I desperately wanted to move, wanted to shut my ears against what was coming, I couldn't seem to make myself go. I'd already told Damian there was no chance of him getting his grubby little hands on the manuscript, and it would be a cold day in hell before he got anywhere near the performance rights. Helen had no doubt relayed that same message again tonight.

I should've known he'd go to Noah next.

Don't do it. The plea stayed firmly behind my teeth. If Noah was going to betray me, it was better to know now.

"Did he?" Noah's tone sounded almost jovial. "No, you did the right thing. Thank you."

Did the right thing? What did that mean? Sure, Noah liked me, but if I had learned one thing about this industry, it was that money trumped personal affection every time. And there was an ungodly amount of money to be made here.

Noah laughed unabashedly. My pulse leaped.

"Then I guess it's a good thing I've never wanted his name

connected to any of my books. And I'm glad we're on the same page, Lou. I don't give a shit what he said—she doesn't want him to have it. Not even to read."

I held my breath. *Maybe...*

"Because I was there when she told him to fuck off. Not that she used those exact words, but that was the gist, and I don't blame her."

A slow smile spread across my face. He chose *me.*

The concept was so wild that it took a moment to sink in. He. Chose. Me. As if the knowledge unlocked my feet, I was suddenly moving toward the office, pushing the door fully open, and standing before Noah.

He sat perched at the edge of the desk, one palm braced on the surface, the other holding his phone to his ear as he looked me in the eye. "He has first right of refusal?"

"I'm not selling the rights. It doesn't matter," I said, electricity humming under my skin like a living, breathing current. His words had done what weeks of flirting and sexual tension hadn't—broken down my last defense. I was done fighting this.

"Did you hear her, Lou?" Noah smiled at whatever his agent said. "Yeah, I'll tell her. Enjoy the rest of your vacation." He hung up and set the phone down on the desk. "She gave him first right of refusal on future deals?" His eyebrows rose in disbelief.

"At the time, she gave *me* first right of refusal. I started the production company with Damian, remember? What did your agent say?" Less than six feet separated us. Any closer, and there wouldn't be any more talking.

"That he's a pompous asshole." A corner of his lips lifted.

"True." I nodded. "What did he offer you?"

"A contract on two of my un-optioned books, which is funny, since I've already shot him down previously." Noah shrugged. "And that was just to get a look at the manuscript."

"You didn't give it to him."

"It's not mine to give." The muscles in his forearms rippled as he gripped the edge of the desk. "And I'll be damned if I'm giving him anything, let alone something that's yours."

I closed the distance between us, took his face in my hands, and kissed him. The hard lines of his mouth were impossibly supple against mine as our lips collided, softened, lingered.

"Georgia," he said against my mouth, my name somewhere between a plea and a prayer as he drew back slightly, searching my eyes.

"You won me over," I whispered, my hands sliding to the back of his neck.

A smile ghosted across his face, and then his lips were on mine, his hands gripping my waist, pulling me against his strong frame.

I gasped, my lips parting for him.

He tunneled a hand through my hair, cradling the back of my head as he deepened the kiss, laying claim to my mouth with thorough, sure strokes of his tongue that set me on fire. A small whimper I barely recognized as mine escaped at the taste of chocolate and Noah.

He tilted my head and kissed me deeper as I arched against him, rising on my toes to get closer. His hand moved to the small of my back as he explored the lines of my mouth with single-minded focus, as if nothing existed outside this kiss.

Need spiraled within me, fierce in its demand as the kiss went on and on. Noah kept me on edge, changing the tempo—hard and deep, then soft and playful, nipping at my lower lip with the gentle scrape of his teeth, only to soothe the sting with a swipe of his tongue.

I'd never been so completely, thoroughly intoxicated by a kiss.

More. I needed more.

I slid my hands from his neck to grip the hem of his shirt and tugged.

"Georgia?" He questioned between kisses.

"I want you." The confession was a whisper, but I'd given it.

Offered my truth up on a silver platter for him to accept or reject.

"Are you sure?" His dark eyes studied mine with equal parts heat and concern, a slightly wild edge to him, as though his self-control was as tenuous as mine.

"I'm sure." I nodded, just in case the words weren't enough, and ran my tongue across my kiss-swollen lower lip as an unwelcome thought slid into my mind. "Do you want..." This had the potential to be up there with the most embarrassing moments of my life if I'd read the signals wrong.

"What do you think?" He pulled my hips into his, and I felt him hard between us.

"I'd say you do." *Thank you, God.*

"Just so there's no confusion, here." His fingers traced the line of my jaw. "I've wanted you from the first second I saw you in that bookstore. There's never been a moment I haven't wanted you." If his words hadn't melted me, the intensity in his eyes would have.

"Good." I grinned and tugged at his shirt again.

He reached behind his head and pulled his shirt off in one smooth motion, leaving him bare from the waist up.

My mouth went dry. Every line of his torso was carved, and the beautifully defined muscles covered by yards of soft, kissable, inked skin. This man was every single one of my fantasies come to life. I ran my fingers down the sculpted ridges of his chest and abdomen, my breath growing choppier with each inch I traveled, then catching at the sight of that deep vee that disappeared into his jeans.

When I finally brought my gaze back to his, the hunger I found there weakened my knees.

He captured my mouth in another kiss, stealing every logical thought with every thrust and swirl of his tongue against mine.

We broke apart only long enough for my shirt to land next to his, and then our mouths fused again, like it wasn't just a kiss but oxygen. My hands flew to the fly of his jeans.

He caught my hands. "We can take this slow." Even the rasp of his voice turned me on.

"Sure. Slow, later. Fast, here. Now." The urgency clawing its way through me wouldn't be satisfied with anything less than hot and hard.

The sound that escaped him reminded me of a growl before he sealed his mouth over mine and kissed me senseless. We were a tangle of hands and mouths, kicking off our shoes before Noah gripped my ass and lifted me like I weighed nothing.

My legs wrapped around his waist, and I locked my ankles at the small of his back as he carried me from the office, striding up the stairs without so much as getting winded. Tension radiated from his muscles as he walked us down the hall and into my bedroom, but his kiss never wavered.

I felt the bed under my back as Noah rose above me, his hands sliding under me to unclasp my bra. Then it, too, was on the floor, followed quickly by my jeans.

"Damn, you're beautiful," he said reverently, sitting back on his knees as he slid his fingers along my throat, down the valley between my breasts, and over my stomach to the thin straps of my underwear. My skin tingled in the wake of his touch.

I mentally gave myself a high-five that I'd gone with the pink lace thong this morning on a whim—then that was gone, too, the lacy fabric quickly replaced by his mouth.

"Noah!" I cried, fisting one hand in his hair as the other clutched at the covers to keep me grounded.

Holy shit, the man's tongue was *magical*. He worked me with sweeping strokes, quick flicks, and even the light scrape of his teeth, cradling my hips as I began to writhe beneath him. The pleasure was too intense, too consuming, too wild, and it only grew as he slid first one, then two fingers inside me. I clenched around him, my eyes slamming shut against the onslaught, my neck arching as he stroked me. It had never been like this for me. Ever. How had I lived without this desperate desire that was turning me molten? I didn't just want him, I *needed* him.

The fire he stoked gathered in my belly, coiling like a spring, winding tighter with every lick, every press of his fingers, until my thighs trembled and my muscles locked. Then he sucked my clit between his lips, and I shattered, the orgasm sweeping over me in long, powerful waves that had me screaming his name.

He pressed a kiss to my inner thigh, then rose over me with a satisfied smile—like *he'd* just had the orgasm of his life, not me. "I could spend days with you under my tongue and still want more."

That flame of need flared back to life, bright and hungry. "I need you." I threaded my fingers through his hair and pulled his mouth to mine, kissing him long and hard.

We separated only long enough for him to strip naked, and I blatantly ogled the lines of his ass as he slipped a condom from his wallet, dropping the leather to the pile of denim at his feet.

I sat up and took the packet from him, ripping it open and rolling it onto his length, stroking over him once before he groaned and captured my hands in his.

"Tell me you're sure." His words were clipped and low as his gaze locked with mine.

"I'm sure." I tugged lightly in his grip, urging him back to me.

He took the hint, sliding over me to rest in the cradle of my thighs. He kissed me deeply, learning my curves with long, caressing sweeps of his hands, lingering on my breasts and sweeping his thumbs over my nipples before teasing the dip of my waist and gripping my hips. "Incredible. That's the only word for you."

He stole any reply I could have made with a kiss, so I rocked my hips in answer, feeling him thick and hard at my entrance.

"Noah," I begged, gripping his shoulders.

He lifted his head slightly, keeping his eyes locked on mine as he rolled his hips, filling me inch by slow inch until I'd captured all of him, my body stretching with a slight burn that was more pleasure than pain.

"You okay?" he asked, a fine sheen of sweat making his skin glow in the soft light of the bedside lamp. Restraint was evident in every rigid muscle as he braced his weight on his elbows, watching me for any sign of discomfort.

"I'm perfect," I assured him, stroking his shoulders and circling my hips as the burn turned to bliss.

"That's exactly how you feel." He withdrew slightly, then thrust home with a groan. "God, Georgia. I'm never going to get enough of you."

"More."

He obliged. My toes curled as I whimpered, and I lifted my knees to take him deeper.

Then words became obsolete as our bodies took over, speaking for us in every way we needed. He took me slow and hard, driving into me in a ceaseless, aching rhythm that had me straining and arching beneath him, my nails biting into his skin as I gave myself over to the mind-blowing sensations he evoked.

As that pleasure gathered again, surprising me with its intensity, he adjusted his angle, sliding even deeper, rubbing over the most sensitive parts of me with every thrust, driving me higher and higher, until my body went rigid beneath his as I hovered on that precipice.

"Noah," I whispered, my body locking.

"Yes," he urged, swinging his hips faster.

I broke apart, calling his name as I came again, gripping him tight and taking him over with me as deeper, stronger swells raced through my body, consuming me—remaking me into something entirely new, entirely *his*.

"Georgia," he groaned into my neck, and I decided that was exactly how I wanted to hear him say my name from that moment on.

This...this was life. This was exactly how making love was supposed to feel, and I'd missed out on it up until now. I'd settled for so much less, not knowing that this kind of need had existed—

that Noah existed.

He rolled us sideways, holding me close as we recovered, our breaths as unsteady as our heartbeats, but those eyes of his were rock solid on mine, lit with the same joy coursing through my own veins.

"Wow," I managed to say between breaths, my fingers lightly skimming over his cheek and across the light rasp of his beard. How did this man just get better looking?

"Wow," he echoed, a grin shaping his lips.

My heart beat wildly, and yet I felt better than I had...ever. *Happy.* I was happy. Not that I was naive enough to think this would last forever. He didn't even live here. That silly glow throbbing in my heart was the result of two knee-melting orgasms, not... *Don't even think the word.* Liking Noah was one thing; falling for him was quite another.

But then my brain played back the sound of him groaning my name into my neck, and I was a goner, not just falling but plummeting into an emotion I wasn't ready to deal with, let alone name.

"The way I see it, we have two choices," he said, brushing my hair back with so much tenderness that a lump formed in my throat. "I can head back to my place..."

"Or?" I trailed a finger down his chest. I liked him just where he was.

"Or we ride out the snowstorm together right here in this bed." He brushed a tantalizing kiss over my lips.

"I'll take option number two," I answered with a smile. No matter where this eventually led, I had him for now, and I wasn't wasting another second.

CHAPTER TWENTY-TWO

December 1941

North Weald, England

"Right now would be great," Jameson said to her belly, down on his knees in front of her in full uniform. "Because right now, I'm here. And I know you want me to be here when you're born, right?"

Scarlett rolled her eyes but ran her fingers through Jameson's hair. Every day he had the same one-sided conversation with their baby—who was about a week overdue by the midwife's estimate.

"But once I leave, it's really hard to get back quickly," he explained, his hands soft on either side of her stomach. "So what do you say? You want to meet the world today?"

Scarlett watched the hope on Jameson's face fade to frustration and stifled a smile.

"She's definitely a girl," he said, looking up at her. "Stubborn like her mother." He pressed a kiss to her belly, then stood.

"He's a boy who loves to sleep in, just like his father," she argued, but looped her arms around Jameson's neck.

"I don't want to go today," he admitted quietly. "What if she's born and I'm not here?" He laced his fingers at the small of her back, which was no small task considering how she was currently shaped.

"You've said the same thing for the last month. There's no guarantee it will happen today, and if it does, then you'll come home to a son. It's not like someone will steal him if you're not in the house when he arrives." Jameson had gone so far as to demand he be in the room with her, but that certainly wasn't going to happen. Though she had to admit, the thought of having him with her was more than comforting.

"That's not even funny to joke about," he deadpanned.

"Go to work. We'll be here when you get back," she urged, hiding her very real fear that he was right. Jameson needed his full wits when flying. Anything less would get him killed. "I'm serious. Get going."

He sighed. "Okay. I love you."

"And I love you," she replied, her gaze skittering over his face just like it did every day, memorizing him...just in case.

He kissed her slowly, thoroughly, as if he wasn't already running late. As if he wasn't about to fly off into some yet-unknown battle, or perhaps escort bombers on a raid. He kissed her as if he would do it a thousand times again, with no hint that this might be their last.

It was the way he kissed her every morning—or night—before he left for the hangar.

She melted, her grip tightening on his neck as she pulled him closer, kissed him for just a minute longer. It was always one more minute with them. One more kiss. One more touch. One more lingering look.

They'd been married for a year now, and she was still utterly besotted with her husband.

"I wish you'd let me put in a phone," he said against her mouth, pulling out of the kiss.

"You're due to repost back to Martlesham-Heath in two weeks. Are you going to have that kind of extravagance in all of our homes?" She brushed her mouth over his.

"Maybe." He sighed but rose to his full height as he tangled his fingers in her hair, letting the strands pass through his fingers until they ended just under her collarbone. "Just remember the plan. Get to Mrs. Tuttle next door and she'll—"

Scarlett laughed, then pushed at his chest. "How about I worry about having the baby, and you go fly the airplane?"

His eyes narrowed. "Fair enough." He took his hat from the kitchen table, and Scarlett followed him to the front door, where he took his coat from the rack and put it on.

"Be safe," she demanded.

He swooped in for another kiss, this one hard, quick, and ending with a light nip of her lower lip. "Be pregnant when I get home...if that's anything you have a say over."

"I'll do my best. Now go." She motioned toward the door.

"I love you!" he called as he walked out.

"I love you!" Only after she'd said it did he close the door.

Scarlett rested a hand on her swollen belly. "Looks like it's just the two of us, love." She arched her back, hoping to relieve a touch of the endless ache at the base of her spine. She'd grown so large that even her maternity dresses barely fit, and she couldn't remember the last time she'd seen her feet.

"Shall we write a story today?" she asked her son as she settled behind the typewriter that had a permanent place at the kitchen table and elevated her feet on the nearest chair.

Then she stared at papers she'd begun storing in an old hatbox. Over the last three months, she'd started dozens of stories, but never seemed to make it past the first few chapters before something else popped into her head and she shifted gears for fear she'd forget that idea if she didn't jot it down.

The result was a hatbox full of possibilities, but not product.

Knock, knock, knock.

Scarlett groaned. She'd just gotten semi-comfortable—

"Scarlett?" Constance called from the front of the house.

"In the kitchen!" Scarlett called back, utterly relieved that she didn't have to get up.

"Hello there, little one!" Constance came around the table and hugged her.

"Hardly little," Scarlett argued as her sister took the chair next to her.

"What made you think I was talking to you?" She smiled and

leaned toward Scarlett's belly. "Have you considered joining us, yet?"

"You're as bad as Jameson," Scarlett muttered, arching her back again. How was the ache getting worse? "No watch today?"

"As luck would have it, I'm off." Her brow knit as she glanced back through the kitchen door. "I can't remember the last time I've had a Sunday off. I'm guessing Jameson can't say the same?"

"No. He left just a bit ago."

"What shall we do?" Constance drummed her fingertips on the kitchen table, and Scarlett did her best to look anywhere but the ring that sparkled on her fingertip. How ironic that something so glitteringly beautiful was the harbinger of so much destruction.

"As long as it involves me not moving, I'm all for it."

Constance smiled, then reached for the hatbox. "Tell me a story."

"Those aren't done!" Scarlett reached for the box, but Constance was too quick—or she was too slow.

"Since when have you ever told me a story that was already finished?" Constance scoffed, digging through the papers. "There must be at least twenty in here!"

"At least," Scarlett admitted, shifting in her seat again.

"Are you all right?" Constance asked, noting the strain on her sister's face with blatant concern.

"I'm fine. Just uncomfortable."

"I'll get you some tea." Constance pushed away from the table, then put the kettle on. "Were you thinking about finishing any of those stories?"

"Eventually." Scarlett leaned far enough to steal the hatbox back while Constance stood at the stove.

"Why not write one to the end, then start another?" She took tea out of the cabinet.

Scarlett had often asked herself the same thing. "I'm always afraid I'll forget an idea, and yet then I can't help but feel like I'm chasing butterflies, always thinking one is prettier, and never catching one because I can't commit to the single chase." She stared at the hatbox.

"There's no rush." Constance's voice softened. "You could always type up your ideas like a briefing summary so you don't lose them, then go back to the butterfly you've chosen to chase."

"That's an excellent idea." Scarlett's brows lifted. "Sometimes I wonder if I just enjoy the beginnings, and that's why I never seem to move past them. The beginnings are what make everything romantic."

"Not the whole falling in love part?" Constance teased, reclaiming her seat.

"Well, that too." She raised a shoulder. "But maybe it's really the possibilities that are easy to fall in love with. Looking at any situation, any relationship, any story, and having the sublime ability to wonder where it will take us is a bit intoxicating, really. There's a rush every time I load a blank sheet of paper. Like a first kiss from a first love."

Constance gave her engagement ring a quick glance before tucking it under the table in her lap. "So you'd rather keep loading the paper than finish it?"

"Perhaps." Scarlett rubbed at the spot just beneath her ribs where her baby often enjoyed testing the boundaries of her body. "I don't know if this baby is a boy or a girl. I think it's a boy, though I can't explain why. But in this moment, I can imagine a boy with Jameson's eyes and his reckless smile, or a girl with our blue eyes. Right now, I'm in love with both, basking in the possibilities. In a few days—at least I'm hoping it's a few days or I swear I'll explode—I'll know."

"And you don't want to know?" Constance arched an eyebrow.

"Of course I want to know. I will love my son or my daughter with all my heart. I already do. But while I've entertained both possibilities, only one is the truth. Once this baby is born, that part of the story is over. One of the scenarios I've spent the last six months imagining won't come true. That doesn't make the outcome any less sweet, but the truth is, when a story is finished, no matter what kind it is, the possibilities are gone. It is what it is, or it was whatever it was."

"So be kind to your characters and give them all a happy ending," Constance suggested. "That's better than anything they'd have in the real world."

Scarlett stared at the hatbox. "Perhaps the kindest thing I could do for the characters would be to leave their stories unfinished. Leave them with their possibilities, their potential, even if they only exist in my own mind."

"You leave the letter unopened," Constance said softly.

"Perhaps I do."

A sad smile curved Constance's mouth. "And in that world, perhaps Edward is actually on leave, sneaking up to Kirton-in-Lindsey to see me."

Scarlett nodded, her entire body tightening with nearly painful emotion.

The kettle whistled, and Constance rose to her feet. "It might be a bit difficult to get published that way," she said over her shoulder with a forced, teasing smile. "I think most people appreciate books with endings."

"I hadn't really thought as far as actually publishing anything." The ache in her back flared, reaching around to the front of her abdomen in a breath-stealing, vicious grip.

"You should. I've always loved listening to your stories. Everyone should get that chance."

Scarlett shifted her weight again as Constance made tea. "I think perhaps we should take that in the living room. This chair isn't agreeing with me."

"We can do that."

The sound of porcelain clicking filled the kitchen as Scarlett struggled to her feet. Little by little, the ache dissipated, and she managed her first full breath.

"Scarlett?" Constance questioned, the tray in her hands.

"I'm okay. Just a bit stiff."

Constance put the tray on the table. "Would you rather take a walk? Would that help?"

"No. I'm sure I just need to stretch my limbs here for a minute."

Constance glanced at the clock. "Why don't we ring for the midwife? Just to be sure."

Scarlett shook her head. "The nearest phone is three blocks away, and I'm fine." She was...until the ache returned and spread again, locking all the muscles of her abdomen.

"You are most certainly not fine."

Scarlett felt a pop, and then warmth gushed down her thighs. Her waters had broken. Fear unlike anything she'd ever known gripped her tighter than the contraction.

"I'll ring for the midwife." Constance took her elbow and guided her to the chair. "Sit. Don't try to walk until I can get you into bed."

"I want Jameson."

"Of course," Constance said in that soothing tone of hers as she made sure Scarlett was seated.

"Constance," Scarlett snapped, then paused until her sister looked her in the eye. "I. Want. Jameson."

"I'll ring the midwife, then the squadron, I promise. Midwife first, unless your husband developed some expertise on delivering a baby?"

Scarlett glared.

"Right. Sit. Don't move. For once in your life, let me be in charge." She ran out the door before Scarlett could argue.

Five minutes. Ten minutes. Scarlett watched the clock tick the minutes by as she waited for Constance.

The front door opened twelve minutes after she'd left.

"I'm here!" Constance called out from the living room just before Scarlett heard the door shut. Her sister wore a large, fake smile as she came through the kitchen door. "Good news. The midwife will pop by in just a bit. She said to get you upstairs into a clean bed."

"Jameson?" Scarlett asked through gritted teeth as another contraction took hold.

"How many contractions did you have while I was gone?" Constance asked, grabbing a few towels from a kitchen drawer and mopping up the mess she'd left.

"Two. This is the. Third." Scarlett fought through it with deep breaths, that pain only the tip of the iceberg. "Where. Is. Jameson?"

Constance threw the towels into the wash bin.

"Constance!"

"Somewhere over the North Sea."

"Of course he is," she said through gritted teeth. She should have told him to stay, but there'd been no reason to—no reason acceptable to the wing leader, at least.

"I won't leave your side," Constance promised as she helped Scarlett to her feet.

She didn't.

Nine hours later, Scarlett was tucked between newly cleaned sheets, absolutely knackered and happier than she'd ever been as she stared down at a pair of bright blue eyes.

"I don't care what those midwives said." Constance peered over her shoulder. "Those eyes are going to stay just that utterly, perfectly blue."

"Even if they don't, they'll still be perfect," Scarlett declared, running her finger across the tip of the smallest nose she'd ever seen.

"Agreed."

"Do you want to hold him?" Scarlett asked.

"May I?" Constance beamed.

"It seems only fair, seeing as you were equal parts nurse and maid today. Thank you." Her voice softened. "I couldn't have done it without you." She lifted her son, swaddled in one of the blankets Jameson's mother had made and shipped to them, into Constance's arms.

"I wouldn't have missed it," Constance said, adjusting the newborn in her arms. "He's perfect."

"We want you to be his godmother."

Constance's gaze snapped to hers. "Really?"

Scarlett nodded. "I can't imagine anyone else. You'll protect him, won't you? If anything...should happen." She was in just as much danger from a bombing raid sleeping in her bed as she was when she'd been in the WAAF. Nothing was certain.

"With my life." Constance's eyes misted over as she looked back at the baby in her arms. "Hello, little one. Hopefully your father will be home soon so we can call you by a real name." She shot Scarlett a pointed look.

Scarlett smiled. She'd refused to discuss his name until Jameson held him.

"I'm your Aunt Constance. I know, I know, I look a lot like your mummy, but she's at least a half-inch taller than I am, and her feet are a full size bigger. Don't worry, we'll come into focus a bit better once you're a few months older." She lowered her face. "Want to know a secret? I'm going to be your godmother. That means I'll love you, and spoil you, and always, always protect you. Even from your mummy's awful cooking."

Scarlett scoffed.

"Now, I'm going to go make something for her to eat." She smiled down at the baby one more time, then handed him back to Scarlett. "Do you need anything before I head downstairs?" She eased off the bed as the bedroom door flew open.

• • •

"Are you okay?" Jameson's strides ate up the distance to the bed as Constance slipped past him out of the bedroom. His heart hadn't stopped racing since he'd landed, or more specifically, since the clerk ran him down and told him Constance had called that morning.

That. Morning. No one had radioed—not that he could have gone off mission and flown back, but he would have. Somehow.

"I'm fine," Scarlett promised, smiling up at him with a mix of radiance and what he assumed had to be bone-weary exhaustion. She looked unharmed, but there was a lot of her he couldn't see under all those blankets. "Meet your son." Her smile widened as she lifted the small, blanketed bundle.

He sat on the edge of the bed and cradled the tiny, breakable baby in his arms, careful to support his head. His skin was pink, the shock of hair he could see was black, and his eyes were blue. He was gorgeous, and Jameson was instantly head over heels.

"Our son." Jameson looked at his wife to find her already watching him, her eyes heavy with unshed tears. "He's amazing."

"He is." She flashed a smile, and twin tears streaked down her face. "I'm so happy you're here."

"Me too." He leaned forward and brushed her tears away, careful to keep his son tucked safely in the crook of his arm. "I'm sorry I missed it."

"Only the messy bits," she countered. "It's only been an hour or so."

"And you're truly okay? How do you feel?"

"Tired. Happy. Like I've been torn in two. Madly in love." She leaned in slightly to gaze down at their son.

"Go back to the torn-in-two part," he demanded.

Scarlett laughed. "I'm fine. Really. Nothing abnormal."

"You'd tell me if something had gone wrong? If you were hurt?" Jameson studied her carefully, weighing her words with her eyes, her face, and the set of her shoulders.

"I would," she promised. "Though he'd be worth it."

Jameson's eyes fell to his son, who looked up at him with quiet expectation. *An old soul, then.* "What do you want to name him?" They'd been kicking around names for months.

"I like William."

Jameson smiled, glancing up at his wife and nodding. "Hi, William. Welcome to life. The first thing you need to know is that your mother is always right, which you probably already know, since she's been saying you were a boy for the last six months."

Scarlett laughed, but it was softer. Her eyelids were drooping, too.

"The second thing is I'm your dad, so it's a good thing you look a lot like your mom." He lowered his lips to William's head and pressed a soft kiss at his hairline. "I love you."

He leaned forward and brushed a kiss over Scarlett's mouth. "And I love you. Thank you for him."

"I love you, too, and I could say the same." Her breaths deepened, so Jameson placed their son in the small cradle next to the bed and tucked his wife in.

"Can I do anything?"

"Just stay," she whispered, fading off to sleep.

That first night was an eye-opener. William was up every few hours, and Jameson did what he could to help, but he couldn't exactly feed him.

They were already awake at seven a.m. when there was a knock on their bedroom door.

"Probably Constance," Scarlett muttered with William at her shoulder.

Jameson glanced back to make sure she was covered, then opened the door to find Constance standing in the hallway, blocking Howard.

"You can wait downstairs," she snapped.

"This can't wait."

"What's going on?" Jameson asked from the doorway.

Howard raked his hand through his hair and looked at

Jameson over the top of Constance's head. "I figured you hadn't turned on the news."

"No." His stomach tensed.

"The Japanese attacked Pearl Harbor. Thousands are dead. The fleet's gone," he said with a slight break in his voice.

"Holy shit." *Thousands are dead.* Jameson sagged against the doorframe. He'd dedicated the past two years of his life to keeping this war from reaching American soil, while another had sucker-punched them.

"Yeah. You know what that means?" Howard's jaw flexed.

Jameson nodded, looking back over his shoulder at Scarlett's horrified expression before facing his friend again. "We're on the wrong side of the world."

CHAPTER TWENTY-THREE

Noah

Scarlett,

How are you, my love? Are you as miserable as I am? I found us a house off-station. Now all that remains are your orders and we'll be together again. I'll wait forever for you, Scarlett. Forever...

My arms and back ached as I rolled my shoulders and neck behind the desk. The storm had dumped three feet of snow over the last two days, and it had taken me the better part of two hours to dig out Georgia's house. Could I have called the plow company? Absolutely, but winter in Colorado made my favorite workout—climbing—impossible, so I'd seen it as an opportunity. I'd also gravely underestimated the length of the driveway.

"Busy?" Georgia popped her head into the open office door, and I forgot every single sore muscle. "I don't want to interrupt your flow, but I didn't hear typing so I thought this might be an opportune moment for lunch." Her smile would have knocked me on my ass if I hadn't already been sitting.

"You can have whatever moments you want." I meant it, too. Whatever she wanted, she could have—including me.

"Well, it's not much, but I whipped up some grilled cheese." She opened the door with her hip, carrying a plate with two sandwiches, and a glass of what I knew was unsweetened iced tea.

"That sounds amazing, thank you." I took the coaster from the top drawer and had it on the desk before she reached me.

Funny how we'd both adapted so easily to the needs of the other over these last few weeks.

"You're very welcome. Thanks for digging us out." She put the plate to the side of my laptop, and the tea on the coaster as I wheeled the chair back a few inches.

"My pleasure." I gripped her hips and pulled her into my lap. God, it felt good to be able to do that—to touch her whenever I wanted. The last two days had cut us off from most of civilization and allowed us to do nothing but indulge in pleasing each other. This was my idea of heaven.

"This isn't going to help you get the book done." She smiled, looping her arms around my neck.

"No, but it's going to help me get my hands on you." I slid one hand up the nape of her neck and into her hair, then kissed her until we were both breathless. My need for her hadn't been sated; if anything, it had only grown. I was completely and totally out of my depth with her, with everything I wanted to happen between us.

The first time I'd seen her, I'd known, and every time I kissed her, it only became more apparent—she was it for me. The one. The endgame. It didn't matter that we lived a thousand miles apart or that she was still healing from her divorce. I'd wait. I'd prove myself. I'd do exactly as I promised and win her over, not just her body, but her heart.

Her tongue danced with mine, and she groaned softly when I sucked it into my mouth. We weren't just well-matched in bed, we were combustible, constantly catching fire for the other. For the first time in my life, I knew I was never going to get enough. This was something incapable of burnout.

"Noah," she whimpered, and my body was *there*, ready. I was hers to do with as she pleased, knowing it would sure as hell please me at the same time. "You're killing me."

"It's a pretty sweet way to go." I moved my lips down her neck, running my tongue over the sensitive lines and inhaling the scent of bergamot and citrus. She always smelled so damned good.

She sighed, rolling her head back, and I kissed the hollow of her throat.

"What are we doing?" she asked, her fingers gripping the back of my neck.

"Whatever we want," I answered against her skin.

"I'm serious," she whispered.

That got my attention. I lifted my head and drew back slightly, studying her expression. Half of what Georgia said never came out of her mouth. It was in her eyes, the set of her mouth, the tension in her shoulders. It might have taken me a few months to learn her cues, but I was catching on, and she was worried.

"We're doing whatever we want," I repeated, shifting my hands to her waist, and ignoring the nearly painful throbbing just beneath my belt.

"You live in New York."

"I do." It wasn't something I could deny. "You used to." My tone softened, the hope I usually kept to myself sneaking in that last bit.

"Never again." She dropped her gaze. "I went for Damian. I was never happy there. You, on the other hand, love it."

"I do. It's home." Or was it? Could it be my home if Georgia wasn't there? If I had to leave her in these mountains she loved?

"Your family's there." She stroked her knuckles down my cheek. It had been over a week since I'd shaved, and my stubble had moved into beard territory.

"They are."

She swallowed, her eyebrows knitting.

"Tell me what you're thinking, Georgia. Don't make me guess." My grip tightened on her slightly, as if I could keep her from slipping away.

Still, she stayed silent, her turbulent thoughts manifesting in the subtle tightening of her jaw.

Maybe she needs you to go first. Right. Time to tell her just how deep I was in this, how willing I was to make it work, and how unwilling I was to let her go.

"Look, Georgia, I'm wild about—"

"I think we should just call this what it really is," she blurted.

We spoke at the same time, her words halting mine.

"And what is it?" I asked slowly.

"A fling." She nodded.

My jaw snapped shut, my teeth clicking with the force. *A fling?* What the hell? I'd had my share of flings. This was *not* one of them.

"We're attracted to each other, working in close quarters... It was bound to happen, and don't get me wrong. I'm glad it did." She lifted her brows and her cheeks pinkened. "Really, really glad it did."

"Me too..."

"Good. I'd hate to feel like this was all one-sided," she muttered.

"Trust me, it's not." And if it was, I was the one on the heavily invested side, which was a first.

"Okay, then. Let's keep it simple. I'm not ready for anything big. I can't just jump from one serious relationship right to the next. That's not who I want to be." Her nose crinkled. "Even if I did just dive from Damian's bed to yours—which is much better, by the way. Everything about you is better." Her gaze skimmed my face. "So much better it's scary."

"You don't have to be scared." I didn't bother pointing out that it had been over a year since she'd been in Ellsworth's bed, because that wasn't what this was about, not really. *Her mother.* She didn't want to be her mother. "We can keep this as simple as you need."

In that second, staring into those crystal blue eyes, I realized I was head over fucking heels in love with Georgia Stanton. Her mind, her compassion, her strength, her grace and grit—I loved everything about her. But I also knew she wasn't ready for my love.

"Simple," she repeated, shifting in my lap but clinging to my shoulders as a tentative smile lifted the corners of her mouth. "Simple is good."

"Simple it is." *For now.* What I needed was time.

"Okay. Good. Then we agree." She pressed a quick kiss to my lips, then slid off my lap. "Oh, you were asking about the original manuscript for *The Diplomat's Daughter*, right?"

"Right." I nodded, feeling more than a little off-balance. We'd agreed that this would be simple? Or was there more inferred?

"I pulled it out of the upstairs closet," she said, taking a shirt box from off the office bookshelves and putting it on an empty patch of desk. "She has all her originals up there."

"Thank you." I knew what she was trusting me with, and on any other day I would have been ecstatic to dig further into the oddest literary puzzle I'd ever stumbled onto, but my head wasn't quite in the game.

"I have a phone call with the lawyers to finalize Gran's foundation in a few minutes, so I'll leave you to it." She came around the desk and kissed me, quick and hard, before walking toward the door.

"Georgia?" I called out just before she reached the foyer.

"Hmm?" She turned and lifted her brows, so damned beautiful that my heart actually ached.

"What exactly did we just agree to?" I asked. "Between us?"

"A book-writing fling," she answered with a smile, like it was obvious. "Simple, no strings, and over when you finish the book." She shrugged. "Right?"

Over when the book was finished.

My hands curled into fists over the arms of the chair. "Sure. Right."

Her phone rang, and she tugged the device from her back pocket. "See you when you hit your word count." She flashed me a smile, answered the call, and closed the door all in one smooth motion.

Now our relationship was on the same deadline as the book, and sure, I'd always planned on leaving after I finished, but being with Georgia had changed things...at least for me.

Shit. The one thing I needed to win her over was time, and I was closer to finishing than she knew. Closer than I was willing to admit.

I finished the book—both versions—four weeks later. Then I sat in the office and stared at two files on my desktop.

My time was up.

My deadline was the day after tomorrow.

I'd done it, somehow satisfying both Georgia's requirement and nailing mine, while keeping my contracted dates, and yet there was no feeling of pride or accomplishment, just sheer terror that I wouldn't be able to hold on to the woman I'd fallen for.

I'd only had four weeks, and it wasn't enough. Georgia was opening up, but the parts of her I needed to trust me were still boarded up tight. We were still a fling to her. Just when I thought she might change her mind, she'd mention making the best of what time we had, and now that time was over.

My phone rang and I answered it on speakerphone. "Hey, Adrienne."

"So you're not coming home for Christmas?" my sister asked, more than a little judgment in her tone.

"That is a complicated question." I closed my laptop and pushed it to the far side of the desk. I'd deal with my existential crisis later.

"It's really not. You're either going to be in New York on December twenty-fifth, or you're not."

"I'm not sure yet." I stood and arranged four of the shirt boxes

I'd borrowed on the desk in front of me, then opened and nestled each of them inside their own lids. I was missing something here. Something right in front of me that was driving me up a wall. The manuscripts were from different points in Scarlett's career. Her edited, published works were smoother, of course, but I couldn't help but be fascinated by the stylistic differences between her earlier works and the later ones, couldn't help but wonder if losing Jameson hadn't just broken her heart, but changed her fundamentally.

Couldn't help but wonder if the same would happen to me if I lost Georgia.

"It's only three weeks away."

"Three weeks and—" I did the mental math. "Four days."

"Exactly. You don't think you'll have the book done by then?"

My jaw flexed at the thought of lying to my sister. To anyone, really. "It's not about the book."

"It's not? Wait, am I on speaker? Where's Georgia?"

I laughed softly. "Which question would you like me to answer first?"

"The last one."

"She's in town, working at her studio." Georgia had been a sight to behold this last month. She worked tirelessly, overseeing the construction in the front end of the studio, and completing pieces she wouldn't let me see—wouldn't let anyone see. She'd set the opening date for her birthday, January twentieth, and I wasn't even sure I'd be here to see it, which was a swift kick to the gut.

"Nice. I bet she's loving life out of the tabloids."

"She is." Which was just another reason she didn't want to go back to New York.

"She hasn't frosted you out yet?" There was a teasing lilt to my sister's voice, and it wasn't like she wasn't aware of the rocky ground Georgia and I had started on.

"You should fly out here and meet her. She's opening the studio next month with a party. She's nothing like what you read in the gossip rags, Adrienne." I sighed, shoving my hands through my hair, then taking the phone with me as I started to pace along the bookshelves. "She's kind, smart, funny as hell, driven to help whoever she can. She's never content to sit idle, she's great with her best friend's kids, and she has no problem putting me in my place, which I know you appreciate." I glanced from picture to picture that lined Scarlett's shelves, pausing on the photo album Georgia had left out. "She's..." I couldn't even put her into words.

"Holy shit, Noah. You're in love with her, aren't you?"

"She's not ready for anything like that," I said softly, flipping through the album.

"You are!" She damn near squealed in excitement.

"Drop it." The last thing I needed was her filling Mom's head.

Adrienne scoffed. "Yeah right. Have you *met* me?"

"Fair point." I rubbed the skin between my eyebrows. "The second I leave here, it's over, and I don't want it to be, but Ellsworth scarred the shit out of her."

"So don't leave," Adrienne stated like it was the simplest answer.

"Yeah, if it were only that easy. She said it herself: this is a book-writing fling. Once the book is finished, so are we." And it was done, just waiting to be attached in an email to Adam.

"Okay, so don't finish the book?" she suggested, her voice pitching upward.

"Helpful." I flipped to the wedding pictures and covered Ellsworth with my hand so only Georgia smiled out at me, then peered closer. She was happy, but that smile wasn't as bright as the ones I'd been gifted with.

"I'm serious. Stay. Push your deadline back for once in your life. I'll bring Mom here for Christmas, you can call in. Trust me, if this gets you married and settled—"

"Adrienne," I warned.

"Eventually," she amended. "Mom will be all about it. We both just want you to be happy, Noah. If Georgia Stanton makes you happy, then fight for it. Fight for her. Pretend you're one of your own characters and help her fix whatever Ellsworth broke."

"Are you done with your inspirational speech?" I teased half-heartedly.

"Do you need me to launch into the rarity of finding someone to truly love?"

"God, no." I glanced back at the laptop. "Don't count on me for Christmas. But I love you."

"I love you, and I'll forgive you for missing out if you give me a sister-in-law!"

"Bye, Adrienne." I hung up, shaking my head and scoffing. If it were that easy to heal Georgia, I would have done it already.

I lifted my hand and stared down at Georgia's wedding picture, hearing her words from that day play like a soundtrack. *There's a warning, a sound your heart makes the first time it realizes it's no longer safe with the person you trusted.*

It all came down to trust with Georgia. Ellsworth had broken hers so completely that she didn't have any left. But she'd given me Scarlett's story. She'd climbed the wall. She'd opened her home. She'd unabashedly offered her body without reservation. She trusted me with everything but her heart, because she'd been left, abandoned—

The first time...

"Oh, shit," I muttered as it hit me. *I never said he did.*

I flew back through the album as her words hit home in a way they hadn't when she'd said them. I passed her high school graduation, the birthday Ava had reappeared, and slowed when I'd backtracked as far as her first day of kindergarten.

The pictures just before showed Georgia living with Ava, her eyes bright, her smile a younger version of the dazzling one she gave me these days. *Real love has to be choked out, held under the water until it stops kicking.* And that's exactly what the pictures showed year after year. The slow drowning of love.

It wasn't Ellsworth who had broken Georgia—it was Ava.

Ava, who had disappeared, then shown up whenever it suited

her.

Whenever she needed something.

"If this were a book, what would you do?" I asked myself, flipping through the pages and landing on that twelfth birthday picture. "You'd use the past to heal the present."

The studio opening—I could fly Ava in. *If you're still here in seven weeks.* Georgia had already given her everything she wanted, and without ulterior motive... It could work. I could slowly start to repair the canyons Ava had left in Georgia, if I started with the cracks. I just had to make sure Ava wanted to be there for Georgia's happiness alone.

I slammed the album shut, then took my seat at the desk, parted the boxes of manuscripts to pull my laptop in front of me, and opened it. How the hell was I going to convince her to let me stay another seven weeks?

I shot a healthy heaping of side-eye at the picture of Jameson and Scarlett that sat on the left side of the desk. "Any advice?" I asked him. "It's not like I can fly her off into the sunset, and let's be honest, you had a hell of a wingman in Constance." It also hadn't hurt that the pair had lived during a time where being reckless was a wise use of whatever time you had left.

I drummed my fingers on the desk, staring at the two finished files on my desktop.

If Jameson had won Scarlett by bending the rules...maybe the same would work to win his great-granddaughter.

I pulled out my phone and called Adam.

"Please tell me you're about to send me the finished manuscript."

"Well, hello to you, too," I drawled. "I'm still two days early."

"You know the print deadline on this is tighter than my mother-in-law's Spanx." I heard his chair creak.

"Yeah, about that..." I cringed.

"Do not tell me that for the first time in your career, you're going to blow a deadline. Not on *this* book. Do you know how

hard it's going to be to edit it? To constantly question if I'm
messing with Scarlett-freaking-Stanton?" His voice pitched
upward.

"You sound stressed. Have you been for a run since I left?"

"You're the reason my blood pressure is high in the first place."

And I was about to ask him to raise it even higher, all so I
had a shot at winning Georgia. What kind of selfish prick did
that to his best friend? *You, apparently.*

"Noah, what's going on?" Adam's tone gentled.

"On a scale of one to ten, how good of friends would you say
we are? Because I'd probably go with—"

"You were the best man at my wedding. You're my best
friend. Now, are you talking to me as your editor? Or as my
kid's godfather?"

"Both."

"Shit." I could picture him rubbing his temples. "What do
you need?"

"Time."

"You don't have it."

"Not mine. Yours. How do you feel about doing twice the
work without twice the pay?" I held my breath, waiting for his
answer.

"Explain."

So I did. I laid it all out to the one person who had served
as a linchpin in both my personal and professional life, barely
finishing by the time I heard the garage door open. Georgia
was home.

"Georgia's back. Will you do it?"

"Damn it," he muttered. "Yes, you know I'll do it."

"Thank you." Every muscle in my body sagged with relief.

"Don't thank me," he barked through the speakerphone. "I'll
get started on what's already there, but you owe me an ending,
Noah."

The office door opened, and Georgia slipped her head in.

"Bad time?" she whispered.

I shook my head, motioning for her to come in. "I know it's a pain in the ass, but I promised."

"Okay, but we're going to run tight with the printers. You have the time you need, but you'd better be prepared for some rushed edits."

Georgia's brow puckered in concern as she unbuttoned her coat.

"I can handle it." I'd handle anything that got me the time I needed with Georgia.

"You'd better. Oh, and Carmen told me to let you know that the kid's Hanukkah presents got here. You know you didn't have to do that, but thank you. We'll miss you for the holidays, Noah."

"Just keep running, Adam. I'd hate to leave you in the dust when I get back." *If I get back.* We hung up and I pulled Georgia into my lap, sliding my hands beneath her coat and sweater to the warmth of her skin.

"What was that about?" she asked, brushing my hair out of my eyes.

God, I loved this woman.

"Time," I answered, kissing her softly. Now all I could do was pray that mortgaging my career had bought me enough.

Her eyes flew wide. "Oh God, your deadline. It's this week, isn't it? Is the book done?" Was that a hint of panic in her voice? Or was I just hearing what I wanted to?

"Not yet." It wasn't, at least that's what I told myself to steal a little more time with her. Sure, it was written, but it wouldn't be *done* until it was through edits. "Don't worry. It's just delivery. Adam's juggling a few things on the calendar and starting with what we have so we don't blow the print deadline while I'm getting these endings just right. Think you can stand having me around for a little bit longer?" *Semantics,* but it still felt like a lie.

Because it was.

But the smile she gave me? Absolutely worth it.

CHAPTER TWENTY-FOUR

January 1942

North Weald, England

Scarlett glanced between the small gift box on the table, her typewriter, and the dishes that lay piled in the sink. She hadn't had a spare moment since breakfast. William had fussed all morning, and was finally down for an afternoon nap, which hopefully gave her at least forty-five minutes to get something done…but all she'd wanted to do was nap right next to him.

The days blurred together with the nights, which one of the other wives had told her was normal when caring for a newborn. She was so tired that she'd fallen asleep sitting at the dinner table last night.

And speaking of dinner…

She sighed, mentally sending an apology to her hatbox of stories as she made her way to the sink, blatantly ignoring the gift box addressed in her mother's handwriting. This was her third kitchen in the past year, and though she appreciated the sizeable yet frozen garden just beyond the kitchen window, she wished it had come with a view of Constance.

They'd been at Martlesham-Heath for over a month now, and she'd only seen her sister twice. It was the longest they'd been apart since Constance's birth. She missed her immeasurably, and while they were only an hour apart in distance, they were years apart when it came to this new stage of life.

Constance was still billeted with the other women, still taking her watches, eating in the officers' mess—and planning a wedding.

Scarlett's closest confidant was now a six-week-old baby who wasn't much for conversation. She really was going to have to get out and make some friends.

She was pleasantly surprised when the house was still quiet after she finished the dishes.

A quick listen told her William hadn't woken—she might just have a few minutes.

It felt rather indulgent, but she slid behind her typewriter anyway. It took her a matter of seconds to load the first crisp piece of blank paper. She stared at it for a moment, contemplating what it would become, what story it would hold.

Perhaps she should do as Constance suggested, and finish something. Maybe publish it.

That hatbox was already half full with semi-formed plots, snippets of dialogue, and ideas that needed execution. It contained stories she should write for other people, endings she could twist and sweeten to make other people happy. Endings like the one Constance should have been given.

Endings like the one she wanted for herself and Jameson and William, but couldn't guarantee. She couldn't even guarantee that there wouldn't be a bombing raid tonight—that she wouldn't be among those counted as casualties.

But she could leave as much of their story for William as possible...just in case.

She started on that hot day in Middle Wallop when Mary forgot to pick them up at the train station. She remembered everything she could, writing even the smallest details about the moment she met Jameson. A smile stretched across her face. If only she could go back and tell herself then where they would end up...she never would've believed it. She wasn't sure she even believed now. Theirs had been a whirlwind romance that settled into a passionate, sometimes complicated marriage.

Jameson hadn't changed much in the last eighteen months... but she had. The woman who had made quick decisions at the planning board, who had been a rock-solid, valuable officer in the WAAF, was now...none of that, really. She was no longer responsible for the lives of hundreds of pilots, only William, not that she was alone in that, either.

When he was home, Jameson was a hands-on father. He held William, rocked him, change nappies—there wasn't anything Jameson wouldn't do for William, which only made her love him more. Becoming parents hadn't stripped them of their personalities, it had given new, deeper facets to them both.

She wrote as far as Jameson asking for their first date before William woke with shrill demand. Hearing that first cry, she removed the paper from the typewriter and put it into the hatbox, adding to the stack she'd been careful to leave on top so it wouldn't get mixed in with the rest. Then she put it away and went to fetch her littlest love.

Hours later, William had been fed, changed, cleaned up and changed again, fed once more, mopped up after another spit up, then fed one last time and burped before he was back to sleep.

She headed into the kitchen to contemplate dinner, pulling out fish to fry, and as though right on cue, Jameson walked in the front door.

"Scarlett?"

"In the kitchen!" The relief was a jolt of energy through her system, just like it was every time he came home to her.

"Hey." His footsteps were soft, but his mood filled the room like a thundercloud, dark and ominous.

"What's the matter?" she asked, abandoning the fish she'd planned on frying.

He strode across the kitchen, took her face in his hands, and kissed her. It was soft, which, considering his mood, only made it that much sweeter. He was always careful with her. Their lips moved together in a soft dance that quickly deepened, intensified. It had been six weeks since William's birth. Six weeks since her husband had shared her body, and not just her bed. According to the midwife, six weeks was long enough, and Scarlett couldn't agree more.

Jameson lifted his head slowly, keeping a tight leash on his self-control. She was so damn beautiful, it was nearly impossible to keep his hands off her. Her curves were lush, her hips grabbable, and her breasts full and heavy—she was every fantasy, every pinup painted on a plane, and she was *his*.

He knew she needed time to heal, and he would never push her to heal faster. He wasn't that big of a bastard. But he missed her body, missed the feel of sliding inside her, the way the rest of the world faded until it was just the two of them, straining together. He craved her taste on his tongue, the way her hips ground against his mouth, the silk of her hair sliding over his face from above as she kissed him when she took the lead. He longed for that little catch in her throat before she came, missed the way her eyes glazed over, her breath caught, her muscles locked, the sound of his name on her lips when she finally let go. He missed the sweet oblivion he found in her body, but mostly he craved just a few moments of her undivided attention.

He wasn't jealous of his son, but he could admit the transition had a few bumps and growing pains. "I missed you today," he said, cradling her cheeks in his hands and sweeping his thumbs across the soft skin.

"I miss you every day," she replied with a smile. "But I saw the look on your face when you came in. Tell me what happened."

His jaw tightened. "Where's William?" he dodged, noting that his little man wasn't in the bassinet.

"Sleeping upstairs." She tilted her head. "Tell me, Jameson."

"We've been denied permission to leave for the Pacific front," he admitted quietly.

Scarlett's spine stiffened against the counter, and he instantly regretted the words.

"You asked permission to go to the Pacific front?" Scarlett asked, stricken and sidestepping out of his reach.

"The squadron did. But I was in favor of it." His arms immediately felt empty. "Our country has been attacked, and we're all the way over here. It was only right that we ask. Only right that if we're needed, we go." It had been a highly contentious debate within the squadron, but the overwhelming majority had demanded they send the request for transfer.

Her chin rose, which meant he was in for a fight. "And at what point were you going to discuss the suggestion with me?" she asked, folding her arms under her breasts.

"When it was deemed a possibility," he replied, "or now that it's not."

"Wrong answer." Fire shone in her eyes.

"I can't just sit here while my country goes to war." He backed away from her, leaning against the kitchen table and clenching the edge.

"You are not just *sitting here*," she fired back. "How many missions have you flown? How many patrols? How many bomber intercepts? You're already an ace. How would you call that just *sitting here*? And the last time I checked, your country was also at war with Germany. You're already where you need to be."

He shook his head. "Who knows how long it will take for American soldiers to arrive? For America to do anything about the German threat? I joined the RAF to keep war from my door, to keep my family safe, to stop it here before it was my country being bombed or my mother becoming another casualty on the report. I came here to guard my home against the wolves, and while I was busy watching the front door, the wolves snuck in the back."

"And that is not your fault!" she snapped.

"I know that. No one saw Pearl Harbor coming, but it happened, and it doesn't change the fact that I might be needed there. If there are plans, I want to be a part of them. I can't risk my life defending your country and not do the same for my own. Don't ask that of me." Every muscle in his body tensed, waiting, hoping she'd understand.

"Apparently I don't get to ask anything at all, since you knew the 71st sent the request without so much as telling me." Her voice pitched higher, breaking. "I thought we were partners."

"William had just been born, and you had so much on your plate—"

"That you didn't want to bother me?" Her eyes narrowed. "Because I have such a poor track record of handling stress?"

He rubbed his hand over his face, wishing he could take back every word since he'd walked in the door—or go back to a few weeks ago and talk this all out with her. "I should have told you."

"Yes. You should have. Did you stop to think about what we'd do here if you were sent to the Pacific?" She gestured to the room above them, where William slept.

"They bombed Americans!"

"And you think I don't know what it feels like to have my country torn to bits by bombs?" She tapped her chest. "To watch my childhood friends die?"

"That's why I thought you'd understand. When England went to war, you put on a uniform and fought because you love *your* country just as much as I love mine."

"I don't have a country!" she shouted, then spun to face the window.

He saw her face crumple in the reflection of the window, and his stomach sank. *Shit.* "Scarlett—"

"I don't have a country," she said softly, turning to face him, "because I gave it up for you. I loved you more. I'm not British. I'm not American. I'm only a citizen of this marriage, which I thought was a democracy. So pardon my surprise when it turns out to be a dictatorship. Benevolent, yes, but a dictatorship nonetheless. I didn't fight free of my father's control to have you step into his shoes." She scoffed and gave him a sarcastic, bitter smile.

"Honey..." He shook his head, searching for something he could say to make this better.

"It's not just you anymore, Jameson. It's not even just *us*. You can be as reckless as you want when you're in the cockpit—I know who I married. But there's a little boy upstairs who doesn't know there's a war going on, let alone that it now spans the globe. We're responsible for *him*. And I understand wanting to fight for your country—I gave that up for us, too. Please don't treat me as less than equal because I chose this family *twice*. If you wanted a wife who would do nothing more than cook your meals, warm your bed, and have your babies, then you chose the wrong woman. Do not mistake my sacrifices for smiling compliance. Also, since I *don't* keep secrets, William received a gift today." She motioned to a small box on the table, then walked out of the kitchen, passing him without another glance, and a few seconds later he heard her footsteps on the stairs.

Jameson rubbed the bridge of his nose and scraped his ego off the floor, where Scarlett had crushed it beneath her foot. He'd been trying to protect her, to ease her, to keep yet another worry from her shoulders, and in doing so, he'd cut her out entirely. From the moment he'd met her, he'd stripped away little pieces of her. It didn't matter if that had never been his intention—the result was the same.

She'd transferred for him, left her first station where she'd had friends. She'd hauled her sister along so she could keep the vow she'd made to Constance, too. She'd married him, lost her British citizenship for it, then had to pull family strings once again to be reposted when he was so she could follow him. When she'd fallen pregnant, she'd given up the work she loved—the work she'd based her worth on—and after she'd delivered, they'd been reposted again, and she'd lost daily contact with Constance...

with anyone outside this house, really.

She'd given everything, and he hadn't protested because he loved her too much to let her go.

He glanced at the small box that rested near his right hand, then picked it up, plucking the note from the top.

My darling Scarlett,

Congratulations on the birth of your son. We were so very pleased to hear the news.

Please give him this token of our affection and know that we cannot wait to meet the newest Wright.

Love,

Mother

Jameson shook his head in disgust, then looked into the box. A small silver rattle rested on a bed of velvet. He lifted the ridiculous toy to see the engraving that etched the handle. A large *W* was flanked by another *W* and a *V*.

Jameson dropped the rattle back in its box before he did something *reckless* and torched the damned thing.

His son's name was William Vernon *Stanton*. He wasn't a Wright. They weren't allowed to claim any part of him.

He pushed off the table and draped his jacket over one of the chairs, then loosened his tie as he walked up the stairs. Light shone from beneath their bedroom door, but not William's. Jameson pressed his ear to the door, and when he heard the soft rustling and one disgruntled protest, he went in and leaned over the small crib.

William looked up at him, tightly swaddled in the blanket his grandmother had sent from Colorado, and let loose a jaw-cracking yawn, then furrowed his brow.

"Yeah, I know what that means," Jameson said softly, picking up his son and cradling him against his chest. How ironic that someone so very small had altered the gravity in his world. He pressed a kiss to the top of his head, breathing in his scent. "Did you have a good day?"

William grunted, then opened his mouth against Jameson's shirt.

"I'll take that as a yes." He rubbed small circles on William's back, knowing that he didn't have what he was looking for. "You might want to give her just a minute, kid. I hurt her feelings pretty badly."

He swayed from side to side, trying to not only give Scarlett a few minutes alone but buy himself precious time to think of what he could do or say. Did he want to leave them here, in a country they weren't legally entitled to, knowing they couldn't get into the one they *were*, while he flew halfway around the world to face another enemy?

No.

The thought of leaving them behind was a knife to the gut. William was only six weeks old, and he'd already changed so much. He couldn't imagine not seeing him grow up, leaving for a year—or more—and not recognizing his own son when he returned. And the thought of not seeing Scarlett? Unbearable.

"I'll take him," she said from the doorway.

Jameson turned to see her backlit against the hallway light, her arms already outstretched. "I like holding him," he said softly.

Some of the ice melted in her eyes. "I would hope so, but unless you can feed him, you're not going to like holding him for much longer." She crossed the room, and Jameson reluctantly surrendered their son.

Scarlett settled into the rocking chair in the dimly lit corner, then looked up at him expectantly. "You don't have to stay."

He leaned against the wall and crossed his ankles. "I don't have to leave, either. I've seen your breasts before. Not sure I've told you lately how magnificent they are."

She rolled her eyes, but he could have sworn he saw color rise faintly in her cheeks. She settled their son to nurse with what had become practiced ease, and stroked his soft, black hair with her fingertips.

"I'm sorry," Jameson said quietly.

Her fingers stilled.

"I should have talked it over with you while it was happening. I can make all the excuses in the world about not wanting to worry you, but they don't matter. I was wrong to leave you in the dark."

She slowly brought her gaze to meet his.

"If we had gone to the Pacific, I would have moved heaven and earth to send you to Colorado until I could come home. I would never have left you without making sure you were safe, and not just physically. I won't make the mistake of leaving you out again."

"Thank you."

"I would…" He swallowed the prickly knot of anger rising in his throat. "I would really like to throw that rattle in the trash."

"All right."

His eyebrows rose. "You don't care?"

"Not in the least. I would have put it with the rubbish myself, except I wanted you to know what was happening." There was no jab in the statement, just facts.

"Thank you." He watched her silently for a moment, choosing his next words carefully. "Your visa appointment is coming up in a few months, right?"

She nodded. "May." Almost a year after they'd begun the process.

"I want you to promise me something," he said softly.

"What?"

"Promise me that if anything happens to me, you'll take him to the States."

She blinked. "Don't say things like that."

He crossed the room, then dropped to her eye level, putting his hands on the arm of the rocking chair. "There is nothing more important to me than your lives—yours and William's. Nothing. You're right—it's not just about us anymore. You'll be safe in

Colorado. Safe from the war, from poverty, from your god-awful parents. So please, promise me that you'll take him."

Her brow knit as she considered the request. "If something happens to you," she clarified.

He nodded.

"Okay. I promise if anything happens to you, I'll take William to Colorado."

He leaned in slowly and brushed a chaste kiss over her lips. "Thank you."

"That doesn't mean I'm giving you permission to die." Her gaze turned stern.

"Noted." He kissed William's head, then rose. "Since you're feeding him, I'm going to go work on feeding you. I love you, Scarlett."

"I love you, too."

He left his wife and son in the nursery and went straight to the kitchen...and threw the rattle in the trash where it belonged.

Scarlett and William were Stantons.

They were his.

CHAPTER TWENTY-FIVE

Georgia

Dear Jameson,

You've only been gone a few days, and yet I miss you as if it's been years. This is so much harder than when we were at Middle Wallop. Now, I know what it's like to be your wife. To lie beside you at night and wake to your smile in the morning. I asked again this morning about the transfer request, but so far there is no news. Hopefully tomorrow. I can't bear being so far from you, knowing that you fly into danger and I can do nothing but sit here and wait. I can't even welcome you home. I love you, Jameson. Stay safe. Our fates are intertwined, for I cannot exist in a world where you do not.

Love,
Scarlett

"Are you ready for this?" Noah asked with an excited smile, straightening his tie as we sat parked in front of the studio, the January snow flurrying by.

"If I'm not?" My eyebrows arched.

"It will be awkward in an hour when everyone shows up, but we can lock the door, turn off the lights, and pretend we're not here." He lifted my hand and kissed the inside of my wrist, sending a jolt of need straight through me. I'd had him in my bed nearly every night for the past two and a half months, and the need hadn't lessened. All he had to do was look at me, and I was ready for him. "But I am willing to offer any bribe you want just to see what you've been creating in there."

"I am pretty proud of my little collection." I'd just about worked my fingers off getting ready for this night. There were a few dozen minor pieces ready for sale, and a few larger ones I'd mostly made for display. Invitations had gone out, replies received, and now all I could do was open the doors and pray I hadn't wasted what was left of my bank account.

"I'm proud of *you*." This time he kissed my lips, sucking lightly on the lower one before releasing it. I was completely and thoroughly addicted to this man. It was only supposed to be a fling—that was the deal. He'd leave as soon as the book was finished, and watching the days tick by only served to remind me that we were living on borrowed time. Every day I expected him to tell me it was done, but it wasn't. Pretty soon he'd be flirting with missing the print deadline if he wasn't careful. "I know tonight is going to be just as amazing as you are."

"Glad one of us is certain." I sucked in a breath and reminded myself that this was Poplar Grove, Colorado, not New York City. There were no paparazzi, no movie stars or execs, no gossip columnists, and no one who feigned interest in me just to get five minutes with Damian. This was mine—only mine—and Noah was going to be the first person I shared it with.

He held my hand as we walked to the door, then blocked the wind as I fumbled with my key to get the heavy glass open. Then I led him inside the dark space.

"Wait right here. Close your eyes." I wanted to see his face when the lights came on.

"You'd think it was my birthday and not yours," he teased.

I laughed, then walked to the light switch once I was certain his eyes were well and truly closed. The space was as familiar to me as my bedroom by now. I could find my way blindfolded if I needed to.

I flipped the switch, and the gallery lit up in a dozen places. There were vases and small sculptures lining the glass shelves on the walls, two bigger tower pieces in each bay window, and in the center, on a pedestal highlighted with its own lighting, sat my favorite piece.

"You can open your eyes," I said softly, then held my breath as Noah's dark gaze swept over the gallery in appreciation, his smile wide as he took it all in, then fixed on the pedestal.

"Georgia," he whispered with a shake of his head. "My God."

"Do you like it?" I slid in to his side, and he tucked his arm around my waist, pulling me tighter.

"It's magnificent."

My favorite piece of the collection was a crown composed of glass icicles ranging from six to ten inches long. "Get it?" A corner of my mouth lifted in a smirk.

"It's befitting of an Ice Queen," he answered with a low chuckle. "Though you're anything but cold. It's incredible."

"Thank you. I never commented on their little digs because there's power in silence and grace in holding your head high, but I figured why not own it? I'm the only person who gets to define me anymore, and besides, maybe I'll make a crown of flames next." I could already see it taking shape in my mind.

"You are incredible, Georgia Stanton." He turned and cradled my face, then kissed me deeply. "Thank you for sharing this with me, and just in case I don't get to say it again before we go home, happy birthday."

"Thank you," I said against his mouth, savoring our last few minutes of privacy before the catering staff arrived.

Within the hour, the doors were open, and the gallery filled with guests from my small town. I greeted the first dozen people, showing them around the space with Noah at my side. Lydia—our housekeeper—and her daughter arrived, then Hazel and Owen, Cecilia Cochran from the library, Mom—

I gasped, my free hand flying to my mouth. Noah's arm came around my waist, steadying me as Mom came through the small crowd, wearing a pale pink sheath and a shaky smile.

"Happy birthday, Georgia," she said softly, hugging me gently, then releasing me with her usual two pats.

"Mom?" Shock wasn't an adequate word.

She swallowed nervously, her eyes flying to Noah's and back. "Noah invited me. I hope you don't mind. I just wanted to be here to wish you a happy birthday and say congratulations. This is quite an accomplishment."

Was that really the only reason she was here?

"You and Ian?" I asked tentatively. Had they fallen apart? Was she only here to pick up the pieces under the guise of patching up mine?

"Oh, he's fine. We're fine," she assured me. "He sends his best. I'm sure you understand why he's not with me."

Because I couldn't stand him and he knew it, which was actually pretty considerate when I thought about it.

"How was the flight?" Noah asked, breaking the tension with that easy way he had.

"It was good. Thank you so much." Mom took a deep breath. "In the spirit of full disclosure, Noah bought my ticket."

"Oh." Full disclosure? She and Ian were fine? "That was really sweet of you," I said to Noah, leaning into his side.

"My pleasure." His hand flexed at my waist. "It's not my present, though. That's waiting for you back at the house."

"I told you not to spend money on me!" I chastised, but there was a tiny thrill of curiosity thrumming in my chest.

"I didn't, I promise." There was that grin again. He was up to something.

"I can't hog the birthday girl all night. See to your guests," Mom said with a watery smile. "Thank you for letting me be here. Your birthdays have always been..." Her smile faltered. "I'm just glad, that's all." Her gaze swept over the gallery. "This is phenomenal. I'm so very proud of you, Georgia."

"Thank you for being here," I told her, meaning every word. "It means a lot to me." The advance had been paid, and any other royalties from the book would go straight to Mom's account. She was happy with Ian. It looked like her life was going well, too, which meant she wasn't here because she needed something from me—she was here because she wanted to be. And sure, it was only one night, in a lifetime of them, but it was enough.

I was all smiles as I made my way around the room, watching the smaller pieces disappear as they were purchased.

"This is awesome!" Hazel wrapped me in a tight hug. "And is that Lydia's daughter behind the register?"

I nodded. "I think it might be going well."

"It is. Trust me." Her eyes narrowed as she stared over my shoulder. "Whoa. Who is Noah—" Her eyebrows hit the ceiling.

I turned around, blinking in confusion as Noah embraced a strikingly beautiful woman near the door. He looked up, searching the room, then grinned as he found me. He said something to the woman, then led her past the ice crown to where I stood with Hazel.

The woman's hair and eyes were as dark as Noah's, and her complexion the same sun-kissed olive. A man with sandy-blond hair, green eyes, and a well-tailored suit came to her side.

"I hope you don't mind that I invited one of my closest friends, too," Noah said with a smile. "Georgia, this is my little sister, Adrienne, and her hostage, Mason."

His sister? Men didn't invite their sisters to meet their flings, did they? My chest warmed, my heart aching with the possibility that this was something more to him, that we could really *be* more, even after he finished the book. Maybe we didn't need the self-imposed cutoff date.

Adrienne arched a single, perfectly plucked brow at her brother, but her smile for me was instant and starbright as she swept me into a tight hug. "And I'm thrilled to meet you, Georgia. He talks about you constantly, even though he meant to say my *husband* Mason," she corrected, releasing me.

"But did I?" Noah teased. "Good to see you, man." He embraced Mason, then hugged his sister so tight, he lifted her off her feet. "You too, squirt. Good flight?"

"You know it. Stop paying for first class. It's a waste of money."

"I'll spend my money however I like." Noah shrugged.

"Hope you like arguing, because they do it a lot," Mason said, offering his hand with an easy smile.

"Going to be honest—I'm a little overwhelmed." I shook his hand, and his smile deepened, revealing a dimple.

"Don't blame you one bit, and your gallery is incredible!" Adrienne said. "Oh, and happy birthday! No rush—it's a little busy in here—but later I need to hear all about how you knocked my brother on his ass in that bookstore."

I laughed and promised her details before she and Mason walked off to look around, taking Hazel and Owen with them.

"Have I told you how beautiful you are tonight?" Noah's lips skimmed the shell of my ear, sending a shiver down my spine.

"About twenty times," I assured him. "Have I told you that I'm going to do devious things to you with that tie you're wearing tonight?" I looked up at him from under my lashes.

"Are you, now?" His eyes darkened. "And here I was making plans of my own." He stole a kiss before I was pulled away again.

The night flew by, and before I knew it, I'd sold every piece I'd marked for sale. The ones for display, the crown and the tower pieces, stayed right where I wanted them—with me. The gallery slowly cleared out, until it was only my close friends and the cleanup crew.

"He gets *major* points for this," Hazel said as she was getting ready to leave.

"Hey now," I teased, hugging her goodbye. "Team Georgia, remember?"

"I am team Georgia," she promised. "That man flew his family out to meet you. Your mom, too," she finished quietly as Noah said goodbye to his sister.

Adrienne had already promised to come by for lunch the next day. She'd refused the guest bedroom, but Mom had agreed to stay with us tonight. She'd already taken her rental car to the bed and breakfast to fetch her things.

"I know. He's..." I sighed, looking over at Noah.

"He's just as much in love with you as you are him," Hazel whispered.

"Don't start." I shook my head, refusing to set myself up for major heartbreak.

"I've never seen you as happy as you are tonight, as you have been for the last few months, actually." She took my hand. "You've been through enough bad, G. You have to let the good in, too."

She hugged me again before I could formulate an answer, then Owen tugged her out the door, mumbling something about them still having a babysitter for the next hour.

The house was dark and quiet when Noah and I got home, but Mom arrived just after we'd hung up our coats. Noah's eyes drifted to my legs, bare under the short black dress I'd chosen from my recently unboxed stash.

"I'm going to head up and call Ian before bed," Mom said with a sly smile, carrying her small bag even after Noah had offered to take it up for her. "You two don't have too much fun. Happy birthday, Gigi."

"Night, Mom." I didn't even cringe at the nickname, glancing over at the twenty-nine roses Gran had sent with a first edition, signed copy of *The Sun Also Rises*.

"It's present time," Noah said, coming up behind me and wrapping his arms around my waist. "It might not be Hemingway, but you had me on a limited budget."

I groaned. "You've already given me enough."

"Trust me, you want this."

I turned in his arms. "I want *you*." If he actually knew how badly, he probably would have run screaming from the house.

He kissed my forehead and took my hand, leading me into the formal living room where he'd pitched his writing skills just a few short months ago. The furniture had been pushed to the side, opening the space, and he'd brought the tall foyer table in to hold a medium, beribboned box off to the side of the fireplace, which he turned on with the flip of a switch.

"Gran added that in the remodel." I nodded toward the gas fireplace. "Said it was a foolish, lavish expense, but she didn't care."

"Well, thank you, Gran." Noah shrugged out of his suit coat and laid it over the wingback chair, which sat opposite the box. "Now, open your present, Georgia." He leaned his shoulder against the fireplace mantel and crossed one ankle over the other.

"The present that didn't cost you anything." I arched a brow.

"Not a penny." His eyes narrowed slightly. "Well, I paid for the box. And the bow. Honestly, it was just something I happened to stumble upon while locating my shoes."

I rolled my eyes but walked over to the box, looking for an opening. "Did you tape it shut?" I teased.

"Nope. Just lift." There was so much excitement in his eyes that I couldn't help but feel it rub off on me.

I gripped the sides of the box and lifted. My heart leaped into my throat and tears stung my eyes. "Oh, Noah."

He came forward and took the box from my trembling hands, but I was too busy staring at my gift to see where he put the wrapping. Then he was at my side.

"Is it..." I was almost afraid to say the words, content to let it be real, even if only in my mind.

"It is." He nodded, his smile soft.

"But how?" I reached a shaky hand toward the vintage record player, running my fingers over the timeworn edge of the casing as it sat open on the table before me.

"I found a panel loose in the back of my closet at Grantham Cottage a couple of weeks ago," he said, maneuvering the arm of the phonograph so it rested above a dustless record. "The same closet where the heights marked on the closet doorframe weren't painted over like the rest of the house."

My eyes flew to his, somehow knowing what his next words

would be. "They were Grandpa William's, weren't they?" I guessed.

He nodded. "My guess is that's why she never sold the cottage. I went to the county and looked up the property records. It was originally owned by Grantham Stanton—Jameson's father. Your great-great-grandfather."

"It's where they lived for the first few years," I whispered, putting it all together. "But Gran said the record player was destroyed."

A corner of Noah's mouth lifted. "Whatever got destroyed, it wasn't this. Scarlett must have hidden it in the wall."

"But she never went back to get it?" My brow puckered. "Come to think of it, I don't know if I ever heard of her going in the house. She'd always had it managed."

"Grief is a powerful, illogical emotion, and some memories are safer left boarded up and undisturbed." He flipped the switch on the record player, and to my complete shock, it turned on.

"You found Jameson's phonograph," I whispered.

"I found Jameson's phonograph." He dropped the arm and the needle made contact, filling the room with Billie Holiday's voice.

My eyes slid shut, imagining them in that field, starting out the love affair that led to my existence, the love that had haunted Gran the rest of her life, even though she'd eventually married again.

"Hey," Noah said softly, backing into the center of the room and holding out his hand for mine. "Come dance with me, Georgia."

I walked straight into Noah's arms, feeling the last of my barriers give way.

"Thank you," I said, resting my cheek on his chest as we moved gently together, rocking to the music. "I can't believe you did this all for me. The dinner, and your sister, and Mom, and the phonograph. It's too much."

"It's nowhere near enough." His voice lowered as he tilted my chin to look in my eyes. "I am completely, wholeheartedly, madly in love with you, Georgia Constance Stanton." The intensity in those words was echoed in his eyes.

"Noah." My heart clenched, and the sweet ache I'd tried like hell to stifle broke free and filled every desiccated, love-starved cell in my body as I let myself believe, let myself love him back.

"This isn't a fling for me. It hasn't ever been. I wanted you from the first second I saw you in that bookstore, and knew you were the one the minute you opened your mouth to tell me you hated my books." He nodded slowly, a smirk playing at his mouth. "It's true. And I don't need you to say it back. Not yet. In fact, please don't. I want you to say it in your own time, when you're ready. And if you don't love me yet, don't worry, I'll win you over." He rested his forehead against mine as we swayed.

Oh God. I loved him. Maybe it was reckless and foolish, and too damned soon, but I couldn't help it. My heart was his. He'd won me over so completely that I couldn't imagine a single day without him. "Noah, I l—"

He kissed me quiet, stopping my declaration. Then he carried me upstairs and made love to me so thoroughly, there wasn't a single inch of my skin that didn't know his hands, his mouth, his tongue.

By the time the sun came up, we were both famished, drunk on a cocktail of orgasms and sleep deprivation as we kissed our way downstairs like a pair of teenagers, staying as quiet as possible so we didn't wake Mom.

We were a total cliché—Noah wearing last night's dress pants while I'd hastily buttoned his shirt over nothing but a pair of boy-cut briefs. I didn't care. I was in love with Noah Morelli, and I was going to make him pancakes—or eggs. Whatever was quicker and got us back into bed.

He kissed me deep and long in the foyer, tugging me toward the kitchen.

"What is that?" I drew back at the sound of rustling paper

coming from the office.

Noah lifted his head, his eyes narrowing at the slight gap in the office doors. "I shut those last night before the party. Wait here." He swept me behind his back, then strode silently to the French doors, pushing one open carefully to look inside. "What the hell are you doing?" he growled, disappearing inside.

I followed, racing through the open door.

It took a second to figure it out. Mom sat in Gran's chair, her cell phone poised above the desk, a shirt box open to her left and a small pile of papers in front of her.

She was scanning the manuscript.

CHAPTER TWENTY-SIX

May 1942

Ipswich, England

William cried, and Scarlett rocked him gently, swinging him side to side as the air-raid sirens wailed above them. The shelter was full and dimly lit, but she imagined her expression mirrored those around her. There were a few children huddled in the corner, playing a game—for the younger ones, this had become routine, just another fact of life.

The adults passed around reassuring smiles that were anything but. The air raids had picked up in the last week, the Germans bombing city after city in retaliation for the bombings in Cologne. Though the raids had never ceased completely, Scarlett had grown complacent over the last few months, and though this wasn't the first time she found herself in a shelter, waiting to survive, or not, this was the first time William had.

She'd known fear before. Felt it in those moments the hangar had exploded back in Middle Wallop, or the times Jameson came home late, or not for days, while they escorted British bombers. But this fear, this terror clenching her throat with an icy fist was a new level, a new torture in this war. It was no longer only her life that hung in the balance, or even Jameson's, but that of her son's.

William would be six months old in a couple of days. Six months, and all he'd known was war.

"I'm sure they'll give us the all clear in just a moment," an older woman told her with a kind smile.

"Certainly," Scarlett replied, adjusting William to her other hip and pressing a kiss to the top of his head through his hat.

Ipswich was a natural target, Scarlett knew that. But they'd been lucky so far.

The sirens stopped, and there was a hum of collective relief throughout the long tube that served as their shelter underground.

The ground hadn't shaken, though that wasn't always a sure way to tell if they'd been hit, only that they hadn't been hit nearby.

"There aren't as many children as I would have expected," Scarlett said to the older woman, mostly to distract herself.

"They built shelters at the school," she explained with a proud nod. "They can't fit all the children, naturally, but they go to school in shifts now, taking only as many children as can fit at once. It's thrown more than a few schedules into upheaval, but…" She trailed off.

"But the children are safer," Scarlett assumed.

The older woman nodded, her gaze flickering to William's cheek.

"I can appreciate that," Scarlett said, holding William just a little tighter.

Six months ago, evacuating the children from London and other major targets had felt so logical to her. If the children were in danger, of course they should be evacuated to safer areas. But holding William in her arms, she couldn't imagine the strength those other mothers must have had to put their children on a rail, not knowing exactly where they would be headed. She couldn't get past her own gut check reaction that William was safest with her, but in her own need to stay close to Jameson, was she ultimately placing William in more danger?

The answer was unequivocally yes, and she couldn't deny it, not seeing as she now held him in an underground air-raid station, hoping and praying for the best.

The all clear sounded through the station, and the crowd began to file out. The sun was still shining as she exited the air-raid station. What had felt like days had only been hours.

"Passed right by us," she heard an older man say.

"Our boys must've frightened them off," another added with pride.

Scarlett knew better, but she didn't say so. Her time plotting the bomber raids taught her that fighters weren't often a deterrent. They just hadn't been the target. It was as plain as that.

She walked the half mile home, talking gibberish to William the entire time while keeping her eyes on the sky. Just because they were gone now didn't mean they wouldn't return.

"It might just be the two of us for tonight, little one," she said to William as she opened the front door. With the increased raids, Jameson hadn't been allowed to sleep off-station in over a week. Their house was only fifteen minutes away from Martlesham-Heath, but fifteen minutes was a lifetime when there were bombers approaching.

She fed William, bathed him, fed him again, and had him put down to bed before she thought about eating, herself.

She couldn't stomach much, especially not knowing where Jameson was. It had been frightening to move his markers across the plotting board, to know when he engaged the enemy, to know when members of his squadron had fallen, but it was worse not knowing.

Scarlett sat at her typewriter, opened the smaller box that she had added to her collection in the past few months, then took out her latest page, and continued writing. This box was for their story—she couldn't just lump it in with the other sketched-out summaries, partial chapters, and unfinished thoughts. If one story had to be kept up-to-date, it was this one, just in case it was all she'd have to give to William.

Perhaps she had romanticized a detail or two, but wasn't that what love did anyway? It softened the sharper, uglier moments of life. She was already on chapter ten, which brought them nearly to William's birth.

Once she finished that chapter, she dutifully put the last piece of paper back into the smaller box, then reached for a fresh sheet.

She'd finally reached halfway, or at least what she thought was halfway, in an actual manuscript. She lost herself in that world, the clack of the typewriter keys filling the house.

She startled at the knock at the door, her fingers freezing over the keys as her head snapped toward the unwelcome sound.

He's not dead. He's not dead. He's not dead. She repeated the phrase in a hushed whisper as she stood, then took the agonizing walk past the dining room, to the front door.

"He's not dead," she whispered one last time as her hand reached for the doorknob. There were plenty of reasons someone might call at this hour... She simply couldn't think of them at this moment.

She lifted her chin and yanked open the door, ready to face whatever fate lay on the other side. "Constance!" Scarlett's hand flew to her chest, hoping to contain her galloping heartbeat.

"I'm sorry to call so late!" Constance threw her arms around Scarlett. "I had just gotten back to the hut, and one of the girls said Ipswich had an air-raid scare. I had to see for myself that you were all right." Her sister held her tight.

"We are all right," Scarlett assured her, hugging her back. "I can't say the same for Jameson, because I haven't seen him in a few days."

Constance pulled back. "They canceled his Sleeping Out pass?"

Scarlett nodded. "He's been home twice since the raids began, but only to grab a clean uniform and kiss William and me goodbye once again."

"I'm so sorry," Constance said, shaking her head and lowering her eyes so her hat obscured her expression. "I should have spent my leave here with you, instead of taking it in London for yet another wedding arrangement session."

Scarlett took her sister's hand in hers. "Stop. You have your own life to live. Why don't you come in, and let's—"

"No, I have to get back," Constance said with a quick shake of her head.

"Nonsense," Scarlett argued, glancing over Constance's shoulder to see the new car parked at the edge of the pavement. "It is already so late, and if you can't spend the night, at least let me make you some tea before you drive back." Her eyes narrowed slightly at the lack of insignia on the bumper. "It's a lovely car."

"Thank you," Constance said with no joy. "Henry demanded I take it. He said no fiancée of his would be dependent on public transportation." Constance lifted her shoulders in a minute shrug as she looked back at the sleek automobile.

A sick feeling slid through Scarlett's stomach as she realized that Constance had yet to meet her eyes. "Come on, poppet, just one cup." She reached across the threshold and tilted Constance's chin up.

Rage filled her heart. She was going to bloody kill him.

With the living room light illuminating her little sister's face, Scarlett now saw the bruise marring Constance's eye. The skin around it was puffy, red in places, and light blue in others, speaking to the bruise that would no doubt appear overnight.

"It's nothing," Constance said, jerking her head out of Scarlett's grasp.

"Get in here." Scarlett tugged Constance inside and shut the door behind them, then led her sister to the kitchen where she put on the kettle.

"It really is—"

"If you tell me it's nothing again, I'm going to scream," Scarlett threatened, leaning back against the kitchen counter.

Constance sighed and removed her hat, placing it on the table next to Scarlett's typewriter. "What would you have me say?"

"The truth."

"There are degrees of the truth," Constance said, folding her hands in her lap.

"Not between us there aren't." She folded her arms across her chest.

"I angered him," Constance explained, her eyes lowering to her hands. "Turns out he doesn't like to be kept waiting, or to be told no."

Scarlett's chest ached. "You cannot marry him. If he does this before you're married, imagine what will happen after."

"You don't think I know?"

"If you know, then why go through with it? I know you love that land, and I know you think it's the last piece of Edward, but Edward wouldn't want you to be battered and bruised to keep it." Scarlett crossed the distance between them and dropped to her knees in front of her sister, taking her hands in her own. "Please, Constance, please don't do this."

"It's out of my hands," Constance whispered, her lower lip trembling. "Announcements have been made. Invitations have been sent. By this time next month, we'll be married."

Scarlett felt tears prick at her eyes but would not let them fall. It wasn't her fault that Henry was an abusive ass, but she couldn't help but feel as though her sister had taken her place at the guillotine.

"There is still time," Scarlett pressed.

Constance's eyes hardened. "I love you, but this discussion is over. I'll happily stay another hour or two, but only if you promise to let it drop."

Every muscle in Scarlett's body tensed, but she nodded. "I'd ask if you need to ring your section later, but I noticed your new rank," she said with a forced smile, nodding toward the insignia on Constance's shoulder.

"Oh." The corners of Constance's lips tugged upward. "It happened last week, I just hadn't had time to see you yet."

Scarlett rose to take the seat next to her sister. "You deserved it long before last week."

"It's funny, really," Constance said with a small pucker

between her eyebrows. "Robbins walked up to me after a watch, handed it to me, and simply said that my new duties would start the next day. Quite anticlimactic, really."

Scarlett smiled in earnest this time. "Will he let you stay in?" she asked, unable to avoid the question.

Constance's smile fell. "I think so. It turns out he doesn't have much of a say as a civilian, since he isn't physically fit to serve. But we both know that if I fall pregnant, well…"

"Yes, well, we know all about that." She gave her sister's hand a squeeze. "Since your immediate future isn't up for discussion, what would you like to do?"

Constance's gaze fell to the typewriter. "Did I interrupt you writing?"

Warmth flooded Scarlett's cheeks. "It's nothing."

The sisters' eyes locked, both knowing that what they'd written off as nothing really meant everything.

"I'd hate to stop you in the middle of the grand masterpiece," Constance said, lifting her eyebrows.

"Hardly a masterpiece," Scarlett replied as the kettle whistled.

"How about you finish up the tea, and I'll be your personal secretary and type?"

Scarlett grinned at the impish look on her sister's face. "You just want to sneak a peek at what I'm writing." Nevertheless, she stood and made her way to the stove.

"Guilty," Constance admitted, taking off her jacket and hanging it over the back of the chair before sitting in front of the typewriter. "Well," she said, sending her sister a poignant look. "Go ahead."

Scarlett looked her sister over, then turned her attention to the tea. She couldn't stop this marriage. She couldn't take the bruises from Constance's face, nor would she ever be able to. But she could help her escape, if only for a little while.

"All right," she agreed. "Read me the last line."

. . .

Jameson brought the Spitfire down in a near perfect landing, though he felt anything but on his game. The Germans had been swift to retaliate, and the bombings had increased tenfold, if not more.

There were now three Eagle Squadrons, full of Americans ready to risk their lives. Rumor had it, by the fall, they'd all be back in American uniform, but Jameson had stopped listening to rumors ages ago.

He taxied, then turned his fighter over to the ground crew. He could've sworn his muscles creaked in protest as he climbed out of the cockpit. The number of hours he'd spent in the sky lately felt like they outnumbered the ones he'd spent on the ground, and his body had taken notice. It had been weeks since he'd been allowed to sleep at Scarlett's side.

The few hours he'd managed to spend with her hadn't been nearly enough. He missed his family with an ache so sharp, it threatened to slice him in half, but every day became more apparent that he should miss them more... That they should be as far away as possible.

"We're off for the night," Howard said with his arms raised in victory. "What do you say, Stanton?"

"To what?" Jameson asked as he removed his helmet.

"Let's get out of here and blow off some steam," Howard suggested as they headed for the hangar.

"If we are really off for the night," Jameson said, "the only place I'm going is home." Just the thought had his lips turning upward.

"Oh come on," Boston chimed in, walking beside Howard with a lit cigarette in his mouth. "Get one of those...what did the Brits call them...kitchen passes."

Howard laughed as Jameson shook his head. "What you

don't get, Boston," Howard said with a grin, "is that Stanton here would rather go home to that gorgeous wife of his than ask for a night out with the boys."

"The last two weeks have been a night out with the boys," Jameson countered. "And if any of you had a woman half as good as Scarlett, you wouldn't be so quick to ask for a kitchen pass, either." Besides, it wasn't just Scarlett he was going home to. William had begun crawling, the changes in his little body happening so fast that Jameson could barely keep up.

"I heard she has a sister," Boston joked.

"A very engaged sister," Howard replied.

Jameson's jaw flexed. Not only was it absolutely abhorrent that Constance was marrying an ogre, but he knew the guilt of it ate Scarlett up and spat her back out daily.

"Flight Officer Stanton," an airman called, waving his hands just in case Jameson hadn't heard him.

"So help me God if they don't let me go home tonight, I'm going to prang an aircraft."

"I'll believe it when I see it," Howard said, slapping him on the back.

Fine, he wasn't actually going to crash an aircraft on purpose, but the thought had its appeal if it got him just a couple of days with his family. He waved the airman over. The kid couldn't have been more than nineteen, or maybe it was simply that Jameson felt decades older than twenty-four.

"Flight Officer Stanton," the kid said between heaving breaths.

"What can I do for you?" Jameson asked, already preparing himself for the possibility of another night without Scarlett.

"There's someone here to see you," the kid announced.

"Does this someone have a name?" Jameson asked.

"I didn't catch it," the kid admitted. "But he's waiting for you in the pilots' rest room. He was really insistent that he see you."

Jameson sighed and ran his hand over his sweaty hair. He hadn't just spent the last few hours in an aircraft, he also smelled like it. "Okay, let me get a shower —"

"No! He said he needed to see you as soon as you landed."

"Great." Jameson kissed the thought of a shower goodbye. "I'll head over right now."

To say he was in a foul mood by the time he walked into the rest room would have been an understatement. He wanted a shower, and Scarlett, and William, and a hot meal, not some secretive meeting in the—

"Holy shit! Uncle Vernon?" Jameson's mouth dropped open at the figure he found lounged in one of the leather armchairs that lined the rest room wall.

"Finally!" His uncle stood with a wide grin and captured him in a bear hug. "I almost had to give up on you. I'm due to leave in the next half hour."

"What are you doing here?" Jameson asked as he stepped back, noting the American uniform his uncle wore.

"Your mother didn't tell you?" Uncle Vernon asked with a sly grin.

Jameson's brows rose as he recognized the insignia. "You joined the Transport Command?"

"Well, I couldn't very well sit home on my backside while you were over here risking yours, could I?" His uncle's eyes swept over Jameson in that appraising way he'd always had. "Sit down, Jameson. You look like hell."

"I've looked like hell for the last two years," Jameson argued, but sat, sinking into the worn leather. "How long have you been flying for the ATC?"

"Almost a year," Uncle Vernon replied. "Started out as a civilian, but eventually the pressure got to me," he admitted, motioning to the rank on the collar of his flight suit.

"At least they made you a lieutenant colonel," Jameson noted.

His uncle grimaced. "It has some privileges, like being able to hold a flight three hours late when your nephew is in the middle of a dogfight. A nephew I heard happens to be an ace."

"Wonder where I got those flying skills from."

"You've surpassed anything I could have taught you. It's damned good to see you, boy. Though even I can admit you're a man now."

Jameson rubbed the back of his neck. "I'd say I would have been here sooner had I known, but I wouldn't have." He'd never leave his squadron in the sky.

"I'm just glad I got to see you. I wish I could have met your Scarlett and my great-nephew, but maybe we can get the Germans to agree not to attack when I come back next month." His uncle flashed a smile that closely resembled his own.

"I'll get right on that," Jameson said as flatly as he could manage before cracking a smile. "So where do you go from here?"

His uncle arched a brow. "Don't you know? That's classified."

"Don't you know? I named my son William Vernon." Jameson lifted his own brow in response. How easy it was to be with him again, as though the last two and a half years hadn't happened. As though they were at home on the porch, watching the stars come out in the Colorado sky.

"I heard something about that." His uncle grinned. "I'll meet up with the rest of the ATC pilots up north, and we'll head back tonight. It's hard to believe that sixteen hours make the difference between being in England and hitting the east coast."

Sixteen hours, Jameson thought. *The entire world could change in just sixteen hours.* "We're grateful," he said, looking his uncle in the eye. "Every bomber you guys ferry over here from the States is needed."

"I know," he replied, his face falling. "I'm proud of you, Jameson, but I wish you didn't have to be here. And I definitely wish you weren't raising my great-nephew where bombs fall on sleeping babies."

Jameson let the back of his head fall against the leather and squeezed his eyes shut. "I'm trying like hell to get them out of here. She's been through the medical exams, we have all the paperwork in order, and they're entitled to citizenship...as long as my government hasn't revoked mine." Scarlett's appointment for her visa was next week. It was already May, and he knew chances were the quotas had already been filled, but he couldn't give up hope.

"They haven't revoked your citizenship," his uncle promised. "America is in this war now, for better or worse. They're not gonna punish those who were brave enough to fight before we were provoked."

"We booked her passage. She has to have her travel arrangements before they'll grant a visa, but that doesn't mean she'll actually get on the ship." Scarlett had made her feelings all too clear when it came to leaving him, but that had been before the latest barrage of bombings.

"I know some people at the State Department," his uncle said quietly. "I'll see what I can do to help move that wheel, but sticking your family on a ship with all those U-boats prowling the Atlantic might be a bigger gamble than letting them sleep in their own beds."

"I know," Jameson said softly, running his hands over his face. "I love her more than I love myself. She is everything to me, and William is the best of both of us. If I can't even save my own son, then what good did I do here? What was it all for?"

The two men sat in silence for several moments, both knowing that neither option was safe. Then Jameson realized there was one.

"I need a favor," Jameson said, turning in his chair to face his uncle.

"Anything. You know I love you like you're my own."

Jameson nodded. "I'm counting on it."

His uncle's eyes, the same mossy green shade as his own, narrowed slightly. "What do you have in mind, Jameson?"

"I want you to help me get my family out."

• • •

"Thank God!" Scarlett exclaimed as she raced into Jameson's arms.

He kissed her before he said a word, lifting her in his arms in their living room. He kissed her over and over, pouring his relief, his love, and his hope into it, until she melted against him.

"I've done the wash, and you have a clean uniform in our bedroom," she said, her hands cupping his cheeks.

"I'll put it on in the morning," he assured her with a smile.

Her eyes lit up. "You can stay the night with us?"

"I can stay the night with you." He would stay every night that was humanly possible between now and the date he'd discussed with his uncle.

Her smile was brighter than he'd ever seen, and she kissed him soundly in reply. "I've missed you so much."

"I've missed you," he whispered before kissing her again.

"I want nothing more than to carry you upstairs and make love to you until we're both limp," he whispered against her lips.

"That plan is brilliant," she replied with a smile. "With one exception."

That exception was currently crawling their way, drool spilling from the corner of his lips.

"He's teething," Scarlett explained with a slight grimace.

Jameson let go of his wife, only to scoop up his son and hug him tight. "Are you getting new teeth?" he asked before blowing raspberries on William's neck.

"Of course he is all smiles for you." Scarlett rolled her eyes. The way Jameson looked at their son stopped her heart. It was equal parts love and awe and only served to make her husband even more attractive.

Jameson's face fell and took Scarlett's stomach with it. "He won't be in a minute," he said softly.

"What do you mean?" she asked.

"We need to talk about something," he said quietly, then dragged his gaze to meet hers.

"Tell me," she demanded, crossing her arms over her chest.

"Your appointment is next week, right?"

Her chest tightened, but she nodded.

"I know you agreed to go to the States if something happened to me, but what do you think about going sooner?" He shifted William in his arms protectively, at odds with his words.

"Sooner? Why?" she whispered, her heart breaking. It was one thing to know that William wasn't safe here, but it was another for Jameson to send them away.

"It's too dangerous," Jameson said. "The raids, the bombings, the deaths. I won't be able to live with myself if I have to bury either one of you." His voice came out as though it had been scraped over broken pieces of shrapnel.

"There's no guarantee I'll even get a visa," she countered, her heart fighting what her mind had already told her was best. "We've talked about traveling before."

Nearly all of the commercial ships had been pressed into military service, and while it had been possible, barely, to book passage across the Atlantic, there was still danger. She lost track of how many civilians had died when the U-boats sank their ships from underneath them.

"I love you, Scarlett. There's nothing I won't do to keep you safe." He gazed lovingly at their son. "Keep you both safe. So, I'm asking you to go to the States. I've found what I think is the safest way to do it."

"You want me to go?" Thousands of emotions hit Scarlett all at once—anger, frustration, sorrow, everything seemed to roll up into one ball and lodge itself in her throat.

"No, but can you honestly tell me it's safe here for William?" His voice faded at their son's name.

"I don't want to leave you," she whispered. She hugged herself tighter, for fear that if she let go even the slightest bit, she would shatter to pieces at his feet. He was right, it wasn't safe. She'd come to the same conclusion yesterday in that air-raid shelter, but the thought of leaving Jameson was a knife in her soul.

He pulled her against him, tucking her in tight into his side as he held their son in his other arm. "I don't want you to go," he admitted in a guttural rush. "But if I can save you, I will. Exeter, Bath, Norwich, York, the list goes on. Over a thousand civilians have died in the last week alone."

"I know." Her hands fisted in the material of his uniform, as if she could stay if she held on just a little tighter, but this wasn't about them anymore. It was about their son, the life they'd created together. Thousands of British mothers had trusted their children to strangers to keep them from harm's way, and here, she had the chance to deliver her son from harm herself. "You want us to take the ship to America?" she asked slowly, tasting the bittersweet words on her tongue.

"Not exactly…"

She looked up at Jameson and arched an eyebrow.

"I saw my uncle today."

Her eyes flew wide. "I'm sorry?"

"Uncle Vernon. He's here flying with ATC. He'll be back in a little less than a month."

Scarlett swallowed. "At which time he'll come to dinner so I can meet him?" she guessed hopefully, knowing that wasn't what he meant.

Jameson shook his head. "At which time he can get you out."

How? How could he be sure she'd get a visa below the quota? How could he be sure he'd get them out? How? The questions hit her at such speed that they all skimmed right over her, because everything in her soul, in the center of her being, had focused on the other piece in this puzzle. "Less than a month?" Her voice was barely a whisper.

"Less than a month." The agony in Jameson's eyes was something she'd never forget, but he nodded once. "If you agree."

It was her choice, but there wasn't one. Not really.

"Okay," she agreed, tears pricking her eyes. "But only because of William." She would risk her life to stay with Jameson, but she couldn't risk her son's if there was any other option.

Jameson forced a smile, then pressed a hard kiss against her forehead. "For William."

CHAPTER TWENTY-SEVEN

Georgia

Dear Jameson,
I miss you. I love you. I cannot bear to be away from you anymore. I know I'll reach you before this letter, but I'm coming, my love. I cannot wait to feel your arms around me again...

I stared in open-mouthed shock as Mom slowly pocketed her cell phone, her cheeks turning pink.

"I will ask you again: what the hell are you doing?" Noah repeated as he marched toward the desk.

"She's scanning the manuscript," I whispered, gripping the back of a chair to remain upright.

"Holy shit." Noah reached across the desk, yanking the stack of papers out of Mom's reach with one hand and taking the box with the other. He quickly thumbed through the stack, not sparing a glance in Mom's direction. "She got the first third of it," he said to me, putting the manuscript back together and securing the lid.

"Why would you do that?" I asked, my voice breaking like a child's.

"I just wanted to read it. Gran never let me, and we weren't on the best terms the last time I was here." Mom swallowed and slid her phone into the back pocket of her jeans.

I tilted my head, trying to make sense of it. "We were on great terms until you walked out after you got what you came for." I shook my head. "I would have let you read it if you'd wanted to. You didn't have to sneak around. Didn't have to—" My face fell, and I felt the blood drain straight out of it. "You weren't scanning it for you."

"He has every right to read it, Georgia." She lifted her chin. "You know that contract states that he has the first right of refusal, and you've withheld it from him. You should have heard him on the phone, heartbroken that you were using business to get back at him."

Damian. Mom was scanning the manuscript for Damian. My stomach knotted, dropping to the floor.

"She's not selling the rights!" Noah's voice rose, tension ebbing from every line of his torso. "It's hard to have first right of refusal on a deal that doesn't exist."

"You're not selling the movie rights?" Mom stared at me in disbelief.

"No, Mom." I shook my head. "He played you." Damian had always been a smooth operator, but I'd never seen someone get one over on Mom.

"Why the hell not?" she fired back, stunning me into silence.

"I'm sorry?" Noah barked, stepping back to stand at my side, the shirt box safely tucked under his arm.

"Why the hell wouldn't you sell the movie rights?" she shouted. "Do you know how much they're worth? I'll tell you. Millions, Georgia. They're worth millions, and he—" She pointed to Noah. "He doesn't own *any* of them. It's just us, Gigi. You and me."

"This is about money," I whispered.

Mom blinked quickly, then adapted, her face softening. "Your party wasn't, baby. But I was here. I really think that this could be the key to getting him back, and he promised to adapt it word for word. Don't you believe him?"

"I don't want him back, and I sure as hell don't believe a word that comes out of his mouth!" I sputtered, fire streaking through my veins as the anger pushed through the armor of my disbelief. "Did you honestly think you could force my hand? *Make* me sell him the rights?"

Mom glanced between Noah and me. "Well, I can't now,

since that's not the finished manuscript." Her eyes narrowed on Noah. "Where's the ending?"

Noah's jaw flexed.

"It's not done yet," I snapped. "And even if it was, you can't force me into anything."

"Millions, honey. Just think of what that could do for us," she begged, coming around the side of the desk.

"You mean what it could do for *you*." I put myself between her and Noah. "It's always about you."

"Why do you even care?" Mom shouted.

"Gran hated movies, and you think that out of all her books, I'm going to sell the rights to *this* one to any producer, let alone the man who slept with everything in a skirt?"

"I don't give a shit what Gran wanted," she hissed. "She sure as hell never gave me a second thought."

"That's not true." I shook my head. "She loved you more than life. She only cut you out of the will when you decided to marry a hopelessly-in-debt gambler, so you'd stop looking like a payday to every guy who crossed your path. She cut you out to give you a chance at finding someone who really loved you!"

"She cut me out as a punishment for making her raise you!" she yelled, jabbing her finger in my direction. "Because I was the reason my parents were on the road that night, coming to watch my recital!"

"She never blamed you, Mom." My heart stuttered to life, aching for everything she'd gotten wrong.

"The woman you adore so blindly doesn't exist to me, Georgia." She looked past me to Noah. "Give me the endings. Both of them."

"I told you, they're not done!" How did she even know there would be two?

Her gaze shifted slowly to meet mine, her features transforming to a look of such pity that I recoiled, stepping back in to Noah. "Oh, you sweet, naive little girl. Didn't you learn anything from the last man who lied to you?"

"This is done. You need to go." I straightened my spine. I wasn't the toddler she'd abandoned during afternoon nap anymore, or even the teary-eyed preteen who stared out the window for hours after she'd disappeared once more.

"You really don't know, do you?" Sympathy dripped from her tone.

"Georgia asked you to leave." Noah's voice rumbled against my back.

"Of course *you* want me to leave. Why the hell didn't you tell her it was finished? What else could you possibly get by keeping it from her?" Mom tilted her head just like I had, and I hated it. Hated that I looked so much like her. Hated that I had anything in common with her.

I needed her to go. Now. Once and for all.

"Noah's not done with the damned book!" I snapped. "He's in here working on it all day, every day! I'm never selling the movie rights, and you can tell Damian to kiss my ass, because he's never touching this story. Ever. Now you can leave on your own, or I can throw you out, but either way, you're leaving."

"You're going to need me when you realize how naive you've been. Why would you lie to her like that?" She studied Noah like she'd found a worthy opponent.

That unnerved me like nothing else could have.

"I learned not to need you a long time ago, right around the time I realized that other mothers didn't leave. That other mothers came to soccer games and helped their daughters get ready for dances. Other moms picked out costumes for Halloween and bought pints of ice cream for broken teenage hearts. I may have needed you at one point, but it passed."

She jolted like I'd slapped her. "What would you know about motherhood? From what I've read, you lost your husband over that issue."

"That's uncalled for," Noah moved, but I leaned back against him.

I shook my head with a small laugh. She had no idea. "Everything I know about motherhood, I learned from my mom. I didn't get it until recently, but I do now. It's okay that you didn't know how to raise me. It really is. I don't blame you for being a kid with a kid. You gave me a really great mom. One who came to the games, helped me pick out dresses for prom, listened to my *hours* of chatter without batting an eye, and never once made me feel like a burden, never wanted anything from me. You taught me that not all moms are called *Mom*. Mine was called Gran." I sucked in a stuttered breath. "I'm okay with that."

Mom stared at me like she'd never seen me before, then crossed her arms under her breasts. "Fine. If you don't want to sell the movie rights...if you don't have enough common sense to take the money, or enough compassion for *me* to do it, nothing I say will make a difference."

"I'm glad we agree." My body tensed, recognizing her preamble for exactly what it was, the moment before she went for the emotional kill.

"But I'd be remiss if I didn't tell you that he's finished the book. Both endings. If you don't believe me, call Helen like I did. Call his editor. Hell, call the mailroom clerk. Everyone knows it's done, just waiting for you to pick an ending." She turned her attention to Noah. "You're a piece of work, Noah Harrison. At least I only wanted money. Damian wanted access to Scarlett's rights. What did you want?" She walked past us, pausing to pick up the bag I hadn't noticed was already packed by the office door. "Oh, and you should send your editor a nice bottle of scotch, because that man is a guard dog. No one's seen it but him." She picked up her bag and walked out of the office.

The front door closed a few seconds later.

"Georgia." Noah's voice held an edge of something I hadn't heard there before—desperation.

Mom had called Helen. Helen wouldn't lie. She had no reason to, nothing to gain from it. Gravity shifted beneath my feet, but

I managed to walk to the window before I faced Noah, putting nowhere near enough distance between us if it was true.

"Is it true?" I wrapped my arms around my waist and stared at the man I'd foolishly allowed myself to fall in love with.

"I can explain." He put the shirt box on the desk and stepped forward once, but something in my eyes must have warned him off, because he didn't move any closer.

"Did you finish writing the book?" My voice weakened.

The muscle in his jaw ticked once. Twice. "Yes."

I heard it in the back of my mind—the gasp, the gurgle, the love that had consumed me less than an hour ago twisting, contorting into something ugly and poisonous.

"Georgia, this isn't what you think." His eyes begged me to listen, but I wasn't done asking the questions.

"When?"

He muttered a curse, lacing his fingers on top of his head.

"When did you finish the book, Noah?" I snapped, grasping onto the anger to keep from drowning in the tide of agony rising in my soul.

"The beginning of December."

My eyes flared. *Six weeks.* He'd been lying to me for six entire weeks. What else had he lied about? Did he have a girlfriend back in New York? Did he ever really love me? Or was it all a lie?

"I know this looks bad—"

"Get out." There was no emotion in my words, no feeling left in my body.

"You had just told me that you wanted us to be a fling, and I was already in love with you. I couldn't walk away. It was wrong, and I'm sorry. I just needed enough time—"

"To what? Screw with my emotions? Is that what gets you off?" I shook my head.

"No! I'm in love with you! I knew if we had enough time, you'd fall for me, too." He dropped his arms.

"You love me."

"You know I do."

"You don't lie and manipulate someone into loving you, Noah. That's not how love works!"

"All I did was give us the time we needed."

"What happened to *I never break my word*?" I tossed back.

"I haven't! Is the draft done? Yes. But the book isn't finished. I've been in here every day, editing both versions, giving us as much time as possible before you have to choose one of the endings. Before you cut us off at the knees because you're scared."

"You lied. Apparently my caution was warranted. Take your laptop and your lies and go. I'll mail whatever else you left, just get away from me." I'd made the mistake of holding on to Damian after that first lie, and he sucked eight years of my life away as a thank-you. Never again.

"Georgia—" He came toward me, reaching.

"Go!" The demand was a guttural plea that scraped my throat raw.

His hand fell away, and his eyes slid shut.

One heartbeat passed. Then two. By the time he opened his eyes, a full dozen had passed, just enough to let me know this moment wouldn't kill me. That I'd keep breathing despite the pain.

He saw it, too, nodding slowly as our gazes locked. "Okay. I'll go. But you can't stop me from loving you. Yes, I fucked up, but everything I said to you is the truth."

"Semantics," I whispered, searching deep for the ice I'd grown in my veins during my marriage, but Noah had taken it all, thawed every last shard and left me defenseless.

He flinched. A breath later, he backed away slowly, rounding the opposite side of the desk and opening one of the drawers. His movements were jerky as he put one binder-clipped packet of paper on the left of the manuscript, and the other on the right.

The endings had been in the desk the whole time. I'd never even thought to look or question him.

He picked up his laptop and walked around the desk, pausing at the chairs to look my way. He had no right to the agony in his eyes, not when he'd lied his way into my heart.

"They're both there. Just let me know which ending you pick. I'll honor your choice."

I hugged myself a little tighter, begging the cracks in my soul to hold it together for one more moment. I could break when he was gone, but I wouldn't give him the satisfaction of watching me crumble.

"Some things you have to fight for, Georgia. You can't just walk away and leave it unfinished when it gets too complicated. If I could fly off and fight the Nazis to win your love, I would. But all I've got to battle with are your demons, and they're kicking my ass. Keep that in mind while you're reading those endings, the good and the...poignant. The epic, rare love story in this room isn't Scarlett and Jameson. It's you and me."

One long, yearning look later, he was gone.

I shattered.

CHAPTER TWENTY-EIGHT

May 1942

Ipswich, England

Scarlett clung to Jameson, her nails raking down his back as he moved within her with sure, deep strokes. There was nothing in the world that compared to the feel of his weight on top of her in these moments where there was no war, no danger, no looming deadline for their separation. In this bed, there were only the two of them, communicating with their bodies when words failed.

She moaned at the indescribable pleasure that coiled tight within her belly, and he kissed her deep, swallowing the sound. They'd nearly perfected the art of quiet sex in the past few months.

"I can never get enough of you," he whispered against her mouth.

She whimpered in reply and arched her hips harder against his, hooking one ankle around the small of his back and urging him on. Close. She was so close.

He gripped her thigh and raised her knee toward her chest, taking her deeper, then ground his hips in maddening circles with every thrust, keeping her on that tight edge of pleasure, hovering without falling.

"Jameson," she begged, burying her hands in his hair.

"Say it," he demanded with a grin and another stroke.

"I love you." She lifted her head and brought her lips to his. "My heart, my soul, my body—it's all yours." It was always the *love you* that shook his control, and this time was no exception.

"I love you," he whispered, slipping his hand between them and using his fingers to push her over the edge. Her thighs locked, her muscles trembled, and she heard him whisper, "Scarlett, my Scarlett," as the orgasm swept over her in waves.

When she screamed, he covered her mouth with his, and a few strokes later, he joined her, tensing above her as he found his release.

They were a tangled mess of sweaty limbs and smiles as he rolled them to the side.

"I never want to leave this bed," he said as he lifted a strand of hair from her cheek and tucked it behind her ear.

"Excellent plan," she agreed, running her fingertips down his chiseled chest. "Do you think it will always be like this?"

He palmed her backside. "An insatiable need to get each other naked?"

"Something like that." She grinned.

"God, I hope so. I can't think of anything better than the honor of chasing you out of your clothes for the rest of my life." He wiggled his eyebrows and she laughed.

"Even when we're old?" She brushed the back of her hand over his jawline, rough with stubble.

"Especially when we're old. We won't have to keep it quiet for the kids down the hall."

At that, they fell silent, both listening for William's imminent call for breakfast, but he was still sleeping—or at least happily silent.

Scarlett's chest tightened. Three days. That's all they had left before she was due to leave. Jameson had gotten the message from his uncle yesterday. How long would they be apart? How long would this war last? What if these were the last three days she would ever spend with him? Each question tightened the vise in her chest until every breath was painful.

"Don't think about it," he whispered, his gaze flickering over her face as though he needed to memorize every feature.

346 the things we leave unfinished

"How do you know what I'm thinking about?" She tried to smile, but it wasn't there.

"Because it's all I think about," he admitted. "I wish there were any other way to keep you with me, to keep him safe."

She nodded, biting her lip to keep the trembling at bay. "I know."

"You're going to love Colorado," he promised, a spark of joy lighting his eyes. "The air is thinner, and that might take some getting used to, but the mountains are so tall, it's as if they're reaching for the sky. It's beautiful, and honestly, the only thing I've ever seen bluer than the Colorado sky is your eyes. My mother knows you're coming, and she has the house set up for you and William. Uncle Vernon will help you through immigration, and who knows, you might even have that book of yours finished by the time I get home."

It didn't matter how pretty the picture he painted, because he wasn't in it, at least not for the immediate future. But she wasn't going to say that to him. Their goodbyes were days away, and she knew she needed to stay strong, not only for Jameson, but for William. There was no use lamenting or whining. Her visa had been approved two weeks ago, their path was set, and now there was work to be done—two lives that needed to be packed.

"I'm not taking the phonograph." It was the one point of contention between them.

"Record player, and my mother told me to bring it back."

She quirked a brow. "I thought your mother told *you* to bring it back with you, alive." She ran her fingers through his hair, committing the feel of the strands to memory.

"Tell her I'm sending it home with my life, because that's what you and William are. You are my life." He cupped her cheek and looked at her with so much intensity that she felt his gaze like a touch. "When we look back on this, it will be nothing more than a blip on our timeline."

Her stomach twisted. The only blips she was familiar with were the kind that showed incoming bomber raids.

"I love you, Jameson," she whispered fiercely. "I'm only willing to go for William's sake."

"I love you, too. And the fact that you're willing to go to keep William safe only makes me love you more."

"Three days," she whispered, already breaking her stay-strong motto.

"Three days," he repeated, forcing a smile. "The cavalry is coming, my love. American forces are on their way, and who knows, by this time next year, this all might be over."

"And if it's not?"

"Why, Scarlett Stanton," he teased. "Are you saying you won't wait for me?" The corner of his mouth lifted into what she would almost call a smirk.

"I'll wait for you forever," she promised. "Will you be okay, here without me?"

"No," he answered softly. "I won't be okay until I'm with you again. You're taking my heart with you. But I will live," he swore, bringing his forehead to rest against hers. "I will fly. I will fight. I will write you every day and dream of you every night."

She tried to keep the pain from overtaking her, shoving it back with the reminder that they still had three days. "That won't leave you much time for taking up with another girl," she teased.

"There will never be another girl for me. Only you, Scarlett. Only this." He pulled her closer. "I just wish I could've taken leave today."

She scoffed. "They gave you last weekend for Constance's wedding, and the day to see us off. I can't really complain."

"Would you call that a wedding? It felt more like a funeral." He grimaced.

"It was both." Constance had followed through, as if there had been any doubt, and married Henry Wadsworth last weekend.

Lord Ladder Climber officially had his foothold in British society, Constance had protected the land she loved so much, and her parents' financial future was secure. "It was an overpriced celebration of a business deal," Scarlett said quietly.

They lay there for another moment as the sun rose higher, the light in their bedroom turning from a dusty pink to a brighter hue. They couldn't put off the start of the morning any longer, though Jameson did talk her into taking a shower with him.

Twenty minutes and another orgasm later, he wrapped her in a towel, then tied one around his waist and began to shave. She leaned against the doorframe and watched. It was a routine she never grew tired of, mostly because he usually did it shirtless. Once he was finished, she headed toward her bedroom to get dressed for her day, just as William let out his first cry of the morning.

"I'll get him," Jameson said, already walking toward William's room.

Scarlett dressed, listening to the sweet sounds of Jameson singing to their son as he got him up for the day.

With Constance's wedding last weekend, and her upcoming travel, it had made sense to acclimate William to a bottle, which came with the added benefit of getting to watch Jameson feed their son, which she did about ten minutes later. The bond between the two was undeniable. Jameson was the recipient of William's biggest smiles when he came home, and the one he favored when he was fussy. Even now, William held the bottle with one hand and tugged at the buttons on Jameson's uniform with the other. She didn't mind the blatant favoritism, though, especially knowing that it might be a year or more before they would see each other again.

Would William have any memory of Jameson? Would they have to start all over again? It was hard to believe that such a primal bond could be weakened by something so indefinite as time.

"Would you like me to fix you some coffee?" Scarlett asked as Jameson cradled their son in a kitchen chair.

"I'll grab some at the station, thank you," Jameson answered with a smile, glancing up at her before turning his adoring gaze back to their son. "He really has the best of both of us, doesn't he?"

Scarlett slipped her hair over one shoulder and looked down at William. "I'd argue that your eyes are a great deal more handsome than mine, but yes, I think he does." Their son had her black hair, but Jameson's sun-loving complexion. He had her high cheekbones, but Jameson's strong chin and nose.

"Stanton blue," Jameson remarked with a grin. "I hope all of our kids have them."

"Oh? Were you planning on more children?" she teased as he tugged her down onto his empty knee.

"We make such pretty babies that it would be a shame not to," he said with a quick, gentle kiss.

"I guess we'll have to see about that once we're all in Colorado." She wanted a little girl with Jameson's eyes and reckless ways. Wanted William to know the joy of having a sibling, too.

"I'm going to take you fishing," Jameson promised William. "And I'll teach you to camp under stars so bright that they light the midnight sky. I'll show you the safest places to cross the creek, and when you're old enough, I'll teach you how to fly, too. You just have to watch out for the bears until I get there."

"Bears!" Scarlett's jaw dropped.

"Don't you worry." Jameson laughed as he wrapped his arm around Scarlett's waist. "Most of the bears are scared of your grandma... The mountain lions, too. But she's gonna love you." He glanced at Scarlett. "She's going to love both of you just as much as I do."

Reluctantly, Jameson handed William to Scarlett and they all stood.

"I'll be back as soon as I can," he said, wrapping his arms

around his wife and son.

"Good." She lifted her face for a kiss. "We're not done discussing the phonograph."

Jameson kissed her soundly, then laughed. "The record player goes."

"As I said," she replied with an arched brow, "we're not done discussing it." Scarlett wasn't superstitious, but most pilots were, and taking the record player home to Jameson's mother felt like inviting bad luck.

"We'll talk about it when I get home," he promised. He kissed her again, hard and quick, then brushed his lips over William's and walked out the door.

"*We'll talk about it* means Mummy is going to win," she told William, tickling him gently.

He gave her a belly laugh that she couldn't help but return.

Jameson rolled his shoulders, attempting to ease what had become a permanent ache in his muscles. Their objective, a target on the German border, had been accomplished, and though the three bombers they were escorting had come under fire, they were currently over the Netherlands and whole. That's what he called a good day.

He glanced at the picture he still kept tacked beneath the gauge and smiled. It was the same one of Scarlett that Constance had given him almost two years ago. He knew she thought it was bad luck to take the record player home, but he had all the luck he needed in that picture right there. Besides, there wasn't anyone he wanted to dance with besides his Scarlett, and there would be plenty of time for dancing once this war was over.

"We're making good time," Howard said over the radio, using their designated squadron channel.

"Don't count your chickens," Jameson replied, looking to the right where Howard flew as blue lead about two hundred yards off. The only thing he liked about the astern formation was flying lead alongside Howard. Today, he was red.

But he was right, they were making good time. At this rate, he wouldn't make it home before dinner, but he might make it in time to put William to bed.

Then, he'd take his wife to bed. He was going to make every single second they had together count.

"Blue lead, this is blue four, over," a voice came over the radio.

"This is blue lead, go ahead," Howard called back.

The thing Jameson hated about the astern formation was it left their newest pilots, those with the least combat experience, in the back.

"I think I saw something above us." The shaky voice broke toward the end. That had to be the new kid, the one who had just come in last week.

"You think? Or you know?" Howard asked.

Jameson looked up through the glass of the cockpit, but the only things he saw on the cloud layer above them were their own shadows from the dying sun.

"I think—"

"Red lead, this is red three, over," Boston said across the radio.

"This is red lead, go ahead," Jameson answered, still scanning the sky above them.

"I saw something, too."

The hairs on the back of Jameson's neck stood at attention.

"Above at two o'clock!" Boston shouted.

He'd barely gotten the words out when a formation of German fighters broke through the cloud cover, firing down upon them.

"Split the flights!" Jameson shouted to the radio. In his peripheral vision, he saw Howard bank hard right, and Cooper, who was flying white lead to the left, banked the same.

Jameson pulled on the stick, climbing sharply, leading his men to higher ground. In a dogfight, he who had the elevation had the upper hand. Clear of the blue flight, Jameson turned to face the enemy, locked the first fighter in his ring sight, and let the world fall away.

He fired at the same time the German did, and the glass just behind him shattered as they nearly skimmed each other in a flyby.

"I'm hit!" Jameson shouted, checking his gauges. Wind whipped through the cockpit, but she held steady. Oil pressure was fine. Altitude, stable. Fuel level, stable.

"Stanton!" Howard's voice broke.

"I think I'm okay," Jameson responded. The fight was below them now, and he banked hard left, heading back into the fray.

The dive brought a new rush of air through the cockpit, ripping Scarlett's picture from the rim of the gauge. It was gone before Jameson could even try to catch it.

The radio was a cacophony of calls as the German fighters headed for the bombers. His goggles protected his eyes, but he felt a warm trickle down the left side of his face and lifted his gloved hand quickly.

It came away red.

"It's not bad," he said to himself. It must've been the glass. He'd be dead if he'd taken a direct shot.

Punching through the cloud cover, he kept his finger on the trigger and sped toward the nearest fighter, who happened to have a Spitfire in his sights.

Adrenaline flooded his system, honing his senses, as he dove faster.

The German's first shot missed.

Jameson didn't.

The German fighter fell from the sky in a plume of black

smoke, disappearing into the thick fog of the clouds beneath them.

"Got one!" Jameson shouted, but his victory was short-lived as another fighter—no, two other fighters—came up behind him.

He pulled back on the stick hard, climbing as he banked right, narrowly missing what he considered to be a standing appointment with death as shots whizzed by.

"That was a close one, baby," he said quietly, as if Scarlett could hear him across the North Sea. Dying wasn't an option, and he had no intention of doing so today.

"I've got one on my tail!" The new kid shouted across the radio as he passed directly under Jameson, the German fighter hot on his heels.

"I'm coming," Jameson responded.

He felt the shot as though someone had hit the bottom of his seat with a sledgehammer, before he even saw the other fighter.

The aircraft still responded, but the fuel gauge began a steady decline that could mean only one thing.

"This is red lead," he said as calmly as he could manage across the radio. "I've been hit, and I'm losing fuel."

He'd landed without an engine before. It wasn't pretty, but he could do it again. The only question was if they were still above land or the sea. Land would be better. Land, he could handle.

Sure, he might get taken as a POW, but he'd grown up in the mountains and his evasion skills were top-notch.

"Red lead, where are you?" Howard called over the radio.

The fuel gauge hit empty, and the engine sputtered, dying.

The world went horrifyingly quiet as Jameson fell from the fight into the clouds below, the sound of rushing wind replacing the roar of his engine.

Calm. Stay calm, he told himself as his beautiful Spitfire transformed into a glider. Down, down, down. He could only steer now—just along for the ride.

"Blue lead, I'm in the clouds." His stomach bottomed out as his visibility turned to shit. "Going down."

"Jameson!" Howard shouted.

Jameson glanced at the blank space where the picture had been. *Scarlett.* The love of his life. His reason for existence. For Scarlett, he would survive, no matter what lay beneath the clouds. He'd make it through for them—Scarlett and William.

He braced.

"Howard, tell Scarlett I love her."

CHAPTER TWENTY-NINE

Noah

Scarlett, my Scarlett,

Marry me. Please have mercy on me and be my wife. Days here are long, but the nights are longer. That's when I can't stop thinking about you. It's odd to be surrounded by Americans now, to hear familiar phrases and accents when all I long for is the sound of your voice. Tell me you can get leave soon. I have to see you. Please meet me in London next month. We'll get separate rooms. I don't care where we sleep as long as I get to see you. I'm dying here, Scarlett. I need you.

Was it coincidence? Proof? Did it even matter? I clicked among the four documents my lawyers had sent over an hour ago. Three death certificates. One marriage license.

My phone vibrated on the desk and my gaze snapped to the screen. *Adrienne.*

I hit the decline button and cursed my asinine hopes for jumping at every call. Of course it wasn't Georgia, but there I was, hoping anyway.

My chest ached at the thought of her, and I rubbed the spot over the physical organ like it would help ease the pain. It didn't. I missed everything about Georgia. Not just the physical things like holding her or seeing her smile, either. I missed talking to her, hearing her perspective—which was always different from mine. I missed the way her voice charged with excitement when she talked about the work with the foundation, the way the light had come back into her eyes as she got her feet under her and started to rebuild her life.

I wanted to be a part of that life more than I wanted my next two contracts.

Adrienne called back.

I declined.

My little sister had stayed by my side while I packed my luggage in the small bedroom at Grantham Cottage. We'd taken the same flight back to New York, not that I remembered much of it through the haze of heartbreak and my own self-loathing screaming in my ears. Despite her best efforts to see me home, we'd parted ways at the airport, and I'd ignored the rest of the world ever since.

Unfortunately, the world wasn't ignoring me.

Adrienne's name flashed across my screen again, and a stab of worry broke through. *What if she's in trouble?* I swiped, answering the call, which automatically transferred into my Bluetooth headphones. "Is something wrong with Mom?" My voice was gruff, thick from disuse.

"No," she answered.

"The kids?"

"No. Now, if you—"

"Mason?"

"Everyone is fine but you, Noah," she said with a sigh.

I hung up and went back to staring at my computer. The images attached to the email were grainy—clearly scanned copies of the originals—and had taken me six days and a call to my lawyers to receive.

Adrienne called again.

Why the hell couldn't everyone just leave me alone? Licking my wounds wasn't a spectator sport.

"What?" I snarled, answering it when I really wanted to chuck the damned thing out the window.

"Open your front door, jerk face," she snapped and hung up.

I drummed my fingers on the desk, wishing it was polished cherry and not contemporary glass and I was about nine thousand feet higher and sixteen hundred miles away. Then I took a deep breath, pushed my chair back, and walked to the front door of my apartment, throwing it open.

Adrienne stood at the threshold, her coat buttoned up to her chin, juggling a carrier tray with two cups of coffee and her cell phone in the other hand, her mouth moving quickly as she pushed her way past me into the apartment.

I jerked my headphones off, letting them hang around my neck as I shut the door.

"—the least you could do is tell me you're alive!" I caught the tail end of her lecture.

"I'm alive."

"Apparently. I've been out there knocking for at least ten minutes, Noah." She arched a brow.

"Sorry. Noise-canceling headphones." I pointed to the set of Bose around my neck and headed back to the office. "I'm in the middle of some research."

"You're in the middle of wallowing," she countered, following me. "Whoa," she murmured as I sank into my office chair. "I thought the Stanton book was done?" She motioned to the pile of Scarlett's books that littered the coffee table in front of the couch.

"It is. As you well know." Hence why I was in the middle of Manhattan and not Poplar Grove.

"You look like shit." She pushed aside two manila files and set the drink carrier on the space she'd cleared. "Have some caffeine."

"Coffee isn't going to fix this." I tossed my headphones onto a pile of research and leaned back in my chair. "But thank you."

"It's been eight days, Noah." She unbuttoned her coat and shrugged out of it, draping it across the chair she'd commandeered across from my desk.

"And?" Eight *excruciating* days and sleepless nights. I couldn't think straight, couldn't eat, couldn't stop wondering what was going through Georgia's head.

"And enough wallowing!" She took a cup from the carrier and leaned back, her posture so much like mine that it was almost laughable. "This isn't you."

"I'm not exactly at my best." My eyes narrowed. "And aren't you supposed to be the compassionate one in the family?"

"Only because the role of stubborn asshole was already taken." She sipped her coffee.

The corners of my mouth lifted.

"Well, look at that, he lives." She saluted me with the cup.

"Not without her," I said quietly, glancing at the Manhattan skyline. Whatever this was, it wasn't living. Existing, maybe, but not living. "You know, I used to think the term *falling* in love was an oxymoron. It should be rising, right? Love is supposed to make you feel like you're on top of the world. But maybe that phrase is so popular because actually making it work is rare. Everyone else just crashes at the end of it."

"It's not over, Noah." Adrienne's face softened. "I've seen you two together. The way she looked at you... There's just no way this is how it ends."

"If you'd seen the way she looked at me in that office, you might think differently. I really hurt her," I countered quietly. "And I promised I wouldn't."

"Everyone makes mistakes. Even you. But holing up in your apartment and burying yourself in whatever this is"—she motioned to the disaster zone of my desk—"isn't going to win her back."

I folded my arms across my chest. "Please, do tell me more about what I should be doing to win back the woman I blatantly, deliberately lied to for weeks."

"Well, when you put it that way." Her nose wrinkled. "At least you didn't cheat on her like her ex?"

"I'm not sure arguing that a liar is better than a cheater is really the way to go on this one." I rubbed the bridge of my nose. "I used my best weapon—words—and played with semantics to get what I wanted, and it bit me in the ass, plain and simple. There's no coming back from that with her."

"So you're saying she's a Darcy?" Adrienne tilted her head in thought.

"I'm sorry?"

"You know...her good opinion once lost is lost forever." She shrugged. "*Pride and Prejudice*? Jane Austen?"

"I know who wrote *Pride and Prejudice*, and I'd argue that Georgia is one of the most forgiving people I know." She'd given her mother chance after chance.

"Good, then fix this." She nodded. "You're right. Love—the good, the real, the life-changing—is rare. You have to fight for it, Noah. I know you've never had to before, that women have always come easily to you, but it's because you never cared enough to try to keep someone around before."

"Fair point." This was all new territory for me.

"You live in a world where you can script everything someone says and one grand gesture makes everything instantly better, but the truth is that relationships are *work* in the real world. We all screw up. We all say something we regret or do the wrong thing for the right reasons. You're not the first guy who might need a good grovel."

"Tell me honestly, have you been saving this speech?" I leaned across the desk and took my coffee from the carrier.

"For *years*," she admitted with a grin. "How did I do?"

"Five stars." I gave her a thumbs-up, then downed the offered caffeine.

"Excellent. Time to rejoin humanity, Noah. Get your hair cut, shave, and please, for the love of *God*, take a shower because it smells like funk and takeout in here."

I gave my shoulder a discreet sniff and couldn't argue. Instead, I glanced at the invitation Adam had messengered over a couple of days ago. As much as I hated it, there was one other person who might be able to answer the question that had been eating away at me for the last couple of months. The question Georgia had never asked Scarlett.

"My job here is done." Adrienne stood and slipped her coat on.

"Rejoin humanity, huh?"

"Yep." She nodded, fastening her buttons.

"Want to be my plus one?" I picked up the invitation and handed it to her.

"These things are so boring," she groaned, but read it over.

"This one won't be. Paige Parker is a major donor." I lifted my brows. "I'll bet you anything Damian Ellsworth will be there."

Adrienne's eyes flared with surprise, her gaze darting to mine, then narrowing. "Someone has to keep you out of trouble. I'm free that night. Pick me up at six."

"You always did like a good show." I laughed.

She scoffed and walked straight out of my office.

I heard the front door shut just as the text alert went off on my phone.

GEORGIA: I read both endings.

My heart stopped as I watched three little dots scroll along the bottom of the message, indicating that she wasn't done typing.

GEORGIA: Go with the real one. You did a great job at portraying her grief, her struggle getting here, and her eventual happiness when she married Brian.

My eyes slid shut against the tidal wave of pain that washed over me. *Damn it.* It wasn't just the loss of my preferred ending, the one that Scarlett and Jameson deserved, but the knowledge that I'd failed to convince Georgia she could have that same happiness in her own life. I breathed through the pain and managed to type out a text that wasn't a thousand apologies and a plea to take me back.

NOAH: Are you sure? The happy one is better written.

Because it had my heart and soul in it. It was the right one.

GEORGIA: I'm sure. This one is trademark you. Don't doubt your ability to rip someone's heart out.

Ouch. She was freezing over again, not that I blamed her. Hell, I'd caused it.

NOAH: I love you, Georgia.

She didn't reply. I hadn't expected her to.

"I'll prove it," I said to myself, to her, to the world.

CHAPTER THIRTY

May 1942

Ipswich, England

*C*lack. *Clack. Clack.* The sound of typing filled the kitchen as Scarlett broke the heart of the diplomat's daughter.

Her heart clenched, as if she could feel the very pain she was putting her character through. She reminded herself that she would put them back together once they had both grown enough to deserve the other. This wasn't a permanent heartbreak. This was a lesson.

The knocks at the door nearly blended into the monotonous clicks of the typewriter.

Nearly.

She glanced up at the clock. It was after eleven, but it was also the first night Constance was scheduled to be back from her honeymoon.

Scarlett pushed away from the table and walked to the door barefoot, steeling her heart for whatever she might find on the other side. Who knew what that monster could have done to her little sister in the last week?

She plastered a smile on her face, then opened the front door.

She blinked in confusion.

Howard stood on her doorstep, dressed in uniform, his face drawn and pale.

He wasn't the only one. Behind him stood other faces she recognized, all in uniform with eagles on their shoulders.

Her stomach pitched, and she gripped the doorframe with white knuckles. *How many?* How many of them were here?

"Scarlett," Howie said, clearing his throat when his voice broke.

How many?

Her eyes jumped from one hat to the next as she counted. Eleven. There were eleven pilots outside her door.

"Scarlett," Howie tried again, but she could barely make out the words.

Jameson usually flew in a formation of twelve. Three flights of four.

Eleven of them were here.

No. No. No. This wasn't happening. It wasn't possible.

"Don't say it," she whispered as gravity shifted beneath her feet. There would only be one reason they were here.

Howie removed his hat, and the others followed suit.

Oh God. This was really happening.

She had the instant, overwhelming urge to slam the door in their faces, to un-open the letter, but the words were already written, weren't they? There was nothing she could do to stop this from becoming what it already was.

Her eyes squeezed shut, and she leaned in to the sturdy wood of the doorframe as her heart caught up to what her brain already knew. Jameson hadn't come home.

"Scarlett, I'm so sorry," Howie said softly.

She took a fortifying breath, then straightened her spine, lifted her chin, and opened her eyes. "Is he dead?"

There were words she'd asked herself hundreds of times over the past two years. Words that haunted her brain, amplifying her worst fear every time he'd be late. Words that taunted her sanity while she'd been a plotter. Words she'd never before spoken aloud.

"We don't know." Howard shook his head.

"You don't know?" Scarlett's knees trembled, but she stayed standing. Maybe he wasn't dead. Maybe there was hope.

"He went down somewhere around the coast of the Netherlands. From what he said on the radio, and what some of us saw, he took a hit to the fuel tank."

Heads nodded, but there weren't many eyes willing to meet hers.

"So there's a chance he's alive." She stated it as fact, and the fraying edges of her composure latched on to the possibility with a ferocity she hadn't known she was capable of.

"The cloud cover was thick," Howard said.

There was a mumble of agreement among the pilots.

"None of you saw him crash?" she asked, a dull roar filling her ears.

They all shook their heads.

"He said he was going down." Howie's face crumpled for a heartbeat, but he sucked in a deep breath and pulled himself together. "He said to tell you that he loves you. That was the last thing he said before he disappeared." He ended in a whisper.

Her breaths came faster and faster, and it was all she could do to keep the panic at bay. He wasn't dead. He couldn't be.

It simply wasn't possible to live in a world where he didn't exist, and therefore he couldn't be dead.

"So what you're saying is that my husband is missing." Her voice seemed to come from outside her body, as though she wasn't the one really speaking. In that moment, she felt cleaved in two. There was one Scarlett speaking, standing in her doorway, seeking any logical reason to believe Jameson might still be alive. The other Scarlett, the one who was gaining ground, screamed silently from the depths of her soul.

"Scarlett?" a higher, familiar voice asked. The gathering of pilots parted as Constance walked up the pavement. "What's going on?" She asked Scarlett first, but when no answer could pass her lips, Constance filled the doorway beside her and faced Howie. "What. Is. Going. On?"

"Jameson's missing." His voice didn't break this time, as though it had become easier to say.

As though he was accepting it.

"Where?" Constance asked, her arm encircling her sister's waist to steady her.

This wasn't right. It was Scarlett's job to comfort Constance, not the other way around.

"We're not a hundred percent sure," Howie admitted. "It was right along the coast of the Netherlands. So we're not sure if he managed to land, or..."

Or if he went down in the sea, Scarlett finished in her own head.

The odds of surviving the crash, and even being taken prisoner, were better than those of outlasting the cold of the sea.

"You're going to look, right?" Scarlett asked, her breath catching. "Tell me you're going to search for him." It wasn't a request.

Howard nodded once, but there was no hope in his eyes. "At first light," he confirmed. "We have the general coordinates from when we were attacked."

Another thread to hold on to. Another sliver of hope. He wasn't dead. He couldn't be.

"And you will tell me what you find." Another demand. "No matter what it is, Howie. Wreckage... Or nothing. You will tell me."

"You have my word." Howie turned his hat in his hands. "Scarlett, I'm so sorry. I never wanted —"

"He's not dead yet," Scarlett blurted. "He's missing. Find him."

The pilots nodded to her and made their farewells, all filing back to the small line of cars they'd driven from the airfield. Howie was the last to go, and he seemed to work with himself, struggling for words, but when they didn't come, he left, too.

Scarlett stood in her doorway, Constance's arm around her waist, as the cars drove out of sight. She needed to go inside. Needed to close the door. They were still under blackout. But she couldn't make her feet move. She was a statue, frozen in that moment, held together only by denial and a cracking, plaster facade of will.

"Come on, love," Constance said soothingly as she ushered Scarlett inside.

"He's not dead. He's not dead. He's not dead." Scarlett whispered the mantra, her heart doing its damnedest to convince her mind not to crumble.

She would know, right? If her heart was still beating, then Jameson's had to be as well. And William... *No. Don't open that door.*

Constance supported most of Scarlett's weight as she brought her to the sofa. "It will be all right," she promised, just as Scarlett had promised her on the supply room floor.

She went blessedly numb as she looked up into her sister's eyes. "I would've left the letter unread."

Constance sank into the sofa beside her, then gripped Scarlett's hand.

There was nothing they could do now but wait.

CHAPTER THIRTY-ONE

Noah

Jameson,

I swear, I felt my heart break into a million pieces the second I watched you leave, and yet every tiny shard of that broken heart loves you. I can't fathom that you're so far away, not when you're everywhere I look here. You're standing beneath the tree, inviting me to fly. You're tucked into the corner booth at the pub, holding my hand beneath the table. You're standing on the pavement, waiting for me when my watch is done. I feel you everywhere. I know you're training the new pilots in Eagle Squadron, not flying combat missions, but please be careful. Stay safe for me, my love. We'll figure this out. We have to.

All my love,
Scarlett

"I didn't think you'd come," Adam said as we hovered on the edges of the charity event, just beyond the crush.

"I almost didn't," I admitted, nodding at an acquaintance across the floor. My brow furrowed slightly, thinking of how small and intimate Georgia's party had been, compared to the see-and-be-seen of all this. "You haven't responded to my email."

Adam sighed. "You spent a month avoiding all mine. Consider it payback." He rolled his neck and tugged at his bow tie.

"She's not going to change her mind." My eyes continued to scan the crowd, seeking the one person I'd come to see.

"Make her." Adam raised his brows.

"No." My eyes narrowed as I spotted the indie film crowd to the left. "Besides, she won't answer my calls. It's been two weeks, so there's a chance it's intentional at this point," I said with a self-deprecating smirk.

"You really want to go down as the guy who let his own ego get in the way of Scarlett Stanton's happy ending?"

"That's not what happened." Nope, he wasn't there, either. I turned toward Adam, but looked over his shoulder, continuing my search.

"Well, that's what it looks like, and that's what all the reviews are going to say." He sighed.

"Is it badly written?" I challenged.

"Of course not, it's you." He shook his head in frustration.

"Then it stands. Copy edits are supposed to be back in a few days, right?" I folded my arms across my chest.

"Yep. And let me tell you just how pleased the copy editor was to have to do *both* versions because you hadn't picked one. Spoiler alert, she was pissed."

"Thank you again for accommodating me." I meant every word.

"She also said the happy one is better," he tossed back.

"On that, we agree." A flash of red caught my eye, and I smiled. Paige Parker. That meant Damian was here somewhere.

"Then why the hell are you—"

"Noah Harrison!" someone called out from behind me.

I looked over my shoulder. *Bingo.*

"Damian Ellsworth," I said in greeting. *Keep it civil. You need information.* This wasn't exactly something I could ask Georgia about—not anymore.

"Imagine seeing you here." He slapped my shoulder and moved to join us. Georgia's ex was just shy of six feet, giving me a good four inches on him as he smiled up at me with teeth so white, they were nearly blue.

"I could say the same, seeing that you have a new baby at home." I forced a smile as bile rose in my throat. This was the man who had ruined the woman I loved, who had told her time and again that she wasn't enough to keep him satisfied.

What a fucking tool.

"That's what nannies are for," he answered with a shrug. "So, how is my wife?" He lifted his drink and took a long sip.

I refrained from shoving it down his throat. Barely.

"I wasn't aware that you had a wife." I blinked in mock confusion.

Adam sputtered on his own drink.

"Ha. Touché." He glanced over me with obvious assessment. "Tell me, does that old grandfather clock still keep time? The one in the sitting room?"

"Sure does." I lifted a brow at the transparent reminder of his past role in Georgia's life. "You know, that reminds me. You knew Scarlett pretty well, didn't you?"

Adam's eyes bounced between us like a ping-pong match, but he stayed silent.

"Sure did. That's why I have ten of her books optioned." He smirked.

"That's right," I said like I'd actually managed to forget that fact. What the hell had Georgia ever seen in this off-brand Nick Nolte? "Then you arrived just in time, because my editor and I were discussing the end of the new book."

"The book no one is supposed to know about?" He half winked, which was just weird.

"The same one."

"Guys. Keep it down. We're going for the whole surprise announcement angle, remember?" Adam warned.

"Right. Of course." I could have kissed him for playing along. "Anyway, Adam and I were discussing the end of…Scarlett's story, and there was one piece of the puzzle I didn't quite get out of Georgia while I was in Colorado." I exaggerated a wince. "Well, you know better than most how open she isn't."

Damian laughed, and my fists clenched, but I kept my arms crossed. "Yeah, she's a prickly one, my Georgia." He smiled wistfully.

My *Georgia, asshole.*

Adam lifted his brows and took a long drink.

"Right. Anyway, I was wondering—for the sake of the story—did Scarlett ever tell you why she waited so long to have Jameson declared..." The word died on my tongue. In my head, the two had lived on, deliriously happy.

"Dead?" he suggested, taking another drink.

"Yeah."

"Isn't it obvious?" He looked at me like I was a moron. "She never gave up hope. Ever. That woman was hard as nails, but man was she a romantic. She checked the mail at the same time every day, hoping there had been some word, some discovery, and that was long after Brian passed on."

"Brian. Right." I nodded. "I guess meeting him finally gave her the push she needed to move on and live for herself. Makes sense. Should have thought of that." My lips curved upward in what I hoped looked like a grateful smile.

Adam choked on his drink, then cleared his throat to cover the sound. That was exactly how I'd written the ending, putting the pieces together from what little Georgia knew about that part of Scarlett's life.

"I wouldn't say *meeting* him. Scarlett knew Brian for years, actually." Damian's beady little eyes narrowed slightly in thought. "They never talked about it, but he moved into that tiny cottage in the mid-fifties. Now that you mention it, she told me once that she couldn't marry Brian that first decade because it felt like her first marriage wasn't over." He shrugged. "Guess she finally realized it was. I mean, I think waiting forty years is long enough, don't you?"

My stomach sank.

"Hey, baby." Paige Parker hooked her elbow through his. "You about ready to sit down?"

"I'm chatting business," he told her, then leaned down to whisper in her ear when she pouted.

The blonde was pretty, but she wasn't Georgia. She didn't

have Georgia's eyes, either, or her wit, or strength. In fact, Paige couldn't even hold a candle to Georgia.

"Are you thinking what I am?" Adam asked quietly.

"Depends on what you're thinking," I answered, spotting my sister and Carmen on their way back from the ladies room. Perfect timing. I'd gotten what I'd come here for.

"Somehow Scarlett knew for certain in 1973 that Jameson wasn't coming home," he whispered. "She knew, and she didn't tell anyone."

"Let's keep that thought between you and me." Even the implication would crush Georgia.

Adam nodded as Paige walked off without so much as an introduction from her husband. *Class act, Ellsworth.*

"Speaking of Scarlett's...life," Damian continued. "When do I get to read the manuscript?" He sipped at his drink casually.

"It releases in March." I was done playing nice.

"You're really going to make me wait until release?" He laughed it off. "Imagine if we announced the movie at the same time as the book. The sales would be astronomical."

"Georgia's never going to let you make the movie." I grinned.

"Of course she is. She's just pissed about Paige. She'll come around. Trust me."

"Trust you. That's funny." I nodded to Adrienne, and her steps quickened as she saw who I was standing next to. "You can trust *me*, Ellsworth. It's not going to happen."

His expression changed, dropping all pretense of humor. "What would it take for you to cough up that manuscript? Maybe lean my way so Georgia does the same? From what Ava tells me, you two are...close."

"I'm in love with her," I corrected him.

"And?" He tilted his head, zero emotion in his eyes. "My offer stands. Happy to kick something back for you, too."

"I'd rather die." I held out my hand to Adrienne. "You ready to go?"

"If you are," she replied.

"I am. Damian Ellsworth, meet my sister, Adrienne. Adrienne, meet Georgia's piece-of-shit ex." I turned away from his beet-red face. "Adam. Carmen. It was great to see you." Pivoting with a smile, I walked away with Adrienne at my side.

"Emotions have no place in business, Harrison," Damian sneered. "Eventually Ava will wear her down. She always does. How do you think I own the other ten options?"

I paused. He'd made five movies and still had five to go. I'd seen the way she dug her heels in for Scarlett's wishes, so then why did she give up... *Sometimes the only way to keep what you need is to let go of what you want.* Her words from that day at the creek.

"Do you now?" My smile widened. What if she'd been referring to something else entirely? *Clever woman.*

"What the hell is that supposed to mean?" he snapped.

"It means I know Georgia better than you do." I didn't bother to wait for his response. "Sorry we aren't staying for dinner," I said to Adrienne, walking her to the door.

"I only came for the show," she said with a shrug. "Did you get what you needed?"

I nodded, moving us through the crowd.

"You don't look pleased."

"Georgia has trust issues." I nodded at another acquaintance as we approached the coat check.

"Obviously." Adrienne blinked up at me.

"What would you do if you knew the only person in the world Georgia trusted completely had lied to her for her entire life?"

"Are you certain?" She paled, her eyes widening.

"About ninety percent." Give or take.

"You have to be a hundred, and then you have to tell her."

I cursed. "That's what I figured." Getting Georgia back just became a lot more complicated.

CHAPTER THIRTY-TWO

June 1942

Ipswich, England

"What are you doing?" Scarlett asked as she walked into the living room.

"Packing your things," Constance answered without looking up. "What does it look like I'm doing?"

Every muscle in Scarlett's body locked at the sight. Constance had one trunk and two cases open between the sofa and the window.

"Stop," Scarlett ordered, her tone shrill enough that William startled from where he sat on the floor.

Constance paused for a moment but finished folding a piece of William's clothing, placing it in one of the cases. "You have to go," she said softly, turning to face her sister.

Scarlett's eyes burned, but she blinked back tears, just as she had for the last two days. "I'm not leaving him."

"Of course you're not. You're taking him with you." Constance looked pointedly at William.

"You know damn well I mean Jameson."

Constance lifted her chin, and in that moment, resembled Scarlett far more than Scarlett resembled herself. "They have searched twice—"

"Twice is nothing!" Scarlett crossed her arms in front of her chest, fighting to hold herself together. "Just because they've searched that stretch of coastline doesn't mean he didn't land somewhere else. It takes weeks for the first confirmations to arrive if he's been taken prisoner. Maybe even longer if he's hiding." Tomorrow. One more search. Two more weeks. Her heart pushed the deadline back every day, fanning the embers of hope that logic denied.

Constance's wedding ring flashed in the sunlight that streamed through the living room window as she rubbed her temples.

"You don't have to stay," Scarlett reminded her. "You have a life."

"As if I would leave."

"You have a new husband. A husband who, I'm sure, is angry to know you're using up all your leave to be here."

"It's compassion leave. It doesn't count. And he'll survive. Besides, he's only my husband. You're my sister." Constance held her gaze, making sure Scarlett saw her resolve. "I'm staying. I'm packing your things. And tomorrow, I will drive you and William to the airfield to meet Jameson's uncle."

"I'm not leaving." How could she possibly abandon Jameson when he would need her the most?

Constance took Scarlett's hands in her own. "You have to."

Scarlett ripped her hands away. "No, I don't."

"I've seen your visa. I know how close you are to the Americans' quota, and I've seen the expiration date. If you don't take this chance, it might not come again."

Scarlett shook her head. "He'll need me."

Constance's expression softened, filling with compassion.

"Don't look at me like that," Scarlett whispered, retreating a step. "He could still be out there. He still is out there."

Constance's gaze flickered toward William, who chewed on the edge of the blanket Jameson's mother had made. "He wanted you to go. He arranged all of this so you and William could be safe."

Scarlett's chest tightened. "That was before."

"Can you honestly tell me he wouldn't want you to go?"

Scarlett looked anywhere but at her sister, trying and failing to pin down one emotion, one certainty. Of course Jameson would want her to go, but that didn't mean it was the right thing to do.

"Don't take it away," Scarlett whispered, her throat aching with all the words she wouldn't let herself say.

"What?"

"My hope." Her voice broke as her vision blurred. "It's all I have left. If I pack those bags, if I get on the plane, I'm abandoning him. You can't ask me to do that. I won't." It was one thing to take William to the States, knowing that Jameson would join them when the war ended. But the thought of not being here when they found him, of leaving him to heal on his own, no matter what condition he was in, was more than she could take. And if she so much as gave in for the tiniest second to the possibility that he wouldn't come home, she would shatter.

"You can wait for Jameson in the States just as easily as you can wait here. Where you are doesn't change wherever he is," Constance argued.

"If there was a chance Edward had survived, would you have left?" Scarlett challenged.

"That's not fair." Constance flinched, and the first tear broke free, sliding down Scarlett's face.

"Would you?"

"If I had William to worry about, then yes, I would have left." Constance looked away, her throat working as she swallowed. "Jameson knows you love him. What would he want you to do?"

Another tear fell, then another, as though the dam had broken, as her heart screamed in silent agony at the truth it was forced to acknowledge.

Scarlett scooped her son into her arms and pressed a kiss to the soft skin of his cheek. For William. "He made me promise that if anything happened to him, I'd take William to Colorado." The tears came in a steady stream now, and William tucked his head in to her neck, like he understood what was happening.

God, would he even remember Jameson?

"Then you have to take him." Constance stepped forward and ran the backs of her fingers down William's cheek. "I don't know what happens to your visa if Jameson is dead."

Scarlett's shoulders curved inward as she battled against the rising sob in her throat. "I don't either." All it would take was a trip to the consulate to answer that question, but what if it canceled her visa? What if William could go but she couldn't?

"If you stay..." Constance had to clear her throat, then try again. "If you stay, our father can have you declared hysterical. You know he would do it if it meant getting his hands on William."

Scarlett's tears stopped. "He wouldn't—"

The girls shared a look, because they both knew he would. Scarlett held William a little tighter, swinging softly as he began to fuss.

"Jameson would want you to go," Constance repeated. "Wherever he is right now, he wants you to go. Staying here won't keep him alive." Constance's words faded into a whisper.

If he even was alive.

"You can't help Jameson. But you can save your son—his son." Constance gripped her sister's forearm gently. "It doesn't mean you're giving up hope."

Scarlett closed her eyes. If she tried hard enough, she could feel Jameson's arms around her. She had to believe that she would feel them again. It was the only way she could keep breathing, keep moving. "If..." She couldn't bring herself to say it. "All I would have in this world would be William, and you. How am I supposed to leave you?"

"Easily." Constance gave her forearm a squeeze. "You let me finish packing you. You let me take care of you for once. And tomorrow, if there is no news, you let me help you leave. You take my godson somewhere he can sleep without fear of the world caving in around him. You can't save him from whatever is coming his way—your way—when it comes to Jameson. But you can save him from this war."

Scarlett's heart lurched at the plea in her sister's eyes. Constance's face was pale, and the skin under her eyes was dark from obvious exhaustion. There was no newlywed glow about her, and though no bruises were obvious, Scarlett hadn't missed the way her sister winced and shifted her weight often. "Come with me," she whispered.

Constance scoffed. "Even if I could, well, I can't. I'm married now, for better"—her gaze dropped—"or for worse." She mustered a blatantly fake smile. "Besides, what would you do? Stow me away?"

"You would fit in the trunk," Scarlett tried to tease, but it fell flat. There was nothing left in her to tease with. She was empty, but empty was better than feeling it. She knew as soon as she let it in, there would be no return to whatever this state was.

"Ha." Constance arched an eyebrow. "Once I finish packing you, there won't be much room. Are you sure this is all you can take?"

Scarlett nodded. "Jameson's uncle said one trunk and two cases." She'd filled Constance in on the plan the day before her wedding.

"Well then." Constance managed a reassuring smile. "We'd better get you packed."

William tugged on a strand of her hair, and Scarlett traded him her hair for a toy. The boy was worse than Jameson when it came to giving up something he wanted. They were two stubborn peas in a pod.

"They could find him today," Scarlett whispered, glancing at the clock. They were still a few hours away from getting any update, if the last two days were anything to go by. "They could find him tomorrow morning," she ended in a whisper. *Please God, let them find him.*

Perhaps the only thing worse than knowing Jameson was truly gone was not knowing. The hope was a double-edged sword, keeping her breathing, but perhaps only delaying the inevitable.

"And if they do, then Jameson can drive you to the airfield tomorrow himself." Constance turned back toward the pile of William's clothes she'd been packing and picked up the next piece. "Is there anything specific you need to take that I don't know about?"

Scarlett breathed deeply, taking in her son's sweet scent. *You and William are my life now.* She heard the words in her memory as clearly as if Jameson had been standing beside her.

"The record player."

S carlett's eyes were swollen and achy as she pinned her hair in place. She'd tried her hardest to fend off the tears, but they'd come anyway.

Her fingers brushed over the handle of Jameson's razor. It felt wrong to leave it all here, but he'd need it when he returned. She walked down the hall and took one last look at William's nursery, her heart bleeding out as she pictured Jameson in the rocking chair with his son. She closed the door gently and headed for their bedroom.

Her handbag was on the bed, neatly packed with all the papers she would need tomorrow. It was surreal, thinking that she would be in the United States in less than twenty-four hours if all went according to plan. They would be a world away, leaving Jameson and Constance behind. The emptiness of it was almost more than she could bear, but she would keep her promise. For William.

She sat on the edge of their bed, reached for Jameson's pillow, and clutched it to her chest. It still smelled like him. She breathed deeply as countless memories washed over her, drowning her in their intensity.

His laughter. His eyes when he told her that he loved her. His arms wrapped around her in sleep. His hands on her body as he made love to her. His smile. The sound of her name on his lips, asking her to dance.

He had brought her to life in every way that mattered, had given her the life that mattered most—William.

It was silly, and wasteful, but she took his pillowcase anyway, slipping it from the pillow and folding it into a neat square. She'd already taken two of his shirts, knowing that he wouldn't mind.

"He'll have mine," she said softly to herself.

There weren't words for the agony that twisted her heart, wringing it dry with harsh, unyielding hands. It wasn't supposed to be like this.

"There you are," Constance said from the doorway with William on her hip. "It's time."

"Can't we give them just a few more minutes?" *Can't we give me a few more minutes?* That's what she really meant.

Today would be the last day the 71st would actively search for Jameson. As of tomorrow, the missions would resume, and surely they'd keep an eye out when they flew over that area, but after today, the unit would move on.

Jameson would be another MIA.

"Not if we want to make it to the airfield in time," Constance replied quietly.

Scarlett glanced over the dresser and the wardrobe that still held his uniforms. "Once, you asked what I would give to walk through that first house we lived in back at Kirton-in-Lindsey."

"I didn't know... I never would have asked if I'd thought this would happen," Constance whispered, her eyes heavy with apology. "I never wanted you to feel this."

"I know." Scarlett ran her fingertips over the folded pillowcase. "This is the third house we've lived in since we were married." Her lips tugged upward at the thought. "Jameson is supposed to clear this house out next week, now that the squadron has completed the move to Debden. Maybe in that way, the timing is fitting. The next house we're supposed to live in together is in Colorado."

William babbled, and Constance shifted him to her other hip. "And you'll be in Colorado waiting for him. Don't worry about anything here. I'll have Howie and the boys pack the rest of the house up for when Jameson gets back."

A familiar burn stung Scarlett's nose, but she fought back another round of useless tears. "Thank you."

"Packing is nothing." Her sister brushed her off.

"No," Scarlett said as she found the strength to stand, slipping the pillowcase into her handbag. "Thank you for saying when, instead of if."

"A love like the two of you share doesn't die so easily," Constance said as she handed William over. "I refuse to believe it ends like this."

Scarlett took in William's sweet face. "It won't," she whispered, then glanced at her sister again. "Always the romantic, aren't you?"

"Speaking of romance, I packed both hatboxes with your typewriter. That trunk weighs a ton, but it's in the car." Howie had stopped by earlier and helped with the luggage before heading to the airfield.

"Thank you." She'd spent last night at the typewriter before Constance insisted on packing it, but she hadn't brought their story up to date. She made it as far as their last day together, but hadn't been able to bring herself to what came next, partly because she hadn't accepted the events of the last three days, and partly because she didn't know how it would end. But for those few hours, she'd let the pain slip away and had fallen into a world where Jameson was still in her arms.

That's where she wanted to live, where that day was her own little eternity.

Holding William in the crook of her arm, she managed to

open her handbag and remove the letter she'd written when she woke this morning. "I don't know where to leave this," she admitted softly, showing the envelope to her sister with Jameson's name clearly inked on the outside.

Constance reached for the envelope, taking it gently from Scarlett's hands. "I'll give it to him when he returns," she promised, then tucked it into the pocket of her dress. With them both out of uniform, Scarlett by force and Constance by choice, since she was on leave, it was easy to believe they'd never put them on. That the war hadn't yet happened. But it had, and though the dresses were softer than the WAAF uniforms they'd both spent so much time in, both women were harder on the inside.

Scarlett adjusted the hat on William's head and tugged on the sleeves of his jumper. It was June now, but still chilly for the little one, and would only get colder where they were going. With one long, last wistful look at their bedroom, Scarlett sent up yet another prayer that God would bring Jameson home to her, and then she walked out.

She held herself together as they made their way to the car, keeping her head high as Jameson would want.

Scarlett slid into the passenger seat and held William close as Constance took the wheel. The engine roared to life, and before Scarlett's heart could overrule her mind, they pulled away from the house, driving toward Martlesham-Heath.

They were barely a few minutes into the drive when the air-raid sirens blared.

Scarlett's gaze snapped toward the sky, where she could already make out the outline of bombers overhead.

Her stomach dropped.

"Where's the nearest shelter?" Constance asked, her voice steady.

Scarlett glanced at their surroundings. "Turn right."

William cried, his face turning a ruddy shade of red as the sirens screeched out their warning.

The pavement filled with civilians, all racing toward the shelter. "Pull over," Scarlett ordered. "We'll never make it with the streets crowded like this. We'll have to go on foot."

Constance nodded, immediately parking the car along the left side. They exited the car, then raced down the street toward the shelter as the first explosions sounded.

There wasn't enough time.

Her heart raced as she clutched William to her chest and ran with Constance at her side.

They were a block away.

"Faster!" Scarlett shouted as another earth-shaking boom sounded behind them.

The word had barely left her mouth when the telltale sound of a high-pitched whistle filled her ears, and their world blew apart.

The relentless ringing in her ears was only broken by the sound of William's cry.

Scarlett pried her eyes open, pushing past the pain that screamed through her ribs.

It took a few disoriented seconds to get her bearings, to remember what had happened.

They'd been bombed.

Minutes. Hours? How much time had passed? *William!*

He cried again, and Scarlett rolled to her side, nearly weeping with relief at the sight of his tearful face wailing beside her.

She brushed the dirt and dust from his cheeks, but his tears only smeared the streaks. "It's okay, love. Mummy is right here," she promised, pulling him into her arms as her eyes swept over the destruction around them.

The blast had blown them into a garden bed, which had miraculously sheltered William. Her ribs ached and her ankle protested, but other than those small inconveniences, she was okay. She struggled to sit, holding William against her chest, and startled at the sight of blood slowly oozing from a gash on her shin, but she gave it only a cursory glance as dread filled her chest, replacing the ache in her ribs.

Where was Constance?

The building they'd been running by was nothing but a heap of rubble, and she coughed when her lungs took in more dirt than air.

"Constance!" she screamed, panic overtaking her.

The iron fence of the garden they'd landed in was broken, and through the gap of the bars, Scarlett caught a glimpse of red.

Constance.

She struggled to her feet, her lungs and ribs protesting with vehemence as she staggered toward the scrap of fabric she recognized as Constance's dress. Her arm caught on something, and she gazed down with confusion. Her handbag was still looped around her arm, and she'd snagged it on one of the iron bars. She yanked it free and stumbled a few more feet before falling to her knees at Constance's side, careful to keep William from the harsh blocks of stone that lay around his aunt... That lay on his aunt.

No. No. No.

God couldn't be this cruel, could he? A scream built up in Scarlett's throat, then ripped free as she used one arm and all her strength to shove the offensive, ugly piece of masonry from her sister's chest.

The warmth drained from her body, her soul, as she stared at Constance's dust-and-blood-covered face.

"No!" she screamed. It couldn't end like this. This couldn't be Constance's fate.

William began to cry harder, as if he, too, felt the light grow dimmer in the world.

She gripped her sister's hand, but there was no response.

Constance was dead.

CHAPTER THIRTY-THREE

Georgia

Dear Scarlett,

Marry me. Yes, I mean it. Yes, I'm going to ask you again and again until you're my wife. It's only been two days since I left Middle Wallop, and I can barely breathe, that's how much I already miss you. I love you, Scarlett, and it's not the kind of love that fades with distance or time. I'm yours and have been since the first time I looked into your eyes. I'll be yours no matter how much time passes before I see your eyes again. Always.

Jameson

"Do you think fifty thousand would cover it for the district?" I asked, wedging the phone between my ear and very sore shoulder as I took notes. I'd pushed it too hard this morning at the gym, but at least I hadn't fallen.

"That's more than enough! Thank you!" the librarian—Mr. Bell—exclaimed.

"You're very welcome." I grinned. This was the best part of my job. "I'll send the check out today."

"Thank you!" Mr. Bell repeated.

We hung up, and I opened the corporate checkbook to the next blank check. *The Scarlett Stanton Foundation for Literacy.* I brushed my finger over the scrolling script, then filled out the check, this time to a school district in Idaho.

The guidelines were simple: schools that needed books got money for books.

Gran would have loved it.

I dated the check March first, then sealed it into the envelope and scheduled a pickup with an overnight courier. *There. Done.* Now I could get to the studio.

A pen with a New York Mets logo rolled as I opened the top drawer, and my heart sank all over again, just like it did every single day. Noah's pen.

Because for nearly three months, this hadn't just been Gran's desk—my desk—it had been Noah's, too. And because throwing that pen away wouldn't change that fact, I put the checkbook in the drawer and shut it again.

The pen was my smallest reminder, anyway.

He was everywhere I looked. I saw us dancing in the living room every time I spotted the phonograph, heard the low timbre of his voice every time I ventured into the greenhouse. He was in my kitchen, making me tea. My entryway, kissing me breathless. My bedroom, making love to me. He was in this very office, admitting that he'd lied.

I sucked in a deep breath but didn't push away the pain. Feeling it was the only way through it. Otherwise I'd be the same shell I'd been after Damian.

The doorbell rang, and I took the envelope to the entryway, but it wasn't the courier on the other side when I opened the door.

I blinked in pure disbelief, my jaw dropping an inch before I snapped my mouth shut with an audible *click*.

"Aren't you going to invite me in?" Damian asked, thrusting a vase of flowers in my direction. "Happy seventh anniversary, sweetheart."

I weighed the gleeful thought of shutting the door in his face with the satisfaction of knowing *exactly* why he was here, and went with the latter, stepping back to let him in, then shutting the door as a frigid breeze swept over my skin.

"Thanks, I forgot how cold it is here," he said, holding the flowers—pale pink roses—with an expectant look.

"What do you want, Damian?" I set the envelope on the entry

table. What ploy was he going to try to use to get what he wanted? Guilt? Bribery? Emotional extortion?

"I wanted to talk business." His brow furrowed as he realized I wasn't taking the flowers, and he put them next to the envelope.

"So logically you got on a plane to Colorado instead of calling?" I crossed my arms.

"I was feeling sentimental," he said in that soft tone he reserved for apologies as his eyes did a once-over down my frame. "You look good, Georgia. Really good…softer, if that makes any sense."

The grandfather clock chimed. "Don't bother taking off your coat. You'll be gone before it chimes again."

"Fifteen minutes? Is that really all I'm worth after everything we've been through?" He tilted his head and flashed a playful dimple. *Emotional extortion it is.*

"Counting the time we dated, I've already given you eight years of my life. Trust me, fifteen minutes is generous."

I'd tried to avoid the comparison the entire time I'd been with Noah, but with Damian standing in front of me, it was impossible not to note the differences. Noah was taller, stacked with lean muscle, and held himself with the constant awareness of his body that had developed from years of climbing. Damian was none of those things.

He looked washed out, and what I'd once considered rather angelic was suddenly…meh. The blue of his eyes had nothing on Noah's dark brown ones. Had I ever really been attracted to Damian? Or was his interest in me what had lured me in?

"I like what you've done with it," Damian noted, glancing around the foyer.

"Thanks." I'd repainted, going with a white and gray theme as I'd slowly transformed the house from Gran's to mine. The master bedroom was next—and last—on the list. "You're using up your time."

His eyes flashed to mine, narrowing slightly. *There you are.* "I was hoping to talk to you about *The Things We Leave Unfinished.*"

"What about it?"

"I want to make you an offer, and before you tell me no, hear me out." He put his hands up, then took an envelope from inside his coat. "For old times' sake."

"Old times," I mused. "Like when you slept with your assistant? Or that one makeup artist? Or maybe when you got Paige pregnant and didn't have the balls to tell me about it, which led to the time I read all about my husband's baby mama from the sixteen billion text messages in the middle of Gran's wake?" I tilted my head. "To which of those *old times* are you referring?"

The veins on his neck bulged above the collar of his coat, and he had the grace to flush. "Those are all regrettable memories. But we have good ones, too. I'm here to help, not hurt, and I have a contract all ready for you to sign. I know Scarlett's money is tied up in all that charity work, so if you need a little extra, I'll even look at some of her other works to option. I don't want to see you suffer."

"How magnanimous of you," I drawled. "But you don't have to worry about me anymore. My gallery is doing just fine since I got back to creating the art I love—you know, when I'm not doing all that *charity work*."

He scoffed. "You can't be serious."

"Deadly." I deadpanned. "I never wanted the money. That was all you. And let me guess, that little contract you're so generously offering me not only gives you the rights to *The Things We Leave Unfinished*, but it also confirms your ownership in the five other options you haven't exercised yet, since I'm no longer part owner of Ellsworth Productions?" I asked sweetly.

"You know." His face went slack.

"I've always known." My voice dropped. "Why do you think I walked away without a fight? There was *nothing* about you worth keeping."

"It won't hold up in court," he bluffed.

"It will. My lawyers have always been better than yours. Gran saw to that when she had those same lawyers word the contract to include *in so far that Georgia Constance Stanton remains co-owner of Ellsworth Productions.* She didn't trust you with her stories, Damian. She trusted *me.* You were just too busy counting dollar signs to read the damn thing yourself." I heard the distinct purr of an engine coming up the drive.

His eyes flared with panic. "Gigi, let's talk about this. You know how deeply I cared for Scarlett. Do you really think this is what she'd want? It would have killed her to know you divorced me. That you gave up on us." His expression changed again. *Ah yes, guilt.*

"Gave up on you? She never liked you in the first place, and this conversation was over the minute the divorce papers were finalized. But I do have one question for you." I shifted my weight, hating to put myself in the position of needing anything from him.

"Anything." He swallowed. "You know I'm not married yet, right?" He stepped forward, and the familiar scent of overpowering cologne hit me like milk left too long in the refrigerator—everything good having turned rancid. "We can work this out. Go ahead, ask me whatever you want."

No thank you.

"Did you know who I was that day we met on campus?"

He startled.

"Did you?" In that moment, I saw myself through his eyes. A nineteen-year-old freshman, desperate for love and validation. An easy mark.

"Yes," he admitted, raking his hand over his hair. "And I know who you are now, Gigi. Yes, I've made some bad choices, but I've always loved you."

"Right. Because sleeping with other women—a *lot* of other women—is definitely how you show you love your wife." I paused, giving myself time for the pain to hit, but it didn't come. "Oddly enough, my mother warned me."

My front door flew open and Hazel stumbled in, her hair

windblown and her eyes wild. "Oh my God, you have to come watch!" She stopped suddenly, her eyebrows hitting the ceiling at the sight of Damian. "What. The. Hell?"

"Hazel." He gave her a wry smile and a nod.

"Asshole." Her eyes narrowed at him as she moved to my side.

"Damian was just leaving," I said with a quick grin as the clock chimed. "His time is up."

"Gigi," he begged.

"Goodbye." I walked to the door and held it open. "Give my best to Paige and…what did you name your son?"

"Damian, Jr."

"Of course you did." I motioned to the open door. "Drive safely, now. The pass gets slick this time of year." The sound of the door shutting was more satisfying now than it had been the day I'd left our New York apartment.

"Did you tell him?" Hazel asked, unzipping her coat and hanging it in the hall closet.

"About the options? I did. It was fun." I grinned and tucked my hair behind my ears. "Now, what did you fly in here in a tizzy about?"

"Oh!" Her eyes popped wide. "You have to get online right now." She grabbed my hand and yanked me into the office, all but shoving me into the chair while she brought up YouTube full screen and typed Noah's name.

"Hazel," I warned her softly. The last thing I needed was to see Noah on video, traipsing around New York like he hadn't broken my heart in a million pieces.

"It's not what you think." She clicked on a video of a popular morning show, and I tapped my toes impatiently through the five seconds of ads before it began playing. "Hold on, it doesn't start until about halfway through, and I damn near spit out my coffee." She clicked toward the middle of the video, skipping the first ten minutes.

"—does he think he is?" the female anchor asked her partner, who shook his head. "You don't do that to Scarlett Stanton. You just don't."

"I'd have to argue that the publisher must have known what they were getting when they hired Noah Harrison to finish it," he countered.

"Oh God," I whispered, my stomach dropping out of my body and off the face of the earth. Knowing Noah might get some negative press for my choice and seeing it were two different things.

"It gets worse," Hazel muttered.

"How much worse?" I wasn't sure I could take it.

"Watch."

"I'm not the only one to cry foul," the anchor said, putting up her hands. "Early review copies are out, and spoiler alert: it's not pretty. *Publication Quarterly* calls it, and I quote, 'An egotistical attempt to outshine the foremost romance novelist of her day.'"

The audience booed, and my hands shot up to cover my mouth. "That's not fair!" I said through the gaps of my fingers.

"It gets worse," Hazel repeated.

"How? Are they going to burn a cardboard cutout of Noah?" I challenged.

"Would it bother you if they did?" she asked with mock innocence.

I shot a glare her way.

"The *New York Daily* took it a step further, saying, 'Scarlett Stanton is rolling over in her grave. Though incredibly well-written and emotionally moving, Harrison's blunt disregard for Stanton's bestselling brand of feel-good endings is a slap in the face to romance fans around the world.' And I can't disagree."

"Make it stop." My hands slid from my mouth to cover my eyes as they flashed a picture of Noah.

"One more minute." Hazel yanked the mouse out of my reach.

"The *Chicago Tribune* weighed in with, 'Not since Jane Austen has a romance author been so internationally loved, yet so disregarded by men. Noah Harrison's painful, emotionally sadistic ending to Scarlett Stanton's own love story is unforgivable."

"Oh, Noah," I groaned, letting my forehead fall into my hands.

"But maybe the best review, as always, comes from Scarlett Stanton herself, who said, 'No one writes painful, depressing fiction masquerading as love stories like Noah Harrison.'" The anchor sighed. "Honestly, what was the publisher thinking? You don't bring a man into a corner of the industry that women had to claw out for themselves amid the slut-shaming mommy-porn jokes and let him walk all over the very thing that defines the genre. You just don't. Shame on you, Noah Harrison. Shame on you." The anchor pointed to the camera, and the segment ended.

"At least they didn't set him on fire," I muttered, staring at the computer screen in horror.

"They just had your gran do it," Hazel noted.

"They're not being fair to him. It's a beautiful, poignant ending." I leaned back in the chair and crossed my arms. "It's a fitting tribute for what she went through in real life. And he had *nothing* to do with trashing the genre. That was all me!"

"News flash, G. No one reads romance for real life." She sighed. "Also, that man is so in love with you that I can't even… anything. I can't." She perched on the edge of the desk and faced me.

"Don't," I whispered as my heart cracked, the hastily constructed scabs breaking open.

"Oh, I'm going to." She moved so I couldn't look away. "That man just trashed his career on an international stage for you."

"He trashed his career out of contractual obligation," I countered, but the damage was done. My entire body ached with missing him just like it did every day. Add on the hatred he was getting over my choice, and I was ready to bury myself in a gallon of Ben & Jerry's.

"Keep telling yourself that." She shook her head. "He's Noah Harrison. If he wanted out of the contract, he would have gotten out. He did this for you. To prove that he would keep his word."

"He lied, and for no good reason." Frustration welled up, doing its best to overpower the pain. "I wouldn't have kicked him out in December if I'd known he'd finished the book. I was already in love with him!"

My hands flew to my mouth.

"Ha!" Hazel jabbed her finger at me. "I told you!"

"It doesn't matter!" My arms fell to my sides. "The ink isn't remotely dry on my divorce. It hasn't even been a year!" My spine stiffened. "Isn't there a rule somewhere that you have to take some time for yourself before shoving all your baggage at the next man?"

"Okay, one, there's no rule. Two, I've seen Noah's arms. He can carry all your baggage and then some." Her face scrunched.

"Shut up." She wasn't wrong.

"Three, you're not your mom, G. You'll never *be* your mom. And honestly, you were pretty much alone in the six years of that shitty marriage. You've had *plenty* of time for yourself, but if you think you need more, then take it. Just do the world a favor and tell the man."

I sagged against the back of the chair. "It's impractical. We live on opposite sides of the country. Besides, it's been three weeks since he tried to call. He's probably over it. His rebound rate is astronomical."

"If by rebound rate, you mean he's only been seen in public with his sister, then I agree." She arched a brow at me. "I love you, but you have to get out of your own damned way. He loves you. He screwed up. It happens. Owen screws up every three days, apologizes, makes up for it, and then screws something else up three days later. You figure it out as you go along." She glanced at her wedding ring and smiled.

"What do you screw up?" I asked.

"I'm perfect. Besides, we're not talking about me." Her phone rang and she stood so she could get it free. "Hey, babe. Wait.

Say that again. Colin did *what* with the scissors while you were in the bathroom? How short is *short*?" Her voice pitched shrill.

Oh shit. I hopped up from the chair and raced for the hall closet, yanking her coat off the hangar and shoving it at her as she strode out the door.

"No, don't try to round it out!" She waved at me frantically in farewell, then opened her car door. "No, I'm not mad, it could have happened to me, too. It'll grow back—" Her voice cut off as she got into the car.

"Good luck!" I called out as she drove the semicircle back to the main road, only to have her spot taken by the courier. "One second!" I said, dashing back inside to grab the envelope, and brought the roses, too. "Here, Tom. Take these for your wife."

"You sure?" he asked, eyeing the roses.

"Absolutely."

"Hold on, I have a delivery for you," he said, exchanging my envelope and the roses for a medium-size package. I signed for it, noting the return address of Gran's lawyer.

Right. It would have been my seventh wedding anniversary. At least she wasn't here to see what a hot mess that had ended up being. I carried the package in, shut the door, then plopped down on the bottom step of the staircase, setting the box next to me.

Noah Harrison's painful, emotionally sadistic ending to Scarlett Stanton's own love story is unforgivable. I sighed and stared at the box, wishing there was some easy answer to all of this. Or maybe there was, and Hazel was right—I was standing in my own way.

I leaned forward and took my cell out of my vest pocket, then opened my messages and typed out a text.

GEORGIA: I'm so sorry about the reviews.

I truly was, but my heart wouldn't stop screaming joyfully that he'd kept his promise.

The message showed delivered, not read. Who knew when he'd get around to seeing it, anyway. Or maybe he'd never open it.

"From Ice Queen to Hot Mess. Not sure that's an improvement," I muttered, picking up Gran's package. The tape gave way easily, which was convenient, since I didn't have Noah...or his pocketknife.

Inside there were three manila envelopes. The one labeled *read me second* was thickest. I set it and the third to the side, then opened the one designated first and pulled out a letter. My heart throbbed, bittersweet at the sight of her handwriting.

Dearest Georgia,

Today is your wedding anniversary. If I'm right about the decline of my health, it's your seventh. That seventh was a big one for your Grandpa Brian and me. He had just been diagnosed, everything went sideways, and it was all we could do to hold on to each other.

I hope your seventh goes smoother.

But just in case it doesn't, I thought it was time you truly understand the depth of love that created you. You, my dearest one, are the product of generations of love, not just the infatuations that some experience but true, deep, soul-mending loves that even time cannot separate.

I hope by now you've cleaned out my closet—no, not that one. The other one. Yes, that one, where all the shirts have been replaced by pages courtesy of that little typewriter that has been my constant companion through the joy and the heartache. I hope you've found the little alcove in the back of the second shelf. If not, go look—I'll wait right here.

Found it? Good. This was the work I could never bring myself to truly end. The work that was started for my darling William. I'm sorry I never let you read it while I was with you. My excuses are endless, but the truth is I was afraid you'd see straight through me.

You'll find that it ends on what had been up until then—the hardest day of my life. The day I lost my sister, my best friend, while still reeling from the loss of the love of my life. That day has only since been eclipsed by the snowy evening that stole William and Hannah. Our family has never been without our share of tragedy, has it?

The story is yours to read now, Georgia. Take your time. I've dabbled with it over the years, adding bits and pieces from memory, then setting it aside. Once you reach the end, once you're there with me on that war-torn street in Ipswich, covered in dust, I want you to read through the letters bundled at the top of the manuscript.

These are the true testament to the love that created you, the fact behind the moments of embellished fiction. Once you feel that love, taste the acrid smoke of the last air raid on your tongue, and are ready for what happened next, open the next envelope in this package. You'll realize you've always known the ending...it's the middle that was muddled.

When you're done, I hope you'll read the third—and last—envelope in this package.

Please forgive me for the lie.

All my love,
Gran

Gran never lied. What was she talking about? My fingers shook as I opened the thickest envelope. I'd already read the manuscript and the letters, wept with gut-wrenching sobs when Scarlett had been notified that Jameson had gone missing, and again when she realized Constance had been killed.

I slipped the stack of papers free and skimmed my fingers over the familiar, hard strikes of Gran's typewriter.

Then I read.

CHAPTER THIRTY-FOUR

June 1942

Ipswich, England

Scarlett wasn't cold anymore. The chill had gradually faded to blessed numbness as she stared at her lifeless sister.

Was this the price for William's life? For hers? Had God taken Jameson and Constance as some sort of divine payment?

"Shh," she whispered in William's ear over the ringing in her own, trying to soothe him. There was no one left in the world who could soothe her. Everyone she loved besides William was gone.

He raised a sticky hand to her face, and Scarlett blinked at the blood on his palm, her heart stopping. Using the hem of her dress, she swiped at his skin, then sobbed in relief. The blood wasn't his.

This wasn't happening. Not really. It couldn't be. She refused to accept it.

She gripped Constance's shoulder and shook furiously, willing her sister back to life. "Wake up!" she demanded, shrieking like a banshee. "Constance!" she wailed. "You can't be dead! I won't allow it!"

To her shock, Constance woke with a heaving cough, gasping for air. She wasn't dead; she'd merely been knocked unconscious.

"Constance!" she cried, her chest heaving as she sobbed in relief, leaning over her sister and balancing William carefully. "Can you move?"

Constance looked up at her with glazed, confused eyes. "I think so," she answered, her voice croaking like a frog.

"Slowly," Scarlett ordered as she helped her sister upright.

Constance's face was battered, blood seeping from a gash above her left eye, and her nose was clearly broken. "I thought you were dead," she cried, pulling her sister into the hardest hug of her life.

Constance lifted her hand to Scarlett's back, reaching around William to hold them both. "I'm okay," she assured her sister. "Is William..."

"He seems okay," Scarlett replied, her gaze sweeping over William and Constance. The cold had returned, and her head swam as though she were underwater.

"Is it over?" Constance asked, glancing at the destruction surrounding them.

"I think so," Scarlett answered, noting the lack of sirens.

"Thank God." Constance hugged her sister once more before drawing back, stricken. The look in her eyes raised the hairs on the back of Scarlett's neck.

"What is it?" she asked as Constance gawked at her blood-soaked hand. Moving William along her hip, Scarlett wiped at the blood with a somewhat clean patch of her dress. Air gushed from her lungs in relief. Lucky. They'd been so lucky today. "It's all right," she assured her sister with a shaky smile. "It's not yours."

Constance's eyes flared as her gaze swept down Scarlett's torso. "It's yours," she whispered.

As if Constance's words triggered Scarlett's body, shattering the rallying defenses of shock, agony ripped through her back, and searing pain exploded in her ribs. Scarlett gasped as it overtook her, her eyes sweeping down the spreading bloodstain across her blue plaid dress—the same one she'd worn for that first date with Jameson.

It all made sense—the cold, the pain, the lightheadedness. She was losing blood. Her balance gave way, and she collapsed on her side, barely managing to shelter William's head from hitting the pavement.

"Scarlett!" Constance yelled, but the sound struggled to cut through the fog in her head.

Instead, she focused on her son.

"I love you more than all the stars in the sky," she whispered to William, who had stopped crying and lay on her arm, staring at her with eyes the same shade as her own. "My William."

In that moment of chaos and shrieking sirens, it all became so clear, as if she could see the threads of fate that had woven this tapestry. Leaving home. Serving beside her sister. Meeting Jameson on that dusty road. Falling head over heels in love. It wasn't their path in jeopardy—that was already set. Only William's was undecided.

"It was all for you, William," she whispered, her throat clogging, forcing a gurgle. "You are so loved. Never doubt that."

Constance hovered above them, her mouth agape as she studied Scarlett's back. Her lower lip trembled as she kneeled closer. "You have to get up. We have to get you to hospital!"

"I'm all right." Scarlett smiled as the pain faded once more. "You have to go," she managed to say through wet, gasping breaths.

"I'm not going anywhere!" The panic on Constance's face tore at Scarlett's heart like nothing else could. This was something she couldn't save Constance from. She couldn't even save herself.

"Yes, you are." She shifted her gaze back to William. "He needs to learn to camp," she said without looking away from his face—Jameson's face. "And to fish, and to fly." That was what Jameson had wanted. For their son to grow up safe from the bombs that had brought this exact moment.

"And you can teach him all of that," Constance cried. "But we have to get you to hospital. Hear the sirens? They're nearly here."

"I wanted more time with you," she said to William, each word harder than the last. "We both did."

"Scarlett, listen to me!" Constance shrieked.

"No, you listen," Scarlett said before a cough wracked her body, blood bubbling past her lips. She managed a waterlogged breath and locked her eyes on her sister. "You swore you'd protect him."

"With my life," Constance repeated the vow.

"Get him out of here," Scarlett ordered, mustering all of her strength. "Take him to Vernon."

Constance's eyes flared with understanding as tears streaked through the dust on her cheeks. "Not without you."

"Promise me you'll care for him." Scarlett used what was left of her energy to turn her head toward her beautiful, perfect son.

"I promise," Constance cried, her voice breaking with tears.

"Thank you," Scarlett whispered, gazing at William. "We love you."

"Scarlett," Constance sobbed, cradling the back of her sister's neck as Scarlett's eyes unfocused.

"Jameson," Scarlett whispered with a faint smile.

Then she was gone.

"No!" Constance screamed, the sound overtaking the shrill wail of the sirens.

William's face scrunched as he let loose the cry that echoed her own.

Where was the ambulance? Certainly something could be done. This wasn't how this ended—it couldn't be.

Bits of debris dug into her knees as she leaned over Scarlett and lifted William into her arms, cradling his head against her chest, unblinking, unfeeling as the world swirled around them.

"Ma'am?" someone asked, crouching at her side. "Are you and your baby all right?"

Constance's brow knit as she tried to make sense of the man's words. "My sister," she said in way of explanation.

The man looked at her with pity, glancing between Scarlett's fallen frame and her eyes. "She's gone," he said as kindly as he could.

"I know," she whispered, her lips trembling.

"Can I get some help over here?" the man called back over his shoulder. Two other men appeared, crouching to her eye level. "We'll take care of her. You need to get to hospital. You're bleeding."

"I have a car." Constance nodded, her eyes wide and unfocused. When the men asked for identification, she handed them her handbag. Her mind had shut down, as though it had reached its limit for trauma, for heartbreak.

Edward.

Jameson.

Scarlett.

It was too much. How could one person feel so much sorrow and not die from it? Why was she kneeling, nearly unscathed amid the rubble that had taken her sister?

Constance staggered to her feet, holding William to her chest as the men loaded Scarlett into an ambulance.

Promise me you'll protect him. Scarlett's words whispered through the cacophony of the street, consumed her very being. She tightened her hold on William, tucking his head under her chin.

This was where it ended.

No more grief, no more bombings, no more loss. William would live.

Ignoring the calls of the men around her, Constance grabbed the handbag at her feet and picked her way across the pavement, slipping twice on shrapnel as people appeared on the pavement, emerging from their shelters.

She had to get William to Vernon. She had to get him on that flight.

Dazed but determined, she walked back to the car, William's cries mixing with the ringing in her ears and the screaming of her own heart.

She slid behind the wheel, noting that she'd left the keys in

the ignition. Securing William in the seat next to her, she headed
for the airfield, blinking constantly against the blur in her eyes.

She didn't remember much of the drive, but she arrived at
the airfield, showing them the pass she kept on the dashboard.
The guard let her through, and she continued toward the hangar,
dazed, drunk on shock and grief. She parked the car haphazardly,
then bundled William in his blanket and climbed out. His foot
caught in the strap of her handbag— No, it was Scarlett's handbag.

Which meant she had William's paperwork, but where was
hers?

With Scarlett. She'd handle that later. She clutched William
and stumbled toward the front of the car, where a tall, uniformed
man rushed her way. He looked too much like Jameson to not
be his uncle.

"Vernon?" she questioned, clutching William reflexively.

"My God, are you all right?" The man's eyes were as green as
Jameson's, and they flared in surprise and shock as he reached her.

"You're Vernon, right?" Nothing else mattered. "Jameson's
uncle?"

The man nodded, inspecting her face carefully. "Scarlett?"

Her heart cracked open, blinding pain slicing through the
fog. "My sister died," she whispered. "She was right there in my
arms, and she just died."

"You were caught in the bombing?" His brow furrowed.

She nodded. "My sister died," she repeated. "I brought William."

"I'm so sorry. That's a pretty nasty gash on your forehead."
He steadied her shoulder with a hand and pressed a handkerchief
to her forehead.

"Sir, we don't have much time. We can't delay takeoff again,"
someone called out.

Vernon muttered a curse. "Do you have everything you
need?" he asked her.

"The bags are in the back. One trunk and two cases, just like
Jameson said—" Her voice broke. "I packed them myself."

Vernon's face fell. "They'll find him," he swore. "They have to. Until then, this is what he wanted." The sadness in his eyes reflected her own.

She nodded. *They won't find him, not alive anyway.* The feeling settled deep. Her heart told her Jameson was with Scarlett. William was alone. What would happen to him?

"Get the bags," Vernon ordered the men standing behind him, then brushed his thumb across William's cheek, then the blanket she'd wrapped around him. "I'd know my sister's handiwork anywhere," he muttered with a small smile as the bags were unloaded and carried toward the runway. He studied her again, his face softening. "Your eyes are just as blue as he described," he said quietly, shifting his gaze to William. "I see you have them, too."

"They run in the family," Constance mumbled. Family. Was she really about to hand over her nephew, Scarlett's son, to a complete and total stranger just because he was a blood relation?

Protect him. Scarlett's voice rang through her ears. She could do this—for her.

"The cut on your head looks to be more bluster than wound," Vernon noted, examining her face as he removed the pressure and the handkerchief. "But I'm pretty sure your nose is broken."

"It doesn't matter," she said simply. Nothing mattered.

His brow puckered. "Let's get to the plane. The docs can check you out before we head to the States. I'm so sorry about your sister," he said softly, moving his hand to her back and leading her toward the runway. "Jameson told me how close you two were."

Everything in her recoiled at his use of the past tense, but she kept moving, kept walking, and soon they reached the runway, where the props spun on a converted liberty bomber she knew the ATC used to ferry the pilots back to America.

A few uniformed officers waited outside the door, no doubt completing the manifest.

"Holy shit," one of the officers muttered, staring at her face.

"What's wrong, O'Connor?" Vernon snapped. "Never seen a woman caught in an air raid before?"

"Sorry," the man mumbled, averting his gaze.

"Don't tell me that baby is going to cry the whole way to Maine," one of the Yanks joked in an obvious attempt to divert the awkwardness.

"*That baby*," Vernon said, motioning toward William, "is William Vernon Stanton, my great-nephew, and he can cry the whole damn time if he likes."

"Yes, sir." The man tipped his hat at Constance and climbed aboard.

"You have all your papers?" Vernon glanced at her handbag—no—*Scarlett's* handbag.

"Yes," she whispered as her stomach pitched and gravity shifted. *Your eyes are just as blue as he described.* Vernon thought she was Scarlett. They all did. She opened her mouth to correct him, but nothing came out.

"Excellent."

The last remaining officer lifted his clipboard and glanced between Constance and Vernon. "Lieut. Col. Stanton," he said with a nod, checking the name off his list. "I wasn't expecting William Stanton to be quite so young, but I've got him here." He checked again. "That leaves us with…"

Protect him.

With my life. She'd promised Scarlett, and that was exactly what she would give—her life for William's. Only Scarlett could go with him, protect him.

She lifted her chin, adjusted William on her hip, and opened the handbag with trembling fingers to find the visa she'd packed this morning. The damage to her face was, in its own way, now a blessing. She handed the papers to the officer, showing him the scar on her palm that matched the description. Then she pressed a kiss to William's forehead and silently begged his forgiveness.

"I'm Scarlett Stanton."

CHAPTER THIRTY-FIVE

Georgia

"Oh my God," I whispered, the last page fluttering to the floor between my feet. My breath came in a stuttered gasp as a pair of tears splattered on the paper.

Gran wasn't Scarlett…she was Constance.

There was a roaring in my ears, as though the cogs in my mind were spinning at quadruple time, trying to process it all, to make sense of what she'd written.

All these years, and she'd never said a word. Not one. She'd taken her secret to her grave, carried it alone. Or had Grandpa Brian known?

I picked up the fallen page, filed it at the end of the chapter, then shuffled it back into the envelope. Why didn't she tell me? Why now, when I couldn't ask?

The seal broke easily on the third envelope, and I nearly ripped the papers in my haste to read them.

My dearest Georgia,

Do you hate me? I wouldn't blame you. There were certainly days where I hated myself, where I signed her name and felt every inch the fraud I was. But this letter isn't for me; it's for you. So allow me to answer the obvious questions.

As we flew over the North Atlantic, William fell asleep, zipped in and warm with Vernon. That's when the reality of what I'd done hit hard. There were so many ways it could go wrong, and yet I couldn't come clean, not with William in the balance. It would only be a matter of time before the truth was revealed and I was forced back to England. All I needed was enough time to meet Jameson's family—to know for certain that William would be in good hands. I had to play the part.

I took paper and pen from the handbag, then bid farewell to Constance, knowing that posting this letter would only serve to help convince my family that William was out of reach.

Two days after we arrived in the States, I posted that letter and stumbled upon a British paper in the lobby of our hotel. It listed the recent casualties from the June air raids. My heart stopped the moment I read CONSTANCE WADSWORTH listed among the dead. That's when I remembered that it was my handbag the ambulance drivers had taken with my sister.

Heaven help me, that's when I realized I could stay with William, not just until he was settled but forever. To my mother, father, and Henry, Constance was dead. No one had challenged it. I was free, but only as Scarlett. My temporary lie became my life.

Vernon took me to immigration, where I was given a new identification card—this time with my picture. My face was still swollen from the bombing, my nose bandaged until the moment the photographer flashed his camera. The other identifying features—the scar and our beauty marks—matched perfectly, as they always had.

Jameson's family was so warm, so welcoming, even in the face of their unbearable grief. I watched the light slowly die in his mother's eyes as the months, then the years passed and no news came from the front about Jameson's disappearance. I didn't have to feign grief—my sorrow was all too real for the loss of Jameson and Edward, but mostly my sister.

From the moment I was born, she'd been at my side. We'd been educated together, sworn to see the war through together, and yet there I was, raising her son in a foreign country that was now my own, practicing her signature over and over, then burning the pages so no one would be suspicious.

The first real challenge came the day Beatrice asked when I planned to begin writing again. Oh, I looked like my sister and even sounded like her. I knew the most intimate details of her life, but writing... that had never been my talent. Perhaps I should have told them, then, but the fear of being separated from William was more than I could bear. So, I pretended to write when no one was looking. I retyped The Diplomat's Daughter page by page, fixing grammatical errors and tweaking a few passages so I could honestly say I'd written something in it. I realized that lies were easier when they were based on truth, so I injected truth at every possible turn.

I didn't submit The Diplomat's Daughter for publication. Beatrice did the year the war ended. The year we finished the gazebo at the bend in the creek where Jameson asked Scarlett to wait for him. That was the year Beatrice accepted what I'd already known. Jameson wasn't coming home. I helped build a gazebo for a future that only existed in my imagination, a future where love and tragedy didn't walk hand in hand.

The problem with signing that first book deal was the request for the second, the third, the fourth. I went through the hatbox, used her partial chapters, her plot notes, and when my own heart failed, I simply imagined she was beside me, hiding in our parents' house, walking the long roads, sitting at that kitchen table, telling me what happened next. In that way, she lived in every book I typed, then the ones I wrote as the hatbox emptied.

I had the house built big enough for Jameson's family, and we moved.

Then Brian came along. Oh, Georgia, I fell for his warm eyes and soft smile that very first year he rented the cottage. It wasn't the same as I'd felt for Edward—that had been a once-in-a-lifetime love—but it was steady, warm, and as gentle as the spring thaw. After Henry...well, I needed gentle.

Beatrice saw. She knew.

William saw it, too. He never voiced his disapproval. Never made me feel guilty. But the year he turned sixteen, he found Brian and me dancing in the gazebo. The phonograph disappeared the next day. He had his father's smile and his passion for life and his mother's eyes and steel will. He was the best thing I'd ever done with my life, and the day he married Hannah—the love of his life—he told me it was time to marry mine.

I told him the love of my life had been taken by the war—that was the truth.

He told me Jameson would want me to be happy—that was true, too.

Every year Brian asked. Every year I said no.

Georgia, there exists within me a gray, shadowy place where I am both the girl I was...and the woman I became that day, both Constance and Scarlett. And in that gray place, I was still married to Henry Wadsworth—though he had remarried and moved his new family onto the land I'd ruined myself to protect. The land where he'd buried my sister in his one and only romantic gesture. And perhaps the girl who had been so egregiously abused took a perverse pleasure that she could bring his life toppling down by simply admitting that she was alive.

The woman I was refused to allow the shadow to dim Brian's light—refused to bring him into a marriage that would ultimately be as fraudulent as I was—but I could never tell him the truth—that would have made him complicit in my crimes. He stopped asking in 1968.

The day I read that Henry Wadsworth had died of a massive stroke, I raced to the veterinary clinic where Brian worked and begged him to ask me again. Only after William had given his blessing did I tell the lawyers to start the paperwork for Jameson.

I married Brian seventeen years after we met, and the decade we were married was the happiest of my life. I found my happily-ever-after. Never doubt that. William and Hannah had tried so long for a child, and Ava was the apple of their eye—and mine. I wish you had known her before the accident, Georgia. Tragedy has a way of breaking gentle things and soldering the shattered pieces together in ways we can't control. Some, it remakes into stronger, more resilient creatures. In others, the pieces fuse before they heal, leaving only razor-sharp edges. I can offer you no other explanation or excuse for the way she's cut you over the years.

You, my sweet girl, were the light of my very long life.

You were my reason to slow down, to live with more intention, less fear.

You, Georgia, who remind me so very much of my sister.

You have her indomitable will, her strong heart, her fierce spirit, and her eyes—my eyes.

I pray that this package finds you happy and madly in love with the man you've deemed worthy of your heart. I also hope you've realized by now that man isn't Damian—not unless he's had an epiphany between what is now your sixth year of marriage, and when you open this on your seventh anniversary. And yes, I get to say that because I'm dead. When I was alive, you were determined, and heaven help the soul who tries to change your stubborn little mind. Some lessons we simply have to learn for ourselves.

So why tell you, now that I'm gone? Why lay this truth at your feet when I trusted no one else? Because you, more than any other Stanton, need to know that it is love that brought you here. I've never seen another love like Scarlett and Jameson's. It was one of those fated lightning strikes, miraculous to see up close, to feel the energy between the two when they were in the same room. That is the love that lives in your veins.

I've never seen another love like I had for Edward—we were twin flames.

But I've also never seen another love like I had for Brian—deep and calm and true.

Or another love like William's for Hannah—achingly sweet.

But I have seen the same love that I had for William the day I stepped onto that plane. It lives in you. You are the culmination of every lightning strike and twist of fate.

Do not settle for the love that hones your edges and turns you brittle and cold, Georgia. Not when there are so many other kinds of love waiting for you. And don't wait like I did, wasting seventeen years because I'd left one bitter foot in my past.

We're all entitled to our mistakes. When you recognize them for *what they are, don't live there. Life is too short to miss the lightning strike and too long to live it alone. This is where my story ends. I'll be watching over you to see where yours leads.*

All my love,
Gran

Tears dripped down my face as I finished the last page, and they weren't the pretty, silent ones. Oh no, I was a snotty mess.

She'd lived seventy-eight years of her life as Scarlett, never being called by her own name. Never letting someone else help carry the burden of what she'd done. She'd borne the deaths of Edward, Jameson, Scarlett, Brian...then William and Hannah, yet hadn't hardened under the grief.

I left the letter on the steps, then clutched my phone and stumbled to the office. Snatching the framed picture of Scarlett and Jameson from the desk, I hit my knees in front of the bookshelf cabinets and dug through the contents to find the same albums I'd shown to Noah months ago.

William. William. William. The first picture of Gran had been taken in 1950, long enough after the Ipswich bombing that no one would question any physical differences. She hadn't just shied away from the camera lens, she'd studiously avoided it.

I studied both pictures, needing to see it for myself.

Scarlett's chin was slightly sharper, Constance's lower lip a bit fuller. Same nose. Same eyes. Same beauty mark. But they were not the same woman.

People see what they want to see. How many times had she said that to me over the years? Everyone had simply accepted that Constance was Scarlett because they'd never had reason to question it. Why would they when she had William?

The gardening. The tiny style differences Noah had spotted. The baking...it all made sense.

I flipped through the album until I found her wedding picture to Grandpa Brian. There was real, true love shining in her eyes. Noah's ending had been truer to life than he could have known... but it wasn't Scarlett's ending, it was Constance's.

Scarlett had died on a ruined street nearly eighty years ago. Jameson couldn't have been far off. They hadn't been apart for long. They'd been together all this time.

I sucked in a shaky breath and wiped my tears on my sleeve as I fumbled with my cell phone.

If Gran had lived a lie to give me this life, then I owed it to her to live it.

The message I'd sent to Noah still hadn't been read, but I called him anyway. Four rings. Voicemail. The guy didn't even have a personalized message, and I wasn't about to pour my heart out on a voicemail anyway. Besides, with the reviews out, it was no wonder he wasn't answering.

I gasped. Reviews were out. Stumbling to my feet, I slid into the chair at my desk, then clicked through my emails until I found Adam's number.

"Adam Feinhold," he answered.

"Adam, it's Georgia," I blurted. "Stanton, I mean."

"I figured it wasn't the state calling," he drawled dryly. "What can I do for you, Ms. Stanton? It's a bit...heavy around here today."

"Yeah, I deserve that," I admitted, cringing like he could see me. "Look, I tried Noah first—"

"I have no clue where he is. He left me a message that he was off on some research trip and he'd be back in time for any release promo we need."

I blinked. "Noah's...gone?"

"Not gone. Researching. Don't stress, he does it every book but yours, since you know, the research had already been done."

"Oh." My heart sank. So much for seizing the lightning bolt.

"You know the guy is pretty much dying over you, right?" Adam said softly. "And I say that as his best friend, not his editor.

He's miserable. Or at least he *was* miserable. This morning he just sounded pissed, but that was after the reviews came out. Christopher is even more pissed, which as editorial director is absolutely possible, trust me."

I was twenty-four hours too late to tell him I'd been wrong. Really wrong. But maybe I could show him. At least I could try. "Did Noah really edit both versions?"

"Yep. Copy edits and all. Told you, he's a mess over you."

"Good." I smiled, too happy to clarify that statement.

"Good?"

"Yep. Good. Now go get Christopher."

CHAPTER THIRTY-SIX

Noah

The only institution slower than publishing was the United States government. Especially when it had to work in conjunction with another country, and neither could agree on who was responsible for what. But six weeks and a couple hundred thousand dollars later, I had the answer to one of my questions.

I was starting to think the other one was better left unanswered.

I cursed as I scalded my tongue on freshly brewed coffee and squinted at the sunlight streaming in the apartment windows. Jet lag was a pain in the ass, and I hadn't exactly been keeping regular hours over there as it was.

I carried my cup-of-lava to the couch, then fired up the laptop and scanned through about a billion emails. Ignoring the real world for six weeks came with some serious inbox complications that I really wasn't feeling up for dealing with yet.

Cell phone, it was. As usual, I went through my texts to find the last message from Georgia.

GEORGIA: I'm sorry about the reviews.

That was one I'd gotten when I landed the day after everyone in publishing simultaneously agreed that I was an asshole, which, in their defense, was true. Just not for the reasons they shouted on every platform. I read through the rest of the conversation, which had become just as routine as coffee.

NOAH: I kept my word.

GEORGIA: I know. I'm taking some time, but call me when you get back.

NOAH: Will do.

That was it. That's where we left it. She was *taking some time*, which roughly translated into leave-me-the-hell-alone, so I did. For six fucking weeks.

How much more time did the woman need?

Also, did that time include today? Was I supposed to call now that I was home? Or give her more time?

It had been three months since she'd raised that stubborn, stoic chin and thrown me out on my ass for the lie I'd been ridiculous enough to tell. Three months since those eyes had welled with tears I'd put there. Three months, and I still loved her so much I ached with it. I couldn't have written a more lovesick character, and I had the circles under my eyes to prove it.

Mom called, and I answered.

"Hey, Mom. I just got back last night. Did you get your copy messengered over?" Usually I took my latest copy myself, but I wasn't sure I could live through seeing her face once she realized what I'd done to Scarlett Stanton's last work.

"It came by courier last night! I'm so proud of you!" Shit, she sounded so happy—because she hadn't read the ending yet.

"Thanks, Mom." My laptop started pinging next to me as the Google alerts filed in with more reviews. I really had to turn that crap off.

"I love it, Noah. You really outdid yourself. I can't even tell where Scarlett's words end and yours begin!"

"Well, I'm sure you'll figure it out once you get to the end. It's pretty obvious," I groaned, sliding lower into the couch. There was a special hell for people who disappointed their mothers. "And I need you to know that I'm sorry."

"Sorry? For what?"

"Just wait. You'll see." I should have stayed overseas, but

even that distance wasn't far enough to save me from the wrath of my mother.

"Noah Antonio Morelli, will you stop talking in circles?" she snapped. "I stayed up all night and read the whole thing."

My stomach hit the floor. "Am I still invited for Memorial Day?"

"Why wouldn't you be?" Her tone grew suspicious.

"Because I slaughtered the ending?" I rubbed my temples, waiting for the ax to fall.

"Oh, stop being humble. Noah, it was beautiful! The moment in the aspen grove when Jameson sees—"

"What?" I sat straight up, my laptop crashing to the floor. "Jameson..." That wasn't what happened. At least, not in the version they'd published. *Adam.* "Mom, do you have the book there with you?"

"Yes. Noah, what's going on?"

"I'm not sure, honestly. Do me a favor and flip to the front, where the copyright is." Adam had to have printed a special edition for her. Holy shit, I owed him big time.

"I'm there."

"Is it a special edition?"

"Well, not if first editions are special."

What the actual hell? I grabbed my laptop off the floor and opened the first Google alert. It was the *Times* and the first line knocked me on my ass.

HARRISON SEAMLESSLY BLENDS STANTON'S VISION—

"Mom, I love you, but I have to go." I clicked down the row of alerts. They all said variations of the same thing.

"Okay. I love you, Noah. You should get more sleep," she said in that kindly authoritarian way she'd always had.

"I will. Love you, too." I hung up and dialed Adam.

He picked up on the first ring.

"Welcome home! How was the trip? You fired up to start

next year's release?" Why was everyone so damned chipper this morning?

"Harrison seamlessly blends Stanton's vision with his own take on classic romance. This one shouldn't be missed. The *Times*," I read.

"Nice!"

"Are you serious? How about this one?" I snapped. "We've been had. How the bait and switch of the decade led to a surprised—and relieved—fandom. The *Tribune*." My hands curled into fists.

"Not bad. Almost looks like we meant to do it, huh?"

"Adam," I growled.

"Noah."

"What the hell did you do to my book?" I roared. It was all ruined. Everything I'd put on the line for her had been ripped away. She'd never forgive me for this—never trust me, no matter how much *time* I gave her.

"Exactly what I was told to do by the only person who had the *contractual right* to tell me to do it," he said slowly.

There was only one person who could approve changes without me, and her time was officially up.

CHAPTER THIRTY-SEVEN

Georgia

"Talk about swoon," Hazel sighed.

"Yeah, that was a good part." I switched the phone to my other ear and finished washing the dirt off my hands. The seedlings were coming along, and in just a few weeks, they'd be strong enough to be transplanted into the garden. Right in time for the weather to be kind enough to allow it.

"And holy wedding-night scene, Batman. I have to know, was that your gran? Or is there a little Noah in there, because it was so hot that I took myself down to Owen's office—"

"Stop right there, because I do not need that mental picture the next time I go to the dentist." I dried off my hands and tried *not* to think of exactly how much of that was Noah. Guess he'd set out to prove me wrong about the *unsatisfying* comment I'd made that day in the bookstore.

"Fine, but seriously. Hot."

"Yeah, yeah," I said as the doorbell rang.

"You sure you don't want to come over for dinner?" she asked as I walked through the hallway and into the foyer. "I hate the thought of you eating pizza on a night like tonight. You should be celebrating. Gran would have loved this book."

"I'm fine, and yeah, she sure would have. Hold up, my pizza is here." I swung open the door. My heart slammed to a standstill, then took off at a gallop.

"Georgia." Noah stood in my doorway, glaring down at me with a smolder that instantly turned my mouth to ash.

"Hazel, I have to go."

"Really? You won't reconsider? Because we'd love to have you."

"Yeah, I'm sure. Noah's here," I said as casually as I could manage given the fact that I couldn't breathe. Three months of longing slammed into me with the force of a wrecking ball.

"Oh, good. Ask him about the sex scene, would you?" she quipped.

He arched a dark brow, obviously having heard her.

"Eh, I think that conversation might have to wait. He looks a little perturbed." My grip tightened on the door handle simply to keep myself standing. Self-preservation demanded I look away from those dark brown eyes, but the laws of magnetics wouldn't let me.

"Wait, you're not kidding, are you?" Her voice lost all its humor.

"Nope."

"Bye!" She hung up, leaving me on my own, staring down the barrel of an incredibly annoyed Noah.

"Are you going to let me in?" he asked, tucking his thumbs into his pockets. It should have been criminal to look as good as he did.

"Are you going to yell at me?" I asked.

"Yes."

"Okay, then." I stepped back as he walked in. I closed the door, then leaned back against it.

He pivoted in the entry, leaving only a few steps between us. That distance was too much and not enough all in the same breath.

"I thought you were going to call me when you got back," I started weakly. I'd been prepared for a lot of things today, but seeing him wasn't one of them, not that I was complaining.

He narrowed his eyes, then reached into his back pocket and whipped out his cell, pushing two buttons.

My phone rang.

"Are you kidding me?" I asked, spotting his name on the screen.

He raised his phone to his ear in blatant challenge.

I rolled my eyes but answered it.

"Hi, Georgia," he said, his voice dropping low and turning my insides to mush. "I'm back."

"When did that happen?" I asked. My cheeks heated as I realized I was actually talking to him on the phone in the middle of my foyer.

He flat-out smirked.

"Ugh," I groaned and we both holstered our phones in our back pockets. "Answer the question."

"Eighteen hours ago," he replied, shoving the sleeves of his sweater up his forearms. "Six of which I've slept. I spent one figuring out what you'd done, then a total of eleven booking a flight, getting to the airport, actually flying, renting a car, and driving all the way from Denver."

"Fair enough."

"Have you had enough *time*?" He stuck his thumbs in his pockets again. "Or would you still like me to leave you alone?"

"Me?" I squeaked. "You were the one who disappeared. I figured you'd be back in a week, maybe two, not *six*. You could have called and told me. Sent an update or a carrier pigeon. *Something*."

"You told me you were taking time and to call when I got back. Those are some pretty specific instructions, Georgia, and it fucking *killed* me to follow them."

"Oh."

"Why did you change the ending of the book?" he asked abruptly.

Here we go. "Oh, right. That." I folded my arms under my breasts, wishing I'd chosen something a little better than jeans and a long-sleeved tee. This conversation called for armor...or lingerie.

"Yes. That." He lifted his brows. "Why did you change it?"

"Because I love you!"

His eyes flared.

"Because I love you," I repeated, this time managing not to yell. "And you were right about the ending. I was wrong. And I didn't want to trash your career because I was being bitter and cold and sharp—"

He was on me before I finished the sentence, his body pressing mine against the door, his hands in my hair, his mouth kissing me into blissful oblivion.

God, I'd missed this—missed him. I kissed him back with everything I had, lacing my arms behind his neck as he picked me up, one hand under each thigh. I locked my ankles at the small of his back. Closer. I needed to be closer.

Over and over, he took my mouth with deep, swirling strokes of his tongue, setting me on fire like a match dropped into a pool of gasoline—like a lightning strike to tinder.

"Wait," he said against my mouth, then jerked back like I'd bitten him. "We can't do this yet." His chest heaved.

"What?" My feet found the floor, and a heartbeat later, he was in the center of the foyer with his hands laced over his head. "What are you doing?"

"This all went to shit before because I hid something from you."

"Awkward time to point that out, but okay." I leaned back against the door, struggling to catch my breath. He hadn't been the only one to keep secrets. "I guess in the interest of full disclosure, I should tell you that I can have kids."

"I thought…" His brow knit, two little lines appearing in his forehead. "Not that it matters, but that was never an issue for me. Biology isn't the only way to parent."

"Well, thank you. But I can. I just…didn't want to have them with Damian, so I didn't go off my birth control. Didn't want to know what kind of mother I'd be in that situation. I also didn't tell him that."

"Huh. Okay. Well, I've spent the last six weeks between England and the Netherlands." He fished a small, white envelope out of his front pocket.

"Doing book research. Adam told me." This was what he'd stopped us for? We could have been naked by now, and he wanted to chat book research?

"Not exactly. I hired a deep-sea exploration company to try to locate Jameson's plane off the last coordinates from the radio calls that day."

"You what?"

"I think we found it last week, and by *think*, I mean I'm pretty damned sure, but there are official channels and a lot of red tape flying around. The Eagles didn't transfer to the American military until September, and he went down in June, so he was still RAF but an American citizen. No one quite agrees who has jurisdiction." He turned the envelope over in his fingers.

"But you think you found him?" I asked quietly.

"Yes...and no." He winced. "It's a Spitfire, but the identifying markers on the tail have worn off and the wreckage was scattered."

"Where?"

"Off the coast of the Netherlands. It's..." He sighed. "It's too deep to recover the entire wreck, but we sent an ROV down." He walked slowly toward me. "We found an aluminum panel of the fuselage and what we think was the cockpit, but no...remains."

"Oh." I didn't know whether to be relieved or devastated. To come so close, and yet still not know. "Then why do you think—"

Noah took my hand, palm up, and tipped the envelope into it. A gold ring slid from the paper and into my hand. It was still warm from Noah's pocket. "Read the inscription."

"J With love, S." My throat tightened. "It's his," I whispered.

"I think so, too," Noah agreed, his voice going rough. "And I'll put it back if you want me to. We were looking for anything that might identify it, and it was right there...like it was waiting to be found, engraving and all. The team I hired said they'd never seen anything like it."

My fingers closed over the band. "Thank you."

"You're welcome. I'm sure you're getting a call this week. American. British. I'm not sure who at this point." He swallowed. "That wasn't the only reason I went to England. I know this might piss you off, and I don't have any proof, but I don't think…" He shook his head, then took a deep breath and started again. "I think the book—our book—was written by two separate people."

"That's because it was." I smiled slowly, feeling the heavy metal of the wedding band against my palm.

Noah's eyes widened and his lips parted.

"The oldest pages—the unedited original ones, were written by Scarlett during the war." I swallowed. "And the newer ones, the edits and additions…those were all made by—"

"Constance," he guessed.

I nodded. "How did you know? I didn't until about six weeks ago." What had he seen that I hadn't?

"The book tipped me off. I wouldn't have figured it out if our book had been the last one she'd written…and not the first. Then, it was the marriage license. She told Damian it took her years to remarry because it didn't feel like her first marriage was over, which was easily interpreted that she was still in love with Jameson…until I found the death certificate for Henry Wadsworth and the years matched up. It wasn't enough—just a hunch, and I didn't want to shatter your trust in her without having a damn good reason, but I decided to stop digging before anyone noticed."

"Gran—Constance told me. She wrote it all down the year before she died and had it delivered. Once I read it, I called you, but you were already gone, so I called Adam."

"And changed the end of the book."

I nodded.

"Because you love me." His eyes searched mine.

"Because I love you, Noah. And because Gran had her happy ending in real life. She fought for it. She didn't need you to craft it for her—she'd already earned it, already lived it. You gave Scarlett and Jameson the story they deserved. The crash, the evasion, the Dutch Resistance—all of it. You finished a story that fate had wrongfully cut short. Gran...she couldn't do that. She left it unfinished because she couldn't let them go—couldn't let Scarlett go. You set them free."

He cradled my face in his hands. "I would have done it for you. Would have given you whatever you wanted no matter what anyone else thought."

"I know," I whispered. "Because you love me."

"Because I love you, Georgia, and I'm done living without you. Please don't make me."

I wound my arms around his neck and arched to brush my lips across his. "Colorado or New York?"

"Autumn in New York. August and September, at least." He smiled against my mouth. "Colorado winter, spring, and summer."

"For the leaves?" I guessed, nipping his lower lip gently.

"For the Mets."

"Deal."

CHAPTER THIRTY-EIGHT

August 1944

Poplar Grove, Colorado

"Be careful around the steps, love," Scarlett said to William as he toddled along the edge of the newly finished gazebo, his hands gripping the individual spokes of the railing as he went.

He grinned over his shoulder and kept going.

She abandoned the record she'd selected and rushed across the floor, scooping him into her arms just before he reached the stairs. "You're going to be the death of me, William Stanton."

William giggled, and she blew a kiss into his neck, then shifted him to her hip as she walked back to the phonograph. The fall breeze rippled her dress, and she tucked her hair to the side to keep it out of William's grasp. The strands were longer now, falling midway down her back, her own personal calendar for how long it had been since she'd kissed Jameson goodbye in Ipswich.

Two years, and no word…but no remains, either, so she held on to hope and the spark of certainty that flared to life in her chest when she thought of him. He was alive. She knew it. She wasn't sure where or how, but he was. He had to be.

"Which one should we listen to, poppet?" she asked their son, setting him down in front of the small collection of records on the table. He picked one at random, and she put it on. "Glenn Miller. Excellent choice."

"Apples!"

"Right you are." The sound of The Glenn Miller Orchestra filled the space as she led William to the blanket she'd spread out on the far end. They snacked on apples and cheese—she wasn't sure she'd ever get used to how much food was available here in the States, but she wasn't complaining. They were lucky.

There were no air-raid sirens. No bombs. No boards to plot. No blackouts. They were safe. William was safe.

She prayed every night that both Jameson and Constance would be, too. Her fingers brushed over the small scar on her palm, thinking of its match in England. Had the cut above her sister's eye scarred over, too? She'd been bleeding when she forced them onto the plane that day the bombs had blasted them out of the street in Ipswich, barely sparing the three of them.

She'd packed up two new dresses for her sister yesterday and shipped them off. It had been nearly a year since Henry had slipped on the staircase and broken his fool neck, and according to her last letter, she'd met a handsome American GI who was serving in the Army Veterinary Corp.

William lay down on the blanket, and Scarlett ran her hands through his thick, dark hair as he drifted into an afternoon nap, his lips parting in sleep just like Jameson's. When she was certain he was out, she untangled herself carefully, then made her way back to the record player.

She knew she'd pay for the indulgence later, that she'd miss him even more, but she changed out the record for Ella Fitzgerald anyway. Her heart stuttered as the familiar song began to play, and for that moment, she wasn't in the middle of the Colorado Rockies, and those weren't golden aspen leaves swaying in the mountain breeze all around them—no, those were the tips of long summer grass in an overgrown field just outside Middle Wallop.

She closed her eyes and swayed, allowing herself one moment to imagine he was there, holding out his hand as he asked her to dance.

"Need a partner?"

She gasped softly, her eyes flying open at the sound of the voice she'd know anywhere. The voice she'd only heard in her dreams for the last two years. But there was only the phonograph before her, William asleep on the floor beside her, and the rush of the creek as it bent around them.

"Scarlett," he said again.

Behind her.

She spun, her dress whipping against her legs in the breeze, and quickly tugged her hair out of her eyes to clear her field of vision.

Jameson filled the entrance to the gazebo, leaning against the support beam, his hat tucked under his arm, his uniform new but travel-worn, no longer RAF, but United States Army Air Force. His smile widened as their eyes locked.

"Jameson," she whispered, her hands flying to her mouth. Was she dreaming? Would she wake before she could touch him? Tears pricked at her eyes as her heart warred with logic.

"No, baby, no." Jameson strode across the space, his hat falling to the deck below. "God, don't cry." He cradled her face in his hands, wiping the tears away with his thumbs.

His hands were warm. Solid. Real.

"You're really here," she cried, her fingers trembling as she grazed his chest, his neck, the line of his jaw. "I love you. I thought I'd never get to tell you that again."

"God, I love you, Scarlett. I'm here," he promised, his gaze sweeping over her hungrily, starved for the sight of her, the feel of her against him. Years and miles, battles and crash landings hadn't changed a single thing, hadn't dimmed his love for her. "I'm here," he repeated, because he needed to hear it, too. Needed to know they'd made it against all the odds that had come their way.

. . .

He tilted her face toward his and kissed her long and slow, breathing her in, tasting apples and home and Scarlett. His Scarlett.

"How?" she asked, locking her fingers behind his neck.

"A lot of luck." He rested his forehead against hers and wrapped one arm around her waist, tugging her close. "And a really long story that involves a broken leg, a resistance operative who took mercy on me, and some very accommodating cows who didn't mind a hidden roommate for three months while my leg healed."

She huffed a laugh, shaking her head. "But you're okay?"

"I am now." He pressed a kiss to her forehead and splayed his hand wide over her lower back. "I missed you every single day. Everything I did was to get home to you."

Her shoulders buckled as a sob slipped past her lips, and his throat closed around the lump that had formed the second he'd seen her swaying with the breeze, waiting where the creek bent around the aspen grove.

"It's okay. We made it."

"Do you have to go back?" she asked, her voice breaking.

"No." He tilted her chin and fell headfirst into those blue eyes. God, no matter how detailed his memories, how perfect his dreams, nothing had come close to how beautiful his wife was. "I couldn't get out until Maastricht was liberated. I spent a year fighting in secret with the Dutch Resistance, and I know too much for them to chance me being captured, which means the only planes I'll be flying belong to my uncle, right here."

"So it's over?" she asked, her voice edged with the same desperation he felt.

"It's over. I'm home." He kissed her again, sinking into her mouth as she gripped the lapels of his uniform, tugging him closer.

"You're home." She smiled, wide and brilliant.

He dipped, locking his arms at the backs of her thighs,

and lifted her to his eye level. Then he kissed her until he'd reacquainted himself with every line and curve of her mouth.

A rustle caught his attention, and his breath stuttered at the sight of William asleep on the blanket, his hand tucked beneath his head. Slowly, he set Scarlett down. "He's so big."

She nodded. "He's perfect. Do you want to wake him?" Her eyes danced.

Jameson swallowed, his throat and chest tight as he glanced between his dreaming son and the love of his life. Perfect. It was all perfect, and better than anything he'd imagined during the long, empty nights and battle-torn days. He sank his hands into the silk of Scarlett's hair and grinned at his wife. "In a few minutes."

Her smile was slow as she leaned up for another kiss.

"In a few minutes," she agreed.

He was home.

CHAPTER THIRTY-NINE

Georgia

Three years later

I smiled and read the last page once more before whispering a quiet goodbye to Jameson and Scarlett. Then I shut the book and returned to the real world, where my real husband was currently getting ready to launch his new book four aisles over.

My thumb trailed across the names on the cover. One, I'd known since birth but never met, and the other I'd met in this very spot and would know for the rest of my life.

"I can tell you how it ends," Noah said in my ear as he came up behind me, his voice low and his arms warm.

"Can you?" I leaned back, brushing a kiss over his jaw. "I heard the ending was even a surprise to the author on release day." I grinned shamelessly.

"Huh. Imagine that."

"Much more *satisfying* sex scenes than his normal books, too." I shrugged.

He scoffed. "Have you read his latest? Pretty sure he got ahold of some excellent inspiration."

"Hmm. I'll have to check it out."

"I'd be happy to give you a private reading."

I laughed so hard, I almost snorted. "Okay, that was just bad."

"Yeah," he admitted. "Definitely not my best. How about, 'Kiss me, Georgia, I have to go sign some books.'"

"That, I can do." I tilted my head and kissed him, keeping it PG-13. Barely. The man was too addictive for public consumption.

His grip tightened and he nipped my lower lip. "I love you."

"I love you. Now go do your thing. I'm going to head next door and do mine." I flashed him a smile and he stole another kiss before disappearing down the next aisle, leaving me dazed for a moment, staring after him as a woman wandered into the romance section next to me.

"That is such a good book," she said, nodding enthusiastically at the one in my hands and clutching Noah's latest hardcover. "If you haven't read it, you have to. Trust me. You won't regret it. Amazing."

"Thanks. I always appreciate a good recommendation. You here for the signing?" I shifted my weight. Pregnancy was doing weird things to my balance, and I was still wiped out from jet lag.

"I came all the way from Cheyenne, Wyoming," she said with a grin. "My sister's holding my place in line. Have you seen him? He's gorgeous." She lifted her brows. "Seriously."

"I definitely wouldn't kick him out of bed," I agreed. I never did. In fact, I spent as much time as possible letting him get me *into* bed. The fact that Noah got more handsome every single day had not escaped my notice—far from it.

"Right? Me either. Oh, it's starting!" She waved and disappeared into the next aisle.

I grinned and slid the book back onto the shelf, right next to the Scarlett Stanton books where it belonged. It was still my favorite of Gran's books—Noah's too. Within those pages, Scarlett and Jameson loved, fought, and most importantly, lived.

Here in the real world, we'd buried Jameson's ring last week under a large, shady tree by a quiet pond in the middle of England next to a marble headstone that read Constance Wadsworth. I couldn't help but feel like they were all finally at peace.

I headed for the door, my eyes locking with Noah's as I passed by the table. Love shined in his gaze, and we smiled at each other like the besotted fools we were. It was our turn to live out our own epic love story, and I treasured every single minute of it.

We both did.

ACKNOWLEDGMENTS

First and foremost, thank you to my Heavenly Father for blessing me beyond my wildest dreams.

Thank you to my husband, Jason, for pulling me through this utter bear of a year. For holding my hand in the darkest moments and making me laugh when I was sure I'd never find anything funny again. Thank you to my children, who have handled quarantines and social distancing for their high-risk brother with grace and love. Never doubt that you are essential to my existence. To my sister, Kate, for always picking up the phone. To my parents, who bring me coffee creamer from a thousand miles away. To my best friend, Emily Byer, for never blinking when I'm on deadline for months.

Thank you to my team at Entangled. Thank you to my editor, Stacy Abrams, for jumping in and taking this book on. You are simply incredible. To Liz Pelletier, Heather, and Jessica for answering endless streams of emails. To my phenomenal agent, Louise Fury, who makes my life easier simply by standing at my back.

Thank you to my wifeys, our unholy trinity, Gina Maxwell and Cindi Madsen—I'd be lost without you. To Jay Crownover for quite possibly being the best neighbor ever. To Shelby and Mel for keeping my ducks in a row. Thank you to Linda Russell for always bringing the bobby pins. To Cassie Schlenk for always being the number one hype girl. To every blogger and reader who has taken a chance on me over the years. To my reader group, The Flygirls, for bringing me joy every day.

Lastly, because you're my beginning and end, thank you again to my Jason. If you're reading this, it's 2021. Enough said.

Discover the heart-wrenching forbidden romance about family, betrayal, and ultimately how far we're willing to go on behalf of those we love.

Turn the page to start reading
Great and Precious Things.

CHAPTER ONE

Camden

M y lungs burned as I drew a deep breath, seeking oxygen that wasn't there, and my fingers itched to hold the cigarette I'd thrown away six years ago. Altitude did that to me every time—at least the breathing part.

The craving for a smoke? That was courtesy of Alba, Colorado, population 649. Or so the sign I'd passed about a mile back proclaimed. Then again, I wasn't about to trust a sign that hadn't been updated since before I'd been born—which was par for the course in my hometown.

Nothing about it had changed since I'd left, which was pretty much the point of the whole town. Just past the paved roads, Alba was the best-preserved ghost town in Colorado, and the tourists who flooded her streets in the summer kept the tiny town alive all winter long.

The total on the gas pump climbed as I stretched my hands toward the late-afternoon sun and the snowcapped peaks above me, willing life back into muscles I'd kept cramped for far too long during the drive from North Carolina. The bite in the March breeze cut through my exhaustion, and I welcomed its icy fingers on my exposed skin. It definitely wasn't T-shirt weather up here at ten thousand feet.

A gasp caught my attention, and I turned toward the minivan that had pulled up behind my Jeep a minute ago. A blonde wearing sunglasses too big for her face and a puffy winter coat gawked with one foot on the concrete and one inside her vehicle, as if someone had pushed pause during her exit.

I lowered my arms, and my shirt slid back into place, covering the inked strip of stomach she'd no doubt gotten an eyeful of.

She shook her head quickly and started to pump her gas.

At least she didn't make the sign of the cross and back away.

Either she'd moved to Alba in the last ten years or my reputation had softened some since I'd joined the army. Hell, maybe the population of Alba had forgotten all about me.

I finished filling my tank and headed inside the small convenience store to grab a drink. God only knew what Dad would have in his fridge.

A set of bells chimed as the door closed behind me, and I nodded in greeting to the older man leaning on the counter. Looked like Mr. Williamson still owned the gas station. His bushy silver brows rose with a quick smile. Then he did a double take, both his brows and smile falling as he blinked in confusion. And then his eyes narrowed in recognition.

Looks like that rep is alive and well.

I quickly chose a few bottles of water from the slim selection and carried them to the counter.

The old man's eyes darted between my hands and the bottles as he rang them up, like I was going to steal them or something. I'd been a lot of things, but a thief wasn't one of them.

The bells chimed again, and Williamson visibly relaxed. "Afternoon, Lieutenant Hall," he greeted his newest patron.

Awesome.

I didn't bother looking. That stubborn, old, judgmental piece of work hated my—

"Holy shit. Cam?"

That wasn't Tim Hall wearing a badge—it was his son, Gideon.

Gid's mouth hung slack, his light-brown eyes wide in shock. It was a similar expression to the one he'd worn that time Xander had shoved us into the girls' locker room the fall of our freshman year. I'd never found a way to properly thank my brother for his attempt at hazing—not that anyone would believe Xander would stoop so low. After all, he was the good son.

"I didn't think police officers were supposed to swear in uniform." I gave him a quick once-over. Unlike his dad, Gid was still too trim to sport a belly over his belt.

"As opposed to soldiers?" he countered.

"Actually, that earns us bonus points, and besides, I'm not in a uniform anymore." I hadn't been for seventeen days. "Does your dad know you stole his badge?"

"Anymore? Does your..." He sighed. "Crap, I've got nothing!" His laughter unleashed my own. "It's good to see you!" He pulled me into a fierce, back-pounding hug, his badge digging into my chest.

"You too." I grinned as we broke apart. "In fact, you might be the only person I'm happy to see."

"Oh, come on. Not Mr. Williamson here?" Gid looked over my shoulder and cringed at whatever expression he saw on Williamson's face. "Okay, maybe not him."

"He's never really cared for me." I shrugged, well aware that he could hear me.

"You did throw someone through that window the last time you were here." Gid motioned toward the glass that had long since been replaced. "Man, how long ago was that? Four years?"

"Six," I answered automatically. Of the few things I remembered about that night, the date was still crystal clear.

"Six. Right." Gideon's expression fell—no doubt remembering why I'd been in Alba last.

Sullivan's funeral.

Grief threatened to rise up and steal what was left of the oxygen in my lungs, but I beat it back for the millionth time since we put Sully in the ground.

God, I could still hear his laughter—

"You going to pay for these waters, Camden?" Mr. Williamson asked.

"Yes, sir," I responded, thankful for the interruption, and turned back to the counter to finish the transaction. I didn't miss the flash of surprise on Williamson's face at my tone or when I thanked him as I took the bag and moved aside.

"That stuff will kill you," I told Gideon as he purchased a six-pack of soda.

"You and Julie, man," he muttered under his breath as he handed over his debit card. "Can't a guy drink in peace?"

Funny. This was more than I'd smiled in the entire last month. "How are Julie and the kids?"

"Driving me to drink." He lifted his soda in the air. "No, really, they're great. Julie's a nurse now, which you would know if you ever joined the social media world."

"No, thank you. What's the point?"

Gideon thanked Mr. Williamson, and we headed outside. "What's the point? I don't know. To keep in contact with your best friend?"

"No, that's why we have email. Social media is for people who need to compare their lives. Their houses, their vacations, their accomplishments. I see no reason to stand on my front porch with a bullhorn to broadcast what I had for dinner, either."

"Speaking of dinner, how long are you in town for?" he asked as we paused between my Jeep and his faded squad car. "I know Julie would love to have you over."

"For good," I replied before I could choke on the words.

He blinked.

"Yeah, it's taking me a little time to process, too." I glanced up at the mountains Alba slept between. Mountains I'd sworn I'd never see again.

"You got out? I figured you'd be career."

So had I. Just another thing to mourn.

"Officer Malone?" a scratchy feminine voice called over the radio.

"Marilyn Lakewood still calls out dispatch? What is she, seventy?"

"Seventy-seven," Gideon corrected. "And before you ask, Scott Malone is twenty-five and a giant pain in my ass."

"What did you expect from the mayor's kid?"

"Mayor's kid? When's the last time you talked to—"

"Officer Malone?" Marilyn repeated, her annoyance pitching her voice higher.

"Do you need to get that?" I motioned toward the radio on his shoulder.

"Malone needs to get that," he muttered with a shake of his head. "It's probably Genevieve Dawson whining about the Livingstons' cat in her yard again. If it's serious, Marilyn will call me. Now, fill me in. When did you get here? You're back for good? As in you've moved back here? The place you called Satan's as—"

"Xander called." I cut him off with the half-truth before he could remind me of yet another reason I'd sworn I'd never come back here. "Since it had been six years, I answered."

"Your dad," Gideon said softly.

"My dad."

A quiet moment of understanding passed between us.

"Gideon Hall!" Marilyn snapped through the radio.

"Lieutenant," he whispered to the sky before responding. "Yes, Marilyn?"

"Since Boy Wonder isn't answering the call, it seems that Dorothy Powers has lost Arthur Daniels again. She woke up from her nap, and he was gone."

My stomach dropped, and my gaze drifted up the mountain. According to Xander, Dad ditched his home nurse a few times a week but never wandered far from the house. It didn't help that Dorothy Powers was older than Dad and probably in need of her own nurse.

"On my way. Call up the usual searchers." Gideon caught my eye, then dropped his hand from the radio.

"My dad." How far could he have gotten?

"Second time this month." His lips flattened. "I'm going to head to the station to grab the four-wheel drive. I won't make it to your place in the cruiser."

"Just hop in with me. I'll take you up," I more ordered than offered, unwilling to wait. My Jeep was lifted and sported massive tires, a V-8 engine, and more than enough four-wheeling capability to survive the apocalypse. Even the road to Dad's wasn't that bad this time of year.

He agreed, and a minute later, we pulled onto Gold Creek Drive, which served as the town's main artery—no stoplights needed but snowmobiles optional.

"How long have you been gone?"

"Six years." I shot him a look. Hadn't I just answered that?

"No, I mean today. When did you leave the house? Was Dorothy awake? Was your dad?" He was already thumbing through his cell phone.

"I wish I could help you with a timeline, but I haven't been home yet." I motioned toward the back seat of the four-door Rubicon.

"You literally just pulled into town?" He took in the bags and boxes that had been my only companions on the two-thousand-mile drive.

"Yep," I replied as we passed the last post-fifties building in Alba. We crossed the bridge that spanned all thirty feet of Rowan Creek, and the snow-packed pavement ended, marking our entrance into the time capsule that kept Alba alive. "Figured it was a good idea to gas up. Someone told me once that it's easier to run from the cops on a full tank."

Main Street opened up on my left. Wooden buildings with metal roofs lined both sides of the dirt road that would fill with tourists in the next few months, all looking to experience a real 1890s old west mining town.

"Someone grew up. Also, please don't make me chase you.

an imprint of Entangled Publishing LLC